Canadian **Dani Collins** knew in high school that she wanted to write romance for a living. Twenty-five years later, after marrying her high school sweetheart, having two kids with him, working at several generic office jobs and submitting countless manuscripts, she got The Call. Her first Mills & Boon novel won the Reviewers' Choice Award for Best First in Series from *RT Book Reviews*. She now works in her own office, writing romance.

Jackie Ashenden writes dark, emotional stories, with alpha heroes who've just got the world to their liking only to have it blown wide apart by their kick-ass heroines. She lives in Auckland, New Zealand, with her husband, the inimitable Dr Jax, two kids and two rats. When she's not torturing alpha males and their gutsy heroines she can be found drinking chocolate martinis, reading anything she can lay her hands on, wasting time on social media or being forced to go mountain biking with her husband. To keep up to date with Jackie's new releases and other news, sign up to her newsletter at jackieashenden.com.

CINDERELLA'S ROYAL SEDUCTION

DANI COLLINS

CROWNED AT THE DESERT KING'S COMMAND

JACKIE ASHENDEN

MILLS & BOON

First Published in Great Britain 2020
by Mills & Boon, an imprint of HarperCollins*Publishers*
1 London Bridge Street, London, SE1 9GF

Cinderella's Royal Seduction © 2020 by Dani Collins

Crowned at the Desert King's Command © 2020 by Jackie Ashenden

ISBN: 978-0-263-27802-6

MIX
Paper from
responsible sources
FSC™ C007454

This book is produced from independently certified FSC™ paper
to ensure responsible forest management.
For more information visit www.harpercollins.co.uk/green.

Printed and bound in Spain
by CPI, Barcelona

CINDERELLA'S ROYAL SEDUCTION

DANI COLLINS

My long-suffering family always deserves a dedication for cheerleading me in this career I've chosen, but when it comes to the nuts and bolts of actually getting a book written there are two people I absolutely cannot do without.

First and foremost, my editor. I've been lucky enough to work with Laurie Johnson on and off in the seven years I've been published. Thank you for helping me turn so many pumpkins into carriages, this book very much included.

Second and no less important, my RMT, Loretta. Thank you for keeping the carpal tunnel and shoulder gremlins at bay, for being a fan of romance, and for recommending I visit Sparkling Hills in Vernon, the spa that inspired the one in this book.

PROLOGUE

JUST ONCE, CASSIOPEIA BRODEUR wished she could be given enough time to sit and think before having to react to whatever catastrophe her stepmother, Maude, had set in motion.

She really wished that when she'd been fifteen and thinking she was welcoming her stepsisters into her family, she hadn't told them her friends called her Sopi.

"Soapy?" Nanette and Fernanda spoke English as their fourth language, but they'd heard the pun and laughed hysterically.

Seven years later, all of Sopi's childhood friends, including the ones who'd given her the nickname when they'd been in grade school, had moved on to university and world travel, interesting jobs and serious relationships and *cities*.

While Sopi was still here in Lonely Lake, scrubbing up after her spoiled stepfamily and the guests of the hotel and spa that bore her name.

Why couldn't Maude and the girls shove off back to Europe and quit destroying what was left of her life? They certainly made no effort to hide their disdain for this "backwater village" in the remote wilderness of the Canadian Rockies.

Oh, right, they had run through all of Sopi's father's

money and had nowhere left to turn. Yet they seemed determined to drive this place into ruin, too.

"*All* the reservations?" Sopi repeated with disbelief. "You canceled *all* of March?"

"Yes."

"On purpose?"

"Sopi." Maude used her most hideously patronizing tone. "We can't have families with children running around when we're entertaining royalty, can we? And we'll need the rooms."

"Royalty?" Sopi asked with a choke of hysterical laughter. "Is that a figure of speech?" The odd aging pop star turned up—emphasis on *odd*—but real celebrities with real money went to Banff or Whistler for their spring skiing.

"Rhys Charlemaine is the prince of Verina."

"Never heard of him," Sopi said flatly, even though it rang a distant bell. She barely had time to keep up with weather reports and the latest safety regulations, though. She didn't follow gossip on fading royalty.

"Honestly, Sopi. Your lack of education." Maude shook her coiffed silver head in despair.

Was she referring to the education that hadn't been paid for because instead Sopi's father's money had been used to keep Nanette and Fernanda in boarding school in Switzerland? The girls' absence had turned out to be a blessing, so Sopi didn't complain much about it, but honestly.

"Why on earth would a prince come here?" Sopi asked.

"Because I've arranged a week of heli-skiing for him."

With what money?

Sopi wanted to scream or maybe cry. She glanced

longingly beyond the windows where February skies were an intense blue over blinding white slopes across the valley. Last season, she'd skied once on the small commercial hill on the far side of the lake. This year she hadn't had a single opportunity—too busy trying to keep the spa afloat.

"And as for the accommodation," Maude continued absently, "the girls will move from the penthouse so he can use it, but they'll stay on the top floor. His entourage will take the rest of the rooms there."

"His *entourage*? Please tell me this isn't *all* complimentary." Sopi knew it would be and felt sick. Sick. Maude never let her peek at the books, but Sopi wasn't blind or stupid. She knew they were in the red and bleeding more every day.

"Of course we won't charge him." Maude's scoffing tone chided her as Silly Sopi. "This is exceedingly good exposure for us. Everyone will want to come here, especially while he's in residence. I've arranged a decent chef. That's long overdue." Her pointed look blamed Sopi for not having made that happen sooner, and Sopi couldn't even imagine what it was going to cost. "You'll need to hire more staff for the treatments."

"Maude." Sopi tried one more time, even though this argument had never made an impact. "There is no one to hire."

The occasional adventurous cosmetician or massage therapist joined them for a season, but the isolation of Lonely Lake wasn't for everyone. Plus, Maude and her daughters were a special kind of hell to work for. Their incessant demands and tantrums over inconveniences like having to wait for deliveries of a desired shade of nail polish impacted the spa's ability to retain qualified employees.

"You always make things harder than they are," Maude sighed. "People will beg to work for gratuities if you tell them who will be staying here."

The spa's bread-and-butter clientele were retirees soaking their arthritis in the hot mineral pools at an affordable price. Sopi couldn't deny that a high-profile guest would fill rooms, but, "Seniors on fixed incomes aren't known for their generous tips. If this prince and his cronies—"

"Cronies?" Maude's head came up. "Sopi, he's *thirty*. Unmarried. And it's time he changed that." Maude had been fingering through a collection of fabric swatches. She held up a square of cranberry silk. "Would this clash with Nanette's hair, do you think?"

As was often the case when Sopi spoke with her stepmother, Sopi's brain was racing to catch up. Even as she tried to formulate arguments against whatever Maude was demanding, she knew the struggle was futile. Her stepmother had gained control of the spa when Sopi's father died and kept a firm grasp on it. Sopi didn't have the resources to fight her for it, and Maude would no doubt clean out what was left of the spa's available cash to repulse an attack. Sopi would be bankrupt whether she won or lost.

Sopi's only choice was to try to keep the place solvent until she had enough in her savings account to mount a proper legal challenge. Maybe it was a fool's dream, but it kept her going.

So she was always mentally planning how to mitigate or adapt to or accomplish whatever ridiculous thing Maude insisted had to happen while doing the math, trying to calculate when she would be able to put her foot down and hold her ground.

Today, amid that familiar scramble, Sopi's brain

crashed into Maude's end goal. Maude wanted to marry one of her daughters to a prince. To a man who lived in a kingdom—or was it a principality? Who cared? It was far, far away.

If one left, they all would.

A tentative ray of hope gleamed like a beacon at the end of a long, dark tunnel, breaking a smile across Sopi's face.

"You know what, Maude? You're right. This sounds like a tremendous opportunity. I'll start prepping for it." Sopi's pulse pounded so hard, her ears rang.

"Thank you," Maude said in a beleaguered tone that echoed with, *It's about time.* "Leave moving the girls out of the penthouse until the last moment. They don't want to be inconvenienced any more than necessary."

Sopi nearly choked on her tongue, but she bit down on it instead. If she played her cards right, and if she threw her stepsisters in front of this Prince Charlemaine or whoever the heck he was, then maybe, just maybe, she could free herself of her stepfamily forever.

It was such an exciting prospect, she hummed cheerfully as she left Maude's office and headed upstairs to strip beds and clean toilets.

CHAPTER ONE

RHYS CHARLEMAINE WOKE before the sun was up. Before any of his staff began creeping into his suite with fresh coffee and headlines and messages that required responses.

He didn't ring for any of them. What privacy he had was precious. Plus, he had withstood enough bustle and fussing yesterday when he and his small army of assistants, bodyguards and companions had arrived. The owner of this place, Maude Brodeur, had insisted on personally welcoming him. She had hung around for nearly two hours, dropping names and reminiscing about her first husband, whom she had cast as a contemporary equal to Rhys's father—which he wasn't. He had been a distant cousin to a British earl and largely unknown.

Blue blood was blue blood, however, and she had clearly been using the association to frame her pretty, well-educated daughters as suitable for a man next in line to a throne. Her daughters had perched quietly while she rattled on, but there'd been an opportunistic light in their eyes.

Rhys sighed. If he had a euro for every woman who wanted to search his pockets for a wedding ring, he would have more money than all the world's tech billionaires combined.

Instead, he had a decent fortune built on shrewd investments, some of it in tech, but much of it in real estate development. Half of it belonged to his brother, Henrik. Rhys handled their private interests while Henrik looked after the throne's finances. They each had their lane, but they drove them side by side, always protecting the other's flank. Rhys might be the spare, a prince to his brother the king, but they were a solid unit.

Even so, he and Henrik didn't always agree. This detour to a tiny off-grid village in Canada had had his brother lifting his brows with skepticism. "Sounds too good to be true," had been Henrik's assessment.

Rhys's antennae were up, as well. On the surface, the property in a valley reminiscent of Verina's surrounding Alps appeared ripe for exploitation, especially with its hot-spring aquifer. That alone made it a unique energy opportunity. The remote location would be a challenge, of course, but there was a modest ski hill across the lake. It drew locals and guests of this hotel, but could also be picked up for a song and further developed.

Maude was claiming she wanted to keep the sale of the spa quiet for "personal reasons," pretending she didn't need the money. Normally, Rhys would steer clear of someone attempting to pull the wool over his eyes. He had his own reason for accepting her invitation, however, and it had nothing to do with whether or not this place was a sound investment.

Rhys shifted his pensive gaze across the frozen lake, searching for answers that couldn't be solved with money and power. He needed a miracle, something he didn't believe in. He was a man of action who made his own destiny, but the only action available to him at the moment was a path littered with disloyalty to his brother, if not the crown.

He supposed he should be thankful the doctors had finally discovered the reason Henrik and his wife, Elise, were failing to conceive. They'd caught Henrik's testicular cancer early enough that treatment had a reasonable chance of success. With luck, Rhys would not assume the throne. Not soon, at any rate, but Henrik would almost certainly be sterile.

That meant the task of producing future progeny to inherit the throne had fallen into Rhys's lap.

Which meant he needed a wife.

He tried not to dwell on how treasonous that felt. Henrik had worked tirelessly to regain their rightful place in Verina. Doing so had nearly cost him the woman he loved. The royalists who had supported their return from exile had expected Henrik to marry an aristocrat, not a diplomat's daughter. Somehow, Henrik had overcome their objections only to come up against the inability to make an heir.

Henrik and Elise deserved children. They would be excellent parents. Given everything Henrik had gone through, the throne ought to go to his child, not Rhys's.

None of this felt right to him.

A blue glow came on below his window, dragging Rhys out of his brooding. The lights in the free-form mineral bath illuminated the mist rising off the placid water, beckoning him.

His security detail had reported that the guest register was swollen with female names, many of them bearing titles or related to one. He wasn't surprised his intention to ski here had been leaked to the press, drawing the usual suspects. He had counted on Maude being canny enough to see the value in a full house. It made the place look successful and ensured she would still have a nice influx of cash even if he turned down her offer to purchase. She might even have thought a bevy of beautiful naked women would sway him to buy.

It wouldn't, but he appreciated the expediency of having a curated selection of eligible women brought to one place for his consideration.

He had no choice but to marry and was down to his last moments of bachelorhood. He decided to make the most of them. He dropped the pajama pants he'd slipped on when he rose and left them on the floor, mostly to reassure his staff that he hadn't been kidnapped. He'd learned to pick up after himself during his years in exile with his brother. He was a passable cook and could trim his own beard, not that he did those things for himself anymore.

He was a prince again, one who had believed his primary function was to ensure his family's economic viability while his brother ruled their country and provided heirs. His responsibilities were expanding, though, and the one duty he would happily perform—taking his brother's place while he battled his illness—was not open to him.

Heart heavy, he shrugged on his monogrammed robe, stepped into his custom-sewn slippers, searched out the all-access card Maude had given him, then took the elevator to the treatment level.

Sopi was so tired, she thought she was hallucinating when the man appeared across the mist rising off the pool. The spa area wasn't yet open, and the locks were on a timer. The only means of entry was the use of a staff card, and she was the employee on shift. The man's robe wasn't hotel issue, either, but that wasn't too unusual. Frequent guests often brought their own robes so it was easier to track where they'd left them.

Even so, she'd never seen anyone show up in anything like that gorgeous crimson with gold trim and embroidered initials.

As she squinted her tired eyes at the man's stern profile and closely trimmed beard, she recognized—

Oh God. He was completely naked under that robe! She should have looked away but didn't. *Couldn't.*

Through the steam rising off the pool, she watched him unbelt and open his robe, drop it off his shoulders to catch on his bent arms. The muscled globes of his bare butt appeared as he turned and slid free of the robe, draping it over the glass half wall that formed the rail around the pool. He was sculpted like an Olympic swimmer with broad shoulders, narrow hips and muscular thighs.

He pivoted back to face her across the pool, utterly, completely, gloriously naked. A shadow of hair accented the intriguing contours that sectioned his chest and abdomen, streaking out to dark nipples and arrowing down his eight-pack abs to—

He dived into the water, shallow and knife sharp, barely making a ripple.

She pushed her face into the stack of towels she held, no longer breathing as she tried to suppress her shock and abject mortification. She fought to push back a rising blush of hot embarrassment and something she didn't even recognize.

Because she had not only seen their special guest, the prince of Verina, in a private moment. She'd seen the crown jewels.

And of *course* she was standing on the far side of the pool where the spare caddy of clean towels was tucked beneath an overhang, next to the bar that operated in the summer months.

To escape, she would have to circle the deck, walk over the little bridge that separated the main pool from the portion that jutted out from the cliff and move past the robe he'd thrown over the rail near the glass doors into the building.

There was a small splash of water breaking as he surfaced near her feet.

"Good morning." His voice was surprised and carried the gravel of early morning.

Oh *God*. She made herself lift her face and briefly—very briefly—glanced his way.

Okay. Only his head and shoulders were visible. That ought to have made breathing possible, but dear Lord, he was good-looking. His cheekbones were carved marble above his sleek beard. Was he deliberately using the short, dark stubble to accentuate how beautiful his mouth was? Because it framed lips that managed to be both well defined and masculine, swirling wicked thoughts into her mind just looking at them. His hair was slicked back, his eyes laser blue and lazily curious.

"En français?" he tried.

"What? I mean, pardon? I mean, no. I speak English. Good morning," she managed *very* belatedly and clumsily.

At least he didn't know who she was. She had put on her one decent dress last night, planning to form part of the greeting party with Maude and her stepsisters. A last-minute mix-up with a delivery had had her changing into jeans and boots to drive two hours each way so she could fetch high-grade coffee beans and other groceries that Maude had ordered specifically for the prince's menu.

"I'm restocking towels." Not staring or tongue-tied or anything. She hurried to shove the stack into the caddy, snatching one back. "I'll leave this one with your robe. Our…um… European hour is actually…um…ten o'clock. At *night*."

"Euro…? Oh." The corner of his mouth dug in on one side. "Am I supposed to wear a swimsuit?"

"Most of our guests do." All of them. "Aside from the few who prefer to sauna au naturel. At *night*," she repeated.

"The sun hasn't come up. Technically, it's still night." He lifted a dark winged brow at the gleam of bright steel along the seam where pearly peaks met charcoal sky.

"Point taken." She drummed her fingers against her thigh, debated a moment, then decided to tease him right back. "But technically the pool isn't open yet. You're breaking our rules either way."

"What's the penalty? Because I don't expect anyone here packed a bikini top. Only a few will bother with bottoms. We don't wear them at the health spas at home. I expect that's where your 'European hour' label came from."

Pressed against the wall of the pool, he looked exactly like every other guest who might fold his arms against the edge and gaze at the view or strike up a friendly conversation with passing staff.

Except she knew he was naked, and his banter was flipping her heart and fanning the nervous excitement in her stomach. She hugged the single towel to her middle, trying to still those butterflies.

"At least I understand why Maude didn't want children running around this week. Apparently, we're hosting a nudist convention."

He smiled, the light in his eyes so warm she curled her toes in her sandals, unable to stem the shy smile that pulled at her own lips.

"You Americans are so adorably prudish."

Oh no, he didn't. She narrowed her eyes. "And you French are so—oh, I'm sorry. Are you not French?" She batted her lashes as his good humor blanked to affront.

Since Maude's announcement that he was coming here, she'd taken the time to learn that Verina was a small kingdom in the Alps between Switzerland, Germany and France. Verinians spoke all of those countries' languages and, having overcome an uprising twenty years ago that had had their neighbors sniffing and circling, trying to extend their borders to encompass Verina for the next fifteen years, were fiercely patriotic to the flag they still flew.

"I find people from *North* America to have very conservative views about sex and nudity," he clarified.

She nodded her forgiveness of his faux pas and explained, "We're not that prudish in Canada. We keep our clothes on because we're cold." She pointed at the lazy drift of tiny flakes hitting the steam off the pool and dissolving. Strangely, she wasn't feeling the chill nearly as much as she usually would, standing out here in the predawn frost. Heat radiated from her middle. Her joints were melting and growing loose.

"You must be in this pool often, though. You've never swum naked in it?"

"Never." She couldn't recall when she had last had a chance to swim at all. She vacuumed and scoured and restocked and never enjoyed the luxury she provided to everyone else.

If I can just get Maude and the girls out of here was her mantra. If she could take control of the books and balance them, quit financing trips and clothing for women who brought no value to the spa, only drama, she could relax instead of burning out.

"It's very freeing. You should try it."

"I'm sure it is." He had no idea of the constraints she was under, though.

"No time like the present."

As she met his gaze with a rueful smile, certain he was mocking her for her modesty, something in his gaze made her heart judder to a stop in her chest then kick into a different rhythm.

He was looking at her with consideration, as though he'd suddenly noticed something about her that had snagged one hundred percent of his attention. As though he was serious about wanting her to strip naked and jump in the pool with him.

More insistent tugs and pulls accosted her midsection. A flush of sensual heat streaked up from her tense stomach, warming her chest and throat and cheeks. Her breasts grew heavy and tight.

She *never* reacted to men—not like this, all receptive and intrigued. Her last date had been in high school and ended with a wet kiss that hadn't affected her nearly as strongly as this man's steady gaze. The dating pool in Lonely Lake was very small unless she wanted to get together with guests, and she didn't do that because they didn't stick around.

That's what this is, she realized, clunking back from a brief, floaty fantasy of a prince taking an interest in a nobody like her. This wasn't *real* flirty banter. He wasn't genuinely interested in her. He was only inviting her to join him in the way male guests occasionally did because she was *here*, not because he found her particularly attractive. How could he? She looked especially hellish this morning. She was frazzled and exhausted, no makeup, clothes rumpled as though she'd slept in them. Joke was on him. She *hadn't* slept.

Maybe this wasn't even happening. Maybe she would wake after being dragged from the igloo room and defrosted from a hypothermia-induced delirium.

"I'm sure you'll have plenty of company soon enough," she said in a strangled voice. She nodded upward at the windows lighting behind curtains as guests began to stir. "I'll check the saunas. They're banked at night, but I'll make sure they're up to temperature for you."

As the owner, Sopi could have asked that he wear a towel around the resort, but she didn't want to introduce herself. She was too embarrassed at thinking, even for a second, that he might genuinely be interested in her.

Besides, if he climbed out to shake her hand, buck naked, she would die.

Rhys watched her walk away with a surprising clench of dismay, even though he knew better than to flirt with the help.

He hadn't even realized anyone had been on the pool deck until he'd surfaced after swimming the length underwater. But there she was, face buried in a stack of towels like an ostrich, her dark hair gathered into a fraying knot, her uniform mostly shapeless except where it clung lovingly to a really nice ass.

Arrogant as he innately was, he didn't expect servants to turn their face to the wall as his father had once told him his great-grandmother had demanded of palace staff.

This young woman had obviously recognized him. Nearly every woman of any age reacted to him—which he made a habit of ignoring. His reputation as a playboy was greatly exaggerated. Affairs complicated an already complex life. When he did entangle himself,

he stuck with a long-term arrangement with a sophisticated partner, one who had a busy life herself. He
kept ties loose until the woman in question began to
suggest marriage would improve their relationship, in-
variably claiming it would "give us more time together"
or "draw us closer"—two assumptions he knew would
prove false.

Sometimes they brought up a desire for children,
and he had had good reasons for putting that off, too.
Until recently.

But until very recently, Rhys hadn't believed he'd
have to marry at all. Staying single had been his greatest luxury and one of the few genuine freedoms available to him. Occasionally, he had thought a wife might
be the best way to stave off the fortune hunters who
constantly stalked him, but marriage and family were
yet more responsibilities on top of an already heavy
mantle. He had thought to indefinitely postpone both.

Besides, he didn't deserve the sort of happily-ever-
after his brother was striving for.

A shrieking giggle from a balcony above had him
glancing up to see a pair of women in negligees exhib-
iting all the excitement of children spotting a monkey
at the zoo. Their bare legs and cleavage flashed as they
posed against the rail and waved.

And so it starts, he thought tiredly.

He looked for the young woman who had seemed
so charmingly real, planning to ask her to lock out the
masses for another thirty minutes.

He couldn't see her, and his irritation ratcheted up
several notches. It had little to do with the looming in-
terruption of his peaceful swim. She was gone, and he
was uncomfortable with how annoyed that made him.
He hadn't even asked her name.

She worked here, he reminded himself. He would see her again, but the knowledge did nothing to ease his impatience.

He shouldn't *want* to see her again. He wouldn't be able to approach her when he did. A guest coming on to an employee was a hard limit. There was an entire hotel brimming with beautiful, available, *appropriate* women if he wanted to get laid.

His nether regions weren't twitching for the silk-draped knockouts hurrying to throw on robes and rush down here, though. He was recollecting a face clean of makeup and eyes like melted chocolate framed in thick lashes. She'd had a tiny beauty spot below one corner of her mouth and what had looked like a man's wedding band on a thin chain in the hollow of her throat. Whose? A father, he imagined. She was too young to be a widow.

She could be married, though. She was very pretty, neither voluptuous nor catwalk slender, but pert with small, firm breasts, narrow shoulders and that valentine of a derriere. He had wondered how tall she would be if he stood beside her. He might get a crick in his neck when he leaned down to taste her pillowy lips—

No.

With a muttered curse, he caught his breath and dived to the bottom of the pool, using the pressure and exertion to work out his animal urges.

It didn't work. She stayed on his mind all day.

Sopi remained emotionally wired until she heard the prince had left the building. She watched the helicopter veer across the valley, climb above the tree line and wheel to the far side of a peak.

Deflated and depleted, she slipped away to her cabin

for a nap. Of the half dozen tiny A-frame guest cottages, this one was farthest from the main building. At some point, probably when the stove conked out, it had become a storage unit for spare mattresses and mini refrigerators. Sopi kept one plugged in for her own use, and the heat still worked, so it was quite livable.

The tiny loft above the storage area was hardly on a par with the rest of the accommodation at Cassiopeia's, though. Even the employees had proper flats in the staff lodge tucked into the trees. That building was boxy and utilitarian, but they each had their own bedroom, bathroom and kitchenette. It was well tended and cozy.

Until her father had died very suddenly when she was fifteen, Sopi had lived in the manager's suite across from the kitchen. Somehow that had been given to the manager Maude had hired to run the spa that first year. Maude had taken over the suite when she came back to run things herself, except her version of managing was to delegate everything to Sopi.

Sopi had meanwhile bounced through guest and staff units as they became available. Eventually, she had wound up on the fringe of the property while Maude's daughters had appropriated the top suite when they returned to complain about having to live here instead of gadding about Europe.

Sopi didn't love tramping through the snow in the dark, but she did love having her own space. She had managed to warm it up with a few cherished items of her mother's—a blue velvet reading chair and a faded silk area rug. Her bed, purchased from the buy-and-sell ads, was a child's bunk bed with a desk beneath. Cartoon princesses adorned it, but they inspired her to dream, so she hadn't painted over them.

A long time ago, a guest had started the silly rumor that the owner of this hotel was descended from royalty. He had thought Sopi's mother had been the daughter of an ousted king or something.

Sopi's mother had already been gone by that point. Her father had only chuckled and shaken his head. It was a nice legend that might bring curiosity seekers to the spa, he'd said, but nothing more.

Sopi sighed and climbed into her bed without eating. The stacked milk crates that formed her pantry were empty. She hadn't had time to buy a box of cereal or replenish the instant soup she kept on hand to make with the kettle that was her most reliable friend.

Her head hit the pillow, and she plunged into a sleep so deep she wouldn't have heard a bomb go off.

Yet when the distant rat-a-tat of helicopter blades began to sound in the distance, her eyes snapped open.

Dang. She'd been dreaming something sexy about hot pool waters sliding silkily across her skin while a pair of blue eyes—

Ugh. She was so pathetic.

And wide-awake now that a mixture of self-contempt and guilt had hold of her. She glanced at her phone. It was full of text messages from staff. Some made her laugh. They all got on really well, but it was work, too. She had a quick shower, dressed and hurried back.

After putting out three proverbial fires, she was in the mani-pedi salon listening to a nail technician complain about an order of decals shaped like high-heeled shoes.

"They were supposed to be more bedazzled, but instead they're this plain black, and when you put clear polish on them, they curl up and fall off."

Sopi frowned and took the polish and decals to a

bench at the back of the salon. All the mani-pedi chairs were full of buzzing women hoping to meet the prince later.

From the time she was twelve, Sopi had apprenticed in all the treatments under a multitude of formally trained staff. She didn't have any certificates on the wall, but she could pinch-hit with nearly any service from foiled streaks to Swedish massage. If there'd been a chair free, she would have pitched in to help with the roster of guests begging for polish, but she had too much to do elsewhere anyway.

At least she'd taken the time last week to give her own toenails a fresh, if unremarkable, coat of pale pink polish. She stuck the decals of high-heeled shoes on each of her big toes and shellacked them in place with clear polish. She bedazzled one with a couple of glinting sequins to see if that would help hold it in place and make it look prettier.

She was curled over, blowing on her toes, distantly listening to a pair of women speculate on what time the prince would appear for dinner and whether he would invite anyone to join his table, when she picked up a call that had her frowning and hurrying barefoot down the hall to the massage therapy rooms.

Karl, their beefy Norwegian masseur, wasn't on the schedule this week, but Sopi spotted him about to enter a closed door.

"Karl!" she whispered. They strongly discouraged any conversation above a whisper in the spa area to ensure the guests enjoyed a relaxing stay. "It's your wife." She offered her phone.

Face blanking with panicked excitement, Karl took the phone and spoke rapidly in Norwegian.

"I have to go," he said, ending the call and trying

to pocket Sopi's phone. "The midwife is on her way. It's time."

"Finally! Hurry home, then." Sopi couldn't help grinning as she stole back her phone. "I hope everything goes well."

"Thank you." He started away, turned back, clearly in a flummoxed state of mind. "My phone is still in there. He's on the table!"

"Karl." Sopi took his arm and spoke calmly and firmly. "Don't worry about your client. I'll cover your massage. Get your phone and go home to your wife."

He nodded, knocked gently and led Sopi into the room.

"Sir, I'm very sorry," he said as he entered. "My wife has gone into labor, but I'm leaving you in good hands. Literally. Ah, there it is." Karl retrieved his phone from the small shelf above the essential oils. He turned to Sopi. "And she did text me, but I missed it because I silence it out of habit when I'm consulting with a client. The prince felt a twist in his lower back while skiing. He wants to be sure it doesn't turn into anything serious."

Sopi nodded dumbly, throat jammed as she avoided staring at the muscled back on the massage table, a sheet draped loosely across his hips and legs.

"Thank you," Karl said to her as he hurried from the room.

Sopi drew a breath and choked on a speck of spit. She turned her cough into a cleared throat, managing to croak, "I apologize for the switch. Karl was on call this week. I don't think he would have come in for anyone else but you."

The prince's shoulders tensed as though the sound of her voice surprised him.

She moved to tug the sheet over his exposed foot and

straightened the rest of it as she moved up the far side of the table. When she started to tuck the edge of the sheet under the band of his underwear, she realized he wasn't wearing any. Big hairy surprise. How was this her life?

CHAPTER TWO

"I'M NOT FORMALLY trained, but I've apprenticed under all of our registered therapists. I have over four hundred hours of treatments."

It was her. She had a touch as light as her footsteps moving quietly around the table. The room held a vague scent of citrus and sage, but he detected a scent beneath it. The sharp bite of nail polish and something more subtle, like sun-warmed peaches.

"Is your injury serious enough I should arrange a doctor or physiotherapist to come in? I don't want to exacerbate anything."

"You can't hurt me." He nearly laughed at the idea, but there was already an uncomfortable compression in his groin that might become a serious ache if he didn't keep a firm grip on his straying thoughts. "I typically ask for a man because women usually aren't aggressive enough. It's only a small twinge. I should have warmed up properly with my swim this morning, but the pool became too busy for laps." Too busy, period. He'd left when the first women arrived and had had to swim up a stream of crestfallen faces on his way to the elevator.

She set a hand on the back of his calf and squeezed, then moved it down to his ankle and squeezed again. It was a silent communication to let him know where she was, but it was surprisingly firm. Confident.

"I'll use our unscented oil. If there's significant inflammation, I can add geranium or yarrow."

He almost suggested she could dress him like a salad, but bit it back. He didn't usually have to filter himself quite so carefully when he was alone with a woman. He was the one naked and facedown, pretty much at her mercy, but an urge to pursue gripped him. He had to be careful.

"Whatever you think is best."

"How was the snow?" She was on his left side.

"Good." Amazing, actually. The sun had come out and the powder had been chest deep, but he barely recalled it now as he heard the click of a cap and the quiet friction of her palms rubbing together. He discovered he was holding his breath with anticipation.

Her fingertips settled in his middle back, light as a leaf coming to rest on the ground. Slowly, she applied pressure until she was leaning into him, prompting him to exhale until there was nothing left in his lungs.

As he drew in his next breath, the warmth in her hands stayed firm, penetrating his skin. She began to move in sweeping strokes, spreading the oil before her touch slowed and grew more exploratory.

Rhys had a massage at least once a month. He was as athletic as possible given his busy life of travel and meetings. He worked out regularly and ran marathons on treadmills, but he had a knack for storing tension in his shoulders and neck.

She found it, squeezing his trapezius muscle on either side, not working it, but acknowledging it. It wasn't supposed to be erotic, but he found her greeting of that tension both teasing and soothing. A comforting warning that she would be back.

It fostered a sense of connection that he instinctively knew would make for both heaven and hell. He probably should have called this massage off right here and now, but the temptation to feel her hands on him was too strong. Even though he doubted he'd be able to relax when—

He grunted with shock as she set her thumb into a spot next to his spine and sent a white-hot blade between his ribs.

"Sorry." Her touch lifted away. "Trigger point. I'll come back to it."

"No." It was as if she'd found something in him no one else had ever discovered. "Do it again."

"I just felt all this tightness here." Her hand got into the crook of his neck and shoulder while she pressed into the trigger point again with the point of—

"Is that your *elbow*?"

"Too hard?" She lifted away.

"No."

The pressure came back, the pain intense for the space of three breaths before it faded into a release of tingles like fairy dust, so profound he groaned in relief.

"There we go," she murmured, hands sweeping to soothe before she moved to the other side.

For the next ten minutes, she worked his shoulders, alternately persecuting and appeasing before she moved into his lower back. She even nudged aside the sheet to get her elbows into the tops of his glutes. It was another pressure point, hurting like hell before the cords in his lower back relaxed and his muscles turned to pudding.

He had never considered himself kinky, but this was bordering on erotic. The whole time he was blinded by intense sensations, he was equally aware of the sensual brush of her breast against his hip and what might have been the tickle of her hair falling against his spine. When he lifted his hips slightly, trying to give himself room to grow, she straightened away and drew the sheet up over his tailbone.

"I'll try going after that area with reflexology." She uncovered his feet. "Tell me if this pressure is too much?"

Her thumbs dug against his instep. He nearly levitated, but the endorphin rush was worth it. By the time she'd gone up his calves and into his hamstrings, he was hers. He'd never been in such a state of sublime arousal. She could have tied him to the bed and shown him a riding crop and he'd have begged, "Yes, please."

She worked his arms, and it took everything in him to keep them lax rather than flexing to drag her close. He ached to touch her as intimately as she was touching him, but he had to stay motionless and let her drive him mad.

This was torture. Genuine torture.

"Would you like to turn ov—"

"No," he growled. He was fully hard. If she looked him in the eye, she would know how badly he wanted to drag her atop him and see how much abuse this table could take.

A surprised pause. "I'll finish with your neck and scalp, then?"

"Yes."

She moved to stand above his head. All he could see through the face cradle was her bare feet.

Each of her big toes wore a silhouette of a woman's shoe against a background of pink. The plain one was peeling up. The other was bedecked with jewels and winked at him as she curled her toes and set gentle fingertips against the back of his neck.

"If I've been too rough—"

"You haven't." He closed his eyes in pleasure-pain. "This is the best massage of my life. I have to cut it short before it turns into something else."

He thought he heard a small *"Eep."* He definitely heard her swallow.

"Stay mean," he growled.

Her laugh was garbled and semihysterical, but she obeyed. She did cruel things to his trapezius muscles, turning snarling pit bulls into docile golden retrievers.

The final act was a merciless grip of all four fingertips of both hands into the muscles at the base of his skull. She held him in a dull headache for what felt like ten minutes before the pain evaporated into a sensation of sunshine dawning after a long, harsh winter.

She speared her fingers into his hair and erased his memory of pain, leaving the tranquil buzz he'd only previously experienced postcoitally.

"Take your time rising and dressing." Her voice sounded throaty and laden with desire, causing a fresh rush of heat into his groin. "Drink some water."

He couldn't move. Wait. He picked up his head, but the door was already closing behind her.

He felt drugged as he sat up, peeved that he hadn't asked her name. Probably for the best. He looked down at his lap, as ready for sex as he'd ever been.

If she could put him through his paces with a massage, what would sex with her be like?

The strong tug between his thighs told him thoughts like that were unhelpful.

As he pulled on his robe, he resented the hell out of his position. Curse tradition and snobbery and an illness that had put the future on his doorstep. Ten years ago, he could have had an affair with a spa worker and no one would have known or cared.

Once he'd moved back into the palace, he'd had to become more circumspect in his choices, but he still could have managed a fling with someone whose connections were less prestigious than his own. There would have been blowback, but an affair wasn't marriage.

That's what Rhys had to court now, though. Any relationship he started would have to be taken to the finish line. Was he really going to go against the grain with a pool-girl masseuse? Refuse to do his duty to his brother and the crown in favor of appeasing his libido?

He cursed, annoyed. One dinner was all he was after, before he made the rounds through the more expected choices of potential brides. Was that so much to ask? One evening to get to know her before he was forced to settle?

It was a selfish rationalization he shouldn't even contemplate.

He poured a cup of water from the cistern and threw it back like a shot of scotch. As he kicked into his sandals by the door, he almost mistook the speck on the tiles for a spider, but no.

He bent and touched his fingertip to it, picking up the silhouette of a woman's shoe, just like the one that had been coming off her toe. Huh.

Pinching it between his finger and thumb, he tucked it deep into the pocket of his robe, considering.

Flushed and confused, Sopi hurried to get as far away from the prince as possible, all the way to the other end of the building, where the service entrance to the kitchen was located. She stood on the back stoop in the cold dusk, trying to bring herself back under control.

She had provided a lot of massages, usually to women, but many to men, and had never once felt so affected by the experience. It hadn't been lascivious, either. It had been…elemental. She'd never become so entranced by a deep and genuine yearning to ease and soothe and heal. Yet touching him had been stimulating, too, keeping her in a state of alert readiness. Like petting a giant cat.

Or a man in peak condition who appealed to her on a primitive level.

She could have stroked her hands over him for hours, like a sculptor lovingly sanding her creation to a fine polish. In those last seconds before she'd asked him to roll over, she had felt a strong urge to splay herself atop him. Blanket him with her body while soaking in his essence.

Truthfully, she'd been lost in her world at that point and had been shocked back to reality when he declined to turn faceup.

I have to cut it short before it turns into something else.

She'd been stunned. Embarrassed that she'd aroused him, but shaken and inflamed by the idea. All the banked sexual energy she'd been suppressing as she administered the massage had suddenly engulfed her in a rush of carnal hunger.

If he hadn't told her to "stay mean," she didn't know what she might have done, but she'd found the concrete knots at the base of his skull. *Heavy is the crown*, she'd thought, wondering what his life was like back in Verina.

She would never know.

A sudden shiver had her realizing she had cooled past comfortable. She went inside, where the kitchen staff was scrambling to prepare for the dinner rush.

Without being asked, she slipped into the change room and put on her prep cook garb, then spent an hour peeling potatoes and scrubbing pots.

She was at her sweaty, sticky worst when she headed back to her cabin for a shower. The sound of squabbling as she approached through the trees almost had her turning back.

"Sopi!" Fernanda said when she spotted her. "Where have you been? I've been texting you."

"Oh?" Sopi pretended to scan her phone.

"She blocks us, you stooge," Nanette said pithily.

"Only when I'm working," Sopi said sweetly as she slid between the two towering beauties to unlock her door. "The paying guests are my priority, seeing as they support us." Hint, hint.

"Well, this has to do with the prince, so you ought to have been paying attention." As she entered uninvited, Fernanda wrinkled her nose at the clutter.

"She wants to make a fool of herself and wants you to help," Nanette informed Sopi with an eye roll.

"Why are you here?" Fernanda charged. *"The same reason."*

"To shower with me?" Sopi asked facetiously. "I don't usually entertain there."

"Shocker," Nanette muttered with an examination of her nails.

Always a joy spending time with family. Sopi bit back a sigh.

"The dining room could use you both to hostess this evening," Sopi said, mainly to Nanette. She never lifted a finger unless Maude pressed her. "We have a full house. Tables will turn over three or four times at least."

"Unavailable. Sorry," Nanette said with a saccharine smile.

"Not even for the chance to seat the prince?"

"He's not eating downstairs," Fernanda jumped in to say. "That's why I'm here. Women are lined up out the door at the salon to get one of these." Fernanda handed Sopi a sheet of toe decals.

Sopi frowned. "They're defective. I was in the salon earlier. They fall off."

"Yes, I know that. That's why *you* have to put it on. To make sure it stays."

Sopi shook her head, almost thinking there was a compliment in there, but definitely a backhanded one.

"If you're not going to help in the dining room, I have to shower and hurry back. Stick it on yourself. It's not rocket science."

"Forget the dining room," Fernanda said with a stamp of her foot. "No one will even show up there. The prince is dining privately. With a woman who has one of these stuck to her toe."

"What?" When she had pushed her feet into her closed-toe kitchen clogs, Sopi had noticed that she'd lost her plain shoe decal during the massage. She had only managed to keep the bedazzled one. She removed her snow boots now but self-consciously kept her socks on.

Nanette straightened from leaning against the decommissioned stove, wiping her hands across her backside as she did. "It seems the prince met someone who interests him, but he doesn't know her name. His assistant put the word out that this woman only has one shoe." She flipped her hair. "Apparently, she knows who she is, and he wants her to come to his suite this evening if she would like to dine with him."

"He—that's silly," Sopi said, hyperaware of the hot blush that flooded into her cheeks. It was a tremendous long shot that he could be talking about her. "Fernanda, he's going to know right away whether you're the woman he is trying to meet. If you don't already have a decal, you're not her."

"Well, his bodyguard doesn't know that, does he? If I can get in to see him, the prince can decide if I'm the right woman or not."

Sopi opened her mouth but couldn't find words. Fernanda wasn't the brightest candle on the cake and tended to be very self-involved. She came across as selfish, but she wasn't mean, just firmly stuck between thoughtless and clueless.

"I tried to tell her." Nanette grew more alert, like a jackal that scented something on the air. She was definitely the brains in the family, calculating and sharp.

"Yet here you are. Wanting the *same thing*," Fernanda hissed at her sister. "So it's not such a stupid idea, is it?"

"Wait." Sopi held up a hand. "Did you say there's some sort of run on at the salon?"

"Yes! Everyone is trying to get one. The girls tried to tell me to come back later, but there's no time. Can you just…" Fernanda unzipped her knee-high spiked-heel boot and dragged off her sock. "Hurry." She wiggled her toes. "I need to dress."

"Fernanda—" Sopi looked to Nanette for backup, but Nanette was also removing her ankle-high snakeskin boot. "I don't even have polish—oh."

Fernanda had absconded with a handful of bottles from the salon. Nanette had brought a tiny tube of fast acting superadhesive. She handed that over with a pointed look. *She* wouldn't lose her decal, come hell or high water.

"You're going to parade to his suite with everyone

else, all wearing one shoe so he can see you have a decal on your toe?" Sopi asked with bemusement.

"I'll wear proper open-toed evening shoes, won't I? Honestly, Sopi." Fernanda rolled her eyes.

Right. Sopi was the one being ridiculous.

Since it was the fastest way to get these two women to leave her private space, Sopi sat on the stairs to her loft. She motioned for Fernanda to set her foot beside her thigh.

"I put a pair of these on earlier," Sopi mused as she very carefully placed the shoe on Fernanda's toe. "I guess I should dress up and come with you. Maybe it's me he's looking for." It was a deliberate effort to provoke a reaction, so she shouldn't have been stung by Fernanda's dismissive snort.

"Oh, right. Have you even spoken to him for one second?"

"I have, actually." Sopi was always annoyed when these two put on that tone that disparaged her as a backwoods hick who lacked their refinement.

"What did you talk about?" Nanette asked, gaze narrowed.

"Nothing much." She shook the bottle of polish. "He didn't even ask my name." It was another dig.

She swiped the brush across the decal, varnishing the shoe into place. When she looked up, Fernanda was scowling with suspicion.

"Have you given any thought to how you'll walk back with wet polish on your toe?" Sopi asked.

"That's why I brought the glue," Nanette said, nudging her sister aside and eyeing Sopi shrewdly. "What would you wear?" she asked.

"Hmm?" Sopi glanced up from trying to break the seal on the glue nozzle.

"To dine with the prince."

"Oh." She hadn't given one iota of thought to actually doing it, but she'd come this far into needling them. She let bravado take her a few more steps. "I have some things of my mother's. There's a vintage Chanel I've always wanted an excuse to wear."

"How am I only hearing about this now? Show me." Nanette sounded genuinely impressed, but maybe Sopi was that desperate to finally take her by surprise.

She finished gluing the shoe to Nanette's toe, then trotted up the stairs to her loft.

In the chest beneath the window, she kept a handful of keepsakes—her parents' wedding album, the Christmas ornaments that hadn't broken over the years and her audition tape to a televised singing contest that might have been her big break if her father hadn't passed away the week she was supposed to appear.

Moving all of that aside, she drew out a zipped fabric box that also stored her summer wear. She dumped her clothes onto the floor and drew out the tissue-wrapped dress.

Sopi bit her lip as she noticed the moths had been into it. Voraciously.

Nanette arrived at the top of the stairs and said, "Oh my *God*. I thought *I* lived in a hovel."

"Don't you *dare*," Sopi said, voice sharpened by the strike of painful knowledge that she had lost a prized possession. This rag only proved she was nowhere near the prince's league. "You live here for *free*. Who do you think *pays* for that?"

"You just said it. It's free. No one is making you live like this. You're the one who plays the martyr all the time. 'Oh, woe. If you don't play hostess, I have to.'"

"'Oh, woe,'" Sopi shot back. "'I can't put a sticker on my own toe.'"

"Exactly," Nanette said with a hair flip and a complete absence of apology. "Set standards for yourself and refuse to compromise them." Her scathing glance dismissed Sopi's handful of possessions and the dress that was definitely not living up to her claims.

Such a cow. If Sopi was the cretin they thought, she would push Nanette down the stairs, taking out Fernanda, who had come up behind her to make a face of amused disgust as she looked around. God, she hated both of them.

"Oh, Sopi, no," Fernanda said when she saw the dress. Her tone held the depth of sympathy one saved for muddy dogs found starving in ditches. "You have to store vintage pieces properly. Otherwise they fall apart when you wear them. Everyone knows that. What a shame."

"Clearly your standards aren't being met here," Sopi said through her teeth. "Kindly leave my hovel and never come back."

"Does this mean you won't do my hair?"

"Seriously, Fernanda?" Sopi glared.

"You don't have to be so sensitive! I don't understand why she treats us like this," Fernanda complained as the two women went down the stairs.

They left, and Sopi hurried to lock the door so they couldn't return. Then she went into the shower and wept over old dresses and lost parents and foolish fantasies about unattainable men.

When she turned off the water, she stared at the bedazzled shoe on her one toe. Stupid. She picked it off so her nail was an ugly, chipped mess, and she left it that way as a reminder to stay grounded.

Then she wished even harder that the prince would marry one of her stepsisters and get them all out of her life for good.

"Say that again," Rhys growled at his assistant.

Gerard shifted uncomfortably. "I did as you asked. I put the word out that you were trying to locate the woman with the little shoe on her toe."

"You said I had met her already? That I knew who I was looking for?"

"Perhaps I wasn't clear on that?" His assistant's shoulders hunched up to his ears. "It seemed self-explanatory, but…" He trailed off, miserable.

"And now there's…how many women in the hall?"

"Fifty? Sixty?"

"All with one shoe on her toe."

"I'm afraid so, sir." Gerard swallowed.

"What am I supposed to do? Walk the line as though inspecting the troops, looking for her among them?" He'd been trying to be discreet. Rather than make it clear he was looking for someone on staff, he had thought he would get word to her through the grapevine. She could then quietly appear in his room if she was interested.

"How did they even get up here in the elevator?"

"The one shoe, sir. The bodyguards—"

Rhys pinched the bridge of his nose. "Suggestions on how to get rid of them?"

"Perhaps if you simply ate in the dining room? Mingled? Gave them a chance to say hello?"

Rhys had no appetite. "That never works. It only encourages them to approach me later." But he had to find himself a wife, and what was he going to do? Put a staff member in the unnerving position of having to walk a gauntlet to reach him for a single date that would go nowhere?

If she was out there and wanted to see him, she would already have knocked on his door. No, she was either too self-conscious or wasn't interested.

What a galling thought. Deep down, however, he knew it was for the best.

It still infuriated him.

"Fine," he growled. "Tell them I'll dine downstairs after all."

When the news came that the prince would in fact need a table, Sopi experienced a rush of panic. She definitely, positively didn't want to see him. After brooding for a solid hour, she had decided that what he must have meant when he cut short her massage was that he thought *she* was turning it into something it wasn't.

Unsurprisingly, her stepsisters both appeared within minutes of the announcement, eager to marshal rivals to terrible tables and have an excuse to brush past the prince's table while he ate. He would sit with the handful of upper-crust bachelors who had accompanied him onto the slopes and were providing further red meat for the marriage-minded women hungry for a good match.

Sopi gladly relinquished the reservation desk and slipped into the laundry room to help fold sheets and towels.

With nearly every guest now rubbing elbows in the dining room, the rest of the building was quiet. She stuck with her friends in housekeeping, joking and exchanging light gossip about the guests as they restocked the linen cupboards and performed the turn-down service in the top-floor rooms.

She did the prince's room herself and, as she plumped

the pillow, noticed the tiny black shoe on the night table. It sat atop one of the burgundy portfolios Maude liked to use for special event meetings. She would make a note from a bride or other VIP guest, then snap it shut and hand it off to Sopi with instructions to make things happen.

Sopi's pulse tripped at the sight of the tiny shoe, but a bodyguard stood by observing her, so she closed the drapes, set wrapped chocolates on the pillow and left.

Eventually, the guests retired from the dining room to hit the hot pools. Most of them were drunk and she resigned herself to a lot of cleanup later but helped the kitchen recover first.

While she was there, Maude pulled her aside with another list of to-dos. By the time they were done, it was time to close the pool and saunas. As Sopi marshaled the stragglers out, fully eight people tried to bribe her into calling them if the prince showed up after hours.

She bundled the last naked nymph into a robe and onto an elevator, then switched everything to service. That locked off the treatment level to all but the staff cards. She sighed in relief, facing miles to go before she slept, but the closing chores were ones she almost enjoyed. She could do them at her own pace and no one ever interrupted her.

Humming, she wheeled the mop from the closet and got started.

Midnight and Rhys was wide-awake, standing at the window, wired.

Wondering.

Swearing at himself. At his brother. At life.

For two hours, he'd been surrounded by beautiful, eligible, well-bred women, none of whom had been the one he wanted to see. It wasn't like him to be so fixated. He didn't like it. He'd seen the dark side of humans who became obsessed.

The darkest night of his life replayed uninvited. His well-practiced ability to block it didn't work this time, and his head filled with the shouts and crashing and what he'd thought had been fireworks inside the palace.

He'd been ten, old enough to take in the full horror of being invaded by soldiers in military garb and the gravity of their holding his parents at gunpoint below. He'd been too young to make a difference, though. In fact, he'd made things worse. He had screamed and rushed to the top of the stairs, where Henrik was being held off by a soldier.

If he had halted beside Henrik, his parents might still be alive. He had gone for the soldier's gun, though, and the soldier had crashed him in the face with the butt of his rifle, splitting his cheek and knocking him onto his ass.

Rhys had heard his mother scream. She had started to race up the stairs to him. A soldier below grabbed her arm and yanked her back. His father intervened, and the tension below erupted into four shots that left his parents crumpled on the floor.

Rhys could still feel the unnatural strength in Henrik as he'd gripped the shoulders of Rhys's pajamas and dragged him backward, behind the half wall of the upper gallery. Rhys had been limp with shock, gaze held by the cold stare of the soldier who had shot his parents so remorselessly.

He would never forget the ugly lack of humanity in that pair of eyes. He would forever carry the weight of guilt that if he hadn't given in to his own impulses, his parents might be alive today.

Distantly, he'd been aware of Henrik stammering out pleas. Promises they would never come back if they were allowed to leave. He'd somehow got Rhys onto his feet and pulled him down the service stairs and out of the palace.

Shock had set in and Rhys didn't recall much of the days after that, but guilt remained a heavy cloak on him. Guilt and loss and failure. He was grateful to Henrik for getting them out, but a day never went by where he didn't feel sick for escaping. For surviving when his parents had died because of his rash actions.

A day never went by when he didn't feel their loss as though pieces had been carved out of his heart. His chest throbbed even more acutely with apprehension over Henrik's diagnosis.

Why Henrik? It should be him staring into the muzzle of a life-threatening diagnosis, not his brother. If he lost Henrik—

He couldn't let himself think it.

This was why he hadn't wanted to marry and have children. This agonizing fear and inability to control the future were intolerable.

He swore under his breath.

If grim introspection was the only mood he could conjure, he needed a serious distraction. He walked across to the folio Maude had given him, the one he had said he wanted to review when he had made his abrupt exit from the dining room earlier this evening.

Maude's eldest daughter, a lithe beauty, had fallen into step alongside him as he departed, offering an excuse about fetching something from her room. Her purpose had been obvious, though. She had deliberately created the impression she was the one he'd been seeking as his dinner companion. In the elevator, she had set her pretty silver shoe next to his, not quite nudging, but definitely inviting him to notice her toe.

This constant circling was exhausting. In the space of a day, he'd come around from thinking he *should* marry to impatience for task completion. Maude's eldest was exactly what was expected of the royal family— well-bred, smoothly sophisticated and picture-perfect beautiful. She struck him as the possessive type, too. Overtures from other women would no longer be a problem. She would make damned sure of it.

"Please allow me to arrange a more peaceful dining experience for you tomorrow," she had offered with the silky sweetness of a white chocolate mousse. "We often close the solarium for honeymoon couples."

Honeymoon was a deliberate choice of word, he was sure. *So* exhausting.

"I'll let you know." He had cut away to his own room, not the least bit compelled to spend another minute with her, let alone a lifetime.

As he flipped open the folio, interest in purchasing this property nonexistent, the tiny black shoe fluttered to the carpet. All the darkness in him folded in on itself, becoming a burst of light with a single focus. *Her.*

He tried to shake it off. He had no business obsessing over anyone, let alone the least suitable woman here. How did he even have the energy to experience a rush of masculine interest? He ought to be physically exhausted from his day of skiing, but he couldn't shake this buzz of sexual hunger. This sense of something being unfinished.

Maybe he could work it out in the pool.

He stripped where he stood and pulled on his robe. This time he had the sense to bring one of his bodyguards and ordered him to stand at the door to ensure he wouldn't be stalked.

The lights were dimmed in the change room, the mirror and taps polished, the floor dry. The music and water feature were both turned off, along with the jets in the tub. It was blessedly silent as he walked past the still water of the indoor pool and hot tub. Through the fogged windows, he saw steam rising off the mineral pool in gentle wafts against the black sky.

Just as he was about to walk outside and dive in, however, he heard a noise down the short hallway that led to the sauna area. A woman was singing.

The scent of eucalyptus carried with her voice on the humid air. A bucket of cleaning supplies stood outside a door to a steam room. The sound of spraying water cut off, and he clearly heard her crooning a modern ballad that reverberated beautifully off the tiled walls.

He stood transfixed as *she* emerged to drop a long-handled scrubbing brush into the bucket. Her hair was in a messy ball atop her head, but tendrils stuck to her damp neck. She wore light cotton pants and a baggy smock, both heavily soaked at the cuffs. Without looking his way, she quit singing and sighed. She picked up the bucket and carried it down the hall and around a corner where an authorized-personnel-only sign hung.

What was she doing cleaning the sauna at midnight? She was a goddess who possessed a healing touch and a siren's voice, not a scullery maid.

He crossed his arms, scowling as he listened to a door open and close. He waited for her to reappear.

And waited.

Had she locked herself in a utility closet? He followed to the end of the hall, where he found two doors. One opened to a closet that was empty of all but fresh linens and cleaning supplies. Her bucket sat on the floor inside it.

The other door read Emergency Exit Only. Door Locks Automatically.

It hadn't set off an alarm when she went through, so he pushed it open. The night was clear, the air bracing. A narrow footpath had been stamped into the snow. He glimpsed a maintenance building in the trees.

Don't, his rational head warned.

He felt for his key card, tried it against the mechanism on the outside and saw it turn green. He stepped into the cold and let the door lock behind him.

CHAPTER THREE

TO HELL WITH IT. That was what Sopi had been thinking the whole time she'd been scrubbing the saunas. She felt grimy and sweaty and resentful and *entitled to enjoy herself.*

Not in the treated waters of the hot pool, though. No, she was going to the source, the original spring that had been formed by long-ago explorers, possibly ancestors of the nearest First Nations tribe. No one knew exactly who had dammed the hot water trickling out of the mossy ground, forming a small bathing pool on a bluff in the woods, but through the 1800s and into the early 1900s the small swimming hole had been used by hunters and snowshoers who heard about it through word of mouth.

Eventually, an enterprising railway baron had built the first rustic hotel here. He had brought in a crew to dig a proper pool by hand, and that hole had eventually become what was the indoor pool today. He had lined it and filled it with snow that he melted and heated by piping water from this tiny hot spring. Since this natural, rocky pool was impossible to clean, the hotel wasn't allowed to let guests use it. It was kept as a heat source and a point of interest. In the summer, the gate next to the pump house was left unlocked so guests could picnic on the bench nearby, enjoying the view of the lake and the soothing trickle of the water.

Tonight, Sopi's were the only footsteps as she veered off the path to the maintenance shed and wound through the trees. The snow wasn't too deep under the laden evergreens, but she was only wearing sandals. By the time she emerged and shoved at the gate to open it against the accumulation of snow, her feet were frozen and aching.

She waded through the knee-high snow the final few yards. As she reached the edge of the pool, she kicked off her sandals and stepped into the hot water. It hurt like mad, but was a relief, too.

She hadn't been to the pool in a long time. Not since she had come out here to cry after getting the news her father had passed from a sudden heart attack. This had always been her sad place, and that moment had been one of her saddest. Since it wasn't something she liked to revisit, she didn't come here often.

She had forgotten how peaceful it was, though. The height of the trees hid it from hotel windows. The only reminders of civilization were the fence and gate and the distant hum of the pump house. She turned her back on those man-made things and faced the lake. The slope fell away, allowing a clear view of its sparkling, snow-blanketed surface.

The longer she stood here, the better she felt. The waters truly were capable of healing, she decided with a sigh of reclaimed calm. She started to pull her top up over her head but froze when she heard the crunch of footsteps.

Really? She almost screamed in frustration. Who? *Why?* She twisted to glare at—

"Oh."

"You're not supposed to swim alone." The prince's

breath fogged against the frosty air. He wore his robe and rattled the gate to open it farther before he took long strides through the snow in his slippers. As he came closer, she was able to read his frown of dismay in the moonlight reflecting as a faint blue glow off the surrounding snow. He abandoned his slippers next to her sandals and stepped into the water, hissing at the bite of heat.

She looked back the way he'd come, expecting at least a few bodyguards and one or two of his cohorts, if not a full harem of adoring women.

"Are you lost? What are you doing here?" she asked him.

"What are *you* doing here?"

"You inspired me," she admitted truthfully, although Nanette's pithy talk of refusing to compromise had also lit a fire of rebellion in her.

"To try skinny-dipping? This is hotter than the pool."

"It is. Too hot in the summer, which is the only time this area is open to the public." She nodded at the sign obscured by a buildup of frozen condensation. "No swimming allowed."

"Ah. I've inspired you to break rules." His mouth barely twitched, but he sounded pleased. "Live dangerously."

"Not really. I happen to know it's tested regularly and is always found to be potable." The fence kept wildlife out, so risk of contamination was next to zero.

"That takes some of the thrill out of it, doesn't it?"

His words made her think of her stepsisters' disparagement of her. Their contempt had gone far deeper than a scoff over a moth-eaten dress. They knew she wasn't any match for a man in his position. *Sopi* knew it. She was standing here prickly with self-consciousness, aware that she was still covered in sweat from laboring in the spa. Definitely not anywhere near his exalted level.

The water beckoned, but she murmured, "It was a dumb impulse. We should go back."

He dragged his gaze from the frozen lake, eyes glittering in the moonlight, but his expression was inscrutable. "I wanted you to join me."

"Here?" She shook her head. Part of her was tempted. Where was the harm in a nude swim with a stranger? And where had such a reckless thought come from, she wondered with a suppressed choke of laughter. But he was the first man to make her consider such rash behavior. Everything about this was a rarity for her.

"For dinner," he clarified. "Did you…get that memo?"

The air that came into her lungs seemed to crystallize to powdered ice. "I didn't imagine for a minute you were looking for me. Besides, every woman here got a decal—"

"I know that," he cut in, sounding aggravated. "Now."

She bit back a smile. "You could have sent me a proper message."

"I didn't know your name. My assistant asked the booking clerk, but Karl was listed as my masseur. Who *are* you?"

She hesitated. Tell him everything? Would he care?

"I know this is inappropriate," he growled into the silence that she let stretch out with her indecision. "That's why I didn't want to make overt inquiries."

Inappropriate? It hadn't been, not really, until he used that word. Now she reeled, astonished that he was making this private conversation into more than she would have let herself believe it to be.

"If I'm out of line, say so. We'll go back right now."

"I don't know what this is," she admitted, hugging herself against the cold, because the hot water on her feet wasn't enough to keep her warm when she was outside at midnight before spring had properly taken hold. "My father bought this hotel for my mother. She named it after me. Cassiopeia. My friends call me Sopi."

"Cassiopeia." He seemed to taste the syllables, which made her shiver in a different way. "Maude is your mother?" He sounded surprised. Skeptical.

"Stepmother. She took control of the spa after my father died. I wasn't old enough to do it myself and... Well, I'd like to challenge her now, but lawyers cost money and... It's a long, boring story." She doubted he would believe the spa ought to belong to her anyway, not when she stood here all sweaty and gross. "I'm really cold. Can we—" She looked for her sandals.

"Yes. Let's warm up." He skimmed off his robe, tossing it to hook on the fence before he made his way farther into the pool. Naked, of course, carefully choosing his footing on the slippery rocks.

She looked to the sky, begging for guidance from higher powers.

"It's deeper than I expected," he said with satisfaction. He sank down as he found one of the rocky ledges that had been set in place for seating. "What are you doing? You said you wanted to try this."

"Alone."

"I'll turn my head." His tone rang with *prude*.

She was wearing a bra and underwear, basically a bikini. She knew that was a rationalization to stay here and swim with a man who intrigued her, but she also liked the idea of proving she *could* interest a prince, even if she was the only one who would ever know it.

Could she?

With an internal tsk, she decided to—for once—do something for herself. She stepped out of the water long enough to drop her drawstring pants and throw off her top.

She gingerly made her way into the pool, one eye on his profile to ensure he wasn't witnessing her clumsy entry. She winced at sharp edges pressing into her soles, bent to steady herself with a hand on a submerged boulder and let out a sigh as she sank to her shoulders and heat penetrated to her bones.

The pool was about four feet deep and maybe six feet wide. The prince had found one of the best perches facing the lake. She bumped her foot into his and he looked at her.

"Cheater," he accused as he noticed her bra strap.

She ducked under, unable to resist the lure of baptizing herself even though her hair would freeze into its tangled bun. Her long, strenuous day began to rinse away as she did it again. She came up with another sigh of sheer luxury.

"I didn't bring a towel. This is literally the dumbest idea I've ever had, but I don't regret it one bit."

"I would be a gentleman and offer you my robe, but then I'd have to streak like a bald yeti across the snow to get back inside."

"I'm pretty sure I saw one of those this morning."

His teeth flashed white. "Have you always lived here? You're Canadian?"

"I am. My mother was Swedish, I think. I don't have much information on her. She was an only child, and my father was funny about her family. Didn't like to talk about them. I don't think my grandparents approved of him."

"Why not?"

"Snobs, maybe? He sold two-way pagers and the early mobile phones into the European markets. Not very sexy at the time, but it was lucrative. That's how he paid for this." She nodded toward the hotel hidden by the spiky trees. "Then Silicon Valley crashed the party. His heart trouble started when my mother passed, and financial worries made it worse."

Sopi didn't know what kind of means Maude had pretended she had, but based on what Sopi had learned since, she believed Maude had misrepresented herself and worked on her father's desire for Sopi to have a mother with the goal of taking over his bank account and assets.

"It's a strange purchase for someone in that industry, especially since you don't have cell service beyond the hotel."

"My mother was struggling as a new mom in a new country. Dad traveled a lot, and she didn't have anyone to rely on. She wasn't working and felt very isolated. She loved her spa visits, though. She came here on one of them, talked to the owner who was thinking of selling. My father bought it for her."

"Romantic."

"Not really. It was worse for wear, and she had a lot of challenges with its remote location. She knew what she wanted, though, and made it happen. It was quite successful until she passed a few years later."

"What happened?"

"A bad flu that turned into pneumonia. Can we not talk about that? I was quite young, but it still makes me sad."

"I understand," he said gravely.

She recalled a bleak line in the history of Verina stating his parents had been killed in an uprising, forcing him and his brother to live in neighboring countries for fifteen years. For the first time, she wondered if the platitude he'd just used was actually true. Maybe he really did understand the hollow ache inside her.

He had braced his elbows on nearby rocks above the surface and tipped his head back to look up at the clear sky.

She took stock of where she was, soaking with a prince in the wilderness, the only sound a distant hum and a closer trickle of water seeping from the seams in the rocks and off a worn ledge into their bath.

"There you are." He tilted his head. "The trees were in the way. Cassiopeia."

Hardly anyone used her whole name, not when they addressed her. She'd begun to think *Cassiopeia* only applied to things that weren't really hers.

"A queen, if memory serves." It was hard to read his expression with the shadows and his beard.

She almost mentioned the silly rumor about her mother being descended from royalty but thought he might think she was trying to elevate herself to his stratosphere.

"A vain one who gets tied to a chair for eternity," she said instead. "Maybe I am vain." She didn't look for the W in the sky, having searched it out nearly every starry night since childhood. "My tiny mind was blown when I learned on the first day of school that not everyone had their own constellation."

He snorted. "I don't."

"Because you're a star on earth."

"Don't," he said flatly. The steam seemed to gust off the water so there was no mist between them, only clear, dry air that stung her cheeks and nose. "Don't put distance between us."

She swallowed her surprise, but a lump lodged in her chest, one that her voice had to strain to speak around. "There is a continent and an ocean between us." Among other things. His mountain of society and stature, her vast desert of education and life experience.

"Rhys," he said, laying down a gauntlet. "If you're going to reject me, use my name so I'm clear that you mean me." It was such an outrageously arrogant statement she wanted to laugh, yet he drew her in as his equal by offering the familiarity. Such an enigmatic man.

"I thought I was pointing out the obvious," she said quietly.

"You're the least obvious person I've ever met. Any other woman would be naked and straddled across me by now, whether I wanted her here or not. You wouldn't even come to dinner with me. Why not?"

Cowardice.

"I didn't think you were serious," she repeated. "Where would this even go? That's not opportunism talking. I don't have affairs with rich, powerful men. You tell me what happens. How long does it last? What happens when it's over?"

His eyes were obsidian, his jaw gleaming like wet iron. With a muttered curse in what sounded like German, he turned his glower toward the frozen lake below.

He didn't tell her she was wrong.

Sopi felt for another of the worn rocks that provided a rough seat and settled onto it. "Do you want the truth?"

"Always," he bit out.

"Maude wants you to marry Nanette. I thought if I

facilitated that, I could get rid of all three of them and finally have my home to myself."

A pulse of astounded silence, then he barked out a humorless laugh. He snapped his head around to glare at her. "I'll marry if and whom *I* desire. It won't be either of them. I promise you that right now."

She kissed goodbye her pipe dream of being free of her stepfamily, which left her to contemplate whether she should allow herself to get closer to this compelling man who, for the moment, at least, was not that far away.

"I don't know what happens, Sopi. I wish I did," he said cryptically.

At the sound of her nickname on his lips, she found herself trying out the sound of his. "Rhys." It caught with tugging sensations in her chest and across her shoulders.

He looked at her.

Everything altered. The air shimmered and the earth stood still. Her scalp prickled and her breasts grew tight and heavy.

"That does not sound like a rejection, *süsse*." His voice melted her bones. He extended a long arm across the surface of the water, palm up in invitation.

She hadn't consciously meant to turn this into anything, but her hand went into his. She floated across the short space between them, drawn by his firm grip to set her hand against his neck. The top of her foot hit a rock, and she reacted with a jerk of her knee, knocking it into his.

He made a noise of concern and gathered her into his lap. His hand cupped her knee and he soothed her kneecap with his thumb. "Tell me," he murmured. "Do you feel the same when I touch you?"

"The same as what?"

The hand behind her back ran up to cradle her neck. With the lightest squeeze, he had her shuddering and turning her torso into his.

"Like that," he growled, lips coming close enough to nibble at her chin. "The way you made me feel on the table today."

Streaks of light and heat seemed to shoot through her at the graze of his whiskers and the mere touch of his mouth on her skin. She cupped his wet beard and searched for his lips with her own, not really knowing what she was doing, only knowing she needed the press of his mouth to her own.

They both moaned as their lips parted and slid and found the right fit. Forever, she thought. She wanted the forceful play of his mouth to consume hers forever. Then his tongue touched her inner lip, delved, and the taste of him shot lightning through her again, spearing a jolt of pleasure straight between her thighs.

She jerked away to catch her breath, stunned, but went straight back after his mouth, pressing the back of his head to encourage him to ravage her.

He growled and they kissed with more fervor, wildly, deeply, a sound rumbling in his chest like a predatory animal. His arms flexed around her, drawing her tighter into his lap and twisting her chest to rub against his.

Her bra shifted as they slithered against one another, abrading and annoying her as it kept her from feeling him with all her skin. She tried to scrabble behind herself with one hand and release it, but his confident fingers met hers and easily unclasped it. She drew back to pull her arms free and he threw it into the snow.

As she pressed herself into him, their mouths crashed together again. His hand swirled a rush of water across her ribs right before his palm flattened against her skin, stroked and shifted, teasing at her waist and shoulder blade and back to her rib cage until she couldn't stand it. She twisted, offering her breast, and finally he claimed the swell in a firm clasp. He shaped and caressed and made her forget everything but the feel of him fondling her so blatantly.

She realized a keening noise was coming from her lips and tried to bite it back, but he caught her nipple in a light pinch and once again she had to break from their kiss to catch her breath—the sensation was so sharp.

"Too much?" He bowed his head over hers as she buried her face in his neck, as though shielding her from something. "You're killing me."

She realized that wasn't just her own heart slamming unsteadily against her rib cage. His was, too. And that hard shape against her hip was him, fully aroused.

She stilled, shocked and stunned and wickedly curious.

"I don't have a condom," he muttered. "This is definitely the best and worst idea you've ever had." He found her ear and flicked his tongue along the rim, making her shudder. "Are you on anything? Should we take this upstairs?"

Dazzled, it took her a moment to realize what he was asking. "I'm not on anything. I don't do this. I've never done it."

"I'm not a guest. You're not an employee. Not right now. That's not what this is. It's two people who can't keep their hands off each other." He cursed and shifted her, but the sound he made was more a groan of suffering. He sucked on her lobe so hard she nearly came out of her skin. Then he applied his teeth, just short of pain, holding her in a tingling state between fear and trust.

If she pulled away, it would hurt, but she didn't want to go anywhere. She petted her fingers across his wet beard, soothing the beast who held her in his tense jaws. Her pulse throbbed in her throat and low in that secretive place between her clamped thighs.

"I mean I've *never* done this," she admitted in a quavering voice. "Made love. With anyone."

His arms nearly squashed her breathless, and a strangled noise came out of him.

"Are you serious?" He took hold of her wet, knotted hair, holding her so her nose was nearly touching his. His eyes were depthless black orbs, threatening to pull her into another universe. Her heart galloped so hard, she thought her chest would explode.

"Who would I sleep with? No one has ever made me feel like this."

"How?" His hand tightened in her hair, pulling her head back to expose her throat. He licked along the artery, and her nipples contracted to such tight points, they felt pierced. She pinched her thighs together.

"Like I'm on fire," she gasped. "Like I need your hands all over me to put it out."

His ragged laugh rang with satisfaction. This time when he claimed her breast, she arched into his touch. He caught her nipple in the crook of two fingers and applied tender pressure until she set her open teeth against his neck.

His caress was so delicious, she found herself sucking the skin of his neck against her teeth before she realized what she was doing and pulled back.

"Mark me, *süsse*." He gentled his touch and circled his thumb around her turgid, stimulated nipple, soothing. "Don't be scared. I won't hurt you. But I do want this." His arms hardened as he lifted her.

Her shoulders and chest came out of the water. As the cold hit her and tightened her nipples even more, he closed his mouth over one. The sudden shifts in temperature and his hard pull sent a jolt of electricity through her. She squeaked and clenched her hand in his hair.

He made a noise of sympathy and drew back to blow and lick circles around her nipple, making her sob under a fresh onslaught of blinding sensation.

She didn't know what to do. Wires of tension pulled in her abdomen and lower. It was more than she could take, but she was greedy, too. She folded her arms around the back of his head and he captured her nipple again, sucking more gently this time, while she moaned in abject pleasure, head falling back so her hair was in the water.

When he finally let her sink back down into his lap, she was trembling and panting. He was so hard against her hip, she thought he must be in pain. Perhaps he was. He was breathing in deliberately measured breaths, and his thighs opened wider to cradle her more deeply against him.

"Do you want me to…" She didn't know what to do. What to offer. But she knew she was dying to touch him.

"I want you to let me do this." His hand slid to catch against the elastic of her underpants. He paused, the fabric pulled far enough from her hip the first ripple of hot water began to caress her bare skin.

Breathless with anticipation, she nodded.

He drew her panties down. The small shift bounced her naked backside against his thighs. Her stomach wobbled at the light abrasion of his leg hair against the sensitive cheeks of her bottom. He pulled the cotton off her ankles and flicked it over his shoulder, joining her bra somewhere in the snow.

"And how does this feel, *süsse*?" His fingertips trailed across her outer thigh to her hip while she absorbed the eddies of hot water moving freely against her most intimate places.

She could hardly breathe. She thought about his touch trailing into those places and shifted restlessly, her nose finding its way into the wet whiskers under his jaw.

"I don't know what to do," she confessed with embarrassment. "I've never touched a man."

"Then by all means, find out what you've been missing." His teeth flashed in a brief smile, but he chucked her chin. "And come here. I want to kiss you again."

She pressed her mouth to his, joyously returning to this wondrous place where she could flagrantly gorge herself on the taste and feel of his lips and tongue and the beard that was rough and silky and utterly compelling.

Shyly, one arm firmly encircling his neck, she let her other hand drift to caress across his shoulder. Those tendons were tight and straining, but not in the way they'd been this afternoon. His pectoral muscles were taut, too, flexing beneath her touch as she dipped her hand below the surface.

Was that his nipple? She scraped her thumb across it, and he made a low sound of pleasure in his throat, one she couldn't help teasing out of him a second time before she shifted to make space for her hand to trail between them, down to the fierce shape pressing so insistently against her hip.

As she closed her fist on the girth of him, his fingers bit into her waist where he anchored her on his thighs. His teeth took hold of her bottom lip, and she felt the rumble of his pleasured groan vibrate in his chest.

How utterly fascinating. She moved her hand, learning the shape of him, discovering what made him hiss or release sounds of delicate agony.

"Am I hurting you?" she broke their kiss to ask.

"No." He stole brief, hungry kisses. "Squeeze tighter."

She looked down at where the dark water obscured her view of him. "I feel cheated."

"So do I." He nuzzled under her chin. Beneath the water, he skimmed his hand along the back of her thigh, but stopped where her leg sat pressed to the top of his.

She tucked her chin and kissed him, squeezed him more boldly and allowed her legs to relax.

His flesh pulsed in her fist and he tilted her, rolling her into a more aggressive kiss that flipped her heart on its edge. Her inner muscles clenched in anticipation, but his fingertips only teased behind her thighs, the barest touch skimming lightly across the fine hairs that protected her folds.

She sobbed with denial. Opened her legs more. Tried to tell him wordlessly what she wanted. He made a low sound of satisfaction and his touch moved to the front of her thighs, stroked inward and upward, until she was the one biting his lip, aching with expectancy.

When his hand finally, firmly covered her, her stomach fluttered and she groaned into his mouth. He seemed to brand her with his intimate touch, claiming her so thoroughly, she had to break their kiss and exchange breathless pants with him.

"If we do this right, we'll do it together," he said in a voice like smoke and velvet. "Yes?"

"Yes," she breathed. Then opened her mouth in a silent scream because he lifted all but one finger from her and gently worked his wicked touch against her.

"Keep stroking me, *süsse*," he urged in a whisper.

"I like it. It feels like this." He found the most sensitive place on her body and pressed without mercy, two fingertips now slowly circling to draw her into a place of mindless pleasure.

She shook, groaning with abandon into his naked shoulder, not realizing she had tightened her hold on him until he gave an abbreviated thrust into her grip and made a ragged noise against her ear.

"Like that, yes." His breath hissed with concentrated pleasure. "We're going to kill each other." He rocked his touch, unhurried as he stoked the fire within her. "I couldn't be happier than to die right here, tonight. Like this."

It was the most singular experience of her life, to communicate completely with touch. To caress him and sense his pleasure as acutely as she experienced her own.

He became her entire world. Nothing mattered in these concentrated seconds except his touch passing across her bundle of nerves, his pulse against her palm, the wall of his iron-hard body shifting with light friction against her skin.

Tension coiled in her abdomen. Through her whole body. She licked his skin and kissed him with abandon, trying to make him understand how exquisite he was making her feel. How he was torturing her beyond what she thought she could stand, yet she never wanted him to stop.

In a subtle move, he hitched her a fraction higher and his touch probed. Her inner muscles tightened at the intrusion of his finger. She shivered despite being so hot she thought she would incinerate. He bit tenderly at her lips with his own, teasing kisses of reassurance as the pressure of his palm rocked where she needed it most.

She saw stars. Gripped him tightly in her fist and matched the rhythm of his thrusts with a lift of her hips against his firm hand. The crisis rose. She tasted copper and thought she might have bitten his lip. She wasn't sure, but he didn't complain. He only kept up the wild caresses that carried them both over a waterfall so they plunged freely off a cliff into the mist.

CHAPTER FOUR

RHYS VAGUELY WONDERED if there was an aphrodisiac in these waters, because he had never climaxed so hard in his life. Despite aching from the force of it, he wanted nothing but to pull Sopi astride him and sink into the satin depths he'd claimed with his touch.

He gently cradled her trembling body against his unsteady heart, trying to find his breath. Trying to find a shred of sense, because all-night lovemaking had a place—and it wasn't a primordial pond in the frozen wilderness.

With a virgin disguised as a woodland nymph.

He didn't disbelieve her about her inexperience, but he was incredulous that such a passionate woman hadn't found someone to share her sensuality with.

No one has ever made me feel like this.

Him, either, and that shook him. He wasn't entitled to this sort of high. His deepest instincts began to war, one side warning him that he couldn't have this. The other, greedier side wanted to mate and mate some more. Grind himself against her until they were nothing but dust.

She posed a very serious danger, this curious, unassuming goddess of a woman.

He rose abruptly, making her gasp at the shock of cold air on her wet skin.

He twisted to ease her back under the warmth of the water, seating her on the flat ledge he'd vacated.

She blinked in surprise, mouth pouted and shiny from their endless kisses, all but her collarbone hidden from his insatiable gaze.

"I'll fetch you a towel and a robe." He waded out of the water, welcoming the bracing slap of winter frost that cleared his head so he could think.

"You don't have to," she said in a small voice behind him.

"I want to," he insisted, pushing his wet arms into his robe and belting it tightly. "Two minutes."

Sopi was reeling from what she'd done with the prince. Her whole body tingled with lassitude, the kind that made her want to groan in luxury at how deliciously sated she felt. She couldn't think of any other experience that had left her so dreamily satisfied.

His abrupt departure caused her a pinch of distress, though. The longer she sat here, the more she began to feel self-conscious about her lack of inhibition. About waiting here like a harem girl for the sheik to return.

When she heard his footsteps crunching through the trees, she sat a little straighter, mouth trembling into a shy smile of greeting.

It wasn't him. It was one of his bodyguards. The clean towel and robe he carried glowed like an armload of snow as he approached.

Throat locked, eyes burning in mounting horror, Sopi watched him look indecisively between the soggy pants and shirt she'd left atop her shoes and the snow-covered bench nearby.

"The prince offers his regrets that he couldn't bring these himself. He said he will speak to you in the morning. Um… Here?" He shook out the items and hung them on the fence, then stepped through the gate and stood with his back to her.

"What are you doing?" she asked, appalled when he stayed there.

"I'm to escort you safely indoors."

Her embarrassment turned to outrage. "I'm fine. *Go.*"

"With respect, I have my orders. Take your time."

She stewed with impotent fury as she realized her choices were to argue while she boiled or end this as quickly as possible. Why was the practical choice always to give in?

And why hadn't Rhys come back himself? Had she turned him off? Had he finished with her already? Was he mad that she hadn't put out with *actual* sex?

Growing more and more horrified by what she'd done, she waded out and shook the robe open, struggling into it without bothering to dry herself. When she scooped up her clothes, she glanced at the thick snow on the far side of the pool and decided to find her underwear in the morning, when it was light.

Moments later, she stomped through the trees toward her cabin, surprising the bodyguard into saying, "Ma'am?" He hurried to follow her new direction.

She ignored him, aware of him trailing her, but she didn't even look at him as she got to her door, unlocked it, then closed it in his face, locking it again from the inside.

With hot, dry eyes and wet, tangled hair, she fell into bed.

Rhys had returned to the deserted spa in time to hear Nanette trying to pull rank on his bodyguard.

"I'm the owner. I can go anywhere I want," she insisted.

"Your mother claims to own it," Rhys had said flatly, moving forward to prevent her from realizing he was coming from the hallway to the building's exit, not the men's room.

Nanette faltered, frosty expression morphed into welcome.

"That's what I mean, of course. My mother is the owner. Your Highness," she added with a sweet smile especially for him. "When I saw your man standing guard, I wanted to be sure you had everything you need."

"Everything but privacy."

Her smile stiffened, and she looked past him. He waited for her gaze to come back and held it with his most unapologetically imperious glare.

She sniffed and said, "I'll leave you to it, then."

"Do." He waited until she was out of earshot before he muttered his instructions to his bodyguard to take a robe and towels to Sopi, aware Nanette would stake out his floor to see whom he brought back to his room.

Rhys rarely took action without considering the consequences. If he did, he would currently be wondering if a deflowered virgin was incubating a royal baby. He'd had the presence of mind to stay this side of sane with Sopi, thankfully, but he wouldn't expose her as his lover to the likes of Nanette until such time as he'd weighed the ramifications for both of them. What little she'd told him about her relationship with Maude meant there could be consequences for her.

She had also left him with the impression that she was the rightful owner of this property, if not legally, at least morally. Her father had bought it for her mother, who had lovingly restored it, but Maude was the one trying to unload it in a private sale under the radar.

That had his mind churning as he took the elevator back to his floor, passing Nanette in a chair in an alcove, hair twisted around one finger, an open book in her lap.

"Good night," she said as he passed, shoe dangling from her toe.

He nodded curtly, entered his room and went directly to the window on the north wall. He thought he might have seen a flash of movement in the trees but wasn't sure.

Annoyed, he went back to the folio Maude had given him.

Lawyers cost money, Sopi had said.

They did but, as it happened, he had an abundance of both.

Sopi's morning went from bad to worse very quickly.

She woke with the worst type of hangover—the sober kind that piled nausea on remorse with none of the blurry celebration of alcohol to dampen her memory or give her an excuse for behaving so wantonly. She didn't even regret the sex part. She had wanted that, but she felt very much like she'd fallen for a line from a playboy who set up conquests like bottles on a log, simply so he could shoot them down.

At least no one would know, she told herself. Then her walk of shame past the pump house turned up fruitless. One of the hotel's maintenance men must have checked the gate and gathered her bra and underwear. She could only pray her things would be thrown away rather than turned in to Lost and Found.

By the time she was heading into the back door of the hotel and passing Maude's office, her phone was exploding with the usual work-related texts. Sopi had her head down, reading complaints about late deliveries and equipment needing repair, and didn't see Maude waiting for her until her stepmother's haranguing voice said, "Sopi."

Hiding her wince, Sopi detoured into Maude's office. "Good morning."

"Two of Fernanda's friends are arriving in Jasper in an hour. They don't want to wait for the shuttle. Can you collect them?"

"Fernanda can't do it?" Wasn't that the obvious solution?

"She's tied up."

Doing what? Sopi didn't ask. She was too relieved to have an excuse to disappear for three hours. Plus, the drive was always pretty. Minutes later, she was admiring the golden gleam of snow off the craggy peaks above her and caught the stub tail of a lynx as it slunk into the trees.

Maude's information on the women's flight was completely wrong, of course. Sopi wound up with time to kill, so she engaged in retail therapy while she was in the bigger center. Then she sat in the airport addressing as many texts and emails as she could.

When the chartered flight finally arrived, there were a dozen women, too many for Sopi's SUV, *and* they'd already arranged for a private shuttle.

Annoyed, but completely unsurprised—this was classic Fernanda—Sopi drove home alone.

Rhys had grown up on the sort of palace intrigue that had resulted in the murder of his parents. The infantile game Maude was playing, trying to sell this property without telling the person it would affect most gravely, was nothing more than a mosquito-like annoyance to him.

Things took a turn into adult parlor games when Rhys decided to play along while he turned the tables. He kept hearing Sopi ask, *How long does it last? What happens when it's over?*

They had barely even started and couldn't really continue, not properly. That infuriated him, but after their intimacy last night, he couldn't ignore the way Maude was going behind Sopi's back. He was convinced Maude would pursue the sale with someone else if he declined, so he decided to go through with it. He had Gerard call Maude first thing and tell her to expect the prince's counteroffer later today.

Rhys then sent his bodyguard to fetch Sopi. He wanted to come clean about his purchase and include her in the negotiations. Maybe they could work out some other arrangement while they were at it. He knew it was next to impossible, though, and that put him on edge.

When his bodyguard returned with Cassiopeia's neatly bagged delicates and the news that she had driven away in a company vehicle, he nearly snapped.

This was the only time they had!

He was in a brooding, foul mood when Gerard knocked and entered carrying his trusty tablet. "I relayed the stepdaughter's details to the palace for the due-diligence investigation, sir. You'll want to see this. The palace investigators dug fairly deeply into the Brodeur background—"

"And Maude is on the run from the law?" he surmised facetiously. "Shocking."

"Um, no, sir. Maude and her daughters don't seem to have a criminal record of any kind. But Cassiopeia's mother is a Basile-Munier."

Rhys snapped his head around. "But they died out."

Nevertheless, his blood leaped as he took the tablet and scrolled through the report. It included an image of a birth certificate and a short article by a historian who had visited this spa some years ago. The man had been trying to prove the owner was the surviving child of a prince who had disappeared from public life after an assassination attempt. That prince and his wife had had a daughter late in life. She'd eloped against her father's wishes.

A marriage certificate and a title search on this property all seemed to indicate Sopi's mother was that same woman.

"Is this real?"

"A DNA test would confirm it, although I'm not sure where we'd get a sample. Miss Brodeur seems to be the only surviving member. But if you scroll to the photo at the bottom, it would seem, um, like mother like daughter. And granddaughter."

Rhys stared at a scan of a dated color photograph of two women who both had Sopi's cheekbones and chin, rich brown hair and gleaming dark eyes.

The room was absolutely still and silent, but he felt as though a gust of wind hit him. Went through him. Nearly knocked him on his ass.

This was too easy. Too perfect. This wasn't how life worked. Not how it should do in any case, not for him.

At the same time, a roaring thrill went through him. He could have her. He *would* have her. His agile brain quickly found the rationale for it. A commoner would have been a fight, but a royal would be accepted without question. Even better, she was a lost princess whose story would pull the spotlight from Henrik. His brother dropping out of public life while he sought treatment would barely be noticed by anyone.

"Forget driving down the price of the spa. I want a swift sale, immediate possession and binding terms."

The checkers game he'd been playing with Maude was flung into the air. This was now grand master chess with a side hand of high-stakes poker.

Within the hour, Gerard had the contract finalized. Maude agreed that the transfer of ownership would remain confidential until such time as Rhys saw fit to announce it. Rhys informed her he would retain all staff but no longer needed a marketing VP or brand ambassadress. The people holding those positions—Nanette and Fernanda—would have to vacate their suite by the end of the week.

"Your late husband purchased this property for his wife?" Rhys asked as he and Maude set their electronic signatures to the final deal. He was curious whether Maude knew of Sopi's royal blood.

"I understood she had an inheritance of some kind enabling her to renovate it. We rarely spoke about our previous marriages, to be honest. I'm just delighted to finally have this albatross off my hands. I run it as a folly, but it's more work than it's worth."

As Gerard double-checked and pronounced everything settled, Rhys said to Maude, "Would you and your family dine with me this evening?"

"Oh, Nanette and Fernanda would love that."

No mention of Sopi, her considerable contribution to the business or how this sale would impact her.

Maude's complete disregard for her stepdaughter incensed Rhys, making his delight in outsmarting her grow exponentially until a bellow of triumph was nearly bursting from his chest.

It was a warning sign that he felt far too strongly about this. About *Sopi*. If he felt anything, it ought to be the comfortable satisfaction that he had uncovered an opportunity that benefited his brother and was moving strategically to seize it before anyone else could.

Even when he had the spa sewn up, however, Rhys's powerful sense of urgency didn't ease. He tried to pace it off, aware that Sopi would be furious with him, but his deal with Maude was the least of the shocks she would receive tonight.

When Sopi returned and confronted Maude over the wasted day, her stepmother frowned and said, "Oh, you know how Fernanda gets distracted when she's excited. She and Nanette have been invited to dine with the prince tonight. That must be why she mixed things up."

It was a prevarication if not an outright lie. Sopi was dying to say, *Oh, really? Because last night, when I was with the prince, he told me he wasn't interested in either of them.*

But she didn't want to reveal she'd been with the prince. She hadn't felt sordid when it happened, but after brooding on it all day, she was convinced she'd behaved like those women he'd spoken of so disparagingly. The ones who straddled him whether he wanted them to or not.

She went about her afternoon checking in with staff and pitching in as necessary. When a handsome young man approached her as she was covering the booking desk, she smiled in greeting, caught off guard when he used her full name, not the *Sopi* on her name tag.

"Cassiopeia Brodeur?"

"Yes." This was more the type of man she ought to aim for, she thought absently. He was polite and well dressed, but his attitude didn't scream wealth and privilege. He returned her smile, but with polite reserve. He didn't move the needle on her body temperature one millimeter, which was delightfully unthreatening if a little disappointing.

"Please call me Sopi. How can I help you?"

"I'm the prince's assistant, Gerard. This is for you." The small envelope he offered was imprinted with the royal crest.

Her heart tripped, and she ducked the envelope below the edge of the desk to hide how her hands began to tremble.

"Thank you," she said in a strangled voice, cheeks scorching. She wanted to glance around guiltily but held his stare and her smile even though it began to feel forced.

"He asked if I could also take your number?" He offered his telephone with a contact already started in her name.

She balked. Rhys had gotten her naked last night, then fobbed her off on his bodyguard when he was finished with her. She wasn't up for a do-over, if that's what this was about.

"Perhaps if you read his message," Gerard suggested, correctly interpreting her mutinous expression.

She withdrew the card, which was a single sheet, not even folded. It was some kind of high-grade linen stock in ivory with raw edges, also embossed with his crest.

His fine-tipped pen had dug in deep and left small trails, as though he'd rushed to write his brief message, barely lifting the pen. Or had written it in anger.

Where the hell did you go today?
Dinner.
No excuses.

Splotch went the ink on the final dot.

She bit her lip and slid the card back into the envelope, glanced at Gerard.

"Seven p.m. in the dining room with the rest of your family? I'll tell him you're confirmed?"

The rest of her family? *Yech.*

He must have read her reaction. "If there are any impediments, please bring them to my attention so I may iron them away."

She resisted asking him to squash her family flat.

"I'll be there," she said, not sure if she was telling the truth. At least she'd bought a new dress today, still stinging over the incident with her stepsisters. The new one wasn't designer or flashy by their standards, but it had come from an upscale boutique and cost more than Sopi's weekly earnings. She had planned to return it on her next trip to Jasper.

"Excellent. And would you be so kind...?" He offered his phone again.

She hesitated, then gave him her number. He tried it, smiling when a ping sounded in her pocket. "Please let me know if I can assist you in any way."

Perhaps he could offer her some strategies on facing the prince after last night?

For the rest of the afternoon, every time she tried to think up a reason to cry off the dinner invitation, she touched the card in her pocket and could hear Rhys's deep voice warning, "No excuses." Why did she find his profanity-laced impatience so reassuring? It brought a secretive smile to her lips every time she thought of it.

At five fifty-five, Maude called her. "Sopi. We have a disaster in the kitchen. You'll have to run out or breakfast won't happen tomorrow morning."

Here was her excuse to skip dinner, but a devilish part of her refused to seize it.

"We're expected to dine with the prince this evening, aren't we?" she asked with a full pound of smugness. "I had a note from him, personally inviting me. I don't want to be rude."

A pause that was loud enough to *thunk*. Maude might have swallowed. "I assumed you would decline. You tend to set yourself apart from us."

Oh, was it was *her* who did that?

Actually, maybe she did. She had never forgiven Maude for keeping her father in Europe or for spending all his money. Still, Sopi pulled the phone from her ear and scowled at the screen. Maude was sounding particularly petty about a simple dinner invitation. Was she that embarrassed of her unrefined stepdaughter?

"Well, tonight I'll join you," Sopi said cheerfully. "Since it's not often I get a chance to dine with royalty." She hung up and stuck her tongue out at the phone.

Then she suffered a churning stomach for the next hour as she showered and dressed. Her hair, which she never bothered to cut because she always wore it up, was ridiculously long, falling to her waist. At least it had a hint of wave, but it tickled her lower back, where her new dress had a circular cutout.

The dress was a sleeveless knit with a high collar, but it made her look fuller in the chest than she was, which balanced hips that were a shade wider than her stepsisters' fashion magazines told her they ought to be.

She wasn't much for makeup, but her cheeks were pale with nerves. She gave them a swipe of blusher and painted her lips with a pink gloss. She hadn't thought about new shoes when she'd been shopping today so she had only the plain black pumps she wore when she played hostess in the dining room.

As she went onto tiptoe in the bathroom, trying to see her bottom half in the mirror, the butterflies in her stomach turned to slithering snakes. She was kidding herself. Not only would she not measure up to Nanette and Fernanda, she would look downright foolish in everyone's eyes, trying so hard to impress.

Just as she started to kick off her shoes, however, Gerard texted that the prince was sending an escort for her.

Sopi choked on her tongue, texted back that it was unnecessary and decided to do what she'd been doing for years now—brave things out for one more day.

She had put up with Maude's proprietary orders and her stepsisters' snobbery because the alternative was to cede the territory to them and wind up with nothing. Cassiopeia's was her home. She would fight for it to the bitter end.

Which came sooner than she'd expected.

What happens when it's over?

It would never be over. Rhys had found the woman he would marry. The knowledge should have afforded him nothing beyond a contented sense of completion. He didn't like the gnawing sense in him that he needed to leap and snatch and hold on tight. Gerard had assured him Sopi had promised to join them for dinner, but she had become so important to him in the last few hours, Rhys feared that if she wasn't in the dining room when he got there, he might well devolve into shedding blood.

He stalked from the elevator across the short bridge that overlooked the foyer below to the dining room res-

ervation desk. He was as combat ready as any of his ancestral knights, vibrating with a drive to claim.

The babble inside the dining room went silent as he
appeared. Everyone rose with a muted shuffle of chairs.
A small pocket of women stood to the side of the reception desk. One of them was backed into a corner
behind a potted palm.

The tension in their small group hit him like a battering ram, but the sight of Sopi's drawn cheeks and
bravely lifted chin reached out to claw into his chest.

"Ladies," he greeted.

Sopi stiffened and skimmed her gaze to a distant
corner, refusing to make eye contact.

"Your Highness," the rest murmured.

So. They'd told her about the sale. And she was taking it badly.

Rhys kept an impassive expression on his face, but
he wanted to catch her by the chin and force her thick
lashes up, so she looked directly into his eyes. He
wanted to ask how she dared let these women take advantage of her. Didn't she realize who she *was*?

No. She didn't. Steps had been taken to bury it too
deeply.

He had thought to make a dramatic announcement
here in the dining room, but as he read the angry hurt
in her, he realized he couldn't spring it on her like that.
She would hate and blame him a little longer, but he
could withstand it.

Any guilt Rhys might have experienced for his un-
derhanded actions in buying the spa dried up, however.
It was past time Sopi learned the truth about her mother
and herself. He couldn't wait for the transformation.

Maude's younger daughter demanded his attention by stepping forward and offering a curtsy with a breathy, nervous giggle.

"Your Highness, some of my friends have just arrived." She waved at a long table with a half dozen women down either side, all looking his way with anticipation. A few empty seats had been saved in the middle. "We wondered if you might enjoy a more lively evening? They're anxious for a chance to meet you."

"Another time." He glanced impatiently at Maude.

"Of course," Maude said smoothly. "We have a quiet table reserved at the back. Sopi?"

"This way." Sopi didn't smile, and her voice was cold and pointed as an icicle aimed at the middle of his chest. She led the way through the staring crowd.

Ingrained protocol nearly had him offering an arm to escort Maude and her eldest daughter, but he shunned them at the last second, moving ahead of them, all his attention on the sensual swish of loose hair across the top of a stunning, heart-shaped ass that swayed provocatively as she wound her way between the tables.

Dear God, that *hair*. How dare she hide such a thing from him? It was an instant fetish he would need a thousand nights to indulge.

It was a good thing the place was filled with mostly women, because if he caught any man, even one of his lethally trained bodyguards, checking her out, he would duel to the death.

He gritted his teeth, trying to suppress this unwelcome surge of possessiveness. Where was it coming from? It was more than his innate preference to act on his decisions the minute he made them. It was positively primeval. It was an aspect of that wildness he knew lurked in any human, and he didn't like it. He only hoped it would ease up once he knew she was his. It had to. Otherwise they were doomed.

He was given the position at the head of the table, Maude on his right, Nanette on his left. Sopi sat on Maude's right and glared at Fernanda, who shrugged across at her in a silent, *Don't blame me.*

"I want to thank you for your hospitality," Rhys said as their champagne arrived and was poured. "I'll be leaving tomorrow."

"You won't stay the week?" Maude murmured, but she was drowned out by Fernanda's, "Us, too, in a few days. Finally!" Fernanda raised her glass.

Sopi choked strongly enough they all lowered their glasses. Her eyes glimmered as she shot hard looks at each of them.

"You suck. You all suck," she croaked.

There was a collective gasp from tables nearby. Maude said a sharp, "Sopi! Consider who you're speaking to."

Rhys said nothing, pleased to see she possessed a spine after all. She would need one.

"*All* of you." She rose and glared directly at him with betrayed hurt sharp as the edge of a knife.

Her hand jerked, but before she could fling the contents of her wine at him, Rhys's bodyguard caught her wrist.

"Stand down," Rhys barked at him, also rising.

Sopi shrugged away from the bodyguard's hold and stepped away from the table. She threw her glass to the floor in a shattering statement.

"Go to hell. Every single one of you." She stalked out.

"*Someone* doesn't know which side her bread is buttered on," Nanette said into her champagne.

"True," Rhys bit out, sending Nanette a dark glower that made her blanch. He set his hands on the table to lean over the three women. "Those who betray others to get what they want should expect the same treatment. Skip the meal and start packing. Be gone by midnight."

"What—"

He ignored the women's cries of shock as he straightened and sent a curt nod to Gerard. His assistant would ensure the staff were notified that Maude and her daughters no longer gave the orders and, in fact, were no longer residents of the hotel.

As the buzz of gossip and speculation spread like wildfire through the room, Rhys jerked his head at his bodyguard to lead the way to Sopi's cabin.

How stupid could she get? She had genuinely thought her worst humiliation was allowing a man with more experience to talk her out of her clothes and take a few liberties with her person. She had thought letting down her physical guard where his sexual intentions were concerned had been the careless act, but no. Last night's dalliance had been some kind of misdirection so she would be blindly ignorant of what Maude was really doing.

What *he* was doing. Of course he wasn't interested in her. He had toyed with her the way some executives spun fidget spinners while brokering a deal.

The pressure in her chest threatened to crack her breastbone, but Sopi refused to scream or cry or release any of the aching sobs branding her throat.

Fine, she'd been thinking for the last twenty minutes, after Fernanda had spilled the beans that Maude had definitely meant to be delivered a few days from now, no doubt after ordering Sopi to load their damned luggage for them. Maude had hissed in warning and Nanette had said, "For God's sake, Fernie. Mummy told you it's confidential."

"What?" Fernanda had had the gall to cast it as a good thing. "She'll be happy. Mummy sold it all to the prince. We'll all be out of your hair by next weekend. You should be happy, Sopi."

Sopi had been utterly speechless, standing there in shock as the prince arrived and everyone stared. She had moved on autopilot, only feeling reality hit her as they reached the table. Instead of holding a chair for their guest the way she would as a hostess, the prince's assistant, Gerard, had moved behind her and held her chair.

It had been so unexpected, it had knocked her out of her stasis and into a plummeting realization that everything had changed. The one dream she had clung to was gone. The only home she had ever known would never be hers.

The nascent fantasy she had had that a prince—a damned royal *prince*—might see something in her beyond a penniless chambermaid had burst like a bubble, leaving her coated in a residue of disillusion and humiliation.

Slamming into her cabin, she kicked off her shoes. Hard. So that one dented a cardboard box and the other went flying toward the bathroom door.

She wrenched at the dress she'd bought with him in mind. It was meant to be pulled on gently to retain the shape and prevent snags in the delicate knit. She dragged roughly at it. Tried to tear it because she hated it. She yanked it off and dropped it where she stood and wiped her feet on it. She was panting and shaking, still trying to catch her breath after her sprint through the snow-laden trees, filled with an endless supply of *hate*.

With a final twist of her foot, she flicked it to the side and shoved at a stack of boxes, freshly delivered this afternoon and left for her to move to a more convenient location. Everything was always left to her to do, and she was *sick* of it. She shoved the stack even harder, so it fell with a tumble.

The crash wasn't nearly as satisfying as she had hoped, especially when it was followed by a loud stomp of a heavy foot leaping onto her stoop. The door flung open to let in a burst of cold air that swirled like a demon around her nearly naked body.

Him. The instrument of her ruin.

"Bastard," she muttered and turned away to take her narrow stairs two at a time.

Below her, she heard the door click closed. She glanced down from the loft and gripped the rail with humiliated rage as she watched him take in the clutter and the mess of boxes. He picked up her dress and gave it a light shake.

"Come right in," she said scathingly. "Act like you own the place."

He lifted his gaze, and she instantly felt naked. Not just physically, which she mostly was, but as though she was utterly transparent. As if he could see through her sarcasm to those puerile fantasies she'd spun in her head. It was so agonizing to be seen this way, she had to hold back a sob and turn away. She yanked out a drawer in her dresser, digging for jeans and a pullover. The stairs creaked as she stuck her legs into her jeans.

He appeared in the loft and flicked his gaze in harsh judgment of her used furniture and what she had always thought of as a cozy living space. As her turtleneck nearly choked her, and she yanked at her hair enough that it had some slack outside her collar, she saw the loft through his eyes and was mortified to realize it wasn't humble. It was shabby.

Angry that he was seeing it and forcing *her* to see it, she said, "I was being facetious. What I really meant was get lost."

What she really meant were two words she had never said to anyone, no matter how badly Nanette had ever baited her, but she was feeling them this evening. She really was.

He draped her dress over the footboard of her bed. "We'll continue this discussion in my room."

"Gosh, I would love to accommodate you, Your Highness, but I have to pack and find a place to live. Because if you think I'm going to work for you, you need to see a psychiatrist about your loose grasp on reality."

"My people will pack for you. Socks," he said, nodding at her bare feet.

"I'm not going anywhere with you."

"*Süsse*, I will carry you out of here kicking and screaming if I have to. We are not talking here."

"There is nothing wrong with the way I live." Everything was wrong with it, but she would die on the hill of defending what was left of her home after the way he had treated her. "This is what a person has to do when they're kicked around by people who have more power than they do."

"I know that!" he shouted, then seemed to pull himself together with a flex of his shoulders and a clench of his jaw. "It reminds me of the way my brother and I lived when we were in exile. I hate it. I won't stay here, but you and I will talk. Am I carrying you?"

Shaken by that completely unexpected admission,

she only hesitated long enough for one brow to go up in a warning that he was dead serious.

She swallowed and told herself she was only cooperating because this was too small a space for the explosive emotions still detonating inside her and radiating off him. She found a balled-up pair of socks and sat on the top stair to put them on with her boots, aware of him looming over her the whole time.

"I don't know what we could possibly have to say to one another," she muttered.

"You will be surprised," he promised in a dark vow. He followed her down the stairs and out the door.

His bodyguard flanked them as they crossed to the hotel and blocked anyone from joining their elevator.

Sopi refused to make eye contact with the wide stares that came at them from every level of the foyer.

"I forgot my phone," she murmured as she realized her hands and pockets were empty.

"It will be retrieved." He let her into his suite himself, waiting while the bodyguard moved through in a swift check of all the rooms. Rhys stationed the man outside his door with, "Only Gerard, and only if the place is burning to the ground."

"Yes, sir."

Rhys let out the sort of breath that expelled hours of tested patience.

Sopi hugged herself and moved to the window where she noted he had quite the view of naked women frolicking in the pool below.

"I was in here last week," Sopi murmured. "Packing Nanette's and Fernanda's things to move them down the hall so you could have this suite. Except that's not what I was doing, was I? You've all been cooking this for ages, and I just did the heavy lifting so they could be on their way faster."

"If they're still here in three hours, I'll set them on the stoop myself."

Taken aback, she realized that whatever fury she was nursing, he had plenty of his own. "If you're so angry with them, why—"

He held up a hand to stop her, pausing in removing his suit jacket before finishing his shrug. He threw his jacket over the back of a chair and loosened his tie on the way to retrieving stapled documents from a stack on the desk.

He dropped one set onto the coffee table. "That's a copy of the offer Maude accepted today." *Slap.* "That's the transfer of Cassiopeia's into your name."

CHAPTER FIVE

"WHAT?" STUNNED, SOPI stepped forward in shocked excitement, unable to believe it. She pulled up as she realized such a thing would have to come with conditions. Her excitement drained away. "Why?" she asked with dread, fearing she already knew.

His beard darkened where he bit the inside of his cheek. His irises glowed extra blue and laser sharp as he branded patterns on her skin with his gaze. "Last night, you asked me where this was going."

"It's not going anywhere. You made that perfectly clear when you didn't come back to the pool afterward." Her heart hammered in her chest.

"Nanette was loitering in the spa. I was protecting you by sending my bodyguard."

"Sure you were," she choked. "That's also what you're doing here, I guess?" She waved at the paperwork.

"I am," he said in a voice so gritty it left her feeling abraded all over. "Nanette knew I was with someone last night. I could have revealed you, but I wasn't ready to. I wanted time to consider exactly how I would answer your question."

"And this is your answer?" She was growing more appalled by the second. How did he manage to hurt her so easily? So *deeply*? Despite last night's intimacy, they were still virtual strangers. He shouldn't be able to impact her like this. "You went behind my back to cut a deal to buy my *home*?"

"I wanted to talk to you about it." Her temper didn't faze him. He stood as an indifferent presence, unrepentant and untouched. "You weren't here. From now on, you're not allowed to be angry with me for actions I take if you don't show up to hear my side of it before I take them."

"Wow. Sure," she agreed, laying on the sarcasm with a trowel. "I will be sure to never be angry with you in future when I *never see you again*."

"Dial back the histrionics. We have a lot to cover, and you don't want to peak too early."

Her blood boiled. She shot her arms down straight at her sides, hands in tight, impotent fists.

"I have a right to be angry, Rhys! You bought property stolen from *me*." She jabbed at her chest. "Now you want to gift it to me like you're doing me a favor—" Her voice caught, but she forced out the rest, each word like powdered glass in the back of her throat. "But I expect you want favors in return, don't you? Virginity is quite the precious commodity these days, isn't it? You make me sick!"

She turned to wrench at the door latch, but he was on top of her, surrounding her and catching her hand in a firm but strangely gentle grip as he caged her. His deep, velvety voice growled into her hair, causing tickles against her ear that made goose bumps rise on her nape.

"It's a wedding gift."

"To who!" She tried to shove her elbow into his gut.

"You." He spun her and pinned her to the door. "Now

settle down before my bodyguard bursts in here and I have to kill him for trying to touch you again."

"You really have lost half the cards from your deck. I'm not marrying you." She pressed her forearms against his chest, forcing space between them, so astounded she didn't have the sense to be intimidated. "We've known each other two *days*. Why would you even suggest such a thing?"

"Because the gradual approach is not open to me." His jaw clenched as he studied her flushed, angry expression.

She didn't want to be aware of his heat and weight pressing into her, but she was. She really didn't want to *like* it. She turned her face to the side, resisting and rejecting.

"You were going to come to my room last night. Weren't you?" His voice was smoke and mirrors, casting a spell she had to work to resist.

"If you had come back to the pool and asked me yourself, I probably would have, yes." She lifted her chin but winced internally as she admitted it, hating herself for that, too. "Were you planning to propose if I had?" she scoffed.

He backed off a fraction. "I wasn't thinking much beyond how badly I wanted you in my bed."

"That's a no, then." She gave him a firm nudge, but he was immovable.

"Everything changed while you were playing hide-and-seek this morning."

"I was doing my *job*." Her voice faded into a discouraged sob that rang in her chest as she realized she no longer had one of those.

He sighed and gave a comforting brush of his thumb against her jaw. "Maude was determined to sell the spa,

Sopi. Someone else would have bought this property if I hadn't. Be happy it was me."

"You people need to quit telling me how to feel about this." A burning ache of blame stayed hot in her throat.

"Don't lump me in with your stepfamily," he warned, not even flinching. He only grazed her cheekbone with his fingertips as he tucked a wisp of hair behind her ear. His voice changed. Gentled. "And hear what I'm saying. Your life would have toppled regardless. Whether you're happy about it or not, I'm offering you a cushion. A velvet one. With gold tassels."

His words, edged in irony, held a quiet finality that shook her to the core. Her world *was* shattered. All she had known had been upended and was sliding beyond her reach.

Her heart began to tremble and she pushed harder on his chest, freshly angry, but scared now, too. "Let me go."

He waited a beat, then stepped back and dropped his hands to his sides, watchful.

She hugged herself, moving into the room to put space between them so she could think, but she remained too anxious and confused to make sense of any of this. Marriage? Really?

"I've always thought that if I were to marry, it would be to someone I love. Someone I *trust*. I'm not going to marry to get a *thing*. Especially not to get something that should already be mine."

"I wanted you to be here while I negotiated with Maude." He sounded brisk but tired as he moved to the bar and poured two glasses from a bottle of whiskey that was already open. "If it were up to me, I would have hired the lawyers you needed to fight Maude, taken a partnership in the business in exchange, but there was no time. Plus, all of my business dealings are scrutinized. I can't foot the bill on a stranger's legal fight—or gift a hotel to a woman with whom I am having an affair—without causing a lot of questions to be asked. Buying this property as a present for my future wife, however…"

She shook her head, unable to take in that he really meant that.

Nevertheless, a distant part of her was processing that *she* would finally be the boss here. All her friends would have secure jobs. That was as important for the village as for the spa. She grew dizzy with excitement at the prospect.

But why her?

"Is this like a green-card thing or something?" she managed to ask. "Would it be a fake marriage?"

He snorted as he came across with the glasses. "Not at all."

"You're genuinely asking me to marry you. And if I do, you'll give me this hotel and spa, all the property and rights to the aquifer. Everything," she clarified.

"If you'll live in Verina with me and do what must be done to have my children, yes," he said with a dark smile.

She was still shaking her head at the outrageous proposition but found herself pressing her free hand to her middle, trying to still the flutters of wicked anticipation that teased her with imaginings of how those babies would get made.

She veered her mind from such thoughts.

"Why? I mean, why *me*?" She lifted her gaze to his, catching a flash of sensual memories reflected in the hot blue of his irises.

"I've already told you. I want you in my bed."

"And that's it? Your fly has spoken? That's the sum total of your motivation?"

His eyes narrowed, becoming flinty and enigmatic. "There are other reasons. I'll share them with you, but they can't leave this room."

That took her aback. "What if I don't want to carry your secrets?"

"You're going to carry my name and my children. Of course you'll keep my secrets. Would you like to tell me yours?" He regarded her over the rim of his glass as he sipped, as though waiting for her to tip her hand in some way.

She shrugged her confusion. "I'm not exactly mysterious," she dismissed. "The most interesting thing that's ever happened to me is happening right now. You realize how eccentric this sounds?"

"Eccentric or not, it's a good offer. You should accept it before I change my mind."

She snorted. "You're quite ruthless, aren't you?" She spoke conversationally but knew it as truth in her bones.

"I do what has to be done to get the results I want. You understand that sort of pragmatism, even if you've pointed your own efforts in dead-end directions. I look forward to seeing what you accomplish when you go after genuinely important goals."

"This is my *home*. It's important to *me*."

"Then claim it."

A choke of laughter came out of her. "Just like that? Accept your proposal and—" She glanced at the paperwork. "I'm not going to agree to anything before I've actually reviewed that offer."

"Due diligence is always a sensible action," he said with an ironic curl of his lip. He waved his glass toward the table, inviting her to sit and read.

Gingerly, she lowered onto the sofa and set aside her whiskey.

Rhys kept his back to her, gaze fixed across the valley as he continued to sip his drink, saying nothing as she flipped pages.

His behavior was the sort of thing a dominant wolf would do to indicate how little the antics of the lesser pack affected him, but she was glad not to have his unsettling attention aimed directly at her as she compared the two contracts. Aside from the exchange of money on Maude's—and the fact that hers finalized on her wedding day—they were essentially the same.

"I want possession on our engagement. *If* I decide to accept your proposal," she bluffed, fully expecting him to tell her to go to hell.

"Done. On condition we begin the making of our children on the day our engagement is announced." He turned, and his eyes were lit with the knowledge his agreement had taken her aback. "We'll keep the conception part as a handshake agreement. No need to write that down in black-and-white."

He brought her a pen. His hand was steady as he offered it. Hers trembled as she hesitantly took it.

"Are you completely serious?" she asked.

"Make the change. Sign it. I'll explain why I want you to marry me. You'll accept my proposal, and Cassiopeia's will be yours."

Inexplicable tears came into her eyes. This was too much. Too fast.

"What if we get engaged and I back out?"

"I expect you to go into this with good faith, Sopi. I will."

And he expected her to sleep with him. Get started

on making his babies. She might not have the option of backing out on their marriage if that happened.

She wanted to sleep with him. That was the unnerving part. Not for Cassiopeia's or a wedding ring or babies. For the experience. To be able to touch him and feel...

She swallowed, hearing him say her life would have changed regardless. He was right about that. Which made her stupid to turn this down. It was probably the best outcome she could anticipate. Her alternative was to let him have Cassiopeia's while she tried to sue Maude for a slice of the purchase price. Good luck with that. Maude was headed out of the country. Sopi would most likely lose any settlement she won to lawyer fees anyway.

She told herself she was only signing as a matter of hearing him out, not really committing to changing her entire life.

Shakily, she made the change and set her signature to the page, feeling so overwhelmed her head swam as she rose to bring the pages and pen to him.

He set the contract on an end table and inked his name next to hers, handing it back to her for her inspection.

She moved away from the intensity of his gaze, trying not to think about the full severity of what she was edging toward. She returned the document to the coffee table and picked up her drink, took a bracing sip of scorching whiskey.

"The floor is yours, Rhys." The alcohol left a rasp in her voice. "Tell me what sort of husband I'll get for the price of a spa."

"No more sarcasm," he said flatly and threw back the last of his drink, then went to pour another. "I offer more than a damned spa in exchange for marriage. You'll have security of every kind. Wealth and power and a type of fame that can be tiresome but has its uses. It can be very effective when used for altruistic acts. I thought that might interest you." He cannily noted the way she swung to face him.

"Why would you think that? You don't know me." She demurred, forcing her gaze elsewhere while she took another nervous sip.

"I know more about you than you do," he said with a cryptic sort of confidence that made her feel as though the floor shifted beneath her. "You want this place because it's your home, not to develop it. You care about your employees and work alongside them because they're your friends. You never ask them to do a task you wouldn't do yourself. In fact, you look after complete strangers better than you look after yourself."

"I'm just trying to keep the place running." She shrugged off his compliment.

"You're self-effacing and self-sacrificing. You'll need that."

"Being nice doesn't mean I'm ready to have children." If she was quick to help others, it came from being bounced into friends' homes when her father had traveled, which had happened frequently. She had learned to pitch in to fit in and be welcomed.

When her father had remarried, she had thought he would finally stay home and they would live more as a family. Maude had had expensive tastes, however, and his business had been declining, forcing him to travel even more. What Sopi had really learned from the humbling experience of losing everything was the importance of ensuring she could offer support and attention to her children before making any.

"If I could give you more time to absorb all of this, I would, but time is a luxury I no longer have. My brother has testicular cancer. It was discovered when he and his wife failed to conceive."

"Oh." She swayed, knocked back by the news but wanting to move toward him, to offer some sort of comfort. "I'm so sorry."

He was steely and still, his frozen demeanor holding her off. She stayed where she was.

"What…?" She didn't know what to ask, how to respond.

"They're pursuing treatment options right now. Obviously, we hope he will survive, but even if he does, he will almost certainly be sterile. I'm next in line, therefore I need an heir. And a spare. Turns out they have their uses," he stated with grim humor.

He sipped, and she copied the motion, stunned to her toes.

"Are you aware of Verina's history?" he asked. "Support for my brother has never been higher, but we still have a handful of detractors looking for a foothold. We can't afford any show of weakness. I have to take action to secure the throne before any of this comes to light."

As whiskey slid down her throat like a rusty nail, she glanced at the contract she'd signed.

"I see the urgency, but I still don't understand why me? I mean…" She had to clear her throat to speak, not wanting to state baldly that he might become king. She certainly didn't want to picture herself at his side if he did. "You're, um, saying your son or daughter is likely to rule Verina. There are thousands of blue bloods to choose from as a mother for those children. There are a hundred in this *building* right now." She waved at the walls.

"True. And I came here expecting to find my bride among those women." He tilted the last of the liquid in his glass. "I'm expected to marry someone with that sort of pedigree." He was eyeing her in that penetrating way again. "Henrik's wife, Elise, is the daughter of a diplomat, schooled much as all the women here." He waved at the walls. "But her father lacks a title, and it was a long, hard-won fight for Henrik to be allowed to marry her."

"Then—" That made her a poor choice, didn't it? She suddenly felt as though the floor was falling away, leaving her grappling with such profound disappointment, she realized that she *liked* the idea of marrying him.

"I don't personally care about bloodlines. If I must marry, I want a woman who will be honest with me and show some integrity, rather than tie myself to someone like your stepsisters. I would much prefer to share my bed with someone I want to share my bed with," he added pointedly.

The hot coals in the pit of her belly seemed to glow bright red, as if he'd blown on them, sending heat through her limbs and up into her cheeks and deep into the notch between her thighs. Her scalp itched and her breasts felt tight.

"I don't even have your sister-in-law's education," she said. "I'm as common as clover. You really want to fight that hard for sex?"

He didn't laugh or reassure her that yes, he wanted her *that much*. Instead, his expression turned even more grave.

"You're not a commoner." He spoke with matter-of-fact solemnity. "Your mother was the daughter of Prince Rendor Basile-Munier. He tried to retake his principality of Rielstek when the USSR fell apart. There was an attempt on his life, and he fled to Sweden, where he lived out his days."

He spoke so confidently a jolt went through her. It evaporated into a pained sense of setback. Of stinging anguish that this marriage really wouldn't happen.

"Someone has been embellishing." Regret sat as an acrid taste in the back of her throat. "Did you overhear a local gossiping? I've never heard names and details like that, but it's pure nonsense."

He cocked his head. "Why do you believe that?"

"Because I would know if my mother was a princess! Instead, I know when and how that rumor got started. A guest claimed to be writing a history of some kind. He asked my father if my mother had been a princess. My father said that, like most writers, the guy had a screw loose. Mom would have told him if she was secretly royal. Even though it wasn't true, I was young enough to be taken by the idea. I told some staff, and it turned into a joke. It's a sort of urban legend, something employees repeat to prank the tourists. It's not true, Rhys."

"Yes, it is," he stated. "That historian was an extremely well-regarded academic. I studied from his textbooks myself. Unfortunately, he passed on before this particular work was published. That's why our staff had to dig to find it and why your heritage isn't common knowledge."

"No." She shook her head, growing agitated. "My mother would have told me. My father would have known."

"Not if her father had actively tried to bury their identity, worried for their safety."

"No, Rhys."

"The property in Sweden is still in your family's name. The caretakers live rent-free. They had no incentive to reach out, but they have provided some documentation to our palace investigators. Our team is looking for a means of DNA testing, but they're quite satisfied with the evidence they have so far—especially once they compared photos from your social media pages to your grandmother."

He took out his phone and showed her a photo of a woman in a tiara and a sash. She could have been Sopi dressed in costume.

Sopi dropped her glass, having completely forgotten she was still holding it.

Thankfully, it only held half an ounce of liquid and didn't break. She scrambled to retrieve it and shakily set the glass next to the contract she had signed. *The one agreeing to their terms of engagement.*

She shoved her butt onto the sofa cushions and set her face in her hands, concentrating on drawing a breath while the whole world spun in the wrong direction, pulling her apart.

"I didn't think you were aware," he commented drily.

"This can't be true, Rhys. Does Maude know?"

"I didn't tell her. If I gave a single damn about her, I would look forward to her reaction when she realizes I'm making you my wife and that any future regard you bestow upon her will be strictly on your terms."

Sopi was convulsively shaking her head. "I can't marry you. You can't really expect me to move to Europe with you? Turn into a princess overnight?"

"I've just explained that's what you already *are*." There was no pity in his voice. "I'm exactly the sort of husband you were meant to have."

"But you can't *want* me! I—"

"I damned well do." He sat on the chair to her left, only one hip resting there so he was crowded into her space. His knee brushed hers, and he forced her hands down so she had to lift her gaze to his. "I've explained what's at stake for me and my country. Hell yes, I want to engage myself to a lost princess. We'll be the feel-good media storm of the year."

"You expect me to tell people?" It was another blow she hadn't seen coming. She was going to have a bruise on her forearm where she kept pinching herself, trying to wake up.

"Of course I do. You're ideal."

"No, I'm not!" She waved at the bargain jeans and top she wore.

"You will be."

"You're not listening to me!"

"I've heard every word. You're shocked by ancestry that has been hidden from you. You're already home-sick because this place is your connection to your parents. You're afraid to become my wife because it feels bigger than you ever expected to be."

"I'm afraid of *you*." She realized she was trembling. "How can I trust you when you're forcing all these things onto me?"

"I'm only giving you what you're supposed to have. Do you want to tear that up?" He pointed at the contract they'd signed.

No, but she didn't want to accept that she had no say over anything, not even who she *was*.

He drew a long breath that tried to neutralize the charged energy between them. "I'm just the messenger, Sopi."

"You're proposing to be my *husband*. Maybe you're fine with marrying a stranger, but I'm not." She was a stranger to herself, and it was so disconcerting her brain was splitting in two.

"We're not strangers," he scolded in that tone that crept past her defenses like wisps of drug-laced smoke, filling her with lassitude.

"Sure, you know everything about *me*." She was trying really hard not to become hysterical. "All I know about you is that you swim naked and get whatever you want!"

He let that wash over him, then snorted as if he found something in it funny. He drew a breath and rose, nodding in a way that suggested he was conceding a point.

He pulled out his phone, said, "Gerard. We'd like the dinner we missed. When do you expect Francine? Good. Send her up. I want Sopi to meet her."

"Who?" Sopi asked as he ended the call.

"The new manager of Cassiopeia's until such time as you make changes."

"This is happening too fast, Rhys."

"I know." Now, he almost sounded as if he pitied her. He stepped closer and cradled her jaw, giving her cheekbone a light caress with his thumb. His hand felt a lot warmer than her face.

Despite being wary of trusting him, she rested in that reassuring palm. She wanted to throw herself into his arms. He was the only solid thing in a crumbling universe.

Murmured voices outside the door had him releasing her to invite a middle-aged woman to enter. She had a sleek blond bob and an elegant figure in a crisp suit. If she was jet-lagged, she didn't show it a bit. Her handshake was firm, her smile friendly. Her English held an accent similar to Rhys's, somewhere between French and German.

"Francine will be your proxy once our paperwork

is finalized and you take possession," Rhys said with a nod to their contract.

"I'll take the first week to observe, then communicate my recommendations." Francine mentioned her credentials, which were stellar. "I've taken possession of the office and all the equipment. I thought to also start an audit, if you agree?"

Sopi glanced at Rhys. "I can't afford her." Maybe after a year of penny-pinching, but not when Maude had just drained the coffers dry.

"You can," Rhys assured her. "Once the press release about us goes out, this place will thrive. Go ahead with the audit," he instructed Francine.

Sopi's chest felt compressed. Agreeing to hire Francine felt like an acceptance of marriage and all the rest.

"Francine will ensure future profits will continue to support her well-deserved but exorbitant salary. Even if you were going to be here, I would recommend you move forward with her as your manager."

I will be here, Sopi wanted to argue. She couldn't hold his unwavering gaze, though. Her eyes were growing too hot and damp.

"We'll come back in a few months," he offered in a gentle coax, as though trying to soften a blow. "The ski hill has accepted my offer to purchase, but they want to finish the season. When I come back to finalize that, you can check in here."

It was a thin lifeline, but she grasped it. "You promise?"

"I do."

She gave Francine a timid nod, pretty sure it was the equivalent of pushing the button that would blow up her bridge back to her old life. Even though it was already on fire.

Francine smiled and departed, revealing the room service trolley had arrived. The bodyguard wheeled it in before returning to his station outside the door.

More out of habit than anything, Sopi began transferring the dishes to the small dining table.

Rhys was right there to help. She stepped back, startled to find him so close. "I can do it."

"So can I. I've waited tables."

"When?"

"When I had to." His mouth pursed and his movements slowed as he took care with the setting of their cutlery. "I've been through this sort of transition, Sopi. Both directions. I wasn't given time to pack a bag or hire staff or worry about anyone beyond myself and my brother."

He spoke in a distant tone, as though consciously removing himself from painful memories.

"Online it says you were ten when the revolution happened. I don't understand how anyone could break into a home and commit violence against innocent people."

"Power is an aphrodisiac. The justification was that my father did nothing for Verina. It wasn't until he was gone that people realized the difference between a leader who serves his country and autocrats who take from it."

She couldn't tear her eyes from his grim face.

"I'm so sorry. How did you cope? Where did you go?" He hadn't had any velvet cushions to land on.

"There's a small lake on our border with France. Some of the servants were escaping in a rowboat and took us across with them. We were taken into a protective custody by French authorities, but several governments squabbled over us through those early years, all eager to wage war on our behalf. The real goal was to take possession of Verina, not that we understood it at the time. We only wanted our parents. Our own beds."

"Are you saying you were political hostages?" She was appalled.

"Pawns. Well-treated orphans on whose behalf they claimed to operate. Eventually, a Swiss diplomat who had been a close friend of our father's was able to take us in. He saw to our education with a focus on politics so we understood what was happening to us and Verina. We quickly realized the only help we should accept from any government was the basic human right to move freely. Henrik was sixteen, I was fourteen when we finally moved out on our own."

"That's when you lived…"

"Poorly. Yes," he said shortly. "It was a frustrating time, some of it typical adolescent rage, but we were realizing how badly we'd been used. That the people who should have helped us were operating from their own motives. The greater loss was hitting us, as well. We were mature enough to see the damage that had been done to all of Verina. The path forward to repair not just our own lives, but those of people who we were meant to protect and lead, was daunting. I honestly don't know how Henrik faced being the one. We were eating out of dented cans, barely making the grade at school because we were working any spare moment we had just to pay rent on a moldy apartment. He proved himself to be worthy of the role, though, showing the necessary leadership, making the hard decisions."

"But you were there, supporting him. That had to be important, too."

"To some extent, I had to become what we both hated. A gambler and a hustler, playing politics and digging at social cracks. Eventually, protesters in Verina forced a proper election. When the legitimate government was reinstated, we returned. Then we had to find our feet as royals all over again in a very different environment."

"Are there still detractors? Are you in danger?"

"No worse than any other dignitary. In fact, we're quite popular, having lived as the common man. We're seen as an inspiration. Plus, we brought prosperity back to Verina. Henrik's resumption of the throne after the conflict makes him an emblem of our country's resilience. We have to work hard every day to maintain stability and goodwill, though."

That stability was under threat by his brother's illness. Rhys had so much to carry—dark memories and concern for his brother and responsibilities to live up to. She searched his face, wondering how *he* managed.

"I didn't tell you all of that to downplay what you're going through. I'm saying I can be your guide as you move from being a hidden royal into the spotlight. I've done it. I know the pitfalls and how to navigate them."

"Why can't I just stay here and be…me?"

"Is that really what you want?" His frown of disapproval struck particularly deep. "After learning all that is available to you, all that is yours *by right*, you want to continue scrubbing floors? Is that who you are, Sopi? A coward?"

CHAPTER SIX

"COWARD!" SOPI REPEATED stiffly, flinching and looking away, then lifting her lashes to throw a scold at him. "I'd think you were above name-calling."

Rhys took it as a good sign that she wasn't curled on the sofa weeping, but on her feet, consistently pushing back while taking most of this on the chin.

"Peer pressure, *süsse*," he mocked lightly.

"Not funny."

"It infuriates me that your grandfather was unable to retake what ought to be yours," he admitted with anger he would always struggle to suppress. "I've been there. I want you to fight for what belongs to you."

"You do see the irony in that statement, I hope?"

"I refuse to apologize for buying this property. It was cheaper and more expedient than hiring lawyers. Less public, too." He drew out a chair for her. "Maude will get her comeuppance in other ways. Sit. Eat. Digest," he suggested drily.

"I don't—" She cut herself off and grumbled, "I'm not hungry."

"So we'll get to know one another and you'll begin to trust me."

After a brief hesitation, she gave a shaky sigh of defeat and sank into her chair.

Rhys stayed behind her, his attention caught by the loop of hair that had been teasing him ever since she had dragged this turtleneck over her head in her squalid little cabin.

He gathered the mass in his fist and gently tugged. She stiffened, then leaned forward so he could work the tresses from inside her shirt. When every last strand was free, he combed his fingers through it, pleased when she shivered in reaction.

"You'll speak to me before you ever think of trimming this," he ordered.

"Even what I do with my hair is up to you now?" Her voice quavered.

The fractures in her composure were showing after all. He wound her hair in a rope around his fist and set a light kiss on her crown.

"That was the teasing demand of a lover, *süsse*. Don't take it so much to heart."

"We're not lovers."

Everything in him wanted to contradict her. Prove to her in the most basic way that the chemistry between them meant that their engaging in a physical relationship was as inevitable as their marriage.

But he heard the tremor of fear that underlay her bravado. Her remark about being unable to trust him had been a slap in the face. He was doing what he could to buffer her from the sharp edges of her new reality, but she was still being knocked around by it.

"We're not the sort of lovers I want to be. The kind I hope we will be very soon." He released her hair so it fell down the front of her shoulder and over the swell of her breast, then set his hands on her shoulders, noting the tension in her, much like an animal ready to bolt. "I'm not going to force you, though. You can relax."

Her shoulders softened slightly, and he thought he glimpsed a pout of consternation on her lips when he released her and moved to take his chair across from her. Mixed feelings? That was progress, at least.

"I do need an heir, though," he reminded her, glancing at the wine in the bucket. The bottle was open and ready to pour. He drew it out and gathered the moisture with the towel.

She choked on a humorless laugh, one that said she had given up. When he glanced back at her, she was staring at him through eyes that glimmered with tears.

"It will be okay, Sopi. I promise you." He poured lightly since she'd already had whiskey.

"What would it even look like? Marrying you?" She gulped before they'd toasted. "Besides the fast track to making babies."

"The wedding or the marriage?" He held his glass for the clink of hers. "Both will brim with protocol and adherence to tradition, I'm afraid, but we'll carve a personal life out of it. Henrik and Elise manage to." He set aside the dish covers, releasing an aroma of sage and roasted apple as he revealed slices of elk with risotto and creamed spinach.

"Would we divorce if it didn't work out?"

"I never undertake anything with a mind-set that I'll fail. Short of a catastrophic betrayal, let's agree we'll make every effort to work out our disagreements. But divorce is legal in Verina, if it comes to that."

"And the baby?" she asked as she picked up her cutlery.

"Babies. Plural, if we might be so blessed. What about them?"

"*Would* you see them as a blessing? Or are children merely something you're ticking off a list? Like 'wife.'" Her gaze was admonishing, but that wasn't why he flinched.

Losing his parents had been the most painful experience of his life. The mere thought of losing Henrik was sending fractures of agony through him. Children were sheer emotional peril, something he would have avoided forever if he could.

"I've always been ambivalent about having children," he prevaricated. "I've met enough in my travels to know they can be moody little brats, but they can also be quick to offer unconditional love to a complete stranger."

"They're like tiny humans that way," Sopi said drily.

"Indeed."

She had relaxed a little. Humor had returned the sparkle to her eyes.

He was tempted to take her hand, make a move, but forced himself to sit back and give her space to relax.

"I was leaving the raising of progeny to Henrik. Aside from not being particularly anxious to marry and not wanting to overshadow him by having children before he did, he was always a more paternal man than I saw myself to be. Maybe that was my impression because he was my older brother and made all the decisions for us in those early years when we lived on our own. He very much wanted children with his wife. Elise wants a family very badly. This has been a terrible blow for both of them. I'm torn up taking this action," he admitted heavily. "It feels like a betrayal to them both."

"Will that affect how you feel toward your children?"

"No," he dismissed with confidence. "I don't know what sort of father I'll make, but I would try to emulate my own. He was caring. Busy and firm and he set very high standards, but he was encouraging and capable of humor and affection. I miss both of my parents every day."

"Me, too. My father worked away a lot, but when he was home, we were always laughing and he was proud of any ribbon or test score I brought home. He talked about me running Cassiopeia's as though it was a given, never saying anything like, *When you marry*, or suggesting I needed a man to look after me."

"Did he never want to bring you with him?"

"He offered to send me to school in Europe. I had my friends here. I think we both thought there would be time later to connect." She twirled her glass, mouth pulling to the side. "There wasn't."

"No," he agreed pensively. Time, that bastard, loomed like a vulture over everyone. "How do *you* feel about children?"

"I guess I pictured myself with a family eventually. I always wanted a brother or sister, so I've always known if I had children, I would have at least two or three. It bothers me that my parents aren't alive to be grandparents, but I miss *having* family." Her mouth tried to smile, but the corners kept pushing down.

That was, perhaps, the thing that terrified him most about his brother's diagnosis. What family would he have if Henrik wasn't here?

He had to reach out then, offering his hand with his palm up, but it wasn't a pass. It was comfort and a desire for it in return. Recognition of affinity.

"I think we've found something I can give you that you truly want, Sopi. I will take care of your children very well. I promise you."

"I believe you, but what about—" She looked at his hand, her own still clinging to her cutlery, knuckles white. "Do you think… Please don't laugh, but I always thought I would be in love when I got married."

Ah, love, that priceless gift that could exact too much.

"I've never been in love. I can't claim to be capable of it." Like every other intense emotion, he was wary of it. "I believe we will come to care for each other, though."

"I don't know if that's enough." She set down her knife and fork. "I'm really scared, Rhys."

"I know."

"But I don't want to be a coward."

"Being afraid doesn't make you a coward. Giving in to fear does. Bravery is pushing forward despite the cold sweat."

"Peer pressure again?"

"You *are* my equal." If not a mirror image, at least a complementary piece that promised a greater sense of wholeness. He hadn't expected to find such a thing, ever.

In fact, it unnerved him to some extent, niggling at his conscience. He reminded himself this marriage was for Henrik and the crown, not himself.

"Trust me," he cajoled. "And I'll prove you're my equal. *You* will."

She bit her lip. Her hand hovered over his so he felt the heat off her palm radiating against his own. He made himself be patient, not reaching to take despite his craving to grasp and squeeze.

Very slowly, the weight of her soft palm settled against his.

He closed his hand in a possessive grip, experiencing a leap of something in his blood. Conquest? Or something even more profound and basic, like finally coming up for air when he thought he was drowning?

He breathed through it and brought her hand to his mouth, setting a light kiss on fingers that went lax with surprise.

"Welcome to your new life, Princess."

Rhys sent her to bed alone, which left her feeling ambivalent. She tossed and turned, waking unrested to the discovery this hadn't been a dream. They ate a light breakfast and she was given a memo to sign advising the staff that she was the new owner, that Francine was the manager and they should proceed with business as usual.

Then she was given a copy of the press release. It announced her as the recently discovered Basile-Munier princess, stateless but newly engaged to Prince Rhys Charlemaine of Verina. She would take up residence in the palace of Verina with her fiancé immediately.

"Leave your phone with Gerard. He'll field all those messages," Rhys said as her dated smartphone began percolating like a boiling-over pot. He frowned at her clammy, nerveless fingers and warmed her hand in a reassuring grip. "A new one will be waiting for you in Verina."

And then what? She almost wanted to say, *Shouldn't we go do that thing now?* They had a handshake agreement, didn't they?

Rhys seemed intent on getting to Verina first. Aside from the bellman, who kept his eyebrows in his hairline as he loaded their luggage into the helicopter, Sopi saw none of the staff or her friends. She gave the bellman a weak smile and a wave before all that she knew fell away below her.

She had never flown before but knew right away that the jet they boarded out of Jasper was not the average commercial experience. Rhys waved her into an ivory-colored leather recliner against a window and took the one next to her. They were served fresh coffee in bone-china cups that rested on a polished mahogany table that unfolded from a concealed cupboard. A large-screen television was muted but ran the news with market numbers tracking across the bottom of the screen. Rhys handed her the remote and invited her to watch anything she liked.

Rhys's assistants and bodyguards remained in the cabin at the front of the plane, in seats that faced the galley and were closed off from this more luxurious area.

That was when Sopi began to see how different her life would be. Ironically, she felt shut out of the place where she belonged, rather than ushered into a higher sphere.

Through the flight, Rhys talked in a dozen languages to a multitude of people. Gerard came back several times to request her approval on things she had no business approving. When they stopped in New York to refuel, a stylist came aboard with half a dozen outfits.

By the time she landed in Verina, she no longer recognized herself. She wore a sheath with a forget-me-not print that had been altered to fit her perfectly. A pair of low-heeled sandals finished the sweetheart look.

When Sopi rejoined Rhys from the stateroom, hair and makeup elegantly disguising how pale she was, he glanced up, did a double take, then clicked off his phone and set it aside.

"You look lovely."

"Thank you," she said shyly. "I feel like an actress in a costume." Playing the part of a woman who said, "Gosh!" and fell out of trees while rescuing kittens.

"The trick is to own the role. If you believe it, everyone will."

"Are you acting?" she asked, unsurprised when his mouth twitched and he said a decisive, "No."

She hadn't thought so. They began their descent, and her stomach knotted so tightly she could hardly breathe.

"Don't be nervous," Rhys said, reaching across when she wrung her hands in her lap while they drove from the airport. "They're surprised by how quickly this is happening, but pleased. Elise is very down-to-earth. You'll like her."

Meeting a king and queen was the least of her nerves. She was *engaged*. She had taken possession of Cassiopeia's. That meant she had to follow through on the rest of her agreement with Rhys. What if she was bad at sex? What if he lost interest after the first time? What if she didn't get pregnant? She had so many what-ifs floating in her head, she couldn't articulate them.

They were shown directly into the formal receiving parlor for the king and queen. The sun was coming up, piercing through a stained-glass window to cast prisms of light around the couple who had risen early to greet them.

Henrik was in his early thirties, a clean-shaven version of Rhys. His innate vitality belied any hint of illness. His wife, Elise, was a delicate blonde with a warm smile.

"Why don't I show you around the palace," Elise said after a few minutes of innocuous conversation about Canada. "I'll help you get your bearings, then leave you in your room to rest."

Sopi shot a look at Rhys. He gave a small nod to indicate she should go with Elise, but her ears were already burning, certain she was being removed so he could speak freely about her to his brother.

"I'm not the storyteller our butler is. Do ask Thomas to take you around when you have a free hour. He conducts the tours when we open the palace and gardens for public viewing in the summer," Elise said.

The main floor of the palace consisted of a grand ballroom, the throne room, a cavernous dining hall and a veranda that overlooked gardens and the lakeshore. Elise pointed to a green door. "Panic ensues if we go below, so try not to."

But that's where I belong, Sopi wanted to protest. Once again, she experienced the sensation of being shut out of her own life. Her real one.

She clasped her sweaty palms together, lips pinned closed while she mentally searched for the words to tell Rhys he'd made a huge mistake. That *she* had.

Elise took her up a wide flight of stairs, where she waved negligently toward one wing. "Our residence. Your room is next to Rhys's." She waved in another direction, where maids were scurrying to move boxes stacked in the hall into a room with open double doors. "Still unpacking. Best to stay out of their way a little longer."

"Unpacking?" It was the first time Sopi had spoken. Her voice cracked. "I only brought one suitcase." Rhys had said the rest of her things from the cabin would follow shortly.

"Rhys said you needed a wardrobe. Those are from my usual designers. My assistant arranged it. The stylist will help you source more."

Sopi felt sick. This was exactly the laissez-faire attitude her stepsisters had taken, buying clothes on someone else's tab that they might never even wear. Sopi couldn't—wouldn't—become like them.

She looked back the way they'd come, pretty sure she could find her way to where Rhys was still meeting with his brother.

"Come. I want to show you my favorite place. I think you'll like it." Elise led her through a door and up a set of spiral stairs that climbed a tower. When they stepped outside, they stood on a wall that overlooked the lake.

The view was breathtaking. A light breeze picked up Sopi's hair and caressed her skin, soothing her ragged nerves.

In a way, it even looked like home with the lake and the surrounding mountain peaks. Verina was a small country, but it packed exquisite scenery into every square inch. As they slowly paced to the far end, the quaintest of villages came into view, one with stone bridges and red roofs and the tall spire of a church. Beyond it, the grassy hills were dotted by patches of snow and grazing goats.

"This is where Henrik proposed to me the day he was allowed back into Verina. He brought me straight up here before showing me anything else. He said he wanted a good memory to replace the one he'd left with. Do you know how they left?"

"I read about it. It's tragic." Her heart still ached for Rhys.

"It is," Elise agreed. A poignant smile touched her lips as she gazed across the valley. "They lived with us for a while."

"Your father is the diplomat who helped them?"

"Rhys told you that?" She studied Sopi openly.

"He was trying to bolster me, explaining that he

hadn't always lived like this. I wasn't born into this sort of life. It's very…overwhelming."

"It can be." Elise nodded thoughtfully. "Did he also tell you why he's rushing you?"

Sopi bit her lip, nodded. "I'm really sorry about Henrik."

She half expected Elise to be angry that Rhys had revealed their private heartache, but Elise only looked anguished and maybe a little relieved not to have to relay the details herself. Her worried gaze switched to the distance.

"They're very close in their own way," Elise said, adding in wry warning, "It can be annoying. They grouse at each other over insignificant things, refusing to talk it out properly. Men." She rolled her eyes. Sobered. "They're fiercely protective of one another, though. It's amazing. To a point. Henrik is worried about him." Now her face was nothing but hollow shadows. The cords in her neck stood out with stress.

"Henrik doesn't think I'm good enough for Rhys." Sopi clasped her suddenly aching stomach. "It's okay. I don't think so, either."

"That's not what I'm saying at all." Elise caught her arm, her grip strong. Urgent. "I'm asking you for a favor. I want Henrik to be confident that Rhys can handle all he faces, otherwise Henrik will step in and try to carry some of his burden. I know that Rhys is taking on a lot. He'll have to cover Henrik's duties to the throne, arrange a wedding. Then he'll have a wife and the making and rearing of children. It's so much to ask of you both. *I know that*. But this is the man I love. He's all I have."

She wouldn't even have Henrik's child. That grief was a dark knowledge lurking in the backs of Elise's eyes. Her anguish twisted up Sopi's conscience so she instantly wanted to ease her mind any way she could.

"Henrik is opting for a very aggressive treatment. It will give him his best chance at surviving, but he needs to give all his focus to getting through it."

"Of course," Sopi murmured. This poor woman had enough on her plate without Sopi whining about having won an ancestral lottery and not knowing how to handle it. "Of course, I'll do whatever I can. I understand the stakes, perhaps not as intimately as you do, but I know how important it is that this marriage take place and—" result in babies "—work. I know Rhys and I have to project the best possible image."

"Thank you." Elise drifted her eyes closed with relief and gratitude. "I wasn't sure if… But Rhys is a very good judge of character. I should have known he wouldn't attach himself to someone who would put her interests ahead of others."

You're self-sacrificing. You'll need that.

She smiled weakly, wondering if the reason she was ideal was less about her blue blood and more about her willingness to shelve her own needs in favor of others'. She was realizing she had done that to her own detriment in the past, but how could she switch gears now? As it turned out, this king and queen weren't a pair of demigods demanding to be served. They were a couple in love who faced a heart-wrenching situation. Sopi genuinely wanted to do anything she could to ease their suffering.

Even if it meant sleeping with a man she barely knew.

Sopi's liquid-eyed glance as she followed Elise from the room stayed with Rhys as his brother remarked, "You're moving very quickly. I expected you to bring her here for further discussion, not drop it into the press as you left the tarmac."

They had stayed on their feet after the women left, both given to pacing during heavy discussions.

"You disapprove of her?" Rhys's hackles went up.

"I don't know yet," Henrik stated with characteristic frankness. "You have to marry, Rhys. That's a fact, but I expected you to explore your options. How could you know within two days that she's the right one?"

"Look at who she is."

"Oh, on the surface, she's perfect. I heartily agree the spectacle of her background works to my advantage. I'm talking about a more personal connection, though. Wouldn't you rather marry someone you care about? *Love?*"

"Not a requirement for me," Rhys rejected bluntly. "I believe Sopi and I will have a very comfortable arrangement in the long run."

"Comfortable," Henrik scoffed. "That's your aspiration for a life partner?"

"I don't wish to be moved by greater forces," he said truthfully, still uncomfortable with the compulsion that had drawn him toward Sopi in the first place.

"You don't want a marriage like mine?" Henrik folded his arms, frowning.

"No one will ever have a marriage like yours." Rhys smiled with sincere fondness for his sister-in-law. "Elise is one of a kind." If there was such a thing as soul mates, Henrik had found his. Because of that, Rhys was as concerned for Elise as he was for his brother. "How is she coping, now you have more information?"

Henrik let out a weighty sigh. "Exactly as she always does. Brave and stubborn and deaf to anything but the outcome she is striving for." Henrik was wry, yet his voice grew unutterably heavy. "I hate myself for doing this to her."

"It's not your fault."

"I still question everything I've ever done." Henrik poured himself fresh coffee, then ignored the cup. Squeezed the back of his neck.

Rhys knew the feeling. Was Henrik's diagnosis a rebalancing of scales for some action Rhys had or hadn't taken? He desperately wanted to believe there was some way he could take control of what was happening and change it.

"I should have convinced her to move on years ago," Henrik said. "If she was married to someone else, she would have the children she wanted by now."

"She doesn't want another man's children." The doctor had floated the idea of using Rhys's sperm, but none of them had been comfortable with that proposal.

No, Henrik had declared. If Rhys's heir would inherit the throne, his brother ought to be married to the mother of his child.

"If Elise was capable of loving another man, that would've happened by now," Rhys said. "I don't know why she's so enamored. You're not as charming as you think you are," he chided. "But she loves you blindly and unfailingly."

Henrik sent him a look of reproof at the insult but nodded agreement. "It's true. I'm luckier than I have a right to be. Happier, too. That's why I want this for you." He turned on the head of a pin, switching from humbled husband to imperious monarch and domineering older brother in the space of a breath. "This life is hard enough. The wrong partner could drain you dry. You want someone by your side who strengthens you. You won't find that with a stranger, Rhys."

Henrik's words caused an unsettled sensation in Rhys's chest. The flip side of caring that deeply was a carrying of the other's pain—*in sickness and in health* went the vow, didn't it? Rhys didn't want the sort of agony his brother and sister-in-law were currently going through, but he couldn't voice that apprehension.

"Sopi is more than meets the eye," he said instead.

"She's up to *everything* that might be asked of her?" Henrik was obliquely referring to taking the title of queen, should it become necessary. "If Elise didn't love me the way she does, she would have left this life a long time ago. Do you realize that, given your plan for a quick engagement and marriage, you're going to have to play the star-crossed lovers who couldn't wait? Is she up for *that*?"

Rhys had realized that. There wouldn't be any announcements about Henrik's condition until Rhys was married with a baby on the way. Typically, a royal wedding would take a year of planning. His and Sopi's would happen a couple of months from now. Six weeks, if they could manage it. Their engagement party would be organized as soon as possible.

"Love at first sight," Rhys declared with an unconcerned smile. "Sopi and I will sell it. Don't worry about any of this. Concentrate on getting through the treatment. For all our sakes. I want my brother, and I want my king."

Henrik grumbled an agreement, and they turned to other things.

CHAPTER SEVEN

SOPI NAPPED AND woke disoriented, desperately needing reassurance. Rhys was tied up with the king, though. When she did hear from him, it was a message from Gerard requesting she dress for a hastily organized, informal dinner to meet Verina's prime minister and a handful of other dignitaries.

Informal it might be, but Sopi was put in a full-length off-the-shoulder velvet gown. It was such a dark shade of indigo it was nearly black. Subtle ruching ensured the otherwise straight fall of sumptuous fabric accentuated her curves, and a slit at the back allowed her to walk. Dozens of shoes had been delivered, and she stepped into a silver pair with mirror-finish heels before moving toward the lounge between her room and Rhys's.

Nervously, she knocked, then entered when she heard him call, "Come in."

He was nursing a drink but lowered his glass as he took in her appearance. Her heart soared at the sight of him in a white jacket with satin lapels and a black bow tie. His beard was freshly trimmed, his demeanor so quietly powerful, he seemed to reach out and grab her from across the room while remaining untouchable himself. Unattainable.

"You look stunning." His voice was as smooth and

rich as the satin-lined gown that caressed her skin as she moved.

"Thank you." Her hair had been wound onto her head in a crown, and she self-consciously touched the amethyst pendant at her throat. "These are beautiful." The weight of the matching earrings told her they hung in her lobes, but she still wanted to clasp them to ensure she hadn't lost them. They were one more extravagance she wasn't comfortable accepting. "Can we talk about…all of this?"

"After dinner? Our guests will arrive any minute. We should be downstairs to greet them." He set aside his drink and came across to offer his arm. "You don't have to knock," he said as he led her from the room. "This is your home. By the time we're married, we'll have taken over this entire wing."

About that, she longed to say, but they were approaching the top of the stairs, where Henrik and Elise had just arrived.

Sopi subtly squeezed Rhys's sleeve as she practiced the deferential nod she'd been taught by the protocol coach. They followed the couple down to the formal receiving room.

They spent the next few hours dining and making small talk with people who acted pleased to meet her, but Sopi wasn't so naive she didn't know she was more a curiosity than anything else.

Through it all, Rhys remained a watchful presence, within touching distance yet rarely touching her. Sopi was intensely relieved when the evening concluded and they retreated to their lounge.

"Be honest," she demanded as he closed the door. "How bad was that?"

"I thought it went well."

"Really? Because every time I looked at you, you were… I don't know. Displeased?" Distant. Aside from offering his arm, he'd been completely hands-off when she had been longing for a sign of approval or affection. Acceptance.

"I would have stepped in if you were floundering. I thought you handled yourself beautifully." He poured fresh drinks.

"Then why are you so…" She studied his guarded expression as he brought her a nightcap. "Tense," she decided. "Like you're trying not to yell at me or something."

His brows went up. His mouth twitched, and some of the stiffness in his expression eased to amusement.

"It's not that type of tension, Sopi. My mind has been elsewhere most of the night." His gaze slid to the door to his bedroom.

Her scalp prickled. All she could say was a faint, "Oh."

He sipped. His gaze was full of laughter at both of them, causing pulls of attraction in her middle.

"I'm really nervous," she admitted into her glass. "Maybe once it's over with, I'll relax."

"Over with." His humor disappeared in a flash of something more feral. "You're not anticipating our love-making?"

"I don't know what to expect, do I?"

His expression softened slightly. "I told you I won't force you. If you have misgivings, let's address them."

She opened her mouth, but nothing came out. All she could see was the obvious love between Elise and Henrik. They weren't heavy with pet names or physical affection, but their smiles at each other were very natural. They glanced at each other frequently and seemed to read each other's thoughts. It spoke of a truly special link—the kind Sopi would have wanted for herself if she'd known such a connection was possible.

"Sopi?" Rhys prompted.

She crossed her arms, not wanting him to think her juvenile with her romantic longings.

"Every time I want to complain about what's happening to me, I think of what your brother and Elise are going through. Then I feel petty. But I always thought my stepsisters were petty, presuming that the world would simply provide all they needed. Dresses and jewelry and fancy dinners." She fiddled with her pendant. It wasn't the whole of her reservations, but it was a big part of them.

"You're not like them," he assured her. "You won't become like them."

"You'll stage an intervention if I show signs?"

"The minute you deliberately flash your cleavage to get a man to break out his wallet, I will draw you aside for a lecture, I promise you." A dangerous, smoky edge imbued his tone.

"Now you sound possessive." And there was no reason she should find that titillating.

"I am," he stated without apology. "It's another reason I want to address any concerns you have. Once you're in my bed, I will be highly resistant to your leaving it."

Until the deed was done? That thought made her melancholy. She realized her feet were protesting the heels and sat to remove them.

"Everything is so *big*, Rhys. I'm twenty-two. I should have room to make mistakes at this age. Date the wrong man and get a little drunk in public." She had barely touched her wine at dinner, terrified of becoming clumsy or loose tongued. "No one this young should get married to anyone."

"She said with wisdom beyond her years." He shrugged out of his jacket and loosened his tie. "This *is* a lot of pressure, Sopi. I'm not going to tell you you're wrong to feel it and struggle with it. The fact that you're aware of the downside of your new position, not blinded by the shine, tells me you're smart enough and strong enough to handle what you face."

"Every time I try to tell you I'm wrong for this, you tell me I'm right," she grumbled. "I'm afraid you only want to marry the person I'm supposed to become, not the person I *am*."

"They're the same person."

"No, they're not!"

"They are," he insisted. "Listen, if you want me to tell you where you're failing, I will. You're limiting yourself," he stated bluntly. "Think bigger. Let yourself grow."

"I can't!"

"Why not?"

"I don't know!"

She hung her head in her hands, embarrassed that she was acting so childish, yelling like a toddler. She didn't even know where her reluctance to reach higher stemmed from. Maybe that stupid audition tape?

She lifted her face, frowned with self-deprecation as she realized that probably was it.

"When I was fifteen, I made a tape for a singing show," she admitted. "It was a lark with a friend. We weren't serious, but I made it to the top ten, and the organizers wanted to fly me to Toronto."

"That doesn't surprise me." His expression cleared at

the switch of topic. "I heard you in the sauna the other night. You have a lovely voice."

Had it only been some thirty-six or forty-eight hours ago that they had kissed and groped each other in the hot pool?

She shrugged off the compliment, mumbling, "Thanks, but it felt like a fluke. It was exciting, though. I started thinking bigger." She gave him a doleful look.

"You wanted to sing? Professionally?" She saw the wheels turning in his head, trying to assimilate this information with the path they were on. "What happened?"

"My father died. I had to bow out, and I was too sad to try again. I think I felt safer staying home. Staying small." She hadn't put that together until now, but she saw how illogical it was to let that experience hold her back. "Maybe I'm still feeling that way."

"I completely understand how losing a parent stunts your growth." He came to sit across from her. "I don't judge you for it. But you have essentially been running Cassiopeia's. And you were doing it without any real support. That's no small task." His expression grew introspective as he studied her. "I'm not surprised those promoters saw something in you. You possess initiative and determination and star quality. One way or another, you were destined for greatness, Sopi."

She shook her head, dismissing that.

He didn't argue, which left her hearing his voice echo in her head. Somehow that held even more impact.

She thought of the sense of expectation she had felt from Elise earlier. From everyone, starting with the maid who had asked what time she should wake her, to the text from Gerard confirming her schedule for tomorrow.

People wanted things from her—they always had. In fact, she had to wonder if Maude had begun putting everything on her plate because Sopi had stepped in to take the lead every time her stepmother had attempted to.

Ugh. Maybe Rhys was right and she had been putting all her efforts into micromanaging in a misguided effort to take the control she instinctively desired.

She scowled at him, starting to think maybe he did know her better than she knew herself.

"Did you always believe you would get back here after you were exiled?" she asked.

"I did," he said with simple honesty. "I had to. I couldn't…" He squinted as though looking into the past. "I couldn't accept that my parents' lives had been lost for no reason. That's why I was angry when we lived so poorly. I couldn't believe that our parents had given their lives so we could live like that, barely surviving. Intellectually, I know life can be cruel and not every wrong is righted, but I had to believe the wrong against us would be corrected. It was the only way I could get through my grief."

She nodded thoughtfully. "I accept that this has to happen. I do. I want to stop fighting it, but I think I'm mourning my old life. Do you ever pine for that simpler time?"

"Occasionally," he admitted. "I miss the pleasure of listening to a live band while pouring beer behind a bar, not filtering every word through the lens of political impact. You're the first person to make me feel like that man again, if you want the truth. As though the veneer is unnecessary. I don't have to be anyone but myself. I can swim naked," he summed up with an ironic smile.

But you're you, she wanted to say. His air of confidence and control wasn't a veneer. It was an innate part of him. She didn't have anything like it.

Rather than protest, however, she basked in the quiet knowledge that she offered him something no one else did. What would he give her, though?

A sudden hollow sensation in her heart made her smile wobble. She longed for the things every human yearned for: passion and emotional bonds and intimacy.

"What if the sex is awful?" she asked with tentative anxiety.

The corner of his mouth dug in. "The sex will be fantastic. You'll have to trust me on that. Until I prove it," he added slyly.

Her inner muscles clenched in a most telling way, causing heat to flood through her. She didn't ask about the rest, but surely if they were talking like this, and shared their bodies, the rest would manifest?

"Okay," she murmured.

He cocked his head, arrested, gaze locking onto her while his whole body seemed to gather like a predator about to pounce. "You want to go to bed? Right now?"

"I'm starting to realize I'll be scared either way, so yes. I think so."

"You're scared of me?" His head went back and his narrowed gaze flashed with something she couldn't identify.

"I'm terrified of all of this," she said with a wave of her hand. "Who you are. How you live. How you expect *me* to live. But I'm realizing that I can't let fear hold me back. I have to confront it."

He swore and looked to the ceiling. Started to speak. Took another moment to find words.

"I don't want to say no to you, Sopi. I want you in

my bed *right now*. But not as some sort of bravery challenge. I want you to *want* to be there. With *me*."

"I do!"

"Do you?" he challenged. "Who do you want to sleep with? The prince or the man?"

"The man. The warm body. The hands that erase all the frightened thoughts from my head," she admitted baldly.

After a long moment of consideration, he stood and held out one of those hands, palm up with invitation. "I can do that."

She set her hand in his. Felt the squeeze in her chest when he closed his grip over her fingers and drew her to her feet.

"I have to know that this much is real, at least," she whispered.

"It's very real." He skimmed a light caress around the shell of her ear and set her dangling earring to quivering. "I want the touch that empties my mind, too. I want that like water and air."

His touch tickled beneath her jaw, inviting her to lift her mouth in offering. She loved the feel of his silken whiskers as she petted along his jaw, drawing him down.

His kiss was gentle—too gentle. She pressed into her toes, wanting the conflagration to consume her.

He was too strong and easily flexed his muscles to draw back from her. One heavy hand on her hip kept her from closing the distance. He teased her by rubbing his lips lightly against hers, and his breath wafted hotly over her mouth as he spoke.

"This is our first time, *süsse*. I'm not going to race you to the finish line." He slowly eased his mouth over hers again, taking his time as he deepened the kiss.

He didn't have to crush her mouth to inflame her, she realized as she melted under his lazy, thorough veneration of her mouth. She grew lethargic, curling her arms around his neck while she leaned her weight into him, wallowing in the sheer freedom to kiss him the way she'd been dying to since their skinny-dip.

When she had her fingers speared into his hair and his embrace was the only thing holding her up, he lifted his head.

"The world outside our bedroom is always going to be a difficult place, Sopi. Even the world inside a bedroom can be complicated. My hope is that ours will be a retreat from the chaos. Out there—" He nodded at the door to the hall. "I need the princess who is willing to play a supporting role. That's convenient, but it's not why I want you. In here…" He drew her to the door of his room. "I want *you*. Just you."

Her heart stumbled as she crossed the threshold into the lamp-lit room.

"I always knew that sex would be a step I couldn't take back. I think that's why I held back from taking it." It was another aspect of her fear of reaching too high.

"That's why I don't want to rush you." He stood behind her and found a pin in her hair, gently extracting it. "If you want to slow down or stop, tell me. If I don't have your trust with your body, I don't have your trust at all." His mouth nuzzled against the nape of her neck, and he inhaled, making her shiver in delight.

"I'm worried you'll think I'm silly or dumb."

"We frolicked like otters in a pond. We're past silly and dumb."

She had to chuckle at that, but when she lifted her hands to help with the pins, he growled a noise of protest.

"Let me do it. There was a comic book in my youth,

one with a Valkyrie whose long hair was always hiding the most intriguing curves and shadows on her figure. I have latent fantasies I'm looking forward to indulging."

"Good thing my fantasies run to comic book nerds, I guess."

He barked out a laugh of enjoyment and slipped his arm across her collarbone, hugging her into his shaking frame. "I've been called worse."

She was smiling, hands on the muscled forearm that held her so firmly, cheek tilted into his strong shoulder. A whimsical, wistful happiness filled her. A sense of possibility.

"This is really why I'm here, Rhys," she confided softly. "I don't think I could have lived with wondering where this might have gone."

He turned her in his arms. His face was solemn as he plucked the last two pins that held her hair. He unwound the long braid and surprised her by looping it behind his own neck, leaving the tail against the front of his opposite shoulder.

"Me, either," he admitted gravely, making her stomach lift and dip.

This time when he kissed her, it wasn't slow and tender and gentle. It was hot. Thorough. Carnal. His beard scoured her chin, and his arms squeezed her breath from her lungs. She grabbed the tail of her own hair where it hung against his shoulder and pulled, tying them together while an aching noise throbbed in her throat.

If she thought to be the aggressor, she had sorely overestimated Rhys's willingness to submit. He cupped her head and ravaged her mouth, raking his lips possessively across hers, delving to taste and not stopping until she was trembling.

When he broke away, they were both panting, and he

wore a satisfied look as he admired her through half-lidded eyes.

"My only regret about the other night is that I didn't get to see you. Not properly." He turned her and flipped her unraveling braid to the front of her shoulder as he unzipped her. Slowly. Inch by inch, cool air swirled into pockets of heat. Sensitive goose bumps rose on her skin.

"Rhys." Each of her heartbeats thudded in a slow pound of anticipation that made her sway under the impact.

"I've been thinking constantly about it. The smoothness of your skin." He parted her dress at her spine, fingertips tickling into the small of her back.

She arched in pleasure, spears of heat thrown like lightning bolts into her loins by his hot, proprietary touch.

"How you were so shy, then not." He found the clasp on her strapless bra and released it. As it loosened, his caress traced where it had sat, moving forward until he took her breasts in his hot palms. "How your nipples felt against my tongue."

They hardened so quickly, they stung. His thumbs passed over them, strumming such a fierce pleasure through her, she squirmed, pushing her backside into his hips. She immediately felt how hard he was and wriggled a little more enticingly.

"And that," he said in a voice growing guttural. "How you give as good as you get. You made me lose my mind. I didn't behave that wildly as a teenager." He held her nipples in a pinch that hovered on the precipice of pain, keeping her very still as her pulse seemed to ring in each of those points, bouncing off the hard palms that cupped her.

"Losing control like that scares the hell out of me."

He scraped his teeth against her nape and thrust into the cheeks of her butt. "I still want to go there with you again."

She covered his hands, unsure if she wanted to stop him or urge him to be more aggressive. He held her in an erotic vise, but all she did was turn her head so he could kiss her. He did, stimulating her until she ached with yearning. She dragged one of his hands down to cup where she was growing damp and distraught with need.

His strong hand stayed there as she rocked, teasing them both until she was shaking with desire.

"You're so close, *süsse*." He nipped at her ear. "What do you need?"

"I don't know," she sobbed. "You."

He growled and released her, turning her and brushing the open dress down. When he nudged her backward, she thought he was helping her step out of the puddled velvet, but he took her farther, until she felt the edge of the mattress against the backs of her legs and sat.

She only wore her panties and found herself knotting her fists in the duvet as she gazed up at him uncertainly.

"Trust me?" he asked.

"I do." She nodded, even though her heart pounded with nerves.

He smiled darkly and pressed her shoulder so she let herself fall onto her back.

"This is what it means to be mine. All of you." He leaned over her to drop a kiss on her chin, her breastbone, little presses of silken beard and soft lips all the way down her middle. Lace abraded her thighs as he stole her underwear while trailing kisses from her navel to her hip bone.

He held her gaze very boldly as he parted her knees and dropped to the floor at the side of the bed. His effortless strength pulled her toward him. Her thighs went onto his shoulders, and she gasped as he stropped his beard on each of her inner thighs, making her shiver with anticipation.

He blew softly on her fine, damp curls, and she trembled again until the damp heat of his mouth settled with ownership against the most intimate part of her. With a small cry, she reflexively tried to close her legs against the intensity of sensation. She had known what sex was, but she hadn't known it was surrender. Not like this. She would belong to him completely after this. She already did, because she struggled to absorb the onslaught of sensation, but she didn't fight it.

He was in no hurry, taking his time building her tension until she ached all over. She hadn't known that arousal had this ability to consume. She could hardly breathe. Her blood was fire in her veins. Each moment was a drawn-out agony of spearing pleasure that coiled her tighter, and then a pulse beat of eternity waiting for it to happen again.

She lost her ability to speak or form conscious thought. She couldn't process how wickedly good this felt as he swept her with starkly intimate caresses. Arching, writhing, she let the crisis overwhelm her, too greedy for it. Too ready. In moments, she was mindlessly saying his name and shuddering under the force of a shattering orgasm.

A beautiful, floaty feeling came on the heels of it. She didn't have the strength to pick up her head but ran her fingers into his silky hair, trying to convey how lovely he had made her feel.

He didn't stop. He switched from soothing to a fresh,

deliberate assault that sent a spear of acute desire twisting through her.

"What are you doing?" she gasped, shocked that she could go from satisfaction to craving in seconds.

"Do it again," he commanded and went back to pleasuring her mercilessly.

"I can't."

His touch penetrated, and the sensations redoubled. She didn't think she could handle it. He tossed her into a place of intense excitement, but her hand in his hair urged him to continue, and suddenly she was soaring again, higher, abandoning any restraint as she released jagged cries of ecstasy.

He soothed her again, letting her catch her breath, but he didn't let her sink into satisfaction. He teased. Made her say his name again so the pleading of it echoed in the room.

He shifted his kisses to her inner thighs, and she could have wept with loss. Her thighs were still twitching, her skin damp and her heart unsteady.

He rose to set his fists on either side of her hips and tracked his gaze avidly over her naked, trembling form. His face was angular and fierce, his smile savage. "We both needed that."

"Do I…do that to you now?"

"Do you want to?" He pushed to stand straight and yanked a hand down his front to tear his shirt open. "Next time," he decided just as brutishly. "The thought of your mouth—" He squeezed himself through his trousers and hissed his breath through his teeth before he dragged at his clothes to remove them. "Still with me, *süsse*?"

"Yes." She swallowed, mesmerized by the way the lamplight gilded his skin to pale bronze. She had only caught a glimpse of him at the side of the pool. Now, staring at him unabashedly, when he was so close she could touch and he was naked and fully aroused, he made her weak.

He started to reach toward the nightstand, caught himself in his fist again, and his breath hissed through his teeth. "My first time, too, *süsse*. Naked. I don't know if I'm going to hang on long enough."

He came down alongside her, his hand sweeping from her hip to her waist to her rib cage while his mouth pressed against her shoulder.

She felt dazed, not having given thought to what this really was. She flashed her gaze up to his, fearful that this was all simply act of procreation for him, not the starkly profound union it was for her.

He was watching her, maybe tracking the myriad emotions accosting her. Nerves and desire and something new and sweet were moving through her, feelings she didn't know how to interpret, but that made her feel incredibly vulnerable.

His eyes were glittering with feral lights of excitement, but there was a surprising gentleness in him as he caressed her now. He picked up what was left of the braid in her hair and turned his wrist to wrap it around his hand. When his grip was tucked close to her neck and she couldn't move her head, he kissed her. The light restraint held her captive for his teasing, barely there kisses. Heat flowed into her loins, and she crooked her knee and rolled her hips into his.

He broke their kiss to glance at her knee. "The way you respond will be my undoing." He released her hair and trailed his hand down to claim her mound. His touch delved into slippery heat, making her jolt.

"Too sensitive?" He eased away so he was only cupping her.

"Not enough," she complained, rolling fully into him and taking hold of the taut shape of him. "I've never felt so greedy in my life," she admitted. "I want to know how it will feel, Rhys. I want you inside me."

She found herself on her back, the agile strength of him caging her. It was intimidating, yet she didn't feel unsafe. Not physically. Everything that made her feel secure in life had long spiraled beyond her control, but here, trapped by him, she was safer than she'd ever been.

He shifted atop her, using his strong thighs to push her legs apart. She felt the shape of him, the heat and hardness against her unprotected flesh. He nipped her chin and cupped her breast, then bent his head to take her nipple into the hot cavern of his mouth.

She groaned with abandon, twisting and scraping her hands across his shoulders. "Rhys, I can't take this."

He lifted his head, shifted and guided himself against her. She felt the pressure. The forging stretch of him pushing into her. She gasped. This was way more intimate than she had expected.

He paused. "Let me see your eyes."

His were nearly black, atavistic. And yet he smiled. A wicked, satisfied smile. Perhaps even conspiratorial, as though he saw something similar in the windows to her soul that was alive in him.

In that second, she had no defenses against him at all. Not physically or emotionally. She felt intensely vulnerable as he pressed, stretching and filling her until they were locked together. Her knees reflexively bent to hug his hips, somehow making him sink even more flush against her, settling deep within her.

She hadn't realized that sex was so raw. So deliberate. It struck her that she had met him mere days ago, but it was a startling moment of alignment. Of sharing an experience.

"Hurt?" he murmured.

She barely heard and barely comprehended. She was lost to the magnitude of the moment. She couldn't keep her eyes open as waves of emotion washed over her. There was a sweet sense of achievement and the stinging discomfort of uncertainty. But there was also a tender yearning that closed her limbs around him, needing the reassurance of his hot body tight against hers.

"When you're ready," he said against her ear. He kissed across her jaw and temple, the pressure light and frustratingly elusive.

Before she consciously knew what she wanted or what she was signaling, her body shifted restlessly beneath his. Her inner muscles clenched, and the golden light from the lamp seemed to fill her. Possibility arrived within her, stoking a slippery heat in her loins, filling her with renewed hunger and yearning.

"Yes," he hissed. "Exactly like that." He licked into the delicate hollow beneath her ear. As he withdrew, everything in her clenched to hold on to him.

He cupped the side of her neck so she felt the pressure of his strong palm against her throbbing artery. She didn't know which was hotter, his skin or hers.

He returned, flooding her with such a wave of pleasurable sensations, she groaned. The arousal that had been banked while she adjusted to this new act spun through her, catching at her with its tendrils, dragging her back into the sharp tumble of acute desire.

He thrust again, and she felt the strain in his back against her palms as she roamed her touch, urging him on. He kept the pace slow, giving her time to adjust, but her body knew what it wanted. The next time he returned, her hips tilted in greeting. Her thighs clenched on his hips, fighting his next withdrawal, making him hiss in a combination of pleasured excitement and disciplined exertion.

She slid her hands to his lower back and lower still, digging her fingernails into his buttocks to drive him into her with more power.

He began to move faster, setting her afire. Their skin dampened with perspiration. They kissed and kissed again, catching at each other's lips while groaning in an earthly mingle of noises. Her reactions were pure instinct. She arched and pressed her tongue into his mouth, locked her calf across his backside and made noises of agony.

With each thrust she lost a little more of herself, but she threw herself willingly into their erotic struggle. Their fight to reach completion together. Her climax approached, and he grew more ardent, as if he sensed it. Her entire world narrowed to the destination they sought, and suddenly it was there, vast and full of endless possibility.

For one heartbeat, she thought the way he stiffened meant he was in paradise without her. Then a profound, crashing wave engulfed her. After that, she didn't know which of them trembled or shook, which pulsed or contracted, only that they were in this maelstrom together. Thrown and tossed, battered and exalted. Both equally, utterly, gloriously destroyed.

CHAPTER EIGHT

As Rhys dragged free of her, the final caressing stroke on his sensitized skin was pure, velvety bliss that jangled against his nerve endings. He landed on his damp back, the blankets tangled beneath him, and listened to Sopi take a full breath and release it as a hum of supreme satisfaction.

He lay motionless, a castaway barely alive on a remote island beach. The storm had left him weak and boneless, fighting to catch his breath.

Beside him, Sopi was still panting. Her damp arm was against his. Somehow their hands found each other, and their fingers entwined in a silent reassurance that they had made it through to live another day.

Warning signals crept through the fog of his recovery, though. He had somehow managed to keep enough wits about him to be gentle and ensure her pleasure, but he had been completely abandoned to their lovemaking. Lost to a pleasure that was even more exquisite and profound than he'd anticipated. Addictive, even.

It was the novelty of being naked without protection, he assured himself, even as his hand tightened on hers, wanting to draw her deeper into his protective sphere. He closed his eyes and fought the sense of a rising force within him that wanted to somehow bind her to him.

He should have realized her effect on him was dangerously intense when he'd tracked her like a damned arctic wolf following the scent of his mate into the snow. With the clarity of hindsight, he saw how he'd leaped on the convenience of her royal blood so he could have this—her naked body beside his own.

Now they'd embarked on the making of a child. The reality of that hit him like a meteor from space, crashing emotions over him—responsibility, concern, pride, excitement and a fear of the unknown. Terror of the uncontrollable.

He threw his free arm across his eyes, hand knotting into a fist as he tried to stave off the maelstrom of conflict. If he reacted this powerfully to the mere possibility of making a child, how would he cope if they'd actually made one?

He had put himself in an impossible position, he realized, and there was no way to change it now.

"Thank you," Sopi murmured, stirring beside him. She rolled and bent her knee so her soft thigh settled on his. Her head turned into his shoulder, and her damp lips pressed against his skin.

His nerve endings leaped and the spent flesh between his thighs pulsed with a fresh rush of heat. The compulsion to gather her up and roll atop her and consume her all over again was nearly more than he could withstand.

This was impossible.

Intolerable.

But he couldn't push her away, dewy virgin that she was. He might hate himself for giving in to his desire for her, but he would hate himself even more if he hurt her.

He lifted his arm from between them and opened his legs so her knee fell between his own, cuddling her into his side.

"*How* was a woman with that much passion still a virgin?" he asked in a voice graveled by satisfaction.

"I was saving it all for you, obviously." Her fingertips drew a lazy circle across his abdomen.

His heart gave a rolling pound of thrill at the thought. He was too rational and forward-thinking to put virginity on a pedestal, but there was something deeply satisfying in the sense of promise in her words.

He was in so much trouble.

"Was it…okay for you?" she asked tentatively.

He groaned and caught her teasing hand. "It was exquisite. You are." He brought her hand to his mouth so he could lightly bite her fingers. "But you should probably go to sleep before I start thinking we should double-check whether it was really that incredible."

She hummed a sensual noise of amusement and moved against him restlessly, drying his throat. "How can I sleep if there's any question in our minds?"

He was still at war with his elemental self, but the primitive won again. He promised himself he would withhold more of himself this time and pulled her atop him.

Her hair spilled around him, and he was lost.

Sopi wasn't so inexperienced that she believed falling in love two weeks into a relationship was a realistic expectation. Even so, she was quite sure she was on her way. Rhys was such a remarkable man!

The more she learned of Verina's history and how hard he had struggled to return to their homeland, the more she admired him for all he had accomplished. He was earnest in his support of his charities and keen to develop green initiatives. He had a dry wit and a sharp intelligence, and he genuinely cared what happened to his country and the world.

When they were in public, he gave her room to find her way while remaining a steady presence, always backing her up when she was unsure. In private, he offered romantic gestures like touching a rose to her chin or putting a ring on her finger while they stood on the palace wall overlooking the lake.

And then there were the nights, the magnificent nights when they couldn't seem to quench their insatiable passion for each other.

How could she not fall for a man who did all those things to her and for her and…

She counted the days again, heart tripping over itself and tripping up her brain.

She was only a day late, nothing to get excited about. A lot had happened lately. She was handling the move to Verina and her new title and all the public attention fairly well, but this was a huge deal. It could easily be throwing off her cycle. She was often late when she was stressed. She certainly didn't feel any different. No nausea or sore breasts, which she knew from friends were very typical signs.

Even so, her hand went to her abdomen and her eyes closed over emotive tears. She bit her smile, trying to keep the beams of happiness from bursting out of her like balls of sunlight.

This had to be love she was experiencing. Why else would she be this elated at the idea of being pregnant? Obviously, love for her child was taking root in her, but a baby was pure wishful thinking at this point. No, this was more. This was a certainty that she wanted Rhys's baby.

Because she loved him.

She waited a few more days before she said anything to him, not wanting to get his hopes up. They were dressing for their official engagement ball in Paris. It seemed a bit overkill when they were marrying in a month, but the party covered the fact that Henrik had come to a Paris clinic for surgery.

When their maids and valets and assistants left them alone, she clutched her hands before her and watched Rhys check his bow tie in the mirror. He turned and tracked a gaze rich with admiration over every inch of her.

"You're stunning."

"I'm late."

He flicked his glance to the clock. "Fashionably. We're the guests of honor. It's expected," he dismissed.

"No, I mean…" She nearly ruined her lipstick, biting back her smile at the way he'd misinterpreted her.

He actually swayed backward as comprehension struck. "Late," he repeated blankly. "Are you…sure?"

He wasn't smiling, and her own smile faltered.

"I'm sure I'm late. I'm not sure of…anything else. Sometimes I'm off if I have a lot going on in my life." She hitched a shoulder, reminding herself that she didn't want to mislead him, but she had rather hoped for more excitement. "I'll…um…make a doctor's appointment when we get back to Verina, but I thought you'd want to know."

She started to move forward into his arms. In the last days, they'd become quite comfortable in offering affection when they were alone, but something in his demeanor made her falter.

"Are you…not pleased?"

"No, of course I am," he assured her. "But if it hasn't been confirmed…"

She nodded, cheeks feeling skinned. In her mind, this conversation was supposed to swirl with excitement and laughter. Her tentative words of love had been on the tip of her tongue. Now her emotions were crashing into each other like a ten-car pileup.

"I don't mean to be lukewarm." He caught her by the elbows and brushed his lips against her cheek. "This is exactly what we want, but Elise had a lot of disappointments. Let's wait to be sure before we celebrate."

Was that really what was going on? She searched his expression, but he avoided her gaze, moving to open the door. He offered his arm again.

"We should go. I want Henrik to be able to leave the party as soon as possible if he needs to."

Rhys kept his emotions firmly locked down, fearful of letting one out lest they all spill. There was a part of him wanting to scream with pride and excitement, but no. It wasn't even confirmed yet, and a thousand things could still go wrong. There could be medical implications for Sopi. Why had he not thought of that before they'd had unprotected sex? How irresponsible of him.

Then there was the guilt, wider and darker and deeper than any of those other emotions, especially when he looked into his brother's eyes and accepted Henrik's congratulatory handshake on his official engagement.

Henrik's words had been a public expression of his approval that Sopi was joining their family, but Rhys felt like a traitor, holding the secret of his potential heir in the shadows of his heart.

Now Henrik was beside him in a more informal capacity.

"You're right," Henrik said, watching Sopi. "She's more than she seems. You chose well."

Rhys couldn't argue. Sopi was fully embracing the woman she had been meant to become. She wore an elegant, one-shouldered gown in champagne silk with sparkling beadwork scrolling around her waist. Her hair was in a knot and adorned with sparkling pins. If Rhys stared at it too long, he began thinking of the silky feel of it slithering across his stomach and thighs—a distraction he couldn't afford.

He dragged his attention from where Elise was introducing Sopi to a founder of a charity and met his brother's shrewdly assessing gaze.

Henrik had stood to toast them and had been the first to cut in when Rhys had started the dancing with Sopi. Henrik had since danced with his wife and made the rounds to speak with guests, but he was pale. Rhys thought he should call it a night.

"You're both quite convincing," Henrik said.

"In what way?"

"That you're in love."

"That's the point," Rhys said, grimly aware that the infatuation he was displaying wasn't nearly as manufactured as he had planned it to be. When he wasn't fantasizing about having sex with Sopi, he was telling Gerard to check in with her, to ensure she didn't need him. Or he was trolling social media, ensuring no one was saying anything that might impact her growing self-confidence.

Meanwhile, she was taking on palace duties and public appearances like a pro, earning goodwill wherever she went. The one time she had prevailed on him for his opinion, she had just received Francine's report on Cassiopeia's. She had wanted him to confirm her instincts, worried she was too invested to be objective. She wasn't.

In every way, she was rising to the challenge of her station. He couldn't be prouder. Now she was likely fulfilling their most important duty, and he didn't know how to handle how vulnerable it made him feel. How guilty.

"Elise is convinced Sopi's in love with you," Henrik commented.

Rhys yanked his attention back to his brother. When their gazes clashed again, his brother's held rebuke.

"I can't control how she feels." And there, too, he was at war with himself. In every way, he wanted to pull her in, hold her tight, but there was that clear-thinking part of him that saw the peril in it.

"Do you return those feelings?"

"Read my diary and find out." They had long ago perfected their ability to speak about private subjects in public and express annoyance with each other without it being readable on their faces. "Why would you ask me something like that? Here?"

"At your engagement party?"

"I don't interfere in your relationship with Elise. Kindly show me the same consideration."

Henrik laughed outright. "We're not counting the three years you badgered me to propose to her?"

"You were miserable. I was concerned about mankind as a whole."

"I was giving her a choice. I didn't know what my future would look like. Would I regain the throne and make her a queen? Lose all those investment gambles we were taking and force her to live in a shack? I didn't know if they would *accept* her. I loved her too much to start our life together on a string of false promises."

"I haven't made any false promises to Sopi."

"Haven't you? As I said, you're very convincing. If you're not *actually* in love…"

Rhys muttered a curse under his breath. "I care about her. Of course I do."

"She more than cares, Rhys. She's putting her heart into this. Into *you*."

He knew that. If she was carrying his child, she was so deeply invested, he couldn't quantify it.

And even though Sopi wasn't a needy person, she did have needs. He had promised to be her anchor and foundation and sounding board, which he was. He couldn't take many steps back from that, but he refused to take further emotional ones forward.

The resulting conflict was both a sense of walls closing in and a rack of tension, pulling him toward a breaking point.

"I would prefer you focus on yourself and your own wife," Rhys said. "I'll worry about Sopi."

"I have never understood your desire to close yourself off this way. What is the worst that could happen, Rhys? Elise is my source of strength. Let Sopi become that for you."

His brother could die. That was the worst that could happen. And the helplessness he felt at the prospect of that was more than he could bear. How was Sopi supposed to help him through such a thing? He wouldn't put that sort of burden on her.

No, he had to maintain what was left of his reserve for all their sakes.

Sopi somehow kept a smile on her face, but she kept looking to Rhys, anxious that his reaction to her possible pregnancy had been so tepid.

He was locked in a discussion with Henrik. Elise

was right. The two were very close. Sopi was both envious and jealous, having always wished for a sibling, especially one she could confide in the way the men seemed to confide in each other.

She was also a teensy bit threatened by their closeness. Elise had found her place in that dynamic a long time ago. She knew how to pry her way between them and where her marriage took precedence over the fealty between the brothers, but Sopi came up against it like a force field.

Until this evening, she had thought that was the source of this distance she sensed between them. An inequality of sorts. Tonight, she had seen the true problem. She might be in love, but Rhys wasn't.

Which turned her engagement party into a nightmare.

The chatty woman monopolizing her finally took a breath. Sopi was able to say, "Will you excuse me? I need to visit the powder room."

On her way down the hall, she veered onto a balcony for a moment to herself. Her arrival interrupted a couple who broke apart with a stammer and a blush before hurrying away. Their clinch had been tame, but their deep embarrassment meant it had been a very private moment. That left Sopi agonizing for a similar emotional connection with Rhys.

Oh, irony, you devil. Initially, she had balked at marrying him, worried this fairy-tale world she'd risen to would be more than she could handle. Now she wanted the whole package. The declaration of love and the happily-ever-after.

It would come with time, she tried telling herself, trying not to cry. Other things were settling into place. Her friendship with Elise was growing by the day, and even she and Henrik shared a laugh now and again. The job of being a princess wasn't proving too onerous. She looked forward to being a mother.

No, this was old-fashioned bridal nerves, maybe even hormonal changes making her feel like she needed more from Rhys.

As she blinked to clear the blurred vision of the Eiffel Tower, a sixth sense made the hairs stand up on the back of her neck. The door clicked behind her and there was a scuffed footstep.

"Well, well, well."

The voice might as well have been a knife blade tracing down her spine. Sopi's back went tense and rail straight. She fought the urge to clench her fists as a hot-cold flush of angry dread washed over her.

She knew instantly who the voice belonged to and stole a brief second to erase any traces of despondency from her expression. In the busy days since she had left Canada, she had only fleetingly thought of her stepmother and stepsisters. Francine had mentioned their names in relation to some unpaid invoices, but otherwise, Sopi had not missed any of them one bit.

With a fresh layer of composure in place, she turned and faced Nanette.

Her stepsister wore a striking black gown that plunged down the front to her belly button. The frothy chiffon skirt had a slit to the top of her thigh. She wore gold evening shoes peppered in bling and her bloodred lipstick matched her nails. Her lips parted in a malevolent smile as she approached with the slink of a stalking cat. Or a slithering snake.

"Fancy meeting you here."

"I didn't know you were invited," Sopi said. If she had, she might have taken steps to change that. She wasn't feeling hostile or vengeful toward her stepfamily, but neither was she eager to speak to any of them again.

"I'm insulted you didn't make a point of inviting us. I had to come as a plus one. But I suppose you can't be expected to grasp the finer points of etiquette, given your rustic upbringing."

Sopi had precious seconds to weigh her options. Making a scene was not one of them, but she couldn't allow Nanette to intimidate her. The little bit of confidence she had developed in recent weeks had already been battered by the knowledge Rhys wasn't falling in love with her the way she was falling for him. But her self-worth was too hard-won for her to let this confrontation knock her flat. Rhys would be disappointed in her if she let Nanette get the better of her, and she would be disappointed in herself.

Which left her taking a similar approach to her old one. She kept the peace by grasping at patience and speaking politely while trying to project the sophistication she was desperately trying to develop.

"It's lovely to see you again either way," she lied. "Where are you making your home now?"

Nanette laughed, but it was the patronizing chuckle of a superior amused by the antics of a lesser creature. "Full marks for *that*."

Sopi didn't let herself be drawn into whatever crass reaction Nanette was trying to provoke. "Your mother and sister are well?" she persevered.

"Oh, we're really doing this? Yes, Mummy leased us a bleak little walk-up in Vienna because she had to take what she could get on short notice. Fernanda and I would prefer to be here in Paris. You might have mentioned the royal bloodline." She narrowed her eyes with malevolence.

"I'm surprised your mother never unearthed it. She's always found my family to be so enriching." Okay, now she was descending to Nanette's level. She glanced to the glass doorway back to the hallway, noting the shift of one of the bodyguards against the glass. She signaled that she was fine and he should let her handle this.

"Well, look who finally grew a pair," Nanette said after a beat of astonishment.

Sopi realized her hands had closed into fists and consciously loosened them. She and Nanette both wore heels, but the other woman was taller. Sopi had to lift her chin to look down her nose at her.

"Someone told me once that I should set standards for myself and not drop below them," Sopi said with a meaningless smile. "This conversation is one of those things plummeting past acceptable. Excuse me."

"Oh, is acknowledging your stepsister beneath you? Now that you have a title and a presumably concussed fiancé?"

"Of course not," Sopi lied, even though alarm streaked through her veins. "You've taken *so many* pains over the years to tell me that you're far too well-bred to behave in a crass manner."

"It's not crass to pay back a double cross," Nanette shot back. "It's survival."

"You're accusing *me* of a double cross?" Sopi choked on a ball of outrage. "You sold my home behind my back!"

"Is that what happened? Because this whole thing feels like a setup. How did you even know him?"

"I didn't."

"You must have," Nanette snapped, growing genuinely angry. "How did he even find out who you were?

Is it even real? I can't believe he actually wants you, title or not. Do you have money? Does he need it?"

"That's enough." A hot flush of temper stung her cheeks. "Stop before this turns ugly."

"Ugly is throwing people out into the snow at *midnight*."

"I didn't ask that you be treated that way." Was she sorry? Probably not as much as she should be.

"You took control of the hotel that night. Of course that order came from *you*, you hideous bitch."

Don't engage, Sopi told herself. Through the windows, she saw another shift of light, but she was determined to handle this herself.

"I didn't order it," she insisted, but she was piqued enough to bite back. "The timing of your departure was always your choice, Nanette. You could have left long ago. Months. *Years*, in fact."

"Oh, does the student think she's becoming the master?" Nanette asked with a hoot of astonishment. "Allow me to demonstrate how much you still have to learn, Sopi. Start compensating me for the insults you've delivered or I will go straight back into that ballroom and tell everyone you're a janitor with a side hustle that looks like brothel work. No one believes you're in *love*," she dismissed scathingly. "You obviously compromised him in some way and now you're blackmailing him."

"*Who* is resorting to blackmail?"

Nanette tilted her head and smiled with false charm. "Make it worth my while to keep my mouth shut or I will."

Sopi moved closer, driven by old anger and new hurt and feelings that were so fresh and raw, she hadn't processed them, but she damned sure wasn't going to be walked on by this harridan ever again. And she wouldn't let Nanette harm Rhys to get at her, either.

"Think about what you're doing, Nanette," she warned in a voice that originated in a grim place behind her heart. She had to tilt back her head and her body was quivering in reaction, but a frightening thrust of power emboldened her. "Look at who I am now. You do *not* want to start a war with me."

"I know exactly who you are. You're a joke, Sopi."

"My name is Cassiopeia." She leaned in. "But *you* can call me Your Highness."

Nanette struck like a viper with a slap that snapped Sopi's head to the side. She was so stunned, she stumbled back a few steps, hardly able to make sense of the fact that she'd been struck, let alone retaliate.

The door behind her crashed open. There was a blur of movement as Rhys took hold of Nanette and thrust her toward a bodyguard.

"Get her out of here. Have her arrested for assault."

"What? You can't do that to me!" Nanette's screech of protest and furious struggle halted when the bodyguard mentioned handcuffs. With one hate-filled glare, she let the burly man escort her from the balcony.

"Are you hurt?" Rhys positioned himself to block any view of her from the windows.

"I think so." She ran her tongue in the space between her teeth and cheek and tasted copper. Beneath her testing fingers, her jaw was scorching hot.

She was shaking, though, and stepped closer to him, expecting him to pull her into his arms.

He only shifted to settle one tense arm around her. "We should get ice on that. Let's go upstairs."

"What are people going to think if we leave? Did anyone see?"

"I'll issue a statement. Don't worry about it."

He looked so incensed, her stomach flipped with apprehension. He moved to hold the door for her.

Thankfully, the balcony was right off the hallway to the elevators and powder room. They only had to cross to where one of his bodyguards was already waiting with an open car. A handful of people glanced and murmured with speculation, but within seconds they were silently traveling up to their suite.

"I'm really sorry," she whispered, heart thudding at his granite profile. "I didn't mean for anything like this to happen. I didn't even know she was here."

He looked to the guard. "Find out who brought her. Blackball him."

The man nodded and touched his ear to repeat the instruction to someone else.

"Rhys." She set a hand on his arm. He was like iron. Marble. The sort of rough diamonds that came out of the earth flawed and hard and only good for drilling into rock. "I don't think whoever brought her is to blame."

"He lied to get her past security. If I'd seen her name on the list, I would have had them turned away."

They arrived in their suite, and he barked at her assistant to get an ice pack.

Wide-eyed, the young woman complied, hurrying back with a compress wrapped in a hand towel. "Should I call a doctor?"

"I'm fine," Sopi insisted.

"Write down these names." Rhys recited Sopi's stepfamily. "I want alerts on all of them. Reports. Where they live, who they're seeing. Financials. Any pressure points. Tell Gerard I want my lawyer and PR on the phone as quickly as possible."

"Yes, sir." She hurried away, leaving them alone.

"I don't think she came here planning to hit me. I provoked her," Sopi admitted miserably. "I should have walked away instead of letting her get under my skin. It was my first chance to push back after all these years and I…" She'd been upset over *him* and his reaction to her news. She had taken it out on Nanette. "I told her to call me…" She cringed. "Your Highness."

"She should. It's who you are," he asserted coldly.

She shook her head. "No, I was stooping to her level. This is my fault—"

"The hell it is." She had never seen him so hard-hearted. "Has she hit you before? You should have told me."

"No! Never. I didn't imagine she was capable of it. That's why I waved off the bodyguard. But I really don't think she'll do anything like it again. You're over-reacting."

"I am *not*," he hurled at her. "This sort of thing gets quashed at the larva stage." He pointed at the floor. "Otherwise it grows into a goddamned siege."

Oh. She started to understand what was driving his pitiless rage. She sank onto the sofa and lowered the ice from her face. "Can we please talk this out?" she asked tentatively.

"There's nothing to talk out. I'm doing what has to be done. We won't go downstairs again. You can undress, have a bath, make yourself comfortable, but keep that ice on your face." His gaze bounced off the spot that was probably hued red by the ice. "I shouldn't have left you alone. I thought you were going to the ladies' room." He flinched with self-recrimination before his expression hardened. "It won't happen again."

"Rhys, this isn't your fault."

Something in the way he gathered himself told her

he was traveling inward to a place that wasn't reachable. Not right now anyway. Not by her.

"A bath sounds nice," she murmured, wanting some time alone herself. "Call me if you need me."

Sopi woke hours later and realized Rhys hadn't come to bed.

Puzzled, she went in search and found him in the guest room.

"I didn't want to disturb you," he said when she hovered in the door. "You should get your rest."

"It's nothing, Rhys. I'm totally fine." A faint red mark, but nothing a sweep of makeup wouldn't hide. She crossed to lift the covers and join him.

He caught them, stopping her. "What are you doing?"

"I want to sleep with you." She released the blankets and crossed her arms to catch up her nightgown, smoothly skimming it up and over her head. She dropped it to the floor and stood nude in the moonlight.

"I'm not at my best, Sopi."

She had noticed, and she didn't know how to change that except to get close to him physically.

She lowered to sit on the bed, hip aligned to his, and began unraveling the hair she had braided before she went to bed. She did it slowly, in the sort of tease he usually enjoyed.

"I'm not in the mood to play." He spoke through his teeth, catching at her hands to stop her. "I'm too wound up."

"Then you need to relax." She shifted to brace her hands on his shoulders, leaning over him. "Want a massage?" That always turned into lovemaking, but that's where she was aiming. She desperately needed to reconnect with him and assure herself they were still okay.

Was this about her possibly being pregnant? About Nanette? Or was it something deeper? Something she had done?

She didn't land the kiss she went seeking. In one lithe movement, he had her on her back and loomed over her.

"You shouldn't be in here, Sopi. I don't have a good grip on myself."

"You sound like a werewolf. I'm not *afraid* of you," she said with a small laugh, petting his beard but catching enough to give a gentle tug. "You would never hurt me. I know that." She slid her hand to the back of his head, inviting him to kiss her.

"No, but—" His fingers dug into her shoulders, and his neck muscles bunched in refusal. He really did need a massage. He was gripped by something rigid and painful and clearly needed release.

She lifted her head to press her mouth to his.

With an animalistic groan, he pressed her flat beneath him and raked his lips across her own.

It wasn't the gentle seduction she was used to. It was raw need. A quest to drag her into some dark place he already occupied. As she moved with greeting beneath him, trying to settle into a more comfortable position, she could feel through the blankets that he was already aroused. He hardened his arms around her, keeping her in place as he scraped his teeth down her neck. His mouth opened in damp suction against her skin before his hand took possession of her breast, plumping it for plundering.

When he sucked, pleasure streaked like golden lightning from her nipple to her loins. They normally built up to this sort of intensity. His boldness threw her into an electrical storm, but she gloried in the wildness of it. This wasn't the civilized man she knew, but she recognized him in a far more primitive way. Her mate.

She grasped at his straining shoulders and back, encouraging him to keep ravaging her. She grew a little rough herself, catching a fist in his hair and dragging him up to kiss her. She stabbed her tongue into his mouth.

He didn't let her become the aggressor. He cupped her jaw and took her mouth with blatant eroticism until she was limp beneath him, pulsing all over with anticipation.

Then, with a noise like a wounded animal, he yanked the blankets from between them. One of his strong arms hooked under her leg, hiking it high so she was utterly helpless as he guided his turgid shape against her wet folds, moving easily in the gathered moisture, stoking the ache and strumming chords of pleasure through her.

"Stop me," he commanded, the crest of his sex demanding access.

She shook her head, too caught up in her own craven need. "Do it," she urged.

With a guttural sound, he thrust, driving easily into her slippery depths. As he came flush against her, he gave an extra pulse of his hips to ensure he was firmly seated inside her.

She had never experienced anything so earthy before. So primeval. He smothered her with a kiss, and when she bent her free knee, he gathered that one on his other arm and knelt to brace above her, pinning her with her legs open as he withdrew and thrust, watching her.

She was surrounded by him. Claimed by him and willing to be whatever he needed in this moment. She lost herself in the pools of his blue eyes as he undulated with power and purpose. She wanted to lift to kiss him, but her hair was pinned under her back, holding her head against the mattress. The restraint added an erotic twist to their coupling. She couldn't move except to caress damp skin stretched taut over hard muscles and sinew and bones.

And she couldn't escape the pleasure he relentlessly wound tight inside her. She grew sweaty and so acutely aroused, she couldn't stand it.

"Rhys," she sobbed.

He shifted, tucked his hands beneath her cheeks to tilt her hips. The new angle meant fresh nerve endings took his next thrust. Lust surged in her. Something pure and sharp and splendid.

He dropped his head to taste her lips, and she licked between his own with utter abandon, submerged in a hot pool of lava, thick and melting and incendiary.

She urged him to keep going, never let this stop, but she couldn't withstand this intensity. Just when she thought she would burst into flames, the world exploded around her.

He plunged deep and stayed there, pulsing hard within her as she twisted in the throes of her own unbearable pleasure, both of them groaning in carnal ecstasy.

Drained, Rhys realized he was crushing Sopi and forced his still twitching muscles to shift him off her.

He had known he was at his worst when he had finished making statements and recalibrating their security. He'd taken a cold shower to cool his temper, but he'd still been too edgy to sleep. He had wanted sex, but Sopi had been asleep, and he had known his mood wasn't gentle. He'd made himself come to this other bed and had been lying here aching with arousal, seriously reconsidering whether they should marry after all, given the way he was reacting.

When he'd heard her moving through the suite, the beast in him had nearly howled for her.

And she had arrived as though in answer, stripped naked and offered herself.

Such a fight he'd put up, too. He'd taken her with all the finesse of a rutting boar. What if she was pregnant?

With his gut aching, he asked with dread, "Did I hurt you?"

"Of course not," she chided, rolling toward him.

"I was rough." He didn't let her touch him, not trusting himself to stay off her. He sat up on the side of the bed.

"Rhys." She came up behind him, knees bracketing his hips. She wrapped her arms around his shoulders so her breasts pressed into his back. Her scent was all around him, almost impossible to resist in its inducement to turn and take her in his arms, especially when she said, "We've been vigorous before. It was exciting."

It had been a snap of something inside him.

He had been lying here berating himself for hesitating at the door to the balcony. He had wanted to give Sopi the chance to assert herself with her stepsister, but the sudden flash of Nanette's swiping hand had nearly turned him homicidal. It had been all he could do to stay this side of civilized and leave Nanette to the authorities.

His feelings for Sopi were becoming way more than he could handle. He couldn't let her go, though. What if she was already pregnant?

She nipped at his shoulder and rubbed her lips to soothe, fanning all his basest instincts. "I would have told you if you were hurting me. Honestly? I liked that you let go for once. You made me feel sexy and desired. Needed." Her voice held a throb. She was a bright woman. She knew he was holding back from her emotionally.

Much as he hated himself for hurting her, he stood to confront her, trying to cement the barriers in place for both of them.

"My losing control isn't a good thing, Sopi."

Even in the dim light he saw the flash of injury in her expression. He heard it in her voice.

"It wasn't *bad*," she argued, but he heard her quaver of uncertainty. "It means we're at a place in our relationship where we can get a little wild and still have full trust. You wanted me to trust you, and I do."

"You might be pregnant!" He paced away, hand going into his hair and giving a yank of frustration.

"For heaven's sake, you weren't *violent*. We just got to the good part a lot faster than usual."

"I was still crude as hell."

"It was uninhibited. Passionate. It was lovemaking at its finest. Literally *love*making. For me, at least," she added with a hesitant lilt in her tone.

"Don't," he commanded, naked and cold in the shaft of blue light from the window. "Don't fall in love with me, Sopi."

"Why not?" she cried in a flash of angry pain that left a mark on his heart.

"Because I can't fall in love with you." And he couldn't stay here and watch her eyes fill with tears like that. "You can sleep here. I'll go to the other bed."

He left before he couldn't.

CHAPTER NINE

SOPI MOVED THROUGH the next minutes and hours and days in a type of shell shock. Rhys didn't love her, didn't want to love her and refused to talk about it.

She made a doctor's appointment for later in the week, now equally as anxious as she was excited by the idea of being pregnant. She distracted herself by staying on top of things at the palace and making appearances with Rhys and having a fitting for her wedding dress—which should have been one of the happiest things she'd ever done, but it was all she could do to hold back sobs of wretchedness.

In public, she and Rhys continued to play the part of devoted lovers, but they were sleeping apart and barely speaking except in stilted bursts. A few times she caught a look of deep regret on his face, but she always looked away and shored up her own defenses, too hurt by his rejection to bear his remorse over breaking her heart.

She should probably regret all of this. A pregnancy would tie her to a man who didn't love her, but the truth was, she *deeply* wanted to be pregnant. Maybe it wasn't the best circumstances, but since leaving Canada, she'd been feeling very rootless. She needed family. She knew that now. A baby would give her the deep connection to another human being that Rhys was so reluctant to provide.

Which was why she was so devastated to get her period while she was dressing for her doctor's appointment.

Reeling in anguish, she tried to dismiss the maid who entered. "Can you leave me alone, please?" she said, trying to stifle the rush of tears.

"Yes, but the prince said when you're ready, he's in the lounge…" She curtsied and hurried away.

Rhys had arranged to take her to the appointment himself. She allowed herself one silent scream into a wet facecloth, then blew her nose and repaired her makeup.

Bracing herself, she walked into the lounge. Found a distant smile for Gerard.

"Will you please cancel my appointment and give us the room?" she asked him.

"Of course." He sent a brief glance of surprise between her and Rhys's arrested expression, then made himself scarce.

Rhys was headed to a meeting after the appointment. He wore a suit and tie. It fitted him as beautifully as every other piece of clothing he owned, but she thought he looked gaunt.

For the first time in days, his shields seemed to thin as he searched her expression. "What's wrong?"

Besides everything? She didn't know how they had gone from so great to so terrible in less than a week, but telling him she might be pregnant seemed to have been the instigator. Was she supposed to be happy that was no longer an issue?

"I'm not pregnant," she announced through a tight throat.

A flash of something that might have been agony

streaked across his features, and he rocked on his heels, nudged off his keel for the first time since the night of their engagement party.

He quickly schooled his expression into something more cautious. "A miscarriage?"

"I told you I might just be late," she said defensively. "It happens when I'm stressed." But even as she dismissed it as no real loss, her heart hit rock bottom. She waited in vain for a hug and some expression of sorrow that came anywhere near to the devastation wrapping itself around her.

She heard him draw breath to say something, but he seemed to change his mind at the last second. She heard it anyway.

Next time.

Her cramping middle knotted even more. She stood paralyzed by torment as the full scope of what she'd done began to hit her. She had agreed to marry him. To sleep with him until she had his babies. Plural. And she would do that while knowing he would never love her. Then she would have to make a life with him and their children.

While he wore a look of such regret, she felt sick.

Her eyes brimmed until she couldn't see him through her curtain of misery.

"We can try again, but not tonight," she choked. "There's no point. I'll tell you when I'm..." Fertile? Receptive? "Able."

"Sopi," he said to her back, but she closed her door. Shut him out as neatly as he'd been shutting her out.

He leaned his hands on the back of the sofa and breathed through the fiery agony that gripped him. This was why he didn't want to fall in love with her. The baby hadn't even been real yet. He hadn't allowed himself to believe she was pregnant, trying to wait until the doctor had confirmed it before he let himself get attached to the idea of being a father, yet he was as devastated as if she'd been months along and he'd already felt the damned thing move.

In his helplessness, he had searched desperately for words that might wipe that anguished expression from her face, knowing a platitude about trying again wouldn't cut it.

She'd heard it anyway and shut him down. *I'll tell you when I'm able.*

He ran his hand down his face, aching to make love to her again. Not to conceive, but to feel her. Hold her and smell her hair and say nonsense things across the pillow.

Henrik was wrong. He hadn't chosen well. He had chosen selfishly. Yes, she ticked all the boxes. A thousand women could have done that. He had allowed his baser instincts to guide him, though. He had given in to the primeval part of himself, manipulated her into their engagement only to cause her all this pain.

He went through the motions of his day, and when he returned to the palace, he ate alone, brooding, trying to see how they could forge a way forward.

He woke to the disturbing news that his brother and Elise were returning within the hour from Paris and wanted to see him the moment they arrived.

Throat dry and appetite nonexistent, he nearly fell over when Sopi hurried into the breakfast room, an anxious look on her face. She wore a jacket with a straight skirt since she was due at a school later today. Her hair was in a rope-twist ponytail, her makeup light.

"Why are they coming back in the middle of his treatment?" she asked, voice thick with apprehension.

"I don't know." He didn't like any of the possible answers.

Whatever she read in his expression had her crossing to him and pushing her cool hand into his stiff one.

"I won't stay if they don't want me there, but I'll come to their room with you."

He should have said it was unnecessary. He was a big boy, but it was all he could do not to crush her slender fingers. He kept her hand in his until word came that his brother had arrived. Then he drew Sopi with him down the gallery to the monarch's wing.

His throat was full of gravel, his chest nothing but broken glass. Thank God for Sopi, because she found a warm smile for her soon-to-be in-laws as they were shown into the private parlor where Henrik was seated. He looked gray. Elise stood beside him, clasping his hand. They were both beaming.

"Oh," Sopi breathed in relief. "We thought you were staying in Paris for the entire course of your treatment. Is everything going well?"

"As well as can be expected," Henrik said with a dismissive flick of his hand. "I toss more than I eat, but the doctors aren't too concerned. I have a three-day break now, and we missed sleeping in our own bed. Plus, we had news we couldn't wait to share." He looked up at his wife.

Elise was blinking tearful eyes at him.

"We're pregnant," Henrik said.

The announcement hit Rhys like a shock wave. Distantly, he heard Sopi's breath rush out as though she'd been punched. He recovered first, probably because he was used to staying on his feet through life's groin kicks. He wanted to hold on to Sopi's hand, somehow protect her from what she must be feeling, but she pulled her hand free of his.

He was genuinely happy for the pair, though. They'd waited so long for this.

"That's amazing." He moved to kiss Elise's cheeks. "No one deserves such good news more. Congratulations." He shook his brother's hand, unable to hide his astonishment.

"We're as shocked as you are," Elise said as she accepted the shaky embrace Sopi offered.

Only Rhys detected how pale Sopi was and how unsteady her smile was.

"We had completely given up trying after my diagnosis," Henrik said. "But we had a last hurrah before my surgery." He winked.

"Henrik!" Elise nudged his shoulder, blushing and laughing. "That's untoward."

"It's a miracle." He caught her hand again and kissed it. "We won't be making any formal announcements, but we wanted you both to know. I've put a lot on your shoulders lately and we have discovered how counterproductive that sort of pressure can be. Better to…how shall I say? Celebrate what you have rather than pin your heart to an uncertain future."

"But never give up hope, either," Elise hurried to add.

"No, you never do, do you?" Henrik said to her with an emotive look at his wife. "How did I ever get so lucky?"

"We'll leave you to rest," Rhys said mechanically as all the implications of this news began to penetrate his skull.

Sopi walked in a daze back to their wing, unaware whether Rhys had offered his arm or not. She was too encased in throes of envy. She was genuinely pleased for them, of course, especially now she'd had a taste of how disappointing it was to fail to conceive. Even so, she had to press the tremble of anguish from her lips.

"That opens up fresh possibilities, doesn't it?" Rhys asked as he closed the door to their lounge in what sounded like an ominous click.

She spun around, gasping for the breath he had knocked out of her even before she knew where he was going with that cryptic statement. She only knew it was bad.

"Like *what*?" she asked.

His hand was in a fist against his thigh. "We don't have to marry now."

It took her a few moments to find words—her ears were ringing so badly.

"Was it always about *having* to and never about *wanting* to?" she managed to ask.

"Yes." He was utterly still, his profile carved from granite. "If I had to marry, I thought it should be you." He swallowed loud enough for her to hear it. "But I'm realizing how self-serving that was. I didn't recognize how many pitfalls there were for you. This is your chance to walk away before any real damage is done."

Her heart being in tatters notwithstanding?

"You're going to put that on me?" she asked, pressing her hand between her breasts. "I can walk away if *I* want to?" What happened to committing in good faith?

"No," he stated flatly. "I'm going to tell you to go. You'll be better off," he had the nerve to proclaim.

"How does that compute?" she asked, voice husked by gall.

He closed his eyes as though suffering something

unbearable. "You don't want to marry me, Sopi. You never did."

"No, *you* don't want to marry *me*," she flung at him. "*I love you.* I would want to marry you if you wanted me, but you *don't*. Is it because I didn't—"

"Don't finish that sentence," he cut in sharply, speaking through his teeth. A muscle pulsed in his jaw. "But that's part of why I'm doing this. It's one thing for a couple to want children and discover they can't make it happen. This damned title puts far too much demand on you to perform. I can't put that on you. Not when I saw how much it hurt you when…" He lifted a helpless hand.

She didn't tell him she could live with that sort of pressure if he loved her. He didn't contradict her on not wanting to marry her, though—which was probably the cruelest thing anyone had ever done to her.

He broke the charged silence by drawing in a deep breath. "I'll make arrangements for you to travel back to Canada."

"Don't bother," she said flatly, no longer the doormat who allowed lesser people than him to walk all over her. "Thanks to you, I have resources of my own." A house in Sweden, for instance.

"I know it doesn't seem like I'm thinking of you, but I am," he said gravely.

"No, you're not!" She really ought to be grateful to him for all he'd done, but she was too angry. "You're doing this because you like *pain*. I don't understand why you feel a need to punish yourself, but fine. I'll lean into it and be the point of agony you need. You're welcome."

CHAPTER TEN

THE FINAL FLIP of Sopi's magnificent hair as she had walked out on him might as well have been a bullwhip that continued to flay him over the ensuing days.

It stung especially deep when he informed his brother and Elise that she was gone. They both stared at him with exasperation and bewilderment.

"But I liked her," Elise protested in an injured tone. "What if the next woman you choose isn't...her?"

Rhys hadn't thought that far ahead. Now the remark was salt in a wound, rubbing and rubbing. Henrik might have an heir on the way, but more children were next to impossible for them. Rhys would still have to marry and make a few spares.

The idea of lying with anyone but Sopi made him sick.

He buried himself in work, trying not to think of her, trying not to let Sopi's absence cause more work to fall on Elise. As for Henrik, Rhys had to stay ahead of him or he would stubbornly refuse to rest.

"You're starting to look sicker than I am. Walk with me," Henrik commanded one morning. He was home again for the weekend, and spring sunshine was breaking through the breakfast room window.

They were no sooner on the path along the lakeshore,

a refreshing breeze skating across the lake, when Henrik said, "What do you plan to do about Sopi?"

"Nothing. We called it off."

"Why? And don't give me your fabrications about things not working out. You didn't have to convince me she was right for you. I saw it with my own eyes, only for you to turn around and tell me you were mistaken. You're never wrong," Henrik said drily. "In fact, I don't think you were acting. I think you genuinely love her."

He loved her so much he couldn't breathe for missing her. She had only been in his bed a few short weeks and he reached for her in the dark every night. When he heard a footstep in the lounge, his heart leaped in anticipation. When Elise had a light spell of morning sickness, he wondered how Sopi would have coped.

He wondered if she would have children with someone else and wondered how he would make his own when he only wanted one woman in this world.

They had arrived on the end of the floating wharf, rebuilt three years ago, but in the same spot where they had climbed aboard a rowboat with the servants two decades ago.

"I do love her." A weight came off his chest as he admitted it out loud for the first time.

"Then go get her, you idiot."

He wanted to. He was barely surviving exactly the sort of loss he had feared when he pushed her away, but cowardice wasn't the only thing that had driven him that day.

"I haven't been coping well with your diagnosis, Henrik. I keep thinking it should be me going through this, not you."

"Don't," Henrik growled.

"*I* was the one who tried to attack the guard." His voice had roots in the horror of *that night*.

"You were a child," Henrik said quietly. "Terrified and reacting in the moment. You can't blame yourself for actions taken by monsters. It took Elise a long time to convince me that my responsibility was for the future of Verina, not its past. Yours, too. We can strive to maintain peace and ensure Verina prospers, Rhys. We can't undo what has already happened."

"I still think… I cost us *them*. Cost *you*. My actions pushed you into all of this long before you were old enough to handle it. You deserve to be happy, Henrik. You've fought so hard for everything. The crown, Elise, a baby. Now you're fighting for your life. I couldn't stomach the fact that everything you have had to struggle so hard for had just fallen into my lap. A woman I love who has a title?" He laughed drily. "For a few days, we thought she was pregnant, and I was so…" He looked into the sun to try to burn back the wetness in his eyes. "I couldn't accept how happy I was. How easily all of that happiness had come to me."

"So you pushed her away to punish yourself? What happens if you have to take the throne? Will you marry someone you hate just so you can feel truly miserable?"

"I don't want to think of it, Henrik." His heart was being crushed in a thorny vise. "I don't want the throne. I want my brother, alive and well."

"Well, today is your lucky day. I'm here. And I'm going to be a good brother and tell you that I want you to be happy. Not pinheaded." He frowned with impatience. "Don't you dare martyr yourself and expect me to praise you for it. Yes, love demands sacrifice. More often, it gives us the strength to crawl through hell and come out the other side. How do you think I got through those early years? How do you think I got out of this palace that night? *You.* I would have died here if I hadn't been so determined to get you out alive."

Rhys's heart lurched, and he swallowed, but the lump in his throat remained. "I felt like a responsibility back then. A weight." That was why he'd worked so hard to ensure they got ahead. "I've always wanted to make up for that somehow."

"And that's what Sopi is? Your payment?" He snorted at the twisted logic. "This will come as a shock, Rhys, but you are not a god. You cannot influence the outcome of what I face. All this hurt you're causing yourself and Sopi achieves nothing."

He was starting to realize that.

"But maybe you're right to let her go. Let her find someone who will love her the way she deserves to be loved."

Rhys snapped his brother a glower.

"Oh, did that sting?" Henrik taunted. "Good."

"You're lucky I'm in a hurry or I'd push you into the lake," Rhys muttered.

He took out his phone as he strode into the palace, dialing for Gerard—who had a standing order to stay in touch with Sopi in case she needed anything.

Or, as the case was right now, Rhys needed *her.*

The caretaker of the Basile-Munier "cottage" was actually a penny-pinching widower who welcomed Sopi with a warm hug. He lived with his daughter in the village and came up daily to garden and check on the place.

The house was, in reality, a mansion of two stories with turrets on either end. It faced the azure water of a fjord and had a cobbled driveway surrounded by natural forest. The cream-colored siding, green tin roof and gingerbread rickrack made it look like a white cake with spearmint frosting. Sopi adored it, especially after she filled the half-barrel tubs with geraniums and discovered the path down the slope to the village.

She had meant to stay only a few days to lick her wounds, but she was thinking of lingering until the midsummer festival. The baristas in the village had told her the sun would set behind the mountains, but only for an hour. Most people stayed up to watch it set and rise, enjoying dancing and food, drinking and song for a solid twenty-four hours.

Hopefully there would be some forgetting among all that.

Sighing wistfully, she climbed past the abandoned house with the sod roof, always inspired by the resilience it symbolized. People had lived there once. They had dug into the hillside and hibernated through the long winters, probably with a half dozen children underfoot.

People survived the most amazing things. She could survive this heartbreak.

Ah. There was a different wildflower. She bent to pluck it. The barista had told her one of the festival traditions was for young women to pick a bouquet of seven different flowers. If she put them under her pillow, her future husband would appear in a dream.

Sopi had a daisy and some clover and what looked like a buttercup. She didn't know the name of anything else she'd found. There was a cluster of delicate pink things with serrated petals and what she thought was thistle, so she had wrapped a tissue around the stem. Now these little crimson things were dangling off a drooping stem like bleeding hearts.

How apropos. Oh. And forget-me-nots, she noted wryly, stooping to pluck a few. That made seven and a rather sorry-looking bouquet, but desperate times.

Adjusting her shopping bag on her shoulder and her sun hat on her head, she finished the steep ascent to the small lawn and the patio where she ate every evening until the mosquitos chased her inside.

"Oh." She halted and the tissue-wrapped bouquet dropped to the grass. Yearning coiled around her, squeezing the air from her lungs.

Rhys sat in one chair and had his feet propped on another. Watchful.

"What are you doing here?" she asked, bracing herself.

"The house was locked. Your cell service is terrible. I've been trying to guess your Wi-Fi." He set aside his phone.

She almost told him it was MoreFishInTheSea, but admitted, "It's one of those nonsensical things with dashes and mixed caps."

She set her bag on the table to dig for her keys and hide her anxiety at him showing up out of the blue like this. "How are Henrik and Elise?"

"Fine."

He wasn't bringing bad news, then. That was good, she supposed, but her tension remained, wondering why he was here. She unlocked the back door, and he came into the kitchen with her.

"This is beautiful." He moved across the open space to the lounge, where the big picture windows looked onto the sloping lawn, the village below and the sparkling fjord winding around a bend in the distance.

"Thank you. I'm having trouble leaving." She loved it rather desperately, maybe for the connection to her mother that it was. She moved to put away her hand-ful of groceries, then poured two lemonades. "I can see why my mother wanted Cassiopeia's. It must have made her feel at home."

He nodded and glanced at the view again, hiding his thoughts.

She set her hat on a stool, then brought the glasses over.

"Thank you," he murmured absently, swinging his gaze back to her as he took the glass. Whatever preoc-cupying thoughts had been in his face creased into a scowl. "Damn it, Sopi, it's been *nine days*."

"Oh." She touched the hair cropped to chin length. "The salon in the village does that thing where they donate hair to kids with cancer." And she'd been *mad*.

She turned to look at the view. Sipped. Felt him blis-tering her profile with his hot stare. Goodness, that was satisfying, even though her heart was still raw.

"See, if you were still my lover, I might have con-sulted you," she dared to taunt. "But you aren't. Would you like to sit outside?" she asked politely. "There's usually a nice breeze."

"The irony is, Sopi," he said through gritted teeth, "I love you most when you're digging in your heels and standing up for yourself. I'm going to hold a grudge about this for a long time. Probably until it grows back, but I love you for doing whatever the hell you want."

She wanted to say something pithy, but her vision blurred. She frowned at the smeared vision of green and blue beyond the windows. Bit a lip that began to tremble.

"What am I supposed to say to that, Rhys?" Her voice was barely a wisp.

"You could say you'll marry me."

"You'll forgive me if I don't leap on that offer *again*." She moved to set aside her glass before she dropped it.

"Tell me to go to hell, then. I deserve it." His glass also went onto a side table. He cupped her face and made her look at him. "You were right. I thought I needed to suffer. I have."

"Why?"

"Because I didn't know how to be happy. Not like that. Not without feeling guilty for it. I was so disappointed that you weren't pregnant, Sopi. So crushed. I don't know how I'll function if we have trouble conceiving. There, I've admitted it. I'm not impervious. I hurt and fear and damn well need you beside me or I can't bear the uncertainties of life."

Each husky word took strips off her heart.

"And I didn't want a baby because I needed an heir. I wanted a baby with *you*. The one that would make us into a little family of our own. But I couldn't accept that desire in me without feeling I was stealing something from Henrik. From people who don't have *this*."

He didn't have to tell her what *this* was. She felt it as a sparkling force field around them. One that made her feel as though she floated four feet above the ground.

"And now?" she asked in a thready whisper, eyes dampening.

"Now I know that living without you is more punishment than people are meant to withstand."

"It felt like you were punishing me. That you didn't want me to be happy. That no one does."

"I know." His expression was agonized, but he gave a little tug to the tendril of hair dangling against her jaw. "But this tells me that you will go after your own happiness somehow, someway. And I hope that means you'll take another chance that I can give you the happiness you deserve."

Her mouth trembled as she wavered.

"This time you know exactly what you're getting," he coaxed. "You know you're my equal. That I want *you*. Because *I love you*."

Her tears brimmed. "I love you, too. A *lot*."

"Thank God," he breathed and caught her as she threw herself into his arms.

Their first kiss was hard, but tender. Apology and reunion, but it slid quickly toward passion until they were practically consuming one another.

He let out a growl and scooped up to cradle her against his chest. "Where's the bedroom?"

She pointed at the stairs.

"Hell, no. I'll save my strength for more important things." He set her on the sofa and joined her, covering her laughter with a kiss.

EPILOGUE

RHYS WAS IN his robe, waiting for his wife, but he quickly discovered she had left their suite. His bodyguard said something about ice cream, and Rhys went down to the darkened dining room and through to the kitchen that had been closed for the night.

"*Süsse*, I thought you were changing?" He didn't mention the pool or they would have company for sure.

"I went to say good-night and was reminded of a promise I'd made." She wore her evening gown and the anniversary diamonds Rhys had given her before they had come away on this business vacation, but she dug the ice cream scoop into the bucket herself, handing cones to each of their three children.

"Will you take a picture of me, Daddy? I want to show Reggie," their eldest, Sarah, asked. She was third in line for the throne after Rhys and her cousin, Reginald. Fortunately, none of them were worrying about taking Henrik's position anytime soon. He'd been pronounced fully in remission last month.

Even so, the early years of a family drawn close by health challenges had made Sarah and Reggie almost like twins. They were close in age, temperament and intelligence and missed each other terribly if they were away from each other more than a day or two. Rhys found it endearing and hoped they never grew out of it.

"It's bubberscutch," Robbie said, getting some on his nose with his first lick. He grinned, always their entertainer.

Rhys wiped the ice cream away with his fingertip, chuckling and dropping an affectionate kiss on his son's messy hair.

"Maybe you could share one with Marcus?" Sopi suggested as their baby held out a hand and said, "Pea?"

Rhys took fifteen-month-old Marcus from the nanny. He'd been a surprise, and there'd never been a more welcome one. Rhys loved all his children so much, he thought he would burst.

And then there was his wife. Sopi made cones for the nannies, then one for herself before she returned the bucket to the freezer and dropped the scoop into the dish pit.

"You've come a long way, Princess," he teased as she rejoined them.

"Right?" She chuckled. "I didn't want to call the chef back just for this." Her tongue swirled along the edge of her cone.

He had plans for that tongue. First, however, they had to get their children back into their room and their beds, if not actually asleep.

"We'll all go swimming *in the morning*," Rhys promised a short while later when they had everyone abed.

He quickly whisked his wife down to the treatment level.

"I was going to put on a bathing suit," she protested.

"Why? You won't be wearing anything for long." He

collected a spare robe and towels—he learned from his mistakes—and they slipped out the door into the falling snow.

Snickering like conspirators, they made their way through the dark to the private hot pool that was more than a source of healing, magical waters. It was a return to the place where they'd fallen in love. They quickly stripped naked and immersed themselves in its warm embrace.

* * * * *

CROWNED AT THE DESERT KING'S COMMAND

JACKIE ASHENDEN

To Dr A R Coates.
So long and thanks for all the fish.

CHAPTER ONE

CHARLOTTE DEVEREAUX DIDN'T often think about her death. But when she did, she'd hoped it would be when she was very old and tucked into bed. Or maybe in a comfortable armchair, quietly slipping away over a very good book.

She hadn't imagined it would be of heatstroke and dehydration after getting lost in the desert trying to find her father.

He'd told her he was going to the top of the dune to get a better view of the dig site—nothing major. But then someone had mentioned that they hadn't seen Professor Devereaux for a while, so Charlotte had decided to go and see if she could find him.

She'd gone to the top dune where he had last been seen, only to find it empty. As all the dunes around her had been.

She hadn't been worried initially. Her father did go off on his own so he could think, and he was a very experienced and eminent archaeologist who'd been on many digs in his time. The desert was nothing out of the ordinary for him and the idea of him getting lost was unthinkable.

As her father's assistant, she wasn't entirely inexperienced herself when it came to a dig and finding her way around it, and yet somehow, when she'd turned around to go back to the site, it had vanished. Along with her sense of direction.

Again, she hadn't been worried—her father had talked

a lot about how the desert could play tricks on a person's perception—so she'd strode off confidently the same way she'd come, retracing her steps, expecting to come across the site pretty much straight away.

Except she hadn't. And after about ten minutes of striding she'd realised that she'd made a mistake. A very grave one.

Of course she hadn't panicked. Panicking wouldn't help. It never did. The trick, when you got lost, was to stay calm and stay where you were.

So she had. But then the sun had got so hot—as if it were a hammer and she was the anvil. And she'd known that she was going to have to do something other than stand there otherwise she was going to die. So she'd started moving, going in the direction she'd thought the dig site would be, yet still it hadn't materialised, and now she was slowly coming to the conclusion that she was lost.

It was a bad thing to be lost in the desert.

A very bad thing.

Charlotte paused and adjusted the black and white scarf she wore wrapped around her head. She hated the thing. It was too heavy and too hot, and gritty due to the sand. It was also usually damp, because she was constantly bathed in sweat, but she wasn't sweating now and that was also a bad thing. Not sweating was a sign of heatstroke, wasn't it?

She squinted into the distance, trying to see where she was going. The sun was beating her to a pulp. A number of black dots danced in her vision. That was probably another sign of heatstroke too, because she was now starting to feel dizzy.

This was the end, wasn't it?

The rolling golden sands were endless, the violent blue of the sky a furnace she couldn't seem to climb out of. The harsh, gritty sand under her feet was starting to move around like the deck of a ship and there was a roaring in her ears.

The black dots were getting bigger and bigger, looming large, until she realised that, actually, they weren't dots in her vision. They were people, a whole group of them, dressed in black and riding…horses?

How odd. Shouldn't they be riding camels?

She took a shaky step towards them, hope flooding through her. Were they some of the assistants from the dig? Had they come to find her? Rescue her?

'Hey,' she yelled. Or at least tried to. But the sound escaped as more of a harsh whisper.

The people on horses stopped, and she must be in a bad way because it wasn't until that moment that she remembered that the assistants didn't ride horses and they certainly weren't swathed in black robes, the way these people seemed to be. Neither did they wear… Oh, goodness, they were swords, weren't they?

Her heartbeat began to speed up, and a chill was sweeping through her despite the intense heat.

Her father, who'd been managing the dig, had warned everyone about how close the site was to the borders of Ashkaraz, and how they had to be careful not to stray too far. Ashkaraz had closed its borders nearly two decades ago and the current regime did not take kindly to intruders.

There were stories of men draped in black, who didn't carry guns but swords, and of people who'd accidentally strayed over the border and never been seen again.

Rumours about Ashkaraz abounded—about how it was ruled by a tyrant who kept his people living in fear, banning all international travel both out of and into the country. All aid was refused. All diplomats and journalists turned away.

There had been one journalist reputed to have smuggled himself into Ashkaraz a couple of years back, escaping to publish a hysterical article full of terrible stories of a crushed people living under a dictator's rule. But that was it.

Basically, no one knew what went on inside the country because no one—bar that journalist, and plenty doubted that he'd even been there anyway—had ever been there and come back.

Charlotte hadn't listened much to the stories, or worried about how close to the borders they were. Mainly because she had been enjoying spending time with her father and was more interested in the archaeology they were doing than in rumours about a closed country.

Now, though, she wished she'd paid more attention. Because if the people approaching her weren't assistants from the dig, then they were people from somewhere else.

Somewhere frightening.

She squinted harder at the group on horseback. Oh, goodness, was that a…a person, slung over the back of one of their horses? It seemed to be. A person with distinctive pale hair…

Her heart constricted, recognition slamming into her. She'd recognise that hair anywhere, because her hair was exactly the same colour. It was a family trait. Which meant that the person currently slung over the back of that horse was her father.

Fear wound around her, as cold as the sun was hot. He must have got lost, like she had, and they'd picked him up. And now they'd found her too…

A tall figure in the middle of the group swung down off his horse—and it had to be a he, given that women weren't generally built like Roman gladiators—the sunlight catching the naked blade thrust through the belt that wound around his hips, and the chill that gripped Charlotte intensified.

He came towards her, moving with the fluid, athletic

grace of a hunter despite his height and build and the shifting sand under his feet. She couldn't see his face, he was covered from head to foot, but as he came closer she saw his eyes.

They weren't so much brown as a dense, smoky gold. Like a tiger.

And all at once she knew that her doubts had been correct. That this was definitely not a search party come to rescue her. A group of men draped in black with swords at their hips could only mean one thing: they were Ashkaraz border guards and they were not here to rescue her. They were here to take her prisoner because she had almost certainly strayed into the wrong country.

The man came closer, looming over her, his broad figure blocking out the hammer-blow of the sun.

But even the sun wasn't as hot or as brilliant as the gold of his eyes. And they were just as relentless, just as harsh. There was no mercy in those eyes. There was no help at all.

You fool. You should have told someone where you were going. But you didn't, did you?

No, she hadn't. She'd just gone to find her father, thinking she'd only be a couple of minutes. It was true that she hadn't been paying attention to where she'd been going, as she'd so often done as a child, lost in whatever daydream had grabbed her at the time, since that had been better than listening to the screaming arguments of her parents as they'd battled each other over her head.

Even now, as an adult, she found it difficult to concentrate sometimes, when she was stressed or things were chaotic, her mind spinning off into its own fantasies, escaping reality. Though those moments of inattention didn't usually have such terrible repercussions as now, when she was left with the choice of either turning and running away from the terrible man striding towards her across the hot sand, or falling to her knees and begging for her life.

What did these guards do to people who strayed over the borders? No one knew. No one had ever escaped. She and her father were going to be taken prisoner and no one would ever hear from them again.

Running was out of the question. Not only was there nowhere to run, she couldn't leave her father. Wouldn't leave him. He'd had no one else but her since her mother had moved to the States nearly fifteen years ago—and, though he wouldn't exactly win any father-of-the-year awards, his career and all the digs he'd taken her on had instilled in her a love of history and ancient peoples that the dreamer inside her found fascinating.

She had a lot to thank him for, so she'd follow him the way she'd always followed him.

Which meant that she was going to have to throw herself on this man's mercy—if, indeed, he had any.

Fear gripped her tight, and darkness crawled at the edge of her vision. Her lips were cracked, dry as the desert sand drifting around her feet, but she fought to remain upright. She was an idiot for wandering away from the site, it was true, but she wasn't going to compound her mistake by collapsing ignominiously at this man's feet.

She would be polite and reasonable, apologise calmly, and tell him that she hadn't meant to wander into his country by mistake. That her father was a professor and she only a lowly assistant, and they hadn't meant any harm. Also, could he please not kill them, or throw them into a dungeon, or any of the rest of the things her over-active imagination kept providing for her?

A hot wind kicked at the black hem of the man's robes, making them flow around his powerful thighs as he came to a stop in front of her. He stood there so still, as if he was a mountain that had stood for millennia, as enduring and unchanging as the desert itself.

Charlotte held tight to consciousness and something about his merciless golden gaze hardened her spine, making her square her shoulders and straighten up.

She tried to get some moisture into her mouth and failed. 'I'm sorry,' she forced out. 'Do you speak English? Are you able to help me?'

The man was silent a long moment, and then he said something, his voice deep enough that she felt it in her chest, a subtle, sub-sonic vibration. But she didn't understand him. Her Arabic was rough, and the liquid sounds bore no resemblance to the minimal words she knew.

She felt very weak all of a sudden, and quite sick.

The man's golden eyes seemed to fill her entire vision, his stare hard, brutal, crushing utterly her hope of rescue and of mercy.

She would get neither from him and that was obvious.

'I'm so terribly sorry,' Charlotte whispered as the darkness gathered around her. 'But I think the man you have on that horse is my father. We're quite lost. Do you think you could possibly help us?'

Then she fainted dead away at his feet.

Tariq ibn Ishak Al Naziri, Sheikh of Ashkaraz, stared impassively at the small body of the Englishwoman collapsed on the sand in front of him.

Her father, she'd said. Well, that cleared up the question of who the man was.

They'd found him unconscious on one of the dunes. After finding him, Tariq and his border guards had then spotted the woman, and had been tracking her for a good twenty minutes. Her zigzag path and the way she'd blundered across the border straight into Ashkaraz made it clear she had no idea where she was going, though what she'd murmured just now clarified things somewhat. She'd obviously been looking for the man currently slung over Jaziri's horse.

Tariq had been hoping she'd turn around and make her way back over the border again, ensuring that she wasn't his problem any more, but she hadn't. She'd spotted them instead and had just stood there, watching him approach her as if he was her own personal saviour.

Given that she was clearly suffering from heatstroke and advanced dehydration, she wasn't far wrong.

He didn't touch her just yet, though, because you could never be too suspicious of lost foreigners wandering over his borders—as the incident with the man who'd been armed and hoping to 'free the people of Ashkaraz from tyranny' had proved only the week before. One of his border guards had been severely injured and Tariq didn't want that to happen again.

It was probably why Faisal—his father's old advisor, who'd now become his—had been unhappy about Tariq approaching this woman himself rather than letting one of his guards do it. But protecting his subjects was his purpose, and he didn't want another injury simply because one guard had been a little careless when dealing with an outsider.

Tariq knew how to deal with them; his guards generally did not.

Especially a woman. They could be the most dangerous of all.

Except this woman didn't look very dangerous right now, crumpled as she was on the sand. She was dressed in a pair of stained, loose blue trousers and a long-sleeved white shirt, with a black and white scarf wrapped around her head, which was paltry protection from the desert sun.

She did actually seem to be unconscious, but since it

could be difficult to tell, and Tariq was naturally suspicious, he nudged her experimentally with the toe of his boot. Her head rolled to the side, her scarf coming loose and revealing a lock of hair pale as moonlight.

Yes, very definitely unconscious.

He frowned, studying her face. Her features were fine and regular and, though he preferred women with stronger looks, she could be said to be pretty. Currently the fine grain of her skin was flushed bright red from the heat and burned from the sun, making the pale arches of her eyebrows stand out.

English, no doubt, given the sunburn. Certainly when she'd spoken he recognised that cut-glass accent, which meant the man they'd picked up was likely English too.

He gave her another assessing look. Neither she nor the man were carrying anything, which meant their camp, or wherever they'd come from, couldn't be far away. Were they part of a tour party, perhaps? Although tour parties generally didn't come this far into the desert—they stuck to the edges, where it was cooler, safer. From where they could easily get back to the air-conditioned luxury of their hotels and away from the sun and the heat and the rumours of a closed country where men patrolled the borders wearing swords.

'Two foreigners in the same stretch of desert,' Faisal said dryly from behind him. 'This cannot be a coincidence.'

'No, it is not. She saw the man on Jaziri's horse. She said something about her father.'

'Ah…' Faisal murmured. 'Then we can safely assume she is not a threat?'

'We assume nothing.' Tariq let his gaze rove over her, scanning for any concealed weapons just to be sure. 'All outsiders are a threat, unconscious or not.'

And it was true—they were. That was why his father

had closed the borders and why Tariq had kept them closed. Outsiders were greedy, wanting what they did not have and uncaring of who they destroyed to get it.

He'd seen the effects of such destruction and he would not let it happen to his country. Not again.

There were always a few, though, who thought it fun to try and get inside Ashkaraz's famous closed borders, to get a glimpse of the kingdom, to take pictures and post them on the internet as proof of having got inside.

There were some who couldn't resist the lure.

They were always caught before they could do any damage. They were rounded up and had the fear of God put into them before being sent on their way with tales of brutality and swords—even though his soldiers never actually touched any of the people they caught. Fear was enough of a deterrent.

Though not enough of a deterrent for this woman, apparently.

'If she is a threat, she is not much of one,' Faisal observed, looking down at her. 'Perhaps she and her father are tourists? Or journalists?'

'It does not matter who they are,' Tariq said. 'We will deal with them as we have dealt with all the rest.'

Which involved a stint in the dungeons, a few threats, and then an ignominious return to the border, where they would be summarily ejected into one of their neighbouring countries and told never to return again.

'This one in particular might be difficult,' Faisal pointed out. His tone was absolutely neutral, which was a good sign that he disapproved of Tariq's decision in some way. 'She is not only a foreigner but a woman. We cannot afford to treat her the way we treat the rest.'

Irritation gathered in Tariq's gut. Unfortunately, Faisal was right. So far he'd managed to avoid any diplomatic incidents following his treatment of outsiders, but there was always a first time for everything—and, given the gender and nationality of the person concerned, Ashkaraz might indeed run into some issues.

England wouldn't be happy if one of its own was roughly treated by the Ashkaraz government—especially not a woman. Especially not a young, helpless woman. The man they might have got away with, but not her. She would draw attention, and attention was the last thing Tariq wanted.

Then there was the issue of his own government, and how certain members of it would no doubt use her as ammunition in their argument on how closed borders didn't help them remain unseen on the global stage, and how the world was moving on and if they didn't have contact with it, it would move on without them.

Tariq didn't care about the rest of the world. He cared only about his country and his subjects. And, since those two things were currently in good health, he saw no need to change his stance on reopening the borders.

His vow as Sheikh was to protect his country and its people and that was what he was going to do.

Especially when you've failed once before.

The whispered thought was insidious, a snake dripping poison, but he ignored it the way he always did.

He would not fail. Not again.

Ignoring Faisal's observation, Tariq crouched down beside the little intruder. The loose clothing she wore made it difficult to ascertain visually whether she carried weapons or not, and since he had to be certain he gave her a very brief, very impersonal pat-down.

She was small, and quite delicate, but there were definite curves beneath those clothes. There were also no weapons to speak of.

'Sire,' Faisal said again, annoyingly present. 'Are you sure that is wise?'

Tariq didn't ask what he meant. He knew. Faisal was the only one who knew about Catherine and about Tariq's response to her.

Given what that led to, he has every right to question you.

The irritation sitting in Tariq's gut tightened into anger. No, he'd excised Catherine from his soul like a surgeon cutting out a cancer, and he'd cut out every emotion associated with her too. Everything soft. Everything merciful.

There was no need for Faisal to question him, because what had happened with Catherine would never happen again. Tariq had made sure of it.

Though perhaps his advisor needed a reminder…

'Do you question me, Faisal?' Tariq asked with deceptive mildness, not looking up from the woman on the sand.

There was a silence. Then, 'No, sire.'

Faisal's voice held a slight hint of apology. Too slight.

Tariq scowled down at the woman. Obviously, given Faisal's clear doubts, he was going to have to deal with this himself.

'I can get a couple of the men to have a look around to see where she and the other foreigner have come from,' Faisal went on, perhaps hoping to assuage him. 'We could perhaps return them both with no one any the wiser?'

It would be the easiest thing to do.

But Tariq couldn't afford 'easy'. He'd instituted the law to keep the borders closed and he had to be seen to uphold it.

A king couldn't afford to be weak.

Hadn't he learned his lesson there?

You should have listened to your father.

Yes, he should. But he hadn't.

'No,' he said flatly. 'We will not be returning either of them.'

He leaned forward, gathering the woman up and rising to his feet. She was so light in his arms. It was like carrying a moonbeam. Her head rolled onto his shoulder, her cheek pressed to the rough black cotton of his robes.

Small. Like Catherine.

Something he'd thought long-dead and buried stirred inside him and he found himself looking down at her once again. Ah, but she wasn't anything like Catherine, And, anyway, that had been years ago.

He felt nothing for her any more.

He felt nothing for anyone any more.

Only his kingdom. Only his people.

Tariq lifted his gaze to Faisal's, met the other man's appraising stare head-on. 'By all means send a couple of men out to see what they can discover about where these two have come from,' he ordered coldly. 'And get in touch with the camp. We will need the chopper to be readied to take them back to Kharan.'

He didn't wait for a response, turning and making his way back to the horses and the group of soldiers waiting for him.

'Perhaps one of the men can deal with her?' Faisal suggested neutrally, trailing along behind him. 'I can—'

'I will deal with her,' Tariq interrupted with cold authority, not turning around. 'There can be no question about her treatment should the British government become involved. Which means the responsibility for her lies with me.'

There were others who remembered the bad times, when Ashkaraz had been fought over and nearly torn apart following Catherine's betrayal, and they wouldn't be so lenient with a foreign woman again.

Not that he would be lenient either. She would soon get

a taste of Ashkaraz's hospitality when she was taken to the capital of Kharan. They had a facility there especially for dealing with people who'd strayed into Ashkaraz, and he was sure she wouldn't like it.

That was the whole point, after all. To frighten people so they never came back.

His men watched silently as he carried her over to his horse and put her on it, steadying her as she slumped against the animal's neck. Then he mounted behind her and pulled her back against him, tucking her into the crook of one arm while he grabbed the reins with the other.

'Continue with the patrol,' he instructed Faisal. 'I want to know where this woman comes from—and fast.'

The other man nodded, his gaze flickering again to the woman in Tariq's arms. Tariq had the strangest urge to tuck her closer against him, to hide her from the old advisor's openly speculative look.

Ridiculous. The doubts Faisal had would soon be put to rest. Tariq was a different man from the boy he'd once been. He was harder. Colder. He was a worthy heir to his father, though he knew Faisal had had his objections to Tariq inheriting the throne. Not that Faisal or the rest of the government had had a choice in the matter since his father had only had one son.

Still. He had thought Faisal's scepticism long put to rest. *It is the woman. She is the problem.*

Yes, she was. Luckily, though, she would not be a problem much longer.

'You have objections?' Tariq stared hard at the older man.

Faisal only shook his head. 'None, sire.'

He was lying. Faisal always had objections. It was a good thing the older man knew that now was not the time to voice them.

'As my father's oldest friend, you have a certain amount of leeway,' Tariq warned him. It would do him good to be reminded. 'But see that you do not overreach yourself.'

Faisal's expression was impassive as he inclined his head. 'Sire.'

Dismissing him, Tariq nodded to Jaziri and a couple of the other guards in unspoken command. Then, tugging on the reins, he turned his horse around and set off back to base camp.

CHAPTER TWO

CHARLOTTE WAS HAVING a lovely dream about swimming in cool water. It flowed silkily over her skin, making her want to stretch like a cat in the sun. It moved over her body, sliding over her face, pressing softly against her lips…

There was a harsh sound from somewhere and abruptly she opened her eyes, the dream fragmenting and then crashing down around her ears.

She was not swimming in cool water.

She was lying on a narrow, hard bed in a tiny room, empty except for a bucket in the corner. A single naked bulb hung from the ceiling. The floor was cracked concrete, the walls bare stone.

It looked like a…a jail cell.

Her heartbeat began to accelerate, fear coiling inside her. What had happened? Why was she here?

Her father had wandered away from the dig site and she'd gone to find him, only to get lost in the desert. Then those men on horseback had turned up, with her father slung over the back of a horse, and there had been that other man in black robes. That powerful man with the golden eyes, watching her. Tall and broad as a mountain. He'd had a sword at his hip and his gaze had been merciless, brutal…

A shudder moved down her spine.

He must have rescued her after she'd fainted—though

this wasn't exactly what she'd call a rescue. He might have saved her life, but he'd delivered her to a cell.

Slowly she let out a breath, trying to calm her racing heartbeat, and pushed herself up.

This had to be an Ashkaraz jail cell. And that man had to have been one of the feared border guards. And—oh, heavens—did they have her father here too? Had they both joined the ranks of people who'd crossed into Ashkaraz, a closed country?

And you know what happens to those people. They're never heard from again.

Charlotte moistened her suddenly dry mouth, trying to get a grip on her flailing emotions. No, she mustn't panic. Plenty of people had been heard from again—otherwise how would anyone know that the country was a tyranny run by a terrible dictator? That its people lived in poverty and ignorance and were terrorised?

Anyway, that line of thought wasn't helping. What she should be concentrating on was what she should do now.

Pushing aside thoughts of dictators and terror, she swung her legs over the side of the horrible bed and stood up. A wave of dizziness hit her, along with some nausea, but the feeling passed after a couple of moments of stillness. Her face stung, but since there was no mirror she couldn't see what the problem was. Sunburn, probably.

Slowly she moved over to the door and tried to open it, but it remained shut. Locked, obviously. Frowning, she took another look around the room. Up high near the ceiling was a small window, bright sunlight shining through it.

Maybe she could have a look and see what was out there? Get a feel for where she was? Certainly that was better than sitting around feeling afraid.

Charlotte stood there for a moment, biting her lip and thinking, then she shoved the bed underneath the window and climbed on top of it. Her fingers just scraped the ledge, not giving her nearly enough leverage to pull herself up. Annoyed, she took another look around before her gaze settled on the bucket in the corner.

Ah, that might work.

Jumping down off the bed, she went over to the bucket, picked it up and took it back to the bed. She upended it, set it down on the mattress, then climbed back onto the bed and onto the bucket. Given more height, she was able to pull herself up enough to look out of the window.

The glass was dusty and cracked, but she could see through it. However, the view was nothing but the stone wall of another building. She frowned again, trying to peer around to see if she could see anything, but couldn't.

Perhaps she could break the glass?

Yes, she could do that, and then...

A sudden thought gripped her. Carefully, she examined the window again. She was a small woman, which had proved useful on many occasions, such as in hiding from her parents when the shouting had got too bad, and maybe it could be useful now?

Or maybe you should just sit and wait to see what happens?

She could—but this wasn't just about her, was it? She had her father to consider. He might be in another jail cell somewhere or he could even be dead. Dead and she would never know.

You really will be alone then.

Cold crept through her, despite the sun outside.

No, she couldn't sit there, helpless and not knowing. She had to do something.

Decisive now, she stripped off the white shirt she was wearing—her scarf seemed to have disappeared somewhere along the line—and wrapped it around her hand. Then she hammered with her fist on the glass. After a couple of strikes against the crack already running through it, the pane shattered beautifully.

Pleased with herself, she made sure that there were no sharp shards there, waiting to cut her, and then before she could think better of it she wriggled through the window.

A large man wouldn't have made it. Even a medium-sized man would have had difficulty.

But a small woman? Easy.

She fell rather ignominiously to the ground, winding herself, and had to lie there for a couple of moments to get her breath back. The sun was incredibly hot, the air like a furnace. Definitely she was somewhere in Ashkaraz, that was for sure.

But then she was conscious of a sound. A familiar sound. Traffic. Cars and trucks on a road…horns sounding. People talking…the first few bars of a very popular pop song currently hitting the charts rising.

Puzzled, she pushed herself to her feet and found herself standing in a narrow alley between two tall stone buildings. At the mouth of the alley there appeared to be a street, with people walking past.

Despite her fear and uncertainty, an unexpected thrill of excitement caught at her.

She was in a closed country. A country no foreigner had seen for over twenty years. No one except her.

As her father's assistant she'd become interested in archaeology and history, but it had always been society and people that had fascinated her the most. Ashkaraz was reportedly a throwback to medieval times, a society where time had stood still.

And you might be the first person to see the truth of it.

Nothing was going to stop her from seeing that truth, and she eagerly started towards the mouth of the alleyway.

Nothing could have prepared her for the shock of seeing an Ashkaraz street.

Part of her had been expecting horses and carts, a medieval fantasy of a middle eastern city, with ancient souks and camels and snake charmers. But that was not what she saw.

Bright, shiny and very new cars moved in the street, beneath tall, architecturally designed buildings made of glass and steel. People bustled along on the footpaths, some robed, some in the kind of clothes she would have seen on the streets in London. In amongst the glass and steel were historic buildings, beautifully preserved, and shops and cafés lined the streets. People were sitting at tables outside, talking, laughing, working, looking at their smartphones.

There was an energy to the place, which was clearly a bustling, successful, prosperous city.

Definitely not the poverty-stricken nation with a beaten-down populace crushed under the thumb of a dictator that the rest of the world thought it to be.

What on earth was going on?

Amazed, Charlotte stepped out onto the footpath, joining the stream of people walking along it, oblivious to the glances she was receiving.

There was a beautiful park up ahead, with a fountain and lush gardens, lots of benches to sit on and a playground for children. Already there seemed to be a number of kids there, screaming and laughing while their indulgent parents looked on.

This was…incredible. Amazing. How was this even possible? Was this the truth that Ashkaraz had been hiding all along?

She was so busy staring that she didn't notice the uniformed man coming up behind her until his fingers wrapped around her arm. And then a long black car pulled up to the kerb and Charlotte found herself bundled into the back of it.

She opened her mouth to protest, but there wasn't even time for her to scream. Something black and suffocating was put over her head and the car started moving.

The fingers around her arm were firm—not hurting, but definitely ensuring that she couldn't get away. Fear, coming a little late to the party, suddenly rose up inside her, choking.

Did you really think you could escape from that jail cell and start wandering around like nothing was wrong?

She hadn't been thinking—that was the problem. She'd got out of that cell and then been caught up in the wonder of the city outside it.

Charlotte slumped back in the seat, trying not to panic. Now, not only was her chance to escape gone but so was her father's.

And it was all her fault.

The car drove for what seemed like ages and then slowed to a stop. She was pulled out of it and then taken up some steps. Sun and heat surrounded her for a second, and then she must have been taken inside because the sun had disappeared, to be replaced by blessedly cool air. Her footsteps echoed on a tiled floor, and there was the scent of water and flowers in the air.

She couldn't see a thing through the black fabric around her head, and her sense of direction was soon gone as she was pulled down more corridors, around corners, and up yet more stairs.

Were they taking her back to that cell? Or were there worse things in store for her? Would they perhaps murder her? Make her disappear? Hold her prisoner for ever?

She was just starting to be very, very afraid when she

was pulled to a stop and the fabric covering her head was abruptly tugged off.

Charlotte blinked in the bright light.

She appeared to be standing in a large room lined with shelves, containing lots of books and folders and filing boxes. The exquisite tiled floor was covered in thick, brightly coloured silk rugs, the walls also tiled, in silvery, slightly iridescent tiles. There was a window in front of her that gave a view onto a beautiful garden, where a fountain played amongst palms and other shrubs, as well as many different kinds of flowers.

A huge, heavy desk made of time-blackened wood stood before the window. The polished surface was clean of everything except a sleek-looking computer monitor and keyboard, and a small, elegant silver vase with a spray of fresh jasmine in it.

This was certainly *not* a jail cell. In fact, it looked like someone's office…

She blinked again and turned around to see two men stationed on either side of the double doors. They were dressed in black robes with swords on their hips, their faces absolutely impassive.

She would have thought the robes and swords only ceremonial, except they didn't have the clean and pressed look she would have expected. The fabric of their robes was dusty and stained around the hems, as were the boots the men wore. And although the edges of the swords were bright, was that…blood she could see on the steel? Surely it couldn't be.

Charlotte stared, her heartbeat getting faster and faster, and then suddenly from behind her came the sound of a door opening and closing.

She turned back sharply to see that a man had come

into the room from a door off to her left, and he was now standing beside the desk, staring at her.

He was very, very tall and very, very broad, built more like an ancient warrior than a businessman. The muscles of his chest and arms were straining the white cotton of his business shirt, and the dark wool of his suit trousers pulled tight around his powerful thighs.

His face was a harsh composition of planes and angles that nevertheless managed to be utterly compelling, with high cheekbones and an aquiline nose, straight black brows and a beautifully carved mouth.

'Handsome' was far too bland a word for him...especially as he radiated the kind of arrogant charisma reserved only for the very powerful and very important.

But that wasn't what held Charlotte absolutely rooted to the spot.

It was his eyes. Burning gold, with the same relentless, brutal heat as the desert sun.

It was the man who'd approached her in the desert. She was sure of it. She'd never forget those eyes.

He said nothing for a long moment and neither did Charlotte, since she couldn't seem to find her voice. Then his gaze shifted to the men behind her and he gave a slight tilt of his head. A couple of seconds later she heard the door shut behind her, the men clearly having obeyed some unspoken order and left.

The room abruptly felt tiny and cramped, the space too small to accommodate both her and the man in front of her. Or maybe he seemed to get larger and more intimidating, taking up all the air and leaving none for her.

She lifted her chin, trying to get her heartbeat under control at the same time as trying to hold his relentless gaze, but she couldn't seem to manage both—especially not when he moved suddenly, coming over to the desk and standing in front of it, folding his arms across his massive chest.

Bringing him quite a bit closer.

She resisted the urge to take a step back, hating how small and insignificant his sheer size made her feel. It was exactly the same feeling that had filled her when her parents had argued and she'd hidden under the dining room table. They'd never noticed that she'd left her seat—which was ironic, since more often than not they had been shouting about her.

Clasping her hands in front of her to prevent them from shaking, Charlotte took a small, silent breath. 'Um…do you speak English?' Her voice sounded thin and reedy in the silence of the room.

The man said nothing, continuing to stare at her.

It was extremely unnerving.

Her mouth had dried and she wished her Arabic was better. Because maybe he didn't understand English. She wanted to ask him where her father was and also to thank him for saving her.

He put you in a cell, remember?

Sure, but maybe that hadn't been him. He might look like a medieval warrior, but the suit he was wearing was thoroughly modern. Perhaps he was an accountant? Or the chief of the jail she'd been put in? Or a government functionary?

Yet none of those things seemed to fit. He was too magnetic, too charismatic to be anyone's mere functionary. No, this man had an aura about him that spoke of command, as if he expected everyone to fall to their knees around him.

Sadly for him, she wouldn't be falling anywhere in front of him.

Except you already have. In the desert.

That, alas, was true.

'I'm s-sorry,' she stuttered, casting around for something

to say. 'I should have thanked you for saving my life. But can you tell me where my father is? We got lost, you see. And I... I...' She faltered, all her words crushed by the weight of his stare.

This was silly. Her father could be dead or in a jail cell and she was letting this man get to her. She couldn't get pathetic now.

Perhaps introducing herself would help. After all, she'd had no identification on her when she'd collapsed, so maybe they had no idea who she or her father were. Maybe that was why she had been put in the cell? Maybe they thought she was some kind of insurgent, hoping to...?

But, no. Best not get carried away. Keep thinking in the here and now.

'So,' Charlotte said, pulling herself together. 'My name is—'

'Charlotte Devereaux,' the man interrupted in a deep, slightly rough voice. 'You are an assistant attached to an archaeological dig that your father, Professor Martin Devereaux is managing in conjunction with the University of Siddq.'

His English was perfect, his accent almost imperceptible.

'You both come from Cornwall, but you live in London and at present are employed by your father's university as his assistant. You are twenty-three years old, have no dependents, and live in a flat with a couple of friends in Clapham.'

Charlotte could feel her mouth hanging open in shock. How did he know all this stuff? How had he found out?

'I...' she began.

But he hadn't finished, because he was going on, ignoring her entirely, 'Can you tell me, please, what you were doing out there in the desert? Neither you nor your father were anywhere near your dig site. In fact, that is the whole reason you are here. You crossed the border into Ashkaraz—you do understand that, do you not?'

She flushed at the note of condescension in his voice, but took heart from the fact that he was talking of her father in the present tense.

'Are you saying that my father is alive?' she asked, needing to be sure.

'Yes,' the man said flatly. 'He is alive.'

Relief filled her, making her breath catch. 'Oh, I'm so glad. He wandered away from the site, the way he sometimes does, and I went to try and find him. I walked up a dune and somehow—'

'I am not interested in how you got lost, Miss Devereaux,' the man interrupted, his voice like iron, his golden stare pitiless. 'What I am interested in is how you somehow got out of a secure facility.'

Charlotte swallowed. Briefly she debated lying, but since she was in a lot of trouble already there was no point in making it any worse.

'I…smashed the glass and crawled out of the window.' She lifted her chin a little to show him that she wouldn't be cowed. 'It really wasn't that difficult.'

'You crawled out of the window?' he repeated, his voice flat, the lines of his brutally handsome face set and hard. 'And what made you think that was a good idea?'

'I've heard the rumours,' she said defensively. 'About how people who stray over your borders disappear for ever, never to be seen again. How they're beaten and terrorised. And I didn't know what had happened to my father.' She steeled herself. 'I saw an opportunity to escape, to see if I could find him, and so I took it.'

The man said nothing, but that stare of his felt like a weight pressing her down and crushing her into dust.

You're really for it now.

Charlotte gripped her hands together, lifted her chin another inch and stared back. 'We're British citizens, you know. You can't just make us disappear like all the rest. My dad is a very well-respected academic. Once people realise we're missing they'll send others to find us. So you'd better tell whoever is in charge here that—'

'No need. All the interested parties already know.'

'Which interested parties?'

His face was impassive. 'Me.'

'You?' Charlotte tried to look sceptical and failed. 'And who exactly are you?'

'I am the one in charge,' he said, without any emphasis at all.

'Oh? Are you the head of the police or something?'

It would explain his aura of command, after all.

'No. I am not the head of the police.'

His eyes gleamed with something that made her breath catch.

'I am the head of the country. I am the Sheikh of Ashkaraz.'

Charlotte Devereaux, all five foot nothing of her, blinked her large silver-blue eyes. Shock was written across her pretty, pink features.

She should be shocked.

She should be quaking in those little boots of hers.

He'd only just been notified of her escape and her jaunt down Kharan's main street, and to say that he was angry was massively to understate the case.

He was furious. Absolutely, volcanically furious.

The fury boiled away inside him like lava, and only long years of iron control kept it locked down and not spilling everywhere, destroying everything in its path.

Because he had no one to blame for this incident but himself. He was the one who'd elected to bring her back to Kharan and not to follow Faisal's advice to return her and her father to the dig site from which they'd come.

No, he'd decided to handle her himself, to make sure she was taken back to Kharan and had the medical treatment she required. Her father had needed more, and was still unconscious in a secure hospital ward. She had been transferred to the facility where they kept all illegal visitors to Ashkaraz.

Normally those visitors tended to be men. They were not usually little women who could wriggle through small windows. He hadn't even known the cell she'd been put in *had* a window.

Not that it mattered now. What mattered was that this woman had escaped and had somehow stumbled unchecked into Kharan, and she had seen through the lies he and his people told the world.

Far from being a nation stuck in time, mired in poverty and war, it was prosperous and healthy, its population well-cared-for and happy.

And it was a wealthy nation. A *very* wealthy nation.

A nation that had to hide its wealth from the rest of the world or else be torn apart by those desperate to get their hands on it—as had occurred nearly twenty years earlier.

He couldn't allow that to happen again.

He wouldn't.

Catherine had been at the centre of it twenty years ago and now here was Charlotte Devereaux, another foreign woman causing another diplomatic incident.

This time, though, he would not be a party to it, the way he had been with Catherine. He'd learned his lesson and he'd learned it well, and he would not be giving this woman the benefit of the doubt.

'Oh,' she said faintly. 'Oh. I... I see.'

Her voice had a pleasant husk to it. Somewhere along the line she'd lost her scarf, so her silvery blonde hair hung in a loose ponytail down her back, wisps of it stuck to her forehead. The angry red of the sunburn she'd got out in the desert had faded slightly, leaving her pale skin pink. It made the colour of her eyes stand out, glittering like stars. She wore the same pair of loose blue trousers she'd had on in the desert, though the white shirt had gone, leaving in its place a tight-fitting white tank top.

It did not escape his notice that, though she was small, she had a surprisingly lush figure.

'I am sure that you do not see,' he said, forcing those particular observations to one side. 'Because your little excursion has put me in a very difficult position.'

She gave him a cool look that pricked against something inside him like a thorn, needling him. 'Indeed? How so?'

It was not the response he'd hoped for. In fact, nothing of her behaviour was the response he'd hoped for. She should be afraid. As any woman—or any person, for that matter—who'd woken up to find herself in a jail cell would be. Especially given the rumours she must have heard about Ashkaraz.

She should be terrified for her life, not standing there giving him cool looks as if he was nothing more than a mere functionary and not the king of his own country.

'Miss Devereaux,' he said, his anger still raw. 'You are not at all showing proper deference.'

She blinked those glittering silvery eyes again. 'Oh, I'm not? I'm sorry. I don't know the customs—'

'You would curtsey before your queen, would you not?' He cut her off coldly. 'I am king here. My word is law.'

'Oh,' she repeated, lowering her gaze. 'I didn't mean

to offend.' Then she made an awkward curtsey, her hands fluttering at her sides.

He narrowed his gaze at her. Was she making fun of him? He didn't think so, but you could never tell with foreigners.

It didn't improve his temper.

Then again, he shouldn't be taking his temper out on her, full stop. A king should be above such things, as his father had always told him. A ruler needed to be hard, cold. Detached from his emotions.

Except he could feel his anger straining at the leash he'd put on it. He wanted her on her knees, begging his forgiveness.

Are you sure that's the only reason you want her on her knees?

Something shifted inside him—a strange pull.

She was…pretty. And, yes, there was a physical attraction there. Perhaps that accounted for the reason this particular woman tried his temper so badly. Not that an attraction would make the slightest difference. As he'd told Faisal out in the desert, he'd treat her exactly the same way he treated every other intruder.

'It is too late for that,' he said implacably. 'You have offended already. You escaped your cell and found your way into the city.'

She was standing with her small hands clasped, but this time the expression on her face wasn't so much cool as uncertain.

'Yes, well…as I was going to explain, I didn't mean to. I just wasn't sure what you were going to do with me or my father.'

'We would have done what we do with all illegal visitors to Ashkaraz. You would have both been sent back to your home country.' He paused. 'But we cannot do that now.'

Her pale brows drew together. 'Why not?'

'Because you have walked down the main street of Kharan and seen the truth.'

'What? You mean all the nice buildings? The new cars and smartphones and things?' Her mouth, full and prettily pink, curved. 'It's such a beautiful city. How is me seeing that a problem?'

'Because you will tell other people, Miss Devereaux.'

What he had to tell her now wouldn't be welcome, yet she had to understand the gravity of the situation.

'And they will tell others, and so it will go on until the whole world learns the truth. And I cannot let that happen.'

She was still frowning. 'I don't understand…'

'Of course you do not. But you will have plenty of time to work it out.'

Another ripple of uncertainty crossed her face. 'That sounds ominous. What do you mean by that?'

'I mean that we cannot send you back to England. We cannot send either of you back to England. You will have to remain in Ashkaraz.' He paused again, for emphasis. 'Indefinitely.'

CHAPTER THREE

CHARLOTTE'S MOUTH HAD gone bone-dry. 'E-Excuse me?' she stuttered. 'I'm sorry, but I thought you said "indefinitely".'

The man—no, the Sheikh—looked at her with the same unyielding merciless stare he'd been giving her ever since he'd walked in here. As if he was furiously angry and trying to hide it. He was doing a very good job of it, but she recognised his expression. It was the same expression her father had used to have when he was furious with her mother and trying very hard not to show it.

Ever since her parents' relationship had broken down she'd become particularly sensitive to suppressed emotion, because even though the shouting had been bad, her parents' silent fury had been worse. It had filled the whole house, making her feel as if she was being crushed slowly in a vice. She'd had to run away when it got like that—except right now there was nowhere to run.

Then again, she wasn't the frightened girl she'd been back then. She'd learned to shield herself from people's inconvenient emotions by being cool and polite. Though that boat had long since sailed in this case.

The Sheikh's relentless golden stare was inescapable. 'I did,' he said succinctly.

'But you can't mean that.' She swallowed. 'You can't just keep us here for...for ever.'

'My word is law, Miss Devereaux,' he said in that implacable way. 'I can do whatever I please.'

A laugh escaped her, even though she hadn't meant it to, and it sounded shrill in the quiet of the office with the fountain playing outside. 'I'm not going to tell anyone what I saw. I promise I won't. Not that I saw anything anyway—a few buildings, nothing much—'

'Your promises are not sufficient.'

There was no answering amusement in his eyes. None in his face either.

Her chest constricted, and there was a kernel of ice sitting in the pit of her stomach. 'That's ridiculous. No one will even believe me anyway.'

'Some people will. And they will tell others. And soon there will be more like you, coming across our borders, wanting to see the truth for themselves. It is attention this country cannot afford.'

Abruptly, he turned away, striding around the side of the desk, moving with the lean grace of a panther.

'No, you cannot leave. You will have to remain here.'

'People will come and find us,' she insisted. 'An eminent professor and his daughter can't just go missing in the desert without someone doing something.'

'Plenty of people go missing in the desert.'

He stood behind his desk, a massive, powerful figure, and the sunlight fell on his glossy black hair. Putting his hands on the desktop, he leaned on them, never breaking eye contact with her.

'They will think you got lost and perished.'

'But not without searching for us,' she argued, because this was insane. Preposterous, even. 'You'll have search parties all along your borders, looking for Dad and me. And everyone has heard all the rumours about Ashkaraz. Don't think people won't be looking your way.'

He said nothing for a long moment and she had the sense that she'd scored a hit. Good. Because right now that kernel of ice in her gut wasn't going away. It was getting bigger, freezing her.

If you'd only waited in the cell...

Charlotte ignored the thought. Instead she took a surreptitious breath and stared back at the Sheikh, completely forgetting the fact that he was actually a sheikh and maybe that was rude. Then again, he'd threatened to keep her prisoner here indefinitely, and that certainly wasn't polite.

'Are you threatening me, Miss Devereaux?' he enquired at last, his voice silky and dark and full of danger.

Charlotte was suddenly keenly aware of how thin was the ice upon which she was standing. She had no power here. None at all. And yet here she was, arguing with the king himself.

'No, I'm not threatening you. I assure you, I wouldn't dare.'

And yet she had to do something. On the one hand she couldn't afford to anger him—not when he was already angry—but on the other she couldn't allow both herself and her father to be buried in a prison cell for the rest of their lives.

Perhaps she should try and appeal to his humanity?

Before she could think better of it, she moved around the side of the desk and put a tentative hand on his arm. 'Please,' she said, looking up at him, trying not to sound as if she was pleading. 'You don't have to do this. You can just let us go and it'll be fine.'

His gaze dropped to her hand on his arm and then moved back up again, and she was suddenly aware that his skin was very warm beneath her hand, that the feel of his muscles was like iron. And she was aware, too, of his scent—

warm and spicy and masculine. He was very large, very powerful, and he was watching her like a predator, intense and focused. His gaze was all gold, like a tiger's, and just as hungry.

Something unfamiliar shifted down low inside her…a kind of heat and a very feminine awareness she hadn't experienced before.

She had never bothered with men. While her friends had been out clubbing and on dating apps she'd preferred staying at home with a book. Because after the front row seat she'd had watching her parents' toxic relationship she'd decided she wanted no part of that. It was easier to retreat between the pages of her book, where there were no arguments, no screaming, no suffocating silences or the kind of seething quiet that presaged a major emotional hurricane—where princes remained fantasies and fantasies ended with a kiss.

She'd never missed having a man in her life. Never wanted one. The only kisses she'd had had been in her imagination, and she'd never met anyone who had made her want to think about more than kisses.

But now, feeling the solidity and strength of the Sheikh's arm beneath her hand, being close to his powerful body, aware of his warmth and rich, spicy scent… She couldn't seem to catch her breath.

'Are you aware,' he murmured, and the soft, silky darkness of his voice was totally at odds with the blazing gold of his eyes, 'that touching the Sheikh without permission means death?'

Oh, dear.

Instinctively she tried to jerk away, but he was too quick, his other hand coming down on hers in a blur of motion, pressing her palm to his forearm.

The heat of his hand against her bare skin was scorching, making her pulse accelerate, and all thought was fragmenting under the pressure of his brilliant gaze.

Was this a distraction?

Was he trying to use his male wiles on her to make her forget what she was saying?

That's ridiculous. He's a sheikh. He can do whatever he likes. And why would he use his wiles on you anyway?

That was a very good point. But, regardless, she couldn't let him get to her. He might very well be the king, but she was a British citizen and she had rights. And surely what he was doing was against the Geneva Convention?

'We're nothing to you,' she said, trying not to sound breathless, hoping to appeal to him in terms he might understand. 'We're insignificant English people. If Dad is unconscious, then he hasn't seen anything, and I don't have a lot of friends so I don't have any people to tell anyway. Your secret is safe with me. And if I accidentally do let something slip, then you…you can come to England and arrest me. Your Majesty,' she added, for good measure.

There was a long and suffocating silence and the pressure of his hand over hers was relentless, burning.

He's not going to let you go.

A small burst of unexpected anger broke through her determined calm. No, he couldn't do this. He couldn't insist she stay here indefinitely, couldn't touch her the way he was doing, and he certainly couldn't keep her prisoner. She wasn't going to allow it.

Determined, Charlotte met his gaze head-on. 'If you let us go now, and without a fuss, I won't tell the media I was held here against my will.'

There was another suffocating silence.

'You,' the Sheikh said softly, 'are either very brave or very stupid, and I cannot tell which it is.'

Charlotte's cheeks burned, but she didn't look away.

She was probably being the latter rather than the former, in issuing him such a threat, but what choice did she have?

She didn't want her father to suffer for the mistake she'd made. He'd been awarded custody of her after his bitter divorce from her mother, and she'd never wanted him to regret that, even though she knew he did.

Perhaps if she hadn't run away that last time, forcing her parents to call the police and causing all kinds of fuss, then she wouldn't have felt so bad about it. But she had run away. And the next day her mother had called it quits and her father had ended up with her.

She'd always tried to be good after that. Never running away again, never causing a fuss. Trying to be interested in all the things he was interested in and later, when she was an adult, becoming his assistant and general dogsbody, doing whatever was required.

Including getting him imprisoned for life by a dictator.

Her breath came shorter, faster, though she tried to remain calm.

'Well?' She lifted a brow, trying to sound as if she was merely waiting to hear whether he'd like a cup of tea or not, rather than asking what he was going to do about her threat of a diplomatic incident.

He said nothing, just watched her as he spread his fingers out, his hand completely covering her own. His skin was hot, like a brand, with the same heat that burned in the merciless gold of his eyes.

She had angered him, that was clear, and she should be terrified by that. But for some reason she wasn't. He was standing very close, huge and strong and so very powerful, and yet there was something in the heat of his gaze that made her breath catch.

She didn't know quite what it was, but an instinct she

hadn't known she possessed told her that she wasn't without power here. That she had the ability to get under this Sheikh's skin.

It made adrenaline rush in her veins, made her want to push, see how far she could go—which was *not* like her at all. She normally ran from anger, not towards it.

His fingers curled around her hand, holding it for a brief, intense moment. Then he pulled it from his arm and let her go, rising to his full height, towering over her.

She could still feel the heat of his fingers as if they'd been imprinted on her skin, and she wanted to put her hand behind her back or in her pocket to hide it, as if it were visible. But there was no hiding from him.

His eyes gleamed briefly, as if he understood something she didn't, making her blush. But all he said was, 'That, Miss Devereaux, is what is commonly known as a threat. And, as I have told you once already, I do not respond well to threats.'

Charlotte opened her mouth to protest, her heart hammering in her chest. But he must have done something—pressed some button on his desk—because the doors had opened and the guards were coming in.

He said something to them—a sharp order she didn't understand—and suddenly they were on either side of her, hemming her in.

She swallowed hard. 'So is this how you treat guests in your country? You get your guards to drag them back to the cells?'

'We do not have "guests" in this country, Miss Devereaux, and you will not be going back to a cell.'

His fierce gaze shifted to the guards and he nodded to them once.

And then there was no time to say anything more as she was ushered firmly out of the room.

* * *

Tariq paced back and forth in front of the window in his office, coldly furious.

It had been a long time since he was quite *this* angry. Then again, it had been a long time since anyone had issued the kind of threat the little Englishwoman had—all cool and polite and straight to his face.

What made her think that she—a mere nobody—could threaten the king of an entire nation? Looking up at him with her big blue eyes, all beseeching, appealing to him as if he had mercy in his heart instead of cold stone.

And then—then!—to put her hand on his arm as if he was an ordinary man…

You are *an ordinary man. You're just angry that you're responding to her as you did to Catherine.*

That the thought was true didn't make it any more welcome. Because he couldn't deny it. He'd ignored the initial pull of attraction, had dismissed it entirely, and yet as soon as she'd touched him he'd felt his body respond as if it had a will of its own.

The light pressure of her fingers on his arm had caused a sudden rush of awareness of her feminine warmth and her small, lush figure next to his. She'd smelled of something sweet and subtle that reminded him of the flowers in the gardens outside—roses, perhaps. And then those eyes looking up into his had got even bigger, her cheeks even pinker, and he'd known she felt the same pull between them that he did: physical chemistry.

He was an experienced man, and he knew well enough when he was attracted to a woman, and he was attracted to this one. Strongly so. Which did not help his temper in the slightest, considering he was supposed to be treating her the way he treated all intruders.

Physical desire, however, was something easily dealt

with. Her threat to him just now and the challenging look in her blue eyes was not. She had him over a barrel and she knew it.

Because if he kept her and her father the British government would certainly have something to say about it, surely?

Yes, their disappearance could be easily explained by some story of their having got lost and perishing in the desert, but search parties would be sent out. Other governments would know the border of his country wasn't far away from the archaeological site, and those rumours that kept people out would also make people suspicious. Enquiries would be made. Questions would be asked. Ashkaraz would receive attention.

And he did *not* want attention—not from the outside world.

The only reason Ashkaraz remained autonomous and free was because its borders were closed and no one knew anything about it. They didn't know about the massive oil wealth upon which the country sat. Or about how that oil was channelled through various private companies so no one would know where it came from. Or about how that wealth came back into the country and was used to pay for hospitals and schools and other social services.

Ashkaraz was wealthy and prosperous but it came at a price—and that price was isolation from a world that would try and take that wealth from them. Because people were greedy. As he knew to his cost.

Tariq came to a stop in front of his desk, his jaw tight, and had to take a moment to uncurl his fingers, relax the tension in his shoulders, dismiss the anger that burned in his gut. He needed to spend some time in the palace gym— that was what he needed. Some boxing or sword practice with an opponent. Or perhaps he needed to call one of the women he sometimes spent the night with, work out his tension that way.

First, though, he needed to decide exactly what to do about his pretty English captive.

He couldn't risk letting her go, so her father would have to stay too—because he couldn't have the man out and about in the world, demanding his daughter's return.

Yes, she might very well promise not to tell anyone about Ashkaraz, but all it would take was one slip, one accidental confession to the wrong person, and curiosity would start. One person would tell another, and then they would tell a couple more, and on it would go. And then, like a rock-slide, it would get bigger and bigger. The border incursions they already had would get worse. Until one day Ashkaraz would no longer remain hidden.

He couldn't risk that. The balance was already fragile; he couldn't allow it to tip.

But keeping them both here would garner unwelcome attention too.

Unless she stays here willingly.

That was a possibility. That way she could contact the British authorities, tell them that she was alive and well and not to look for her, because she had chosen to stay here.

It would be the perfect answer to all his problems but for the tiny fact that she was *not* willing.

So how to make her?

The answer to that was obvious: her father.

He could let Professor Devereaux go—he, after all, had seen nothing—on the understanding that his daughter would tell the British government that she was alive and well and perfectly happy to stay in Ashkaraz.

The idea solved his little diplomatic problem quite nicely, and he was feeling pleased with himself—until thirty minutes into a meeting with Faisal, when his advisor said, 'You won't like what I'm going to say, Your Majesty, but Almasi wants a decision made about his daughter.'

Tariq, who had been standing with one hip propped against the edge of his desk, his arms folded, was instantly irritated. Almasi was a high-ranking member of his government who'd been angling to have his daughter considered as potential sheikha for the past couple of months. His government in general had been putting pressure on him for a couple of years to marry and secure the succession, but Almasi had been particularly vocal. Mainly because he had an of-age daughter whom he thought would be perfect as Tariq's wife.

Tariq disagreed. Almasi's daughter was a nice woman, but he didn't want anything to do with Almasi himself, or his grasping family. That was the problem with the majority of eligible women in Kharan, and in Ashkaraz in general—they were attached to families who wanted to have a stake in determining the way the wealth of their little nation was distributed. Which would have been fine if it was for the good of the country. But Tariq knew it wouldn't be. It would be for the good of only particular families, and that he wouldn't stand for.

Greed wasn't confined only to outsiders.

Catherine's family had certainly been grasping, so he preferred any woman he might consider marrying not to have such connections.

'I am not going to marry his daughter, no matter what he or the government thinks,' Tariq said, his tone absolute.

Faisal was quiet a moment. Then, 'There is the issue of succession,' he said delicately. 'It must be dealt with, as you know.'

Of course he knew. It was a perennial theme.

'The succession does not have to be dealt with now.'

But the other man's dark gaze was far too perceptive. 'I

understand why you have been reluctant, sire. After Catherine, who would not be? But, forgive me, you are not getting any younger. And Ashkaraz needs an heir.'

Something dark coiled tightly in Tariq's gut. He didn't want to think about this now. In fact, he never wanted to think about it. And it didn't help that the old man was right. Ashkaraz *did* need an heir. He just didn't want to be forced into providing one. The fact that it was all to do with Catherine and what had happened between them he knew already, but it didn't make him any less reluctant.

A ruler had to separate himself, keep himself apart, and that had always seemed to him the very antithesis of marriage. But then, a royal marriage didn't require much involvement beyond the getting of an heir. Or at least, that was what his father had told him. And since Tariq's mother had died when Tariq was young, and he'd never had an opportunity to observe a marriage for himself, he had no reason to disbelieve him.

Certainly, though, if he wanted to secure the future of his country an heir would need to be provided whether he liked it or not—or, indeed, whether any of the candidates presented for the begetting of said heir were suitable or not.

And they weren't. None of them were.

'If you want an heir, then you must bring me better candidates for a bride,' he said impatiently.

'There are no more suitable candidates.' Faisal seemed unmoved by his impatience. 'As our borders are closed we have removed ourselves from the world stage, so you cannot get a bride from elsewhere.'

Again, his advisor wasn't wrong. About any of it.

Tariq bared his teeth. 'Then where do you suggest I get a bride from? The moon?'

As soon as he said the last word a memory caught at him…of a lock of hair the colour of starlight showing from underneath a black and white scarf. Hair that had caught on his black robes as he'd lifted her onto his horse.

There is your answer.

It was a preposterous idea. Marry the little English-woman he'd found in the desert? An archaeological assistant. A woman who wasn't rich or titled? Who wasn't anyone important in any way? A nobody?

She is perfect.

The thought stuck inside him like a splinter.

Catherine hadn't been a nobody. She'd been a rich American from a wealthy family, beautiful and privileged. She'd certainly thought herself entitled to the love of his father the Sheikh, and when that Sheikh hadn't given her what she wanted she'd set her sights on the Sheikh's teenage son...

She'd been greedy, and his father, fully aware of that greed, had kept the secrets of his country's wealth from her. But Tariq hadn't.

She'd promised to stay with him for ever if only he'd tell her how Ashkaraz had got so rich.

And so he'd told her.

A week hadn't even passed before her family and the companies they'd owned had begun to put pressure on Ashkaraz and its parliament, demanding oil rights for themselves by bribing a few of the right people.

It had nearly ripped his country apart.

But Charlotte Devereaux had only her father, and a mother who'd moved away long ago. There were no brothers or sisters. No elderly relatives. There'd be no one to come after her and try to grasp a piece of Ashkaraz's wealth. And, because she wasn't associated with any of the families here either, there'd be no family members in Ashkaraz trying to get rich.

Yes. She was perfect.

You would like her in your bed too.

The memory of her heat next to him coiled itself tightly inside him. That would not be…unwelcome. It would be a good outlet for his physical desire and, because she was an outsider, he would never be in danger of wanting more than that. She would remain a constant reminder of his failure with Catherine. A constant reminder of the dangers of emotion.

The government wouldn't be happy, and the old families whose influence he was trying to negate would be even less so. But he wasn't here for their happiness. He wasn't here for divisiveness or self-importance. For one family putting itself above another.

He was here to protect his people, and the government would have to accept his choice of wife whether they liked it or not.

The only issue remaining was how to get her to accept it. Because if she hadn't liked the thought of being *held* here indefinitely, she would like the thought of being *married* to him indefinitely even less.

Then again, he wasn't just anyone.

He was the king.

And he had her father. If he made letting the old man go conditional upon her agreeing to marry him she'd naturally have to accept.

He'd have a suite of rooms set aside for her here in the palace, as befitted her future station, and she'd have access to his considerable wealth and power.

Her life here would be very comfortable indeed.

Certainly better than a shared flat in Clapham.

In fact, the more he thought about it, the better the idea became. Marrying Charlotte Devereaux would solve a great many of his existing problems.

'Not the moon, sire,' Faisal said, oblivious to Tariq's stillness and silence. 'We shall simply have to—'

'No need,' Tariq interrupted, pushing himself away from his desk. 'I have a suitable candidate in mind already.'

Faisal didn't often appear shocked, but he certainly seemed so now. 'I thought you said you had none?'

'One has suddenly occurred to me.' Moving around the side of his desk, Tariq sat down. 'Call a meeting of the council,' he ordered, and then smiled. 'I have an announcement to make.'

CHAPTER FOUR

CHARLOTTE WAS TAKEN to what was quite obviously a library—and, given that it was a very beautiful library, she wasn't quite as scared as she otherwise might have been.

Ornate carved wooden bookshelves lined the walls, stretching from the floor to the ceiling, and there were low couches and divans scattered here and there, strewn with brightly coloured silk cushions. Small tables stood near each couch, the perfect height for cups of tea, and if reading palled there was always the view. Because, like the office she'd been in, the library faced the beautiful walled garden and through the open windows the liquid sound of the fountains played.

It was an extremely pleasant place to sit, even with the two armed guards on either side of the door, though it was an odd choice for a place where the Sheikh might keep a prisoner. Not that she was complaining, since it was a million times better than the jail cell she'd expected to be dragged back to.

She wasn't sure how long she'd been there, but it was enough time for her to have inspected the bookshelves and found quite a few English language books in various genres. She would have been happy to curl up with one on one of the divans.

She'd had enough time to wonder, too, what was going on and what the Sheikh was going to do with her.

She should never have threatened him—that had been a mistake. She couldn't think why she had done so, or even where her bravery had come from. She'd only been conscious that for some reason she affected him, and she'd let that little taste of power go to her head.

And now both she and her father would pay for it.

The fear she'd been ignoring collected inside her once more, and it was still there when hours or minutes later—she wasn't sure which—the guards took her out of the library and down some more of the echoing, beautifully tiled and arched hallways. They passed glittering rooms and ornate alcoves, went down some elegant staircases and past yet more colonnaded gardens and fountains.

The Sheikh's palace was beautiful, and if she hadn't been afraid for her life she would have loved looking around it. But she *was* afraid, and all the beauty around her only made her more so.

She had very much hoped she wouldn't be taken back to that jail cell, and she wasn't. Instead she was shown into a series of interconnected rooms like a hotel suite, with big French doors that opened out into yet another walled garden, though this one was smaller. It had a fountain, too, and delightful beds of roses and fruit trees. The rooms were tiled in subtle, glossy variations of white, giving the walls a lovely textured feel. And there were more beautiful silk rugs on the floors dyed in deep, jewel colours, and low couches to sit on strewn with silken cushions.

Charlotte tried to ask the guards what was going on, why she was there and not in a cell, but either they didn't speak English or they'd been instructed not to speak to her, because they ignored her questions, leaving her alone in the rooms before going out and locking the door behind them.

So, still a prisoner, then, but now her cage was a gilded one.

After they'd gone she explored a little, finding that one of the rooms had a huge bed mounded with pillows standing against one wall, while another contained a beautiful tiled bath and a large shower.

She couldn't understand why the Sheikh was holding her here, in rooms that seemed more appropriate for a visiting head of state than for some illegal alien he'd picked up unconscious in the desert.

None of it made sense.

Left with nothing else to do, Charlotte paced around the main living area of the suite, her brain ticking over. She didn't know why she was here and not in a cell, and she didn't know what was going to happen to her or her father other than that the Sheikh wasn't letting either of them go.

That made her feel cold inside—not for herself, but for her father. He was an eminent professor with a career back in London, and lots of friends and colleagues, and he would hate to be separated from any of it.

Especially when he finds out that all of this is your fault.

The cold inside her deepened.

She'd been the one to break the window and go looking around outside. If she had simply stayed put, then her father would be safe and so would she. Maybe they'd even be on their way back to the border and none the wiser about Ashkaraz.

But that wasn't what had happened.

And if it's your fault, then it's up to you to fix it.

That was true. But how?

She came to a stop in front of the windows, looking at the pretty rose garden outside, thinking.

There really was only one way to fix it. She was the one who'd blundered out onto the street and seen what she shouldn't have, not her father. He was blameless. Maybe she could convince the Sheikh to let him go if she agreed to remain here? She didn't have a career, like her father did, or friends. No one would miss her.

Your father wouldn't miss you either.

Charlotte pushed that thought aside, hurrying on with her idea. The professor surely wouldn't argue with her, and she could reassure him that everything was fine so he wouldn't think she was being held against her will. She could reassure the British authorities too—keep them away from Ashkaraz's borders, appease the Sheikh.

An unexpected shiver went through her as she thought of him again. Of his intensely masculine, powerful physical presence. His large hand over hers, his palm burning against her skin. The hard muscles of his forearm and his fierce golden stare. The anger she had sensed burning inside him no matter how cold his expression.

Could she appease a man like him? Did she have the power? But she'd got to him in some way earlier, she knew it, so maybe she could do it again.

If she wanted to save her father she would have to.

And what about you? Staying in a strange country all alone for the rest of your life?

Charlotte ignored that. She'd deal with it later. Right now, making sure her father was safe was more important.

The time ticked past and she spent it exploring the small suite of rooms and admiring them in between wondering what on earth was going on and trying to keep her feelings of panic at bay.

At last the doors opened, admitting two exquisitely robed women. One carried a tray of food, the other an armful of silvery blue fabric. The woman with the tray put it down on a small table near the window, while the other laid the fabric across a low divan nearby.

'Tonight you will dine with His Majesty, Sheikh Tariq Ishak Al Naziri,' said the woman near the tray in lightly accented English. She gestured at the fabric spread out on the divan. 'His Majesty has provided suitable attire for you and some refreshment in the meantime. I will come and collect you at the designated hour.'

Charlotte stared at the woman in astonishment. Attire? Refreshment? *Dining?*

What on earth was going on?

'But why?' she burst out. 'And what about my father? Why am I being kept here? What does the Sheikh want with me?'

But the woman only smiled and shook her head, and then she and the other woman turned around and went out, leaving Charlotte alone again.

Okay, so clearly no one was going to answer her questions. Which meant she would have to get answers from His Majesty Sheikh Tariq himself. And she was not going to be put off again by his golden stare and his gentlemanly wiles. She would insist he answered her and then she'd request that he send her father home.

The thought made her feel a little better, so she helped herself from the small tray of food—flatbread still warm from the oven and spicy dips, along with some fresh fruit. Once she'd eaten, she wandered into the bathroom to examine it in greater detail—and then decided that if the Sheikh was housing her in such luxurious accommodation she was going to take advantage of that fully.

So she stripped off her dirty clothing and had a long, hot shower, using delicious rose-scented body wash and shampoo. After her shower, wrapped in a big fluffy white towel, she went back into the living area where the 'suitable attire' had been spread over the divan near the window.

The 'attire' proved to be very pretty robes in silvery blue silk, with roses embroidered around the edge in heavy silver thread. Charlotte put out a hand and gently touched the fabric. It was cool and soft beneath her fingertips. But he'd provided this for her, and part of her didn't want to wear it purely because he'd told her to. Part of her wanted to turn up to this dinner in her own filthy clothes and to hell with him.

But she didn't allow herself such petty rebellions these days—plus, there was no point in angering him needlessly. Not when she had her father's safety to consider as well as her own. Also, she didn't know his country's customs, and causing offence purely because she was angry would be stupid.

Better to wear the robes…be polite, courteous. And then tell him what was what.

Besides… She stroked the fabric again, enjoying the feel of it. The robes were beautiful and she'd never worn anything like them before. Princesses in fairy tales always wore beautiful dresses, and as a child she'd often wished she could have a beautiful dress too. But her mother had never been particularly interested in what Charlotte had wanted. She'd never been interested in Charlotte at all.

You're a prisoner in a strange country, with no idea of what the future will hold for you, and yet you're thinking about how nice it will be to wear a pretty dress?

Well, why not? Her own clothes were filthy, and who knew what was going to happen to her afterwards? She might never get the opportunity to wear a pretty dress ever again.

Dropping the towel, Charlotte dressed herself in the robes, feeling the fabric deliciously cool and smooth against her skin. Then she went to stand in front of the full-length mirror in the bedroom and adjusted the material. She looked…nice, she had to admit. And she felt a little more in control now she was clean and dressed—even in 'suitable attire'.

If she was going to beg a favour from a king, she'd better look the part.

The robed women didn't come back for a long while, and Charlotte tried to fill in the time by examining every inch of her suite and then by having a small nap.

At last the light began to fade, and then a knock came at the door. It opened to reveal one of the robed women.

Charlotte pushed herself up from the divan she'd been sitting on, her heart thumping hard in her chest. The woman gave her a brief survey and there was a satisfied look in her eyes that made Charlotte feel a tiny bit better. Obviously her choice to wear the robes had been a good one.

'His Majesty will see you now,' the woman said. 'Please follow me.'

Nervously clasping her hands in front of her, Charlotte did so, noting the two guards that fell into step behind her as she left the suite.

The corridors were silent but for the sound of the guards' boots on the tiled floor. Her own steps were muffled by the pair of silver slippers she'd put on, which had come with the robes.

She tried to take note of where they were going, but after a few twists and turns, more stairs and more long corridors, she gave up, looking at the high arched ceilings instead, and the glittering tiles on them that caused the light to refract and bounce. They were beautiful, and she got so lost in them that for a couple of minutes at least she forgot that she was going to meet the terrifying man who was king.

Eventually the hallway opened up, and to her delight Charlotte found herself stepping out into the colonnaded garden she'd seen through the windows of the Sheikh's office. The air was as cool and soft as the silk she wore, and laden with the scent of flowers and the gentle sound of the fountains splashing.

The woman led her along a path to the central fountain itself, and then stopped and gestured.

Charlotte's breath caught.

In the dim twilight, tea lights in exquisite glass holders leapt and danced. They'd been set on a low table, their flames illuminating the multitude of cushions set on the ground around it and glittering off glasses and cutlery. Bowls full of food sat on the table—sliced meats and dips and more of the flatbread.

It was like something straight out of one of her favourite books, *The Arabian Nights*, and for a second she could only stand there and stare.

Then she became aware of the man sprawled on one of the cushions at the table, watching her. He rose as she approached, fluidly and with grace, until he towered over the table and her, the candle flames making his golden eyes glow.

He wasn't wearing the suit trousers and shirt she'd seen him in earlier that day but black robes, their edges heavily embroidered in gold thread. They suited him, highlighting his height and the broad width of his shoulders, and the sense of power that rolled off him in waves.

The flickering light illuminated his face, and his features were set in a fierce sort of expression that made her heart race. He wasn't angry now, it seemed, but he'd definitely decided something—though what it could be she had no idea.

What jailer set out a beautiful dinner like this if a prison cell was all that awaited her? It didn't make any sense.

'Welcome, Miss Devereaux.'

His deep voice prowled over her skin, soft and dark as a panther.

'Thank you for joining me.'

Charlotte resisted the urge to shift on her feet, uncomfortable as his intense gaze roved over her. She didn't know how she knew, but she had the sense that he liked what he saw. Which made it difficult to think.

'Well,' she said stoutly, pulling herself together. 'It wasn't like I had a choice.'

The corner of his hard mouth curved and for a second Charlotte couldn't do anything but stare at him, her breath catching at the beauty of his smile.

'That is true,' he acknowledged. 'But I am glad you came without the necessity of guards dragging you.'

It was very clear that if she had refused then, yes, the guards would have dragged her to meet him.

Fear flickered through her, and the old urge to run away and hide gripped her. But she ignored it, steeling herself. Best to get this out of the way first.

'Your Majesty,' she began formally. 'I've been thinking and I want to—'

'Please,' the Sheikh interrupted, gesturing to the table. 'Sit.'

'No, thank you.' Charlotte's palms were sweaty, her heart showing no sign of slowing down. She needed to say this and fast—before she changed her mind. 'I know that you've decided not to let my father and me leave, but I have a request to make.'

His expression was impassive. 'Do you, indeed?'

'Yes, I think—'

'Sit, Miss Devereaux. We shall have this discussion as we eat.'

'No. I need to say this now.' She took an unsteady breath, meeting his fierce golden stare. 'If you let my father go, I'll stay here. And I'll do so willingly.'

Tariq said nothing, watching Charlotte Devereaux's pale face in the flickering candlelight. It was obvious she'd been thinking hard in the time she'd been cooling her heels in the sheikha's suite. And he had to admire her courage; it couldn't be easy, facing a lifetime in a strange land, even if it meant her father went free.

But that was good. She would need that courage and she would need strength too, for the role he would give her. The sheikha would need both.

She certainly made a pretty picture, standing there in the robes he'd chosen for her. The silver-blue suited her pale skin and deepened the colour of her eyes. She'd clearly washed her hair, and it lay soft and loose over her shoulders and down her back, the pale mass curling slightly.

He was pleased she'd worn the robes, and pleased that she'd decided to make an effort. Because that was all part of his plan.

The council had been in an uproar at his abrupt choice of wife, as he'd expected, so he'd deliberately had the robes sent to her, and then had her walked through the palace so everyone could observe the picture of quiet elegance and strength that she presented.

He hadn't been certain she would wear the robes, or that she wouldn't make a fuss about attending his dinner, but he'd counted on her English manners preventing her from making a scene and so far he'd been proved right.

He was pleased with that too.

And now she'd just volunteered to stay willingly if he let her father go, which made things even easier.

Don't feel too pleased with yourself. You haven't told her about the marriage yet.

No, he hadn't. He'd hoped to take his time with his proposal, feeding her the excellent food his chefs had provided and pouring her wine from his extensive cellars. And then perhaps some civilised conversation to set her at ease.

But, judging from the fear in her pretty blue eyes and the way she had her hands clasped together, spinning it out might not be such a good idea. Her finely featured face was set in lines of determination and she was standing very straight, as if bracing herself for a blow, so maybe he should deliver it. A quick, clean strike.

The candlelight glittered off the silver in her robes and glimmered in her lovely hair, making her look like a fall of moonlight in the darkness of the garden. And it prompted something to shift uncomfortably inside his chest—something that felt a lot like sympathy.

Which was wrong. He couldn't afford to be sympathetic. He had been sympathetic with Catherine the night he'd found her weeping beside this very fountain, and his heart—the traitor—had twisted inside his chest at the sight of her tears.

Sympathy was not the only thing you felt that night, remember?

Of course he remembered. How could he forget? He'd also been angry, burning with a frustrated rage that he hadn't been able to control. A volatile cocktail of emotion that had turned dangerous in the end.

He wouldn't do that again.

He had to be hard, cold. Ruthless. He couldn't risk being anything else.

'That is certainly a brave request,' he said, ignoring the tightness in his chest. 'You might change your mind when you hear mine.'

She blinked in surprise. 'Y-Yours?'

Tariq dropped his gaze to the cushions opposite. 'Sit down, Miss Devereaux.'

He didn't make it sound like anything less than the command it was, and after a brief hesitation she took a couple of faltering steps towards the table, then sat down awkwardly on the cushions.

Satisfied, he sat down himself, studying her pale face.

And, even though he thought he'd shoved aside that brief burst of sympathy he'd experienced, he found himself pouring her a glass of the cool white wine and then putting a few tasty items of food on a plate for her.

It was the custom in Ashkaraz for a prospective groom to woo his potential wife by feeding her, so the dinner had been organised very deliberately, to make sure everyone knew exactly what his intentions were. But right now all he was conscious of was that she was quite pale, and that possibly the food he'd had sent to her room hadn't been enough. She really needed to have something more substantial—especially given what he was going to tell her.

He pushed the wine glass in her direction, and then the plate of food. 'You should eat.'

Her pretty mouth tightened, full and lush and pink. 'No, thank you. I'm not hungry.'

Her chin had lifted and there was a slight but unmistakable glow of defiance in her blue eyes.

Faintly amused by her show of spirit, despite himself, he nearly smiled. 'If you want to spite me, there are other, better ways of doing so.'

Colour tinged her cheeks. 'Oh, yes? And what are those?'

'Any number of things—but if you think I am going to tell you what they are, you are mistaken.'

She narrowed her gaze, ignoring the food and the wine. 'Excuse me, Your Majesty, but what is all this for? This dinner? The rooms I was locked in? These…clothes?'

One small hand went to the embroidered edge of her robe, the tips of her fingers running over it. She liked it, he could tell, even though she probably didn't want to.

'I thought I was your prisoner.'

'If you were truly my prisoner you would be back in that jail cell.'

'But you said I was to be here indefinitely. That I was—'

'That is part of the request I have to make,' he interrupted calmly. 'Though perhaps you should have a sip of wine and something to eat before we discuss it.'

Little sparks glittered in her eyes. 'Like I said, I'm not hungry.'

Well, if she didn't want to eat he certainly wasn't going to force her, and nor should he draw this out any longer than he had to.

What happened to a quick, clean strike?

She and her white face had happened.

She and the sympathy that seemed to sit in the centre of his chest whether he wanted it to or not.

'Do not eat, then.' He shoved that sympathy aside once again. 'It makes no difference to what I have to say to you.'

Her gaze narrowed even further, but she didn't speak, merely sat on the cushions, as straight-backed and dignified as the sheikha she would soon be.

'The safety of my country is of paramount importance to me, Miss Devereaux,' he began, holding her gaze so he could see that she understood. 'And protecting it is my purpose as king—a purpose I take very seriously indeed. So when the safety of my country is compromised I must take certain steps.'

'I see. Such as keeping me here, despite the fact that I'm not a threat?'

She was still angry, and he supposed he couldn't blame her. Not when she didn't know the history of the country she was dealing with.

Or your role in it.

But she didn't need to know that. No one did. It was enough that he was working to fix the mistake he'd made, and fix it he would.

'It is not you who gets to decide what is a threat to Ashkaraz and what is not.' He didn't bother to hide the chill in his voice. 'That is my decision.'

Again, colour crept through her cheeks, but she didn't look away. 'You were talking about certain steps. What are they?'

'Keeping you here is definitely one of them. But there are other threats to my kingdom that have nothing to do with you.'

'Okay—fine. I get that. But I still don't understand what this has to do with giving me dinner.'

'A kingdom can be threatened from within as well as without. And there are certain families who put themselves first, over the people of this country.'

He could feel the anger gathering in him again. Cold and terrible anger at the web of alliances that had been forged purely for personal gain and how those very same people who had taken advantage of his father's generosity now looked to take advantage of his.

'I will not have it,' he went on, his voice on the edge of a growl. 'I will not have my council or my government divided, and I will not have one family being awarded more importance than another.'

Her defiance had melted away, and he saw a bright curiosity burning in her eyes. 'No. I can imagine not. But I'm not sure what this has to do with me.'

He bared his teeth. 'If you let me finish, I will tell you.'

She gave a little sniff. 'I wasn't interrupting. Please, go on.'

Her hand moved to the wine glass and she picked it up, taking a sip. Then she looked down at the plate he'd set in front of her and idly picked up an olive, popping it into her mouth.

Clearly she was hungrier than she'd said. Satisfaction

moved through him that she was finally eating the food he'd presented to her, allaying his anger somewhat.

'I need a wife, Miss Devereaux,' he said, watching her. 'The royal succession must be ensured and my council wish this to happen soon. But I will not give in to factions—which means I cannot choose a bride from within my own country. There is no shortage of candidates, but none are suitable.'

Her brow wrinkled as she put the olive pit on her plate, then picked up another olive, chewing thoughtfully. 'That's unfortunate. Can't you choose a bride from outside the country?'

'Our borders are closed—so, no, I cannot.'

'That's *very* unfortunate, in that case.' Once she'd finished the olive she picked up some flatbread, dipping it in the hummus he'd spread on her plate. 'Isn't there anyone you can choose?'

'Not from among the candidates that have been put before me. They all have families who are greedy, grasping. Who want political influence.'

'You can't just tell them no?'

There was no anger at all in her expression now. Her attention was focused on the puzzle of finding him a wife. And if she found it strange that he was discussing it with her, she didn't show it.

Why are you explaining yourself to her? You are the king. Your word is law. Simply tell her she will be marrying you and be done with it.

The thought needled at him. Because explaining was exactly what he was doing and he wasn't sure why.

Perhaps it had something to do with her initial fear and then that little spark of defiance. And the way she'd absently started eating, no matter that she'd made a point of telling him she wasn't hungry.

There was something artless and innocent to her that he found attractive, and it was very much the opposite of what he was used to from the people around him. They were all greedy, all wanted something from him, and they were never honest about it. They lied and manipulated, as Catherine had done, to get what they wanted.

No wonder his father had taught him that isolation was the best lesson for any ruler. To rely on his own judgement and not be swayed by anyone or anything, still less the promptings of his own heart.

Once he'd thought his father had been wrong—but that had been before Catherine, before he'd learned otherwise, and now he filled his heart with marble and his will with steel. Nothing got through. Nothing made him bend.

How does that explain the sympathy in your heart for this woman?

He didn't know. And he didn't like it.

'I cannot "tell them no",' he said flatly. 'Not outright. That would cause more division and dissension, so I must be cautious.'

She frowned. 'Then how are you supposed to find a wife?'

Did she really have no idea what he was leading up to? Did she really not understand?

Tariq searched her face, seeing only puzzlement. 'I have found one.'

Only then did something flicker in her eyes—a flash of apprehension. 'Oh?'

He stared at her, looking for what he didn't know. 'You are not going to ask me who it is?'

Her mouth opened and then closed, and then she tore her gaze from his, looking down at her plate. Her hands dropped to her lap. The candlelight glittered off her pale lashes and her hair, giving her an ethereal, fragile air.

And that strange feeling in his chest, that sympathy that wouldn't go away, deepened. He fought it, because it couldn't gain ground in him. He wouldn't let anything like it take root inside him again.

There was silence and he waited.

Because she'd guessed—he was sure of it—and he wanted her to say it.

'You can't…' she murmured, not looking up. 'You can't mean…me.'

'Can I not?'

Her lashes quivered against the smooth, pale skin of her cheeks and she went very still, tension radiating from her. 'I don't understand,' she said eventually.

'What is there to understand? I need a wife, Miss Devereaux. I need the succession secured and I need my council happy. And I need to put those aristocratic families seeking to use their position to their advantage back in their place.' He paused, making sure that soft, weak feeling inside him was gone. 'I had no suitable candidates, no prospect of any, and then you turned up. You are perfect for the role.'

There was more silence, broken only by the splashing of the fountain. She didn't move, kept her gaze on the table, but he could almost feel her shock.

'You have no family except your father,' he went on. 'And, more importantly, you have no family here. Which means there will be no one using you to better themselves or their position. You are an outsider with no connections, and that makes you ideal.'

Her long, pale throat moved. 'But…but I'm just a woman you picked up in the desert. A nobody.'

'Which is precisely why you are perfect.'

She looked up suddenly and he thought he saw a flicker

of hurt in her eyes. But then it was gone and the anger was back.

'You can't marry me,' she said. 'I'm sorry, but you just can't.'

'Give me one good reason.'

'I don't even know you, for God's sake.' Her face had become quite pink. 'We only just met this morning.'

He shouldn't, but he couldn't deny that he liked her sudden display of temper. He preferred a woman with spirit, and outrage was better than fear.

'Knowing someone is not any prerequisite for a royal marriage that I am aware of,' he said calmly. It would no doubt aggravate her, but she could do with a little more aggravation. It would give her something to fight against. 'And we will have plenty of time to get to know one another.'

'You're assuming I'm going to go through with it,' she shot back. 'Well, just a heads-up for you: I'm not. And you can't make me.'

He wished he didn't have to. But he was going to.

'*Au contraire*, Miss Devereaux. I can certainly make you. For example, if you do not agree, then your father will remain here as my guest. Along with yourself.'

The pink in her cheeks deepened, creeping down her neck. 'So you're going to use Dad to force me to marry you? Is that what you're saying?'

For a second he allowed himself a shred of regret that he had to do this to her, that he couldn't simply let her go back to her life in England along with her father.

Then he excised that regret from his soul. He couldn't let her return to her life. He had a duty to his country to fix the mistake he'd made all those years ago, when he'd put his own feelings ahead of what was best for his nation.

It was a mistake he would not make again.

'Yes,' he said, making his voice hard. 'That is exactly what I am saying.'

Temper glittered in her eyes, stronger this time. 'What about me? What about my wishes? What if I don't want to marry you?'

He met her furious blue gaze. 'I am afraid that you do not get a say. If you do not agree, I will keep your father here.'

She took a little breath, her jaw tight. 'Then maybe he'll have to stay here. He might even like it. It might be just the kind of thing he'd enjoy.'

It was a bluff and they both knew it.

'Are you saying that your father would enjoy being cut off from his colleagues?' Tariq asked. 'From his position as professor? He is an eminent man. He is used to having respect—used to having intellectual discourse with his peers. How will he cope being cut off from all of that? And what will he think of your choice? Because as much as I am choosing for you, you are choosing for him.'

That lovely lush mouth of hers tightened again, and the glow of anger in her eyes was even more intense. She wasn't so much a fall of moonlight now but an angry storm, full of lightning and thunder. A passionate woman.

You will enjoy exploring just how passionate.

Oh, yes, he would. Very much so.

Oblivious to the tenor of his thoughts, she said angrily, 'You have an answer for everything, don't you?'

'Of course. I am the king.' He softened his voice to mollify her. 'It will not be so bad, *ya amar*. As my wife, you will be sheikha. You will have access to my wealth and power. You may live whatever life you choose as long as it does not threaten this country or its people.'

She remained determinedly unmollified. 'Essentially, though, I will still be your prisoner.'

'You will be my prisoner whether you marry me or not.'

His patience was beginning to fray now, because people generally did whatever he wanted them to do, and if he told them to jump they asked *How high?* They did not sit there arguing with every word he said.

'The only thing you have to do, Miss Devereaux, is determine your choice of cage.'

CHAPTER FIVE

Charlotte sat across from the Sheikh, conscious of only one prevailing emotion: anger.

She simply could not believe what he'd said.

Marry him? Marry the *king*?

Her heart was fluttering like a furious bird in her chest, her pulse wild beneath her skin, and she had a horrible feeling it wasn't only anger that she was feeling. But, since anger was preferable to anything else, she clung on tightly to it.

He'd explained why he'd chosen her and yet it still didn't make any sense.

Yes, she was a nobody, with no connections—a foreigner, an outsider. But did he really need to keep emphasising how alone and common she was? Or was that in order to make her feel isolated? So that she felt she wouldn't have any choice but to marry him?

Not that his motives were the most important thing right now.

Not when all she could think about was the word 'marriage'.

It made her feel cold all over. Because all she could think about was her parents, screaming at each other. And when they hadn't been screaming, there had been dreadful silences full of resentment and bitterness.

Not all marriages were like that, she knew, but her par-

ents' marriage had put her off for life, and nothing she'd
seen so far had made her want to change her mind—
still less the thought of being married to this...complete
stranger.

She didn't want to marry him.

She didn't want to marry anyone.

You might not have a choice.

It certainly seemed that way, since it was obvious he
felt very strongly about protecting his country. In fact, the
way he'd spoken about his purpose had fascinated her, and
she'd been intrigued by the conviction glowing in his eyes.

Until he'd spoiled it by telling her that she was going
to be his wife.

He was staring at her now, apparently impervious to the
anger rising inside her. The planes and angles of his face
were impassive, his golden stare cold. He looked like a god
of ancient times, weighing the contents of her soul, determining whether she would go to heaven or hell.

Except that it was she who had to make the decision.
Or at least he'd given her the illusion that she did. And illusion it was, since either she married him or he kept her
father in Ashkaraz.

*How is this any different from you staying here in return
for your father's freedom?*

It was *very* different. Before, she'd imagined she'd simply be allowed to have a life here—and, though she hadn't
thought about that life in any detail, it hadn't seemed as
depressingly final as marriage.

She had a brief vision of herself doing something completely and uncharacteristically violent, such as hurling
the contents of her wine glass in his face or upending the
table, but that felt far too close to something her mother or
her father might have done, so she ignored it.

Instead, she forced herself to sit very still, her jaw tight, her back rigid. 'And if I decide to be a prisoner and not marry you?'

The food she'd eaten sat uncomfortably in her stomach. His straight dark brows drew together and the effect made her breath catch. He was forbidding in his black robes and that slight frown only made him more so.

'Then you are quite welcome to return to the cell you escaped from.' His voice was as dark and deep as the ocean. 'And your father with you.'

A quiver went through her. Return to that small, cramped, bare room? With the bucket in the corner? And the hard bed? And her father too... He would hate it and she knew he would. The horrible Sheikh was right. He would hate being cut off from his colleagues, from his work, from his life back in England.

Another thing to blame you for.

Charlotte swallowed. She'd tried so hard to be good for him, but sometimes she wondered if it would ever be enough. Perhaps this sacrifice finally would be? After all, it *was* her mistake that had got them into this mess.

You're seriously contemplating marriage to this man?

Maybe. Maybe it wouldn't be as bad as she thought. Her parents had once thought themselves in love, and that was why it had gone so wrong—or at least that was what her father had told her. Love turned toxic, was a recipe for disaster.

This would be a different kind of marriage from the one her parents had had right from the start, since she barely knew this man, let alone loved him. There would be no toxic emotion since she had no emotion about him to begin with.

That's a lie.

Charlotte chose to ignore that particular thought.

Her hand shook as she reached for her wine glass, taking a sip of the cool liquid. It was pleasantly dry, as she preferred her wine to be, and soothed her aching throat.

The Sheikh merely watched her with those predatory tiger's eyes.

'Why are you bothering with this?' she snapped in sudden temper, uncomfortable and not knowing what to do with herself. 'The dinner? The robes? Why are you even bothering to ask me? When you could simply drag me down the aisle and make me say "I do" right now?'

'Because I am not a monster—even though I might appear to be one. And I thought you would appreciate at least the illusion of choice.'

'Yes, well...' She put the glass down with a click, splashing the wine slightly. 'I don't appreciate it.'

He tilted his head, watching her. 'You are angry.'

'Of course I'm bloody—'

'Angry rather than scared. Why is that?'

She didn't want to answer. Because she had a horrible feeling that she was, in fact, scared, and that if she thought too much about it she'd end up scurrying away like a frightened mouse. And she couldn't do that. Not in front of a predator like him.

Instead, she clutched her courage and lifted her chin higher. 'There's not much point in being scared, is there? That's not going to get me very far.'

'Anger will not either,' he pointed out. 'Though anger is a far more useful emotion.'

'It's not very useful right now. Especially since I'm assuming that emptying my wine glass in your face will result in my death?'

Unexpectedly a flicker of something crossed his features. It was gone too fast for her to tell what it was, but she caught the gleam of it in his eyes, fierce and hot and completely at odds with the cold expression that had been there before.

It was almost as if he liked her anger, even approved of it, which was a strange thing to think. Yet she couldn't shake the thought, and for reasons she couldn't have explained knowing that somehow eased her fear and bolstered her courage.

'I would not recommend doing it.'

A thread of something she didn't recognise wound through this dark voice.

'So, I take it you accept my proposal?'

She glared at him. 'Do you need my acceptance?'

'No.' There was no sympathy in the word, and yet no triumph either. It was simply a statement of fact.

'So why the need for all...' she waved a hand to encompass the table and the robes she wore '...all of this?'

The fierce glow in his eyes was still there, and the way he sat back on the cushions, large and muscular and dangerous, sent an inexplicable thrill arrowing down her spine.

This man was going to be her husband.

And you know what that means, don't you?

It should have occurred to her before, and yet it hadn't— the realisation that marriage didn't just mean standing up and vowing to love one another till death do you part. There was another part of a relationship that marriage brought, wasn't there? A part she'd had no experience with whatsoever.

Sex.

An unfamiliar feeling twisted, right down deep inside her, and though fear was a part of it, it wasn't the only part. There was something else too—something to do with that thrill at the warmth of his body she'd experienced earlier that day and the feel of his arm beneath her hand. The awareness of him, of the amount of space he took up, an entirely physical awareness...

Her mouth went dry and she wanted to look away, suddenly sure that he could see exactly what she was thinking, exactly what realisation she was only just now coming to. Because those golden eyes would see everything.

She reached for the wine again, picking it up and taking another desperate sip to moisten her throat, her heartbeat thudding in her ears.

He couldn't want her to have sex with him, surely? She wasn't beautiful. She wasn't experienced. He would have his pick of lovely women as king, and he definitely wouldn't ever have picked her—not if she hadn't turned up so conveniently out in the desert.

He's mentioned securing the succession.

Yes, he had, but still...

'You have a question?'

His voice wrapped around her, velvety and soft in the darkness, as if he knew exactly what she was thinking.

'Ask me.'

She should, she knew that, but she couldn't bear the thought. She didn't know what she would do if he told her that, no, sex with him would not be required. Or what she would do if he said that, yes, it would.

Probably burst into flames with embarrassment either way.

'N-No,' she stuttered. 'I don't have a question.'

She steeled herself to meet his gaze. And she didn't understand the glitter in his eyes, because it looked like anger, and yet she didn't think it was. It was far too intent, far too focused.

'Open your mouth, *ya amar*,' he ordered quietly.

It was not what she'd expected him to say and it took

her by surprise—so much so that she'd already opened her mouth to obey him before she realised what she'd done.

Snapping it shut almost immediately, she gave him a suspicious look. 'Why?'

He leaned forward and picked up one of the strawberries sitting in a silver bowl. 'It is the custom in Ashkaraz for a prospective groom to feed his chosen bride. So open your mouth, Miss Devereaux, and signify your acceptance.'

This time there was no doubt about the sharp-edged glitter in his eyes. It was all challenge. And even though she didn't want to obey him, she felt something rise up inside her in response.

It was just a stupid strawberry. And maybe it was a custom here, but it didn't mean anything to her.

It means you accept that you will marry him.

Well, she had no choice about that. And if she had to stay here indefinitely surely it would be better to stay here as the sheikha—whatever that meant—than it would be as a prisoner in a cell.

And who knew? If she was queen maybe she could even change things for herself. Influence him to open up the borders so she could go home eventually. It was an idea. She didn't have to simply bow to his wishes for ever.

The decision hardened inside her and she caught his gaze with hers, letting him know that she wasn't going to lie down and be his doormat no matter what he thought. Then she leaned forward slightly and opened her mouth.

A flame leapt in his eyes, and though she didn't know what it meant, something deep inside her did, and it was making her heartbeat race, all her awareness focus abruptly on him.

He held out the strawberry, brushing the fruit along her mouth at first, tracing her lower lip in an almost-caress that made her mouth feel full and oddly sensitive, made another little shiver snake down her spine.

She went still as he did it again, this time tracing her upper lip with the strawberry before placing it gently in her mouth and holding onto the stem.

'Bite down, *ya amar*,' he ordered, and she did, sweetness bursting onto her tongue. Then he withdrew his hand, taking the stem with it, his fingers brushing her lower lip and leaving a trail of hot sparks in its wake.

Charlotte swallowed the strawberry, but she wasn't concentrating on the taste. All she could feel was the brush of his fingers on her mouth, and she nearly raised a hand and touched her lips herself.

He was watching her, and she didn't know what he'd seen in her face but something had satisfied him, she was sure. That hot, golden glow was burning in his eyes again and she still didn't know what it meant.

You do. Come on.

Maybe. But she didn't want to think about that. Didn't want to think about why her mouth felt so sensitive and why her heart was beating so hard. Why there was an unfamiliar ache down low inside her.

'Well?' she said thickly, trying to pretend that ache wasn't there. 'Is that all I need to do, then?'

He dropped the stem back in the bowl 'That is all.'

'Good.'

Her hands were shaking and she didn't like it. Suddenly all she wanted was to be alone, away from here. Away from *him*.

'I—I'm tired, Your Majesty. If you don't mind, I'd like to go back to…' She gestured at the doorway into the palace, then pulled at her robes, getting awkwardly to her feet without waiting for his agreement.

He rose far more fluidly than she and her heartbeat became a roar as he moved around the table towards her, all tall, dark muscularity, the hem of his robes flaring out around his booted feet.

'Oh, no...it's okay.'

She took an unconscious step back, as if putting some physical distance between herself and him would separate her from the strange feeling careering around in her chest. A feeling that she suspected might be excitement even though it also felt like fear. A feeling she didn't want, whatever it was.

'I can find my way back myself.'

The Sheikh stopped, candlelight flickering off the gold embroidery of his robes, and she thought she caught amusement in his eyes. But then it was gone.

'Very well.' He raised a hand and instantly the robed woman stepped out of the shadows of the doorway, as if she'd been standing there waiting for his command all this time. 'Amirah, please escort Miss Devereaux back to her suite.' In the darkness his eyes gleamed, a tiger on the prowl. 'Sleep well, *ya amar*. Tomorrow you will be busy.'

Heartbeat thumping, Charlotte let herself be led away.

'Excuse me, Amirah,' she said hesitantly as they went down the echoing, dimly lit corridors. 'What does *ya amar* mean?' It had been bothering her.

'It means "my moon",' Amirah murmured. 'Or "my most beautiful". It is an endearment.'

Charlotte felt her cheeks get hot. His "most beautiful"? Well, that was a lie. She wasn't beautiful and she certainly wasn't his.

But soon you will be.

Charlotte ignored the shiver that went down her spine at the thought.

It wasn't excitement. It just wasn't.

* * *

She didn't see the Sheikh over the next couple of days, which was a good thing. And she might have spent those days pacing around in her suite, reflecting over and over on the wisdom of her decision, had not Amirah turned up at her door the next day, informing her that she was now to be Charlotte's assistant and had been asked to help her with the list of tasks His Majesty had assigned to her. Then she'd brandished said list and Charlotte, craving distraction, had grabbed it with some relief.

The Sheikh had asked her to familiarise herself with the history, customs, people and language of Ashkaraz, which made sense since she was going to be queen. And since she'd always found learning interesting she'd thrown herself into study with abandon, especially as it involved spending a lot of time in the beautiful library she'd been taken to when she'd first got to the palace.

There were also culture and protocol lessons—which she found very interesting too—not to mention a lot of scrubbing and oiling of her body—which she found less interesting—including plucking and face masks and hair wraps. The beautification process for an Ashkarazi bride, apparently.

In between all of this the Sheikh sent updates on her father's condition and then, on the third day, a note to say that the professor had been taken to the border and would be released within hours. She was to send him an email, confirming her decision to stay in Ashkaraz, as well as an announcement that she would be marrying His Majesty, Tariq ibn Ishak Al Naziri.

Typing it felt unreal, as if it was happening to someone else, and a burst of homesickness made her wish for a phone call and the sound of her father's voice to steady her. But when she asked Amirah if a phone call was possible she was advised that it was forbidden.

At first she was merely annoyed, but as the day went on, with yet more beauty treatments that included being poked and prodded and then a fitting session for a wedding gown that involved being swathed in yards of white silk, Charlotte's annoyance soon turned to anger.

Everything was new and strange, and it was going to take her a while to get used to her new position in life. All she wanted was the sound of a familiar voice. Some reassurance that she was doing the right thing. That wasn't too much to ask, was it?

She'd already asked Amirah to beg the Sheikh for special dispensation for a call, especially since she had no idea when or even if she'd see her father again, but apparently 'forbidden' really meant forbidden.

There would be no phone calls for her.

Charlotte tried very hard to force her anger away, but for some reason she couldn't ignore it. Nor was it helped by her homesickness. And by the time the afternoon rolled around her emotions had begun to bubble away inside her like a saucepan full of water boiling on a stove.

She'd been preparing for a visit to the historic and apparently very beautiful palace baths, but as her anger had risen she'd decided to find the Sheikh first and tell him exactly what she thought of his phone call ban.

Over the past few days a steady stream of clothing had arrived in the suite—not only traditional robes, but expensive designer dresses, tailored trousers and shirts, blouses, as well several pairs of jeans and T-shirts. There was also underwear, silk and lace, in various pretty colours, which she'd tried to ignore because she felt strange about it. It was even stranger to wear the clothing and find that it was all the right size and fitted her perfectly.

In amongst the items she'd unearthed a very lovely bikini that had jewels sewn all over it. She had no idea if the jewels were real—if so, then the bikini wasn't very practical for swimming in, although it wasn't practical even if they weren't real—but still, it was the only bathing suit she had, and if she wanted to go to the baths, then that was what she'd have to wear.

Amirah had laughed and told her not to be so silly. Bathing naked was the done thing, and no one would bother her once it was known that the sheikha-to-be was bathing there. But there was no way she was bathing naked in public, so she pulled on the bikini, then a gauzy silver robe over the top of it, and, belting the robe around her waist, she went in search of the Sheikh.

However, he was nowhere to be found, and people seemed reluctant to tell her where he was. After half an hour's fruitless search, even more furious than she'd been initially, Charlotte decided to visit the baths anyway and look for him later. Certainly that would give her some time to cool off, and that was a good thing when it came to asking for a favour.

Except as she approached the arched entrance to the baths she saw two black-robed guards standing on either side of the door. She knew who they were now: the sheikh's personal guards. Which, of course, meant that he was inside.

Her temper was not improved by the news, since she'd been hoping to calm down in some peace and quiet. And a part of her was very tempted to simply turn around and go back to her rooms. But running away wouldn't get her a phone call, so she steeled herself, opening her mouth to demand entrance.

Yet before she'd even managed to get a word out, the guards stood aside for her, their faces impassive.

Charlotte shut her mouth with a snap, lifted her chin, and swept on past them, entering an echoing, humid space with high arches and columns set around a huge tiled pool. The walls had the same beautiful tiles as the rest of the palace, though these were in gorgeous shades of blue, and steam wreathed the huge columns that lined the edges of the pool. Light drifted down from the ceiling through hidden windows, illuminating the baths with a diffuse light.

A man was swimming in the pool, his stroke clean and powerful, his large muscular body moving through the water with all the deadly grace of a shark.

It was him. The Sheikh.

An unexpected shiver rippled through her, and the anger sitting in the pit of her stomach twisted strangely. There was something about him she couldn't take her eyes off, and instead of calling to interrupt him she found herself standing at the edge of the pool and watching him swim instead.

But he must have noticed her anyway, because his stroke slowed and gradually he came to a stop, standing up in the water and raising a hand to push his wet black hair back from his face.

And Charlotte realised she'd made a grievous error.

She very carefully hadn't thought of that night beside the fountain, losing herself instead in the tasks he'd set her over the past couple of days. Hadn't thought about the feelings he'd evoked, the anger and the strange sense of excitement as he'd brushed that strawberry over her lips, the fierce rush of adrenaline as he'd stared at her, challenge burning in his golden eyes.

And if he had accidentally found his way into her thoughts she'd distanced herself from him, turning him into the tall, dark and intimidating Sheikh instead, swathed in his robes of state. Safely removed from her by his position.

Yet it wasn't the robed Sheikh who stood in front of her now, but a man.

A magnificent, completely beautiful man.

Water streamed down his powerful body, outlining every perfect muscle from his wide shoulders to his broad chest, to the chiselled lines of his abs. His bronzed skin was marked here and there by scars, but nothing could detract from the fact that he was a work of art. There was not an ounce of fat on him and he was muscled like a Greek god, radiating the same sense of arrogant power.

And yet although he might look very much a man in the pool right now, every soaking wet inch of him was a king.

The distance she'd put between herself and her feelings felt abruptly tenuous, fraying as the diffuse light ran over his magnificent body. Her skin prickled with an undeniable heat. Her hands itched, as if she wanted to touch him, to see if he felt as hard and as smooth and as hot as he looked, forcing her to fold her arms and tuck her hands firmly into her armpits to stop herself from reaching for him.

'Good morning, Miss Devereaux.'

His deep, dark voice echoed in the tiled space and his golden stare caught hers, a knowing look in it.

'Have you come to join me for a swim?'

The prickling heat crept up her neck, warmed her cheeks, and she was very conscious that the humid air of the pool was making the gauzy fabric of her robes stick to her skin, and that all she had on beneath it was the silly, impractical little jewelled bikini.

'No,' she said stoutly, folding her arms tighter across her chest, determined not to let him get to her. 'I'm here to discuss the fact that you won't allow me a phone call with my father before he leaves.'

'Really?'

His gaze dropped down her body in a way that made her face feel even hotter.

'And yet you seem to be wearing the bikini I had sent to you.'

Damn him for noticing.

Charlotte shifted uncomfortably, felt the tiles warm and slick beneath her feet. 'Yes, well…you're already in here and I prefer to swim by myself. Now, about that phone—'

'Do not let me stop you,' he murmured. 'I would hate for you not to enjoy the water because of me.'

Another tiny shiver swept over her at the silky note in his voice and she couldn't seem to drag her gaze from the way the light fell on his wet skin.

Heavens, what was wrong with her? This man was a stranger to her, she'd barely even spoken to him, and yet all she could think about was what he would feel like beneath her fingers.

You're attracted to him. A good thing, considering he's going to be your husband.

She felt breathless at the thought, which irritated her, because she didn't want to feel anything at all about the man who'd essentially kidnapped her and was now holding her prisoner in his country.

'I don't want to swim right now,' she said primly. 'I want to talk about this phone call.'

Something gleamed in his eyes. 'Come into the pool, *ya amar*, and we will discuss it.'

Oh, she recognised that look. She'd seen it before, that night beside the fountain, when he'd told her she was to marry him. Fierce challenge. A dare.

And, much to her annoyance, she could feel a part of herself wanting to answer that challenge, to surprise him, make him see that she wasn't just his prisoner but a force to be reckoned with.

A stupid thing to want when she didn't care what he thought of her.

She didn't want to swim. She didn't want to get anywhere near him. And she wasn't his 'most beautiful', so he could stop calling her that too.

All she wanted was to talk to her father on the phone—that was it.

'I have already told you I don't want to swim,' she said, knowing she sounded sulky and yet unable to help it. 'Why do you keep insisting?'

'Because I have been neglecting you for the past couple of days.' The water rippled around his narrow hips as he moved closer. 'And I would like to catch up with what you have been doing.'

'I've been doing everything you asked me to do.' It seemed to take immense effort to keep her gaze on his face, not to look down and follow the muscled lines of his body. 'That's all.'

'Amirah tells me you have been diligent in your reading and an apt pupil in your language and protocol lessons.'

Charlotte shrugged, trying to ignore the way the light was moving over his chest as he breathed, his skin glistening. 'I like to study.'

He moved closer still and she couldn't help herself. Her attention dropping down over him again and… Was he wearing swimming trunks?

She blinked and looked away, her face suddenly flaming. No, he was not.

He's naked. He's standing in the water, naked.

Her pulse sounded loud in her ears—so loud it was a wonder he didn't hear it himself—and her mouth was bone-dry. Amirah had told her the custom was to swim naked, but Charlotte had never expected that to apply to the Sheikh himself. That she'd find him swimming naked and completely unashamed of the fact.

Not that he had anything to be ashamed about, from the looks of things.

Don't look at him, idiot.

That was a very good plan. Because the more she looked at him, the more breathless and unsteady she felt, and she didn't like it. Not one bit. She preferred to be in control of both herself and her feelings, not at their mercy.

Perhaps she'd simply pretend he was standing in front of her fully dressed and not…not…

'Is there something wrong?'

His voice was laced through with a fine thread of amusement that scratched at her thin veneer of calm, threatening to crack it.

'No, of course not.' She steeled herself to meet his gaze again, determined not to let him see how he affected her. 'What makes you say that?'

'You are blushing very hard, Miss Devereaux.'

Oh, yes, he was very definitely amused, damn him.

'Why is that?'

Curse her pale skin. And curse him into the bargain.

Well, there was no point pretending now. Might as well give him the truth. 'Because you're naked, that's why. And, no, I'm very much *not* swimming with you. Not like that.'

'Why not?' One dark brow arched. 'Are you afraid?'

The question echoed off the tiled walls, and the deep vibration of his voice set something vibrating inside her too.

Was he making fun of her? Or was this about something more?

Oh, but she knew the answer to that. He was challenging her, pure and simple, and the part of her that wanted very much to answer that challenge was getting stronger.

Because wouldn't it be satisfying to set his arrogance back on its heels?

Using your fear, though. That's a clichéd move.

Yes, it was—which meant that the only real response was to stay cool and calm, turn around and walk out.

Yet she didn't. She stayed where she was, rooted to the spot, angry and getting angrier. At herself for her conflicting emotions and at him for making her feel this way. Because it was definitely his fault. She'd never had any trouble controlling her anger before—never had anyone get under her skin the way he was doing right now.

And the real problem was that the longer she stood there, the more she revealed—and he knew it. In fact, he was looking at her now as if he could see her every thought, knew her every feeling, knew that she was afraid and that he was the cause. And he liked it.

'I will not touch you,' he said softly. 'If that is what you are afraid of.'

Oh, yes, he could see her fear. Bloody man.

Her jaw felt tight, aching. 'I am *not* afraid.'

'Get in, then. And we will discuss your phone call.'

She didn't want to. But she couldn't stand there doing nothing any longer.

Before she could think better of it Charlotte moved to the edge of the pool.

Then dived straight in.

CHAPTER SIX

TARIQ HAD NOT expected that. He'd been baiting her, admittedly, and it was probably unfair of him, but she'd turned up during his private swimming time, her silver-blue eyes glowing with anger, wearing a gauzy piece of nothing he could see straight through and the tiny jewelled bikini he'd provided for her on a whim, and… Well, he was a man. And she was very much a woman.

If he thought about it, he'd no doubt find it a little disturbing, how affected he was by her.

But he'd decided not to think about it.

Her vulnerability was the issue, not her anger, and with her standing there arguing with him, the transparent robe clinging to her small curvaceous figure and all that silvery hair curling in the humidity of the baths, it hadn't seemed a bad thing to indulge his urge to push her, bait her just a little. Stoke her anger to see how hot it flared and whether she would burn along with it.

And indeed she had—beautifully, as it turned out.

Her response to him was all he could have hoped for, and he very much liked how uncomfortable his nakedness had made her. Because it was obvious why she was uncomfortable, and it wasn't due to her not liking his body. He knew when a woman wanted him, and his pretty little fiancée very much did, whether she was aware of it or not.

Still, he'd expected to have to drag out some more ultimatums before she finally got in the pool with him. And even then he'd thought she might slip in quietly, perhaps a little hesitantly.

He hadn't thought she'd dive right in, barely making a splash.

She came to the surface, water coursing down her body, the gauzy robe now completely transparent and sticking like a second skin to her lush curves. With her hair lying silky and wet over her shoulders, and water drops caught on her lashes, she looked like a mermaid.

His body tightened, hardening as she lifted her arms to push her hair back. Her breasts rose with the movement, and the jewels on her bikini top glittered only slightly less brightly than her sapphire eyes as she met his gaze.

She was all challenge now, no longer calm and prim, the way she had been on the edge of the pool, and he felt something in him wanting to push her even harder, to see exactly what she was made of.

Because he had a feeling it was of stronger stuff than he'd initially anticipated. She'd been shocked at the ultimatum he'd presented her with the night he'd given her dinner, but then she'd got angry, giving him a glimpse of steel, and he'd very much liked that.

'So,' she said, holding out her hands. 'As you can see, I am now in the water. Can we have a conversation about my phone call now?'

Perhaps she didn't know the effect she presented in this moment—all pale, gleaming skin, her every curve highlighted by the gems on her swimsuit. Because if she had she might have requested more from him than a mere phone call. But plainly she didn't, and that was just as well since he might have given it to her.

She was a such a pretty, pretty thing.

And in addition to her steel he'd also had a glimpse of

her passion that night beside the fountain, and he wanted to test it. Wanted to see if that passion truly did extend to him. Because her desire was going to be fairly crucial when it came to the provision of an heir; he would never force himself on an unwilling bride.

He'd held that strawberry out towards her, a challenge for her to accept, and accept it she had. He'd taken advantage, brushing the strawberry over her luscious mouth, watching her eyes grow round and then glow bright. Watching as her small white teeth had sunk into the flesh of the berry, taking a bite. When he'd withdrawn his hand he'd allowed his fingers to brush her lower lip, and it had been just as soft and silky as it had looked.

The memory of that mouth had taunted him for the past two days, no matter how many meetings and other duties he'd immersed himself in, and he couldn't seem to stop looking at it now. It was just as full as it had been that night, just as pink, and now sheened lightly with water.

Perhaps he needed to test her again, push her further. See how receptive she was so he knew what he'd be dealing with come their wedding night.

Slowly, he moved over to where she stood, then stopped in front of her. She tipped her head back to look at him, folding her arms again, but he saw the movement of her throat as she swallowed and noted the flicker of apprehension in her eyes as he came close.

He'd seen that same apprehension that night beside the fountain, but he'd put it down to shock. He had, after all, delivered an ultimatum with which she hadn't been at all happy. However, it surely wasn't shock now, so what could it be? She liked his body—that wasn't the issue—so it had to be something else. But what?

'I thought you said you were not afraid of me,' he murmured.

She blinked. Clearly she hadn't expected him to notice. 'I'm not.'

'But you are afraid?'

'N-no.'

The stutter was slight, but he caught it, narrowing his gaze and studying her more intently. 'Do not lie to me, Charlotte.'

She shifted in the water as he said her name, as if the sound of it affected her in some way.

'Well, okay. I suppose I am a little…apprehensive. But that's only because you're not wearing anything.'

'I will be your husband,' he pointed out. 'My not wearing anything is something you will have to get used to.'

Her blush deepened. The line of her shoulders was tense, and he had the odd urge to put his hands on her and stroke that tension away, ease her fear. But that would set a dangerous precedent, and not one he could afford.

And besides, he had the sense that it wasn't actually his nakedness that was the problem.

He took another experimental step towards her, watching as her eyes widened and her mouth opened slightly. And then something else flickered to life in the deep blue of her gaze.

Oh, she was bothered by him—of that he had no doubt. But it wasn't because she was afraid of him.

'So,' she said, quickly and sharply, as if she were using the words to stop him in his tracks. 'What do you want for a phone call?'

Momentarily distracted, he did stop. 'What do you mean?'

'You're very fond of ultimatums. *"Marry me or your father stays here. Get in the pool if you want to discuss a phone call."'* Her chin lifted even higher. 'So now I'm in the pool, what do you want in return for giving me that call? Because I can sense an ultimatum coming already, believe me.'

He might have found fault with the accusing note in her voice had he not already decided that she was using the phone call issue as a distraction. He also knew what she was trying to distract him from. But, unfortunately for her, it wasn't going to work. Since he'd decided on marriage se-curing the succession was going to be important, and he couldn't leave anything to chance.

Such as her being bothered by her own response to him.

'What is disturbing you, *ya amar*?' He took another step closer. 'Tell me the truth so we can discuss it.'

'The phone call—'

'It is not the phone call,' he interrupted flatly, taking yet another step, until mere inches separated them. 'You are afraid, and I do not think it is me you are afraid of, but yourself.'

She hadn't moved, yet her tension was obvious as her head tipped back so she could look up at him. The colour of her eyes had darkened and her mouth was slightly open, the pulse at the base of her throat racing.

'I…' she said hoarsely. 'I don't know what you're talk-ing about.'

'I think you do.' He reached out and slid a careful hand behind her head, pushing his fingers through her wet hair and cradling the back of her skull in his palm.

She stiffened, and he could feel the tension in her neck, see it in the awkward way she was trying to hold herself away from him.

'Your Majesty…'

'"Your Majesty" is unnecessary. You may call me Tariq.'

Her throat moved as she swallowed, her gaze pinned to his. 'I'm happy with Your Majesty.'

Stubborn girl.

'You cannot call your husband *Your Majesty*,' he said, amused. 'Say my name, Charlotte.'

He stroked his thumb over the tight muscles at her nape, watching as her eyes darkened even further, her pupils dilating into black. Oh, yes, she was certainly responsive to him, and it was exactly the kind of response he'd been hoping for.

'T-Tariq.'

His name was soft and smoky sounding, the slight stutter of it somehow erotic.

Ah, perfect.

He could feel himself harden, his own pulse beginning to ramp up. The slow melt of her resistance was unexpectedly seductive. Going slowly and carefully had never appealed to him much before, but he could certainly see the allure now.

'That's better.' He drew her close, so they were almost touching, continuing to stroke the back of her neck, soothing her. 'You know, do you not, that wanting one's husband is perfectly acceptable?'

She was breathing very fast, her gaze dropping to his mouth and staying there. 'I... I don't want you.'

He nearly smiled at the obviousness of the lie. 'Of course you do not. That is why you have not told me to stop.'

Charlotte drew in another shaky little breath, yet her gaze didn't move from his mouth and her head lay heavy in the palm of his hand, the tension bleeding out of her muscles completely.

'I should.'

'Why?' He searched her flushed face. 'Physical desire is nothing to be afraid of.'

She gave him a brief, fleeting look before she looked away again. 'I wouldn't know. I've...never felt it before.'

So... All of this was new to her. Perhaps she was even a virgin...

A deep possessiveness he hadn't known was inside him stirred, along with a satisfaction that would have disturbed him if he'd thought about it in any depth.

But he didn't want to think about it in any depth, so he didn't.

'You feel it now.' He didn't make it a question.

Her lashes fell, her gaze once more going to his mouth, as if she couldn't help herself. She didn't speak. But then she didn't need to. He knew the answer already.

Of course she felt it.

'Say it again,' he murmured. 'My name.'

'Tariq…'

The word had barely left her lips before he'd bent and covered them with his in a feather-light kiss. A mere brush across her mouth. To taste her and tempt her. To test their undeniable physical chemistry.

She went very still, her body trembling.

He'd intended to end the kiss almost as soon as it had started, thinking that would be sufficient, and yet he found he couldn't pull away, that something inside him was catching fire.

He touched his tongue to her bottom lip instead, tracing the line of it the way he'd traced it with that strawberry, and she trembled even harder. Then her lips were softening, opening for him, and he couldn't stop himself from deepening the kiss, allowing his tongue to sweep in and taste her.

Oh, so sweet… Like that strawberry. Like honey. Like the late-summer wine that came from the vineyards in the valley to the south.

He spread his hand out on the back of her head, his fingers pushing into her hair, holding her still as he kissed her more deeply, chasing that sweetness.

She gave a little throaty moan. The sound made all the blood in his body rush to a certain part of his anatomy, and all of a sudden the kiss turned hot—far hotter than he'd intended.

This was supposed to be a test. For her, not for him. And yet he found that he was the one on the edge of control.

He wanted her robe gone. Her bikini gone. He wanted her naked and up against the wall of the pool. He wanted to be inside her.

Her hands touched his chest, her fingers pure electricity on his skin.

If you do not stop now, that is exactly what will happen.

And it must not. He knew what happened when he didn't control himself...when he let passion get the better of him. Distance—that was what his father had taught him. Distance and detachment. And that was not what was happening now.

It took every ounce of will he had, but he managed it, tearing his mouth from hers and letting her go.

She was staring at him in shock, her mouth full and red from the kiss, her eyes round as saucers and dark as midnight.

'I will arrange your phone call,' he said brusquely.

Then he turned around and left the pool before she could say a word.

'I don't like it, Charlotte.'

Her father's voice sounded cracked and tinny down the phone.

'I don't like it at all.'

Charlotte gripped the phone Tariq had handed to her hard and tried to ignore her future husband, standing on the other side of the desk, his face impassive.

He'd been as good as his word in arranging the call, though he'd offered no explanation for his sudden change of heart. She thought it might have something to do with what had happened between them in the baths the day before, but she wasn't sure.

She was trying *very* hard not to think about that herself. Though it was difficult when he'd insisted on remaining in the room while she spoke to her father, watching her with his intent golden stare.

'It's okay, Dad,' she said, trying to be reassuring. 'Like I was saying, we met and…f-fell in love, and he asked me to marry him. And I said yes.'

'But it's only been three days,' her father pointed out, sounding cross.

'Isn't that how long it took you to decide to marry Mum?'

Her parents had had a mad, passionate, whirlwind romance—at least that was what her father had said, always bitterly—followed by a quick wedding. And then, years later, an acrimonious divorce.

With her in the middle.

She was suddenly even more conscious of Tariq, just on the other side of the desk, staring at her intensely. His presence was intimidating, pressing in on her, making her skin prickle with heat at the memory of his mouth on hers, the feeling of his hand cradling the back of her head, his body tall and powerful and so achingly close.

Speaking of mad and passionate…

That had been her yesterday, at the baths. Her heartbeat had been frantic, her skin too tight and too hot. She'd been overwhelmed by him, by the taste of him—something indescribable that reminded her of dense, rich, hot chocolate. Sweet and decadent and dark.

She should have stopped him, but when he'd touched her she hadn't even been able to remember why it was wrong to want him anyway. He'd told her that physical desire wasn't anything to be afraid of and in that moment, with the way he'd held her and the gentleness with which he'd explored her, fear had been the last thing she'd felt. All she'd been conscious of was her hunger. For him.

Her pulse was beating hard now, almost drowning out her father's voice.

'Yes, that's true,' he was saying. 'But look what happened there. That woman ruined my life and nearly destroyed my career, while she got to swan off with her divorce settlement, footloose and fancy-free.'

Meaning without the millstone of her daughter hanging around her neck, presumably, though Charlotte didn't ask him that. She knew his thoughts on the matter. If she hadn't got so afraid and run off during one of their more bitter arguments, staying out the whole night while her parents called the police, trying to find her, her mother might have continued to fight the custody battle and would probably have won.

But her mother hadn't continued to fight. She'd deemed Charlotte too much of a problem and left her with her father.

'Well,' her father went on crossly, not waiting for her to speak, 'I suppose if that's what you want to do, then that's what you want to do. But now I'll have to find myself a new bloody assistant.'

So he might never see his daughter again and all he could think about was hiring a new assistant?

Did you expect it to be different? For him to care?

No—and that was the sad thing. She didn't. He'd never made a secret of how unhappy he'd been when he was granted full custody of her, how she'd limited him in terms of his career, and how if she hadn't gone running off that night things would have been different.

The fact that she'd tried very hard *not* to be an impediment to his career as a kid, and then as an adult—had actively tried to help him with it, in fact—didn't seem to register.

'Sorry, Dad,' she said, not knowing what else to say. The pressure of Tariq's gaze was like a weight, pressing down on her.

'Can't be helped, I suppose,' her father muttered. 'Look, I'd better go. These soldiers look like they're ready to get rid of me. Speak soon.'

The call disconnected.

He doesn't care and you know it.

Her eyes prickled, which made her angry. Because, yes, she did know it. She always had. The professor resented her, so why she kept trying to change his mind about her she had no idea.

He's all you have—that's why.

But that didn't bear thinking about—especially not with Tariq still staring at her so intently. She didn't want him knowing how little she was valued by the only important person in her life, and she especially didn't want him seeing her tears.

So she swallowed down the lump in her throat, blinked the moisture from her eyes and handed him back the phone. 'Thank you,' she said, pleased that her voice at least sounded level. 'I don't think there will be any repercussions for you.'

He took the phone and slid it back into his pocket, but his gaze didn't leave her face. 'What did he say to you?'

So he'd picked up on her upset. Wonderful.

'I don't think that's any of your business.'

'You will be my wife soon,' he said flatly. 'Everything you do is my business.'

There was a stillness to him, an intensity that unnerved her. Though that wasn't the only unnerving thing about him. In suit trousers and a black business shirt open at the neck, displaying bronze skin and the beat of a strong pulse, he had a charisma that was undeniable.

She found herself staring at that pulse and thinking about what it would be like if she brushed her mouth over it. What his skin would taste like. What he would do if she did that…

'Charlotte,' he said softly. 'Up here.'

She jerked her gaze up to his, her cheeks hot with embarrassment. Because of course he'd know exactly what she was thinking—like he had in the baths yesterday. She'd tried to hide it, tried to distract him with her request for a phone call, but he hadn't been deflected. He'd been relentless, getting the truth out of her whether she wanted to give it to him or not.

You liked giving it to him.

The taste of him was suddenly in her mouth, the memory of his lips on hers scorching.

'He said nothing,' she murmured thickly, trying to shove the memories from her head. 'Just that he'd have to get a new assistant.'

The gold of Tariq's eyes was molten, the heat in them like the desert sun. As if he was angry. But she couldn't imagine why he would be.

'That is all?'

'Yes.'

'It upset you?'

'Of course it upset me.' She tried to keep her voice level. 'He's my father and now I'll never see him again.'

Tariq's gaze narrowed. 'I do not think that is why you are upset.'

But she didn't want to have this particular conversation. She felt too raw, too uncertain. There was the pain of her father's dismissal and her own anger, as well as the press of that unfamiliar hunger every time she looked at the Sheikh, standing behind his desk. The memory of his kiss still burned in her mind and she didn't want it there.

She looked away. 'Perhaps we could talk about this at a different time? I have to—'

She didn't hear him move, but he must have done because suddenly one large hand was cupping her cheek, his thumb brushing over her skin. 'You hoped for more from him?'

Her heart was beating loudly in her ears again and his body was inches away. His palm against her skin was hot, and part of her wanted to jerk away while another part wanted to lean into his touch. It had been such a long time since anyone had touched her quite like this. A long time since anyone had been interested in her feelings.

'Yes, I did,' she said, not sure why she was telling him this when she'd been so determined not to. 'I hoped he might be upset that he wouldn't see me again rather than because he'd have to get a new assistant.'

His thumb brushed her cheek again and she didn't want to look at him. Because he was too close and that raw feeling in her chest wouldn't go away. Those golden eyes of his would see her vulnerability all too easily, and he'd know how badly her father's easy dismissal had hurt.

And then he'll want to know why.

Yes, he would. And she didn't want to tell him.

'He knows that he will not see you again?' Tariq asked.

'I told him.' She swallowed, gathering herself, then pulled away from his touch and forced a smile on her face. 'He's absent-minded a lot of the time, so I'm not sure he listened. Anyway, that's that, I suppose. What made you change your mind about giving me the call?'

Tariq's hand dropped and he remained where he was, making no move towards her. But he continued to study her, his gaze unsettling in its intensity. 'Maybe it was your kiss,' he murmured.

And any relief she felt that he'd dropped the subject of

her father vanished as heat filled her at the reminder of what had happened the day before. She was conscious once again of the throb of hunger down low inside her.

The space between them suddenly felt electric, crackling with a strange static charge that had her breath catching.

'If you are thinking that our marriage will be in name only, you are wrong, Charlotte,' he went on, his voice even lower and deeper. 'You do understand that, do you not?'

Don't pretend you don't know what he's talking about.

Her mouth was dry and she couldn't seem to find any air. Because of course she knew what he was talking about—and it was something she'd conveniently not been thinking about. At least not until he'd kissed her.

He meant sex.

And he meant that he intended to have sex with her.

Heat swept through her, burning everything in its path, and she had to turn away so he wouldn't see the way her face flamed.

'Of course I understand,' she said automatically. 'Goodness, look at the time. I have to—'

'I would not want there to be any misunderstanding.' There was no mistaking the intent in his words, or the dark hint of sensuality that threaded through his tone. 'We have a certain…chemistry, *ya amar*. And I fully intend to explore that as thoroughly as possible.'

A certain chemistry…

He wants you.

The thought blazed in her brain for a second, bright as neon. She hadn't thought about how she might affect him— mainly because she'd been too busy thinking about how he affected her. But he'd kissed her for a long time yesterday, and the kiss had soon turned hotter, deeper. He'd become demanding, and his grip on her had tightened, his body responding. And then he'd let her go abruptly, with something blazing in his eyes that had looked like anger.

She hadn't thought about why he might have been angry—hadn't thought at all about why he'd let her go either. She'd tried to put it out of her mind entirely.

But maybe she should think about it. Maybe she had was some power she'd never expected to find.

'I see,' she said slowly, turning over the discovery in her head.

'Do you? Look at me, Charlotte.'

There was no resisting the command and she didn't, turning back to him, her gaze clashing with his. And for a moment she was back in the desert, with the sun a hammer-blow of heat, crushing her with its force.

'Tell me you understand,' he said.

She met the ferocity in his eyes, for some reason feeling less vulnerable than she had a moment ago. The knowledge that she wasn't without power here was giving her a courage she hadn't expected to feel.

'I understand.'

He stared back at her for a long, uncounted moment. Then he turned around and went back to the desk.

'I suggest you do some research on the marriage customs of Ashkaraz,' he said, sitting down. 'Amirah will show you which books to read in the library. Some of them you should find quite interesting.'

His attention was on his computer screen now, which obviously meant that she was dismissed.

But that was good.

She had a lot to think about.

CHAPTER SEVEN

TARIQ HAD NEVER been one for weddings, and he hadn't been particularly interested in the preparations for his own. Not when it was the wedding night he couldn't stop thinking about. To a disturbing degree.

Then again, focusing on physical pleasure had been better than going over his behaviour in his office the day she'd spoken to her father, and how he'd given in to the disturbing urge to comfort her.

He still didn't understand why he had, or why the need to do so had hit him so strongly. All he'd seen in her blue eyes was a flash of pain. And then she wouldn't tell him what the problem was, so he'd gone around the desk, reaching for her and cupping her cheek before he'd been able to think better of it.

A mistake.

He couldn't afford slips like that and he knew it.

So for the past week he'd distanced himself from her, busying himself with his duties as well as with preparations for the wedding. And there had been a lot to prepare, since he wanted the whole business over and done with as quickly as possible.

As per royal custom, the ceremony itself was being held on the palace steps, in full view of his people.

Charlotte was robed in gauzy white silk, embroidered all over with silver and belted at the waist with a silver sash that had long sparkling tassels falling almost to her ankles. Her hair was loose, as was also the custom, and gleaming in the sun, and she wore a simple platinum circlet around her brow, with one of Ashkaraz's rare blue diamonds in the centre.

Her face was very pale as she appeared, and it went even paler as she saw the assembled crowds. But she didn't hesitate as she was led to where he stood, alongside the officiant who would conduct the ceremony.

His people hadn't been given much time to come to terms with their Sheikh marrying a foreigner, but as soon as Charlotte appeared they gave her a hearty cheer. Apparently they were as susceptible to a white wedding gown as he was.

And he was.

He couldn't take his eyes off her as she joined him on the steps, all silvery and white and bright as the moon. Beautiful, too, and delicate. He hadn't thought that would affect him, but it did.

And as she recited the complicated vows without a single hesitation he was conscious of that dark satisfaction sweeping through him again—the same feeling he'd had in the baths that day. A feeling he'd not experienced about a person before. Not when his life had been all about feeling nothing for individual people at all.

It was the whole that was important—at least that was what his father had taught him. His country and his people were what he ought to have uppermost in his mind. He did not need to concern himself with specifics.

Yet he was aware, as her vows were being said, that he was feeling something very specific now—and that feeling was centred entirely on a person.

Mine, the feeling told him. *She is mine.*

He hadn't had anything that was his before—not one

single thing. All of it had been for 'the Sheikh' rather than the man. All except Catherine. And even she had been his father's first. Never his.

But Charlotte was. Charlotte was his completely.

He felt almost savage as the vows were completed and their hands were joined. Her delicate fingers were cool in his, and he was already thankful for the traditions of Ashkarazi royal marriage that required the bride and groom to retire immediately after the wedding to an oasis in the south, sacred to the royal family, for three days, to ensure the getting of an heir.

It should have been disturbing to feel this intensely about a woman, but it had been some time since he'd taken his pleasure, so it was no wonder that was all he could think about.

After the vows and rings were exchanged, and the people had cheered their new sheikha, Tariq wasted no time in taking Charlotte's elbow and whisking her from the palace to the helipad, where his helicopter stood ready to take them to the oasis.

She gave him a startled look as his guards fell into step around them and he urged her along the path to the helipad. 'Where are we going? Isn't there a reception or a party? I read that—'

'You read, presumably, about what happens directly after a royal wedding here?'

She flushed, the colour standing out beautifully on her pale skin. 'Oh, the sacred oasis. Of course.'

The shy way she said it only made the savage feeling inside him grow more intense, and it was a good thing that there was no more opportunity for talk as they came to the helicopter.

He helped her into it, bundling the long white skirts of her wedding robes around her, and a few minutes later they were in the air, soaring high over the city of Kharan and then following the long valley down to where the oasis was situated.

It was about an hour from the palace, in isolated, rocky desert, and surrounding the bright green and blue jewel of the oasis were palm trees and grasses.

The chopper took them down, and when it had landed Tariq helped Charlotte out. Palace staff had spent the last day or so setting up the tents that contained all the facilities both of them would need for three days alone, and a couple were still there to help unload their luggage from the helicopter.

Charlotte was silent as Tariq led her over to a low divan set under some shady palms, then went back to help with the unloading of the helicopter. He didn't have to do it, but he couldn't sit still waiting for everyone to leave. He wanted them gone, and quickly.

Another couple of minutes later and the chopper was rising into the air and heading back up the valley to Kharan, leaving Tariq finally alone with his bride.

She'd remained sitting on the divan under the palms in a pool of white and silver silk, her hands clasped in her lap, her silvery hair loose down her back. A smile curved her mouth as he stalked over to her, though he could see it was forced.

'So,' she said breathlessly, 'I guess this is where we are. In the oasis.'

He stopped in front of her, studying her face. A fine sheen of sweat gleamed on her brow, because it was only late afternoon and still suffocatingly hot, despite their proximity to the water. It wouldn't cool down till well after dark.

But he didn't think it was entirely the heat that was making her sweat.

She was nervous.

His own need was beating inside him like a drum, and the urge to pick her up and take her to the bedroom tent was almost overpowering.

Why the impatience? You have plenty of time.

That was true. They did have three days, after all. And maybe it would even do him good to practise some restraint—especially after the incident in the baths when he'd almost forgotten himself. He was supposed to remain detached, after all.

Yet he didn't feel detached now. He wanted her skin damp and slippery from something other than the heat and her silver-blue eyes full of fire. He wanted more of the kisses he'd taken from her, and the taste of her latent passion on his tongue. He wanted to rouse it, stoke it. Make it burn for him and only for him.

And why not? She was his wife now. And he'd told her that their marriage would not be in name only. She had always known what would be expected.

But it was not her choice to marry you—remember that. You railroaded her into it.

He didn't know why he was thinking about that now. Not when his body was hardening, desire and possessiveness coursing through him. And it wouldn't change the fact that although she might not have had a choice about the marriage, she still wanted him. He hadn't forgotten the throaty moan she'd made when he'd kissed her in the baths, or how her mouth had opened beneath his, wanting more.

Her attention was on him, she was watching him, and she must know what he was thinking because he could see that familiar flicker of apprehension in her eyes. But the heat he remembered from the baths was burning there too.

Oh, yes, she wanted him. But she was afraid of it.

'Do not look so frightened, *ya amar*,' he said, a rough

edge creeping into his voice. 'I have already told you that I will not hurt you.'

'I'm not frightened.' Her hands twisted in her lap, her gaze darting around, looking everywhere but at him. 'Could we perhaps go for a swim first? I'm rather hot.'

His patience thinned, irritation coiling with the desire twisting inside him. 'You are lying, Charlotte. And I have told you already that will not work. Not with me. And definitely not now we are about to consummate our marriage.'

Her lashes fell. 'I'm not lying.'

'Then why are your hands twisting in your lap? And why will you not look directly at me?'

She was already flushed with heat and now her cheeks went even pinker. With a deliberate movement, she unclenched her hands, laying them flat on the white silk of her skirts. Then her lashes rose and she looked at him.

'There. Is that better?'

'No,' he said impatiently. 'Do not play with me.'

'I'm not playing with you,' she shot back, and there was the slight edge of temper rising in her voice. 'I'm only trying to—'

'And do not try to placate me either.'

He didn't want to stand there arguing with her. He wanted to take her to bed. But her nervousness and vulnerability were making his chest tight and he didn't like it.

Detachment—that was what he had to strive for. Detachment and isolation. Not being concerned with another person's feelings.

'I'm *not* trying to placate you.' Charlotte pushed herself to her feet, her cheeks red, her blue eyes full of anger. 'I'm nervous, if you must know. I told you the truth in the baths when I said I hadn't felt anything physically for a man before. I haven't. But I feel something for you and I... I don't know what do.' She stopped, took a breath, and glanced away. 'I'm a virgin. And I… I don't want to disappoint you.'

He went very still.

She is yours completely.

He'd suspected she was innocent already, and yet the possessiveness that deepened and broadened in response to her confession was almost shocking.

Yes, she was his. Completely. And why she would think he might find that disappointing was anyone's guess.

'You should have told me,' he growled. 'That is something I need to know. And as for disappointing me…' He stared hard into her flushed face. 'Why would you think that?'

Her jaw tightened, her discomfort obvious, but she didn't look away this time. 'You didn't choose me because you wanted me, Tariq. You chose me because I was convenient.'

'But you must know that I want you. Surely that kiss in the baths told you that?'

'That doesn't change the fact that you wouldn't have married me if I hadn't accidentally wandered into your kingdom.'

'No, I would not.' He couldn't lie; it was the truth. 'But what does that have to do with anything? Do you want me to feel something for you? Is that what you are asking?'

Emotions flickered over her face, but they were gone so fast he couldn't tell what they were.

Then her gaze dropped again, her shoulders drooping. 'No,' she said. 'That's not what I'm asking. Forget I said anything.'

It was not what he'd planned. And it wasn't what he wanted. That tightness in his chest was back, and he didn't know why the sight of her looking so defeated affected him the way it did. It reminded him of the expression on her face that day in his office, during her father's phone call, the bright flash of hurt.

Which shouldn't matter to him. Her self-doubt had nothing to do with him. And yet he couldn't let it go.

He reached out, took her chin in his hand and tilted her head up so her gaze met his. 'Do not change the subject. Answer me, Charlotte. Why do you think you would be a disappointment?'

'You...are stuck with me.' There was a catch in her voice. 'And let's just say that hasn't worked out well for me before.'

Her skin was so soft, so silky. He rubbed his thumb gently along her lower lip, unable to stop himself from touching her, the need inside him becoming even fiercer.

But this was too important to interrupt. 'Tell me,' he ordered quietly.

She let out a soft breath, her lashes falling again, the sunlight turning them to pure silver. 'My parents had a very bitter divorce. My mother decided not to contest custody so Dad ended up with me. He was not...happy about it. Said it would affect his career.'

Tariq frowned, staring down at her lovely face, conscious of yet another unwanted emotion threading through him: anger. On her behalf. Because what kind of father would say that to his child? What kind of father would make sure his child knew she wasn't wanted?

His own father had been strict, and Tariq had been so angry with him—yet Ishak had done what he had because he'd wanted Tariq to be the best king possible. Of course Tariq had ended up disappointing him in the end, but that hadn't been his father's fault. And he was making good now.

And so was she. Sacrificing her freedom in return for her father's. Making the best of marrying a complete stranger.

Throwing herself into all the tasks he'd set her, learning his language and his customs without complaint.

She is trying. Like you are trying.

The need inside him twisted, deepened, ached. Became something more.

'Well, you are not a disappointment to me,' he said before he could stop himself. 'You are the opposite. You are beautiful and loyal and you have done what you could in a situation you did not choose and did not want. You are everything I want in a wife.'

There was something fearfully hopeful in her gaze as it searched his, as if she couldn't quite bring herself to believe him yet wanted to.

'But I'm not experienced. I don't know—'

Tariq put his thumb gently over her mouth, stopping the words. 'I do not need you to be experienced. I have enough experience for both of us. Now...' He paused, letting her see what burned inside him: the desire for her. 'I am tired of waiting, Charlotte. And I do not want to talk. What I want is to take you to bed.'

Her lips were soft and full beneath his thumb, the blue of her eyes darkening. There was already a sheen of perspiration on her skin and wisps of hair were sticking to her forehead—not a good thing when what he was planning to do to her would make her even hotter.

He frowned. 'Perhaps you do need cooling down first, though.'

'Oh, but I'm not—'

Decision made, he didn't wait for her to finish, dropping his hand and giving in to the need to get close to her by gathering her small, curvy figure in his arms.

She gave a soft gasp, but didn't protest, tipping her head back against his shoulder as his grip tightened, her eyes very blue in her flushed face.

'I thought you were tired of waiting?'

'Who says I will wait?' He began to stride through the palms, anticipation coiling inside him. 'A swim can involve all kinds of things.'

She blinked, obviously thinking about this. 'Oh. So you might…um…?'

'Consummate our marriage in the water?' he finished. 'I might.'

Judging by how hard he was right now, it might even be inevitable.

He didn't want to pause to undress her, so he walked straight into the oasis, wading out into the middle, still carrying her. The water was deliciously cool against his own hot skin, making his wedding robes stick to him, and as it flooded over her she gave a little gasp, wriggling against him.

'But I'm still dressed!'

'I realise that.' He moved deeper, until the water was at his chest and she was clutching at him, white silk floating all around her, her breathing fast at the shock of the water.

'But what about a swimsuit?'

'You do not need a swimsuit.'

Her weight in his arms was slight, her body warm, her hands gripping his robes tightly.

He glanced down at her, noting how her flush had receded. 'You are feeling cooler now?'

'Yes, much better, thank you.'

A crease appeared between her fair brows as she met his gaze. The water was lapping at her hair, making it float around her like fine silver thread.

'You're really quite kind, aren't you?'

He wasn't sure what went through him in that moment. It was a wave of something he wasn't familiar with. Almost as if he…liked what she'd said. Which was strange.

Because he wasn't kind, and nor did he want to be. Kindness reminded him of mercy, of sympathy, of the soft feelings he associated with Catherine. Of his weakness when it came to his own emotions. Anger. Desire. Need.

But he wasn't going to think about those things.

Instead, he shoved away the warmth that threatened, concentrated instead on the desire burning like fire in his blood.

'No,' he said, adjusting his hold on her to reach for the silver belt at her waist. 'Kind is one thing I am not.'

And then he pulled hard, systematically beginning to strip her robes from her body.

CHAPTER EIGHT

TARIQ'S FINGERS ON her were firm as he stripped away her heavy, water-soaked robes, but it was the look on his face that made her breath catch.

His jaw was tight, tension radiated from him, and his features looked as if they'd been carved from granite. The only thing that wasn't hard and cold was his gaze, and a kind of molten intensity was burning in his eyes.

Burning in her too.

What had she said? That he was kind? He'd been kind to her that day she'd spoken to her father, and he'd been kind to her just before, underneath the palm trees, as nervousness and the strangeness of the whole day had got to her. As she'd been overwhelmed by the fact that she was now married to a king and that he was going to take her virginity, probably right where she stood.

He'd looked so stern, so forbidding as the helicopter had left. And the courage that had carried her through the wedding ceremony in front of seemingly the entire city had deserted her.

She'd tried to pretend she was fine, but suddenly, under his intimidating stare, all she'd felt was doubt. In herself, and in what was going to happen, and in the intensity of her own desire too.

It had only occurred to her then that, as much as she hadn't had a choice in their marriage, perhaps neither had he. He needed an heir, and he hadn't been able to choose a wife from his own people because he had an entire country he had to protect. And she'd been convenient.

Really, when she thought about it, it seemed he'd been stuck with her the same way her father had been stuck with her.

It shouldn't matter, but somehow it did. She didn't want him to be stuck with someone he was only going to be disappointed in—and she *would* end up disappointing him. She wasn't one of his people and she didn't speak his language. She didn't know his customs or what was expected of her.

She was a virgin with no experience whatsoever.

How could that not be disappointing to a man like him?

And yet he'd cupped her cheek in his hand, his gaze fierce with conviction. And he'd told her that she was beautiful. That she was loyal. That she was everything he'd hoped for.

He *was* kind, no matter what he said, and she didn't know why that made him so angry.

Maybe you should ask him?

She probably should—except now was not the right time, given the way he was looking at her, as if he wanted to eat her alive.

A shiver coursed through her and it had nothing to do with the water lapping around her. Even forbidding and hard, the impact of him was like a gut-punch. She'd felt it the moment she'd met him on the steps of the palace, just before the ceremony. He'd been dressed in white, as had she, but his robes had been embroidered with gold. The white had set off his inky black hair and his bronze skin, and the gold thread had struck sparks from the deep gold of his eyes as he'd looked at her.

And for a second she hadn't been able to breathe. Because he had been so...overwhelming. Beautiful, and strong, and powerful. So achingly charismatic. He had drawn every eye, commanded all the attention.

She found it difficult to breathe now, as he stripped the long-sleeved over-robe off her, let the water move silkily over her bare arms, then began to pull at the ties of the long sleeveless tunic she wore.

'What's wrong with being kind?' she asked, not knowing she was going to say it until it was out and then, given how his features hardened still further, regretting it.

'There is nothing wrong with being kind.'

He pulled off the tunic, then tugged down the long, loose trousers that she wore underneath.

'But you're angry.'

She stared up into his face, trying to figure out why a simple compliment should bother him quite so much, but his expression remained impassive. Again, except for his eyes. They burned brilliant gold.

'Now is not the time for conversation, *ya amar.*'

His voice was rough and full of authority, and she couldn't help shivering as his hands stroked up her bare legs, his palms hot against her skin in stark contrast to the cool water.

'I know, but—'

She stopped abruptly as his hand slid around her, deftly undoing the clasp of her white lace bra and stripping it from her. The water licked over her skin, making her nipples harden, and everything she'd been going to say vanished from her brain.

'But what?' His gaze dropped to her bare breasts, his eyes glittering, heat flaring higher in them.

And she couldn't think.

Couldn't even form one rational thought.

Because he was tugging down the scrap of white lace

that was her knickers, and then they were gone too, and there was nothing at all between her and his merciless golden stare.

She was naked now. Naked in front of her husband.

He adjusted his hold on her again so she was lying back in his arms, her body stretched out, completely bare to his gaze. And she trembled slightly, waiting for the urge to run and hide, to cringe away.

But it didn't come. Instead she wanted to stretch out under his hot stare, to watch the flames in his eyes burn higher. Wanted to see how she affected him. Because she did, and it was obvious. The beautiful lines of his face were sharpening with hunger.

How strange... Though she was in the water, and completely naked, she felt more powerful than she had standing before him fully dressed. Like that day in his office, when she'd got an inkling of how much she affected him. Though that had only been a ghost of what she felt now.

Now her power was fully realised.

Brave in a way she hadn't been before, she lifted her hand and touched one carved cheekbone, running her fingers along his smooth, warm skin.

Something ignited in his eyes and he made a growling sound deep in his throat. Then abruptly he turned, carrying her out of the water and towards the little cluster of tents pitched in the shadow of the trees.

He ducked inside the biggest one, and Charlotte had an impression of a floor covered in silken rugs, with low couches and cushions set up in one corner, before Tariq threw her, still dripping wet, onto a huge bed with a carved wooden base. It was made up with fresh white cotton sheets and piled high with pillows, and it was incredibly comfortable. Not that she was particularly concerned with comfort right now.

He didn't follow her right away, his hands going to his own soaking wet wedding robes and stripping them off carelessly, leaving them in a heap on the floor. She found herself watching him, unable to look away.

She knew what he looked like naked because of the baths, and he was every bit as magnificent as she remembered. Yet this time, as he shoved down the loose trousers he'd been wearing, and with them his underwear, she was able to see what the water of the baths had been concealing.

Heat leapt inside her. Her face was burning…everything was burning.

He made no attempt to hide the long, hard length that curved up between his thighs, stepping naked and arrogant from his wet clothes. She couldn't stop looking at him.

He'd told her that it wasn't wrong to want him, that physical passion wasn't anything to be afraid of, but she couldn't help the apprehension that coiled inside her now. And it wasn't because she was afraid of him. She was afraid of herself, and of the hunger inside her getting deeper. Stronger.

After her parents' divorce intensity had always scared her, so this was frightening. She wanted him so much. Part of her wished he'd push her back on the bed and take her the way she imagined kings took their brides. Hard and fast, with no mercy. Then she would have no choice but to give everything to him. No choice but to surrender to that hunger and not think about how to ignore it or force it away.

Not think about where that hunger might lead.

Except Tariq didn't make a move towards her. He stood there, staring at her, his demanding gaze hot on hers.

'Come to me,' he commanded.

Heat pulsed down her spine before spiralling into a tight knot down low between her thighs. She found herself obeying almost helplessly, pushing herself off the bed and walking the few steps that separated them. Her pulse was hammering in her ears as she came close, deafening her, and her mouth was bone-dry. She felt dizzy, but she didn't think it was the heat of the sun this time.

No, it was him.

Her husband.

He was so tall, towering over her, a wall of heat, hard muscle and bronzed skin. And the expression on his face was ferocious.

'You want me,' he said.

It wasn't a question, but she answered all the same. 'Yes…' Her voice sounded hoarse and thick, the word unsteady.

'Say it,' he ordered, relentless.

Her heartbeat was racing, the strength of her own need building like a storm. He was going to demand an acknowledgement from her, that was obvious, which meant the time for pretending was over and she knew it. It would be pointless anyway—especially when he saw straight through her.

'I…want you,' she whispered.

His eyes gleamed, and his obvious pleasure made something hot glow inside her chest.

'Then go down on your knees, *ya amar*, and show me how much.'

Tariq knew he was indulging himself. That he didn't have to make his virgin wife go on her knees before him. But what she'd said to him out in the oasis had stuck in his head.

'Kind', she'd called him.

And so he'd stripped her bare, trying to prove—to her, to himself—that he was nothing of the sort. Yet even then, naked and wet in his arms, she'd looked up at him as if she knew something about him that he didn't, lifting her hand to touch his cheek.

And perhaps she did know something he didn't. Because

the second her cool fingers had touched him something had opened up inside him—a hunger he hadn't realised he felt. A hunger that had nothing to do with sexual desire. And he had known all at once that she was more dangerous than he could possibly have imagined.

No one had touched him like that since his mother had died. Not without any sexual intent, not casually or just because they'd wanted to. Not even the succession of nannies who'd brought him up had done so. They'd been given strict orders not to touch him or to comfort him—no reassurance or support had been allowed. Because he'd had to learn self-sufficiency, to find consolation in detachment and isolation, since that would be his life as king.

It had been a very hard lesson, but he'd learned it in the end. And it had taken Catherine to finally hammer it home. Since then he hadn't missed it—hadn't wanted the comfort of another person's touch. He'd had lovers to meet his physical needs and that was all he'd required.

Until Charlotte. Until her cool fingers had touched his cheek. Her touch delicate, tentative. Gentle.

He'd guarded himself against *her* vulnerability; he had just never dreamed she would discover something vulnerable in *him*.

What was clear was that he couldn't let that happen. He couldn't let her take that power from him. Which meant he had to show her where the power truly lay: with him.

She'd already given him the acknowledgement that she wanted him, and it clearly wasn't a stretch for her to obey him as she dropped to her knees on the soft rugs of the tent floor.

She was breathing very fast, the sound of it was audible in the tent, so he reached down and grasped her chin, tilting her head back so he could see her face, look into her eyes. They were very dark, the silver blue of a daytime sky turning to midnight. It was immensely satisfying to see how badly she wanted him.

'Open your mouth.' He pressed his thumb to the centre of her bottom lip for emphasis. 'Take me inside.'

'I… I haven't done this before.' Her cheeks were pink and she sounded breathless, a little uncertain. 'I'm not sure what to do.'

'That is why I will instruct you.' He stroked the softness of her lips, admiring her courage, because this time he couldn't see any apprehension in her at all. 'Do as you are told.'

She took a little breath, then opened her mouth obediently.

Ah, she made such a pretty picture, kneeling before him, naked and wet, her nipples pink and hard, her thighs spread, giving him a tantalising glimpse of the nest of blonde curls between them.

He was aching as he took himself in hand, guiding himself to her mouth. He gritted his teeth as she leaned forward, touching him with her tongue, tentative and hesitant. And then heat wrapped around him, slick warmth, as she took him into her mouth, and his heartbeat was as loud as a drum in his head, pleasure licking like a velvet whip up his spine.

He growled, unable to help himself, shoving his fingers in her hair and holding her, guiding her, as she began to suck him. She was inexpert and uncertain, but there was an eroticism to her inexperience that made pleasure burn like hot coals inside him. And knowing that he was the first man she'd ever done this to made it even more intense.

The first man. The *only* man.

His lips pulled back in a snarl as the thought hit him, and as her tongue curled around him it came to him all of a sudden that perhaps he'd made a mistake. Perhaps what had been intended to put her at a distance had only served to

draw her closer. Because she had the power to undo him—
he knew that now. With her hot mouth and her innocence,
with her hesitant tongue and her cool fingers.

She could undo him completely right where he stood—
and that was not what he'd intended at all.

Tariq tightened his grip, pulling her head away.

Her eyes widened in surprise. Her mouth was full and
pink and slick from taking him.

'Did I—?' she began.

But he didn't let her finish, hauling her to her feet and
kissing her hard and deep and territorial. She gave a little
moan, shuddering in his hands, arching her body into his.

Ah, but he had to take control. He needed her to be
the one desperate for him, not the other way around. He
couldn't allow her to get to him any more than she had already.

He picked her up, holding her warm body against him.
Her skin was still cool and damp from the oasis, but now
she was starting to warm up. Silky little woman. He was
going to have to go slowly and carefully if he wanted this
to last.

Crossing the few steps to the bed, he lowered her onto
the mattress and followed, coming onto his hands and knees
over her, watching the expressions across her face shift like
the wind on the surface of a lake.

She was panting, her breasts rising and falling fast, her
pretty nipples were tight and the flush in her cheeks had
spread down her neck and over her chest. Her thighs had
fallen open, baring her sex to his gaze: slick pink skin and
a cluster of silver-blonde curls.

Beautiful. Delicate.

Yours.

He looked into her eyes, watching her as he lifted a
hand and brushed her throat with his fingertips, then ran

them lightly down the centre of her body, stroking her satiny skin. She shuddered, goosebumps rising in the wake of his touch, her breasts and stomach quivering. He didn't stop, and he didn't look away as his fingers brushed the soft curls between her thighs and then the slick, hot folds beneath them.

She gasped, her hips rising to his hand, her eyes going wide. Her pleasure was obvious. The musky, sweet scent of her arousal was like a drug, turning his hunger sharp as knife. But it wasn't his desire he wanted to sharpen. It was hers. So he parted her gently with his fingers, finding the hard bud that would give her the most pleasure and teasing it lightly. She groaned and jerked, panting.

'Arms above your head,' he ordered softly. 'And do not take them down until I say.'

'T-Tariq, I don't know if I—'

'Trust me, *ya amar.*'

She took another shuddering breath, then slowly raised her arms and let them rest on the pillows behind her head. Her gaze was on his, as if he was the centre of the entire universe, and he liked that. Liked the way she trusted him. Liked it far, far too much.

'Yes,' he murmured, stroking and teasing her. 'Look at me. Keep looking at me.'

She shook, gasping as he slid his fingers over her slickness, her hips lifting restlessly. 'Tariq…' Her voice was thick and desperate. 'Oh… I can't… This— This is…'

He lowered his head and stopped her words with his mouth, kissing her hard and deep. She groaned, letting him in. The taste of her was the same as it had been in the baths, achingly sweet, and it made him feel wild, made his restraint feel thin and tenuous.

But he was used to testing himself, so he kissed her harder, letting his fingers find the slick entrance to her body and circling it, tantalising her, before gradually easing inside. She was tight, her body clamping down on his fingers, and the hot, wet heat of her pulled hard on the leash he'd placed on his control.

She arched beneath him, moaning, her hands gripping onto the pillows above her head and twisting. He took his mouth from hers and kissed down the delicate arch of her neck, tasting the salt in the hollow of her throat, and then further, between her breasts. He covered one nipple with his lips and sucked, teasing it with his tongue as he stroked his fingers in and out of her.

She called his name, gasping. Her eyes were closed, her head thrown back, her silver hair sticking to her forehead and neck.

Beautiful. Desperate. His.

He moved his mouth to her other breast and at the same time pressed his thumb down on that small bud between her thighs, sliding his fingers deep. She cried out, her body stiffening as the climax washed over her.

Her taste was in his mouth and her scent was all around, the sound of her pleasure loud in his ears.

And his control hung by a thread.

He could not wait any longer.

Pulling his fingers from her body, he knelt between her thighs and slid his hands beneath the shapely curve of her bottom, lifting her, fitting himself to the entrance of her body.

He put one hand down on the pillow beside her head and leaned over her, looking down into her eyes.

Then he thrust deep and hard inside her.

CHAPTER NINE

CHARLOTTE GASPED, ARCHING against the deep, firm, relentless push of Tariq inside her. The sensitive tissues of her sex stretched around him, taking him. Then she cried out, shuddering. Because it was overwhelming and strange and yet somehow so good she didn't have words for it.

He was stretched out above her, his golden eyes burning down into hers, and for a moment an intense sense of wonder was all there was. Her friends, whenever they'd talked about sex, had mentioned that the first time could be painful, but that it was in the end very pleasurable. But they'd never mentioned this sense of…closeness. Of connection. The intense intimacy of having another person inside you.

She didn't feel pain right now, only that sense of connection blazing through her and into him, joining them together in a way that wasn't possible at any other time, in any other way.

It wasn't anything like she'd expected. She'd had a glimpse of it as she'd knelt at his feet, taking him into her mouth, the taste of him rich and salty on her tongue. His expression had been so fierce, and she'd loved the pleasure she'd seen flare in the golden depths of his gaze. But then he'd pulled away, and she'd thought that perhaps she'd done something wrong—until he'd taken her on the bed and put his hands on her. And then she hadn't thought at all, completely lost as he'd touched her…made the world explode behind her eyes.

But this was different—this was mutual. Giving to each other.

He held her gaze—held it so completely that it felt as if he was touching her both inside and out—and then he shifted, gripping her wrists and holding them down on the pillows above her, adjusting himself so he could push even deeper.

She couldn't speak—didn't have the breath…didn't have the words either. All she could do was look up at him in amazement that this was happening between them, that it could feel like this.

And it wasn't frightening. It wasn't frightening in any way.

Strange and a little uncomfortable, yes, but not scary.

He began to move, drawing his hips back and then pushing in again, the slide of him inside her making her gasp. She could feel her body adjustiing to him, and soon it wasn't uncomfortable or strange as pleasure began to radiate, curling through her. She began to move with him, responding to an instinct that felt as if it had always been there, and it made the light in his eyes blaze brighter.

He murmured something in his beautiful language, the liquid whisper of sound almost a caress in itself. She wanted to touch him, run her hands all over him, feel the hard strength of his muscles and taste his skin, but the way he was holding her down and the movement of him inside her made that impossible.

She moaned as the pleasure gathered strength, urging him to move faster, and he did, going deeper, harder, and it was so good. So very, *very* good that even the thought of how afraid she'd been of this was impossible to imagine.

This wasn't shouting or bitterness. This wasn't anger or pain. This was wonder and joy and connection.

Careful. Be careful.

But she couldn't think about that now. She couldn't think at all as pleasure spiralled higher and higher, gathering inside her, tighter and tighter.

She wound her legs around Tariq's lean hips and moved with him, becoming demanding, getting desperate, calling his name and not caring, giving herself up to the relentless build of sensation.

And then he shifted, lifting one hand from her wrist and slipping it down between her legs, touching her where all the pleasure seemed to centre at the same time as he thrust one last time, deep and hard. And the world exploded into flames around her, making her scream his name as the molten gold of his eyes seemed to consume her whole.

She lost herself after that, dimly aware of him suddenly moving hard and fast, and then the stiffening of his body and the sound of her name as he found his own pleasure.

Then he was on top of her, heavy as a mountain falling, his breath hot in her ear, and the heat of his body was burning her alive. He remained like that for a couple of breathless seconds and she didn't mind at all. His weight and the hard muscle against her was making her feel safe. Bringing her back to earth and anchoring her.

Then his arms came around her and she was held fast against him as he turned over onto his back, taking her with him so she was at last resting on his broad chest. And they remained like that for long minutes, not speaking, with the silence of the desert filtering through the thin tent walls.

'Did I hurt you?' he asked after a long moment, his fingers trailing in a long caress down her back.

His chest was so warm, his skin so smooth, with a light prickle of hair, and he smelled salty and musky and absolutely delicious. She couldn't stop herself from pressing her mouth to his skin.

'No, not at all.' She kissed him again, then glanced up, smiling a little shyly. 'It was amazing.'

He didn't smile back, the set of his mouth grim. Yet she could see the after-effects of pleasure glowing like hot coals in his eyes. Something tight collected inside her. Had he not enjoyed it? It had seemed as if he had, and yet his expression said the opposite.

'It wasn't amazing?' She swallowed, searching his face. 'I tried not to disappoint—'

She broke off as his fingers tangled abruptly in her hair and he lowered his head for a hard kiss, his mouth ravaging hers with an intensity that left her breathless.

'You did not disappoint,' he growled, releasing her.

Panting slightly, she stared at him, bewildered. 'Then why are you looking like you'd never had a worse experience in your life?'

His eyes glittered, the expression in them still impossible to read. 'You are dangerous, *ya amar*. Do you know that?'

'Dangerous?' she repeated blankly, not understanding. 'How am I dangerous?'

'A king is supposed to be isolated. He should remain detached or else face having his judgement impaired.' He untangled his fingers from her hair, and one thumb stroked the back of her neck in an absent movement, as if he couldn't help himself. 'I cannot risk my judgement being impaired.'

She leaned back into his hand, loving his caress, yet remaining puzzled by his words. 'What's that got to do with me being dangerous?'

'You are a threat to my detachment.' His voice had got lower, rougher, and the fierce glow in his eyes was burning bright. 'And to my judgement. So you need to understand that this marriage will be a physical one only. Is that clear?'

Something in her gut twisted, as if in distress. Which was strange, because she hadn't expected anything from this marriage at all. But this didn't sound bad. In fact, if sex was like that every time, then there didn't appear to be a down side. It was good, even. If it was only sex, then there was no risk of feelings entering into the mix—no risk of it turning poisonous like her parents' marriage.

'Yes,' she said, folding her hands on his chest and resting her chin on them. 'I understand.'

'Good.'

The starkly beautiful lines of his face relaxed and he ran the backs of his fingers down her cheek in a light caress that made goosebumps erupt everywhere.

'Now, tell me why such a passionate woman has remained a virgin so long.'

She let out a long breath. It didn't feel so bad to be telling him—not here, not with his big muscular body spread out beneath hers.

'I told you that my parents had a very bitter divorce? Well, their relationship was…uh…volatile, to say the least. Lots of shouting at each other. Lots of screaming. Especially towards the end.' She rubbed her thumb across his skin, tracing a little circle. 'I thought if that was what a relationship was all about, then I didn't want anything to do with one.'

'Understandable. You can have sex without a relationship, however.'

'I know.' She lifted a shoulder. 'I just never met anyone I wanted enough.'

His gaze was very focused, very intense. 'Never met anyone you let yourself want, you mean.'

Charlotte sighed. 'I suppose you're right. I didn't want to risk getting involved with anyone, considering how bad it had been with Mum and Dad. And it's probably a good thing—especially now.'

'Why especially now?'

She could feel her cheeks redden. Did she really have to explain it to him? Surely he would know?

'Well, sex is pretty amazing, isn't it? I mean, I don't know how you could experience that and not get involved with someone.'

Something flickered in his eyes, and again she couldn't read it.

'You say that like it is always that way. It is not, Charlotte.'

She waited for him to elaborate, but he didn't. And suddenly she understood. What she had felt between them— that sense of connection—he must have felt too. And it wasn't usual.

That's why you're dangerous to him. And that's why he is dangerous to you too.

'Oh…' she said faintly, the tangle of emotions in her gut knotting tighter. 'I didn't know.'

'Of course you did not.' His expression didn't change, his focus remaining on her. 'But it is a good thing that you do now. And it is also a good thing for us that we have such physical chemistry.'

She could hear what he didn't say.

Because there will be no one else for either of us.

Knowing that didn't upset her—not as she'd thought it might. The fact was that she didn't want anyone else. Even the thought of having another man touch her, be inside her the way Tariq had been, made her feel cold.

But that connection you felt with him will only ever be in bed.

Of course it would. That was fine, though. She didn't need to have that sense of connection anywhere else.

She met his gaze and smiled. She ignored the small kernel of ice that sat in the pit of her stomach. 'You didn't mind that I was inexperienced?' she asked.

'No, *ya amar*. Not in the slightest.'

'Why do you call me that? I'm not your "most beautiful".'

'Yes, you are,' he disagreed. 'Now you are my wife you will always be my most beautiful. And because your hair is silver, and you are so pale, you are like the moon, Charlotte.'

The words made something warm glow in the centre of her chest. She'd never been given an endearment like that before. She'd never been given an endearment at all, and she liked it. Especially the idea of being his moon when he was the sun.

'What about you?' She stared up at him, suddenly curious. 'What were your parents like?'

A shadow crossed his face, gone so quickly that if she hadn't been looking she might not have seen it at all.

'My mother died when I was very young, so I did not know her. And my father was…very strict.'

Her curiosity tightened at this odd hesitation, which seemed uncharacteristic for him. 'Oh? How so?'

But he only shook his head, reaching for her again. 'Not now.' His hand cupped the back of her head and exerted pressure, urging her towards him. 'Now I need to make certain that my people get the heir I promised them.'

And then her mouth was on his and there was no more talking.

He kept her in the tent for a few more hours after that, making her desperate for him over and over, making her forget about everything but her frantic need to have him inside her.

And after that, when twilight had begun to fall, he arranged her outside on the divan beneath the palms, and made her sit there with a glass of wine while he prepared the food that had been delivered by palace staff.

Solar-powered lighting strung around the palms gave the oasis a soft illumination and later, after they'd eaten a delicious meal and the darkness had closed in, Tariq lit a fire with capable hands, then wrapped her in a blanket that he'd brought from the tent, making her lean back in his arms as they talked.

He was not forthcoming about his family, but he was passionate about his people and his country, talking at length about his plans to keep Ashkaraz thriving. There was no doubting his conviction or his vision, and his drive to protect his people was incredibly attractive.

He was incredibly attractive full stop.

'Why do you keep the borders closed?' she asked after a small lull in the conversation, with her hands wrapped around a mug of the most delicious hot chocolate she'd ever tasted. 'And why do you give the outside world the impression of being a narrow and vicious ruler?'

He'd risen to put more wood on the fire, wearing only a pair of loose black trousers. The flames played over his impressive chest, making her fingers itch to touch him again, but the answer to this was important. Too important to be distracted from.

Crouching, he added another stick to the flames from the pile beside him. Firelight limned the fierce planes and angles of his face in gold, making him look like a hero of old, bringing fire from the gods for the good of mankind.

'You have not read our history, then?' he asked, not looking up from what he was doing. 'That is what you were told to do.'

She flushed. 'I know—and I did. But I started way back,

when Ashkaraz first became Ashkaraz. I haven't got to any recent history yet.'

'All you need to know will be in the books.'

There was a note of warning in his tone, an edge that made her gaze narrow. 'You don't want to tell me yourself?'

'No.' The word was flat and hard. The command of a king.

Puzzled, Charlotte gazed at him. Recent history seemed a strange thing to be recalcitrant about, but she was reluctant to push it since they'd reached a pleasant equilibrium. Perhaps she should leave it. She was enjoying sitting out here with him, watching him do things for her and talking with him about all kinds of trivialities. He had a dry sense of humour that appealed to her, and he knew far more about the outside world and its politics than she'd thought he would.

Pushing him would definitely make things tense, and she did hate that. Then again, he'd been constantly pushing her since she'd arrived in Ashkaraz, and much to her own surprise she hadn't backed down. So why should she now? He'd made her reveal her father's disappointment in her—why shouldn't he give a little in return?

Why should you care?

Not wanting that particular thought, Charlotte shoved it away.

'Why not?' she asked carefully. 'If I'm going to find out sooner or later, I'd much rather hear it from you first.'

The fire glowed in the darkness, radiating heat, casting a warm light over Charlotte, wrapped in a blanket. Her hair lay loose over her bare shoulders and he was very aware that she hadn't bothered to dress. That she was naked underneath that blanket.

It would be easy to go over to her, pull away the blanket and lay her down before the fire. Make her scream his name to the stars above their heads the way he had in the tent earlier. But there was a danger in that too—as he'd discovered the minute he'd pushed inside her. When he'd looked down into her eyes and read the wonder and amazement in them as she'd looked back at him. Staring at him as if he'd given her all the secrets of the universe.

'Dangerous' he'd called her, and she was.

But at least in bed he could keep it all about physical pleasure. Out here by the fire, with her lovely face lit by the flames, her gaze level and very direct, there were no such comforting lies.

Why are you so reluctant to tell her the truth? Why does it matter?

He didn't know. What he did know, however, was that he could not allow his reluctance to win. He had to be very careful with her around, to ensure his detachment was solid—especially considering how she threatened it.

Which meant, of course, that he had to tell her.

Ignoring the strange reluctance that pulled at him, Tariq straightened up. 'What is there to say? My father had an American lover whose family was very keen on knowing the secret of our wealth, so she tried hard to get that secret from him. But he would not tell her.'

He looked at Charlotte over the flames.

'So she turned her sights on me. I was seventeen and... angry with my father for various reasons. So I let her seduce me. And when she asked where our country got its wealth from I told her about the oil reserves in the north.'

Charlotte frowned. 'You meant to tell her?'

'I was in love with her.'

You were not. You told her because you wanted to punish your father.

The thought was a whisper in his head, highlighting the

lie he'd just told Charlotte. The lie he'd always told himself. But it wasn't really a lie, was it?

His father had denied him something he'd wanted passionately and desperately and he'd been *so* angry. So he'd allowed Catherine to seduce him. Allowed her to get under his skin. Allowed himself to give away his country's secrets. Because he could blame it all on love.

Except it hadn't been love. It had been selfishness—his own needs put before his country's.

Sympathy glowed in Charlotte's eyes, and an understanding he didn't deserve.

'Oh, Tariq,' she murmured. 'I'm so sorry.'

'What are you sorry for?' he said brusquely. 'It is not your fault.'

'No, but you think it's yours, don't you?'

'It *is* mine.' More than she knew.

'You were only seventeen.'

'Old enough to know better.'

He knew he sounded cold, but he couldn't afford to make it any different. Nor could he afford to lean into that sympathy and understanding he saw in her face.

'I sold my country out for love.' Which was not entirely untrue. 'It will not happen again.'

The flames played over her pretty face, lighting her pale with a golden glow, and the searching way she was looking at him made him want to push her back on the sand and take her hard, to distract her.

'That's not all there is, though, is it?' she said quietly. 'There's more to the story.'

How she knew that, he wasn't quite sure. But it wasn't anything he'd share with her. She didn't need to know the true extent of his pettiness.

Why should it matter what she thinks anyway?

He ignored the thought. 'There is nothing that you cannot find out from the books in the library,' he said, and stepped around the fire, coming over to where she sat, her hands still wrapped around the mug of hot chocolate he'd made for her.

She tilted her head back, looking up at him. 'Why won't you tell me?'

The question was so simple, so honest and open. And something within him wanted to respond. To tell her the truth about the aching loneliness of his childhood. The need he'd had for someone—anyone—and how that had always been denied him. Until one day he'd broken.

You cannot tell her. A king must be self-sufficient. Detached. Alone.

He knew it—had learned his lesson and learned it well. Catherine had been his teacher in that, even though she hadn't realised it herself. She'd given him what his father had never allowed: someone to talk to, confide in. And he *had* confided in her, and part of him had known his error even as he'd told her about the oil. Known and yet he'd done it anyway. Because he had been angry.

Because you couldn't bear to be lonely and you hated your father for the way he kept you isolated. You were a selfish boy and you nearly destroyed your country because of it.

Charlotte frowned, and he had the strange impression that she could read every thought in his head, because she put her mug down in the sand and rose to her feet, her blanket caught awkwardly around her. She stepped forward and put her arms around him, leaning her head on his chest.

There was nothing sexual in it. It was merely a hug.

He'd never been hugged before. Not by his father, nor by the nannies who'd brought him up. So the feel of Charlotte's arms around him shocked him. Made him freeze in place. He felt as if there was an animal inside him, struggling to get free of a cage, and as if any move he made would spring the cage door wide open.

He didn't know what would happen if that animal got free.

You know what happens.

Yes, he did. Disaster.

His instinct was urging him to shove her away, but that would hurt her, and for some reason the thought of hurting her caused him actual pain. So he was forced to stand there and endure the hug she was giving him, even though he didn't want it.

'I'm sorry,' she said, her voice muffled against his chest. 'You don't have to tell me if it's painful.'

He had no idea how he'd given himself away. And no idea of what to say to her now either. Earlier that day she'd told him about the way her father had treated her and he'd seen how painful that had been for her. How her parents' bad marriage had made her afraid of getting involved with anyone.

He'd thought initially that was a good thing, that her fear would prevent her from getting too close. But the way she was holding him now made it clear that it wasn't as simple as that.

She wasn't afraid to ask him about the things he didn't want to talk about. Or to offer him comfort. She wasn't afraid to show him she cared. And she wasn't thinking of herself or her fear right now. She was only thinking of him.

His heart ached, raw and painful in his chest.

He wanted to tell her his secrets. Wanted to share those hours he'd spent in the desert at a young age, taken out and left there alone so he could develop self-reliance. Those days of silence in the palace, when he had been forbidden company so he could learn how to deal with loneliness. Days of not seeing anyone. Not speaking to anyone.

Sometimes he would hear laughter, the shouts of children in the courtyards outside, and he'd wanted so much to go out and play. But he had never been allowed.

Alone, his father had told him. *A king always stands alone. Because he is stronger that way.*

She was warm against him, all soft, silky bare skin and the sweet scent of her body.

Telling her the truth only means something if you let it.

And it didn't have to, did it? After all, it had happened a very long time ago. He was making amends for his mistake now. He wouldn't let it rule him. So what did it matter if she knew about what he'd done? It might even be a lesson to her to keep her distance. He'd told her back in the tent that they would never have a normal marriage, but it wouldn't hurt to drive that message home.

Tariq could feel his body already responding to her nearness, but all he did was raise his hands and gently put her from him. He would not make this about sex now. Not yet, at least.

She frowned and opened her mouth, but he laid a finger on her soft lips, silencing her.

'I was not entirely truthful,' he said quietly. 'I did love Catherine. But…that was not the reason I told her about my country's wealth.'

Puzzlement flickered over Charlotte's features. 'Oh?'

'My father had…set ideas on how a ruler should be brought up. He believed that a king must always stand apart, and that is how he raised me. Always apart. I was not allowed friends, or companions of any kind, and no comfort from any of the nannies who looked after me. A king has to be used to loneliness, so he made sure I got used to it from a very early age.'

Charlotte stared at him in obvious shock. 'No friends? None?'

'No.' He refused to allow the expression on her face to affect him. 'It was not so bad as a child. But as I got older I found it more…difficult. My father had always stressed the importance of a good education, so I thought I could at least get a taste of what life would be like if I was not a king and go to university. I applied to Oxford, unbeknownst to my father, and was accepted. But…'

He'd thought his anger long since blunted by now, but it wasn't. Even after so many years he could still feel its sharp edge. It deepened his voice to a growl.

'My father would not let me go. I argued with him, shouted at him, but he would not be moved. He even put guards on my door in case I tried to sneak away.' Tariq looked down into Charlotte's pale face. 'I was so angry. So very, *very* angry. And when one night I saw Catherine, weeping beside a fountain in the gardens, I knew I'd found an opportunity to get back at him. She wanted me and I let her seduce me. And when she asked me about Ashkaraz's secret, I told her.'

'Oh, Tariq…' There was nothing but sympathy in Charlotte's expression.

'I told her because I was angry,' he went on, so she fully understood. 'Because I was petty. Because I was selfish. I told her because I had not learned the lessons my father had tried to teach me about detachment. About not letting my emotions control me or affect my judgement. I did what a ruler is never supposed to do, and that is to put his own feelings before his country.'

There was no judgement in Charlotte's eyes, only distress. She reached out and put a hand on his chest.

'Of course you were angry. You wanted some time to be a normal teenager.'

But he didn't want her pain on his behalf. Didn't want her sympathy. Not when he didn't deserve any of it.

'That is no excuse. I should have listened to what he was trying to teach me, yet I did not. I was just a spoiled boy who wanted something his father would not give him.'

'No!' Charlotte shot back, suddenly fierce. 'You weren't spoiled, Tariq. You were lonely. Terribly, desperately lonely.'

'I betrayed my country, Charlotte.' He made it explicit, because it was clear that she did *not* understand. 'Out of nothing more than selfishness. There can be no excuses for that. No forgiveness. There is only atonement and my dedication to make sure it does not happen again.'

She closed her mouth, but the distress in her eyes lingered and he didn't like it, didn't want her to feel it—because it made that animal inside him claw at the cage, wound the tension in his shoulders even tighter. Made him want to take her in his arms and hold her, take the distress away.

But he couldn't allow himself that. And there was one way he could get rid of that look in her eyes. One way to ease her distress.

Tariq put his palm over hers on his chest, then lifted his other hand, tugging the blanket from around her. She made no move to grab it, standing there warm and naked in the firelight.

'Tariq…' she whispered.

But whatever else she'd been going to say was lost as he reached for her, gathering her up in his arms. And then he stopped her mouth entirely with his, and made them both forget about history and pain and loneliness.

At least for a little while.

CHAPTER TEN

CHARLOTTE SAT IN the palace library on one of the low couches near the window, with the sound of the fountain drifting in from the garden outside. The early-evening air was warm and full of the smell of flowers, and she could hear a couple of the gardeners out amongst the rose bushes, talking in low voices.

Her Arabic wasn't good enough yet for her to be able to tell what they were talking about, but she recognised the odd word here and there. Something about football.

It reminded her of her flatmates in England and made her smile—at least until a wave of homesickness hit her. Strange to feel that way about a place where she hadn't much enjoyed living anyway, but she did. And it didn't help that she'd spent the last couple of weeks since getting back from the oasis on her own. Tariq had disappeared into the endless meetings and official business that took up a lot of his time, and she barely saw him at all during the day.

It wasn't as if she'd been completely left to her own devices, though. She had her own royal duties as sheikha, and that was taking some getting used to, plus she had a lot of study to do in order to get up to speed on the customs and history of Ashkaraz, as well as more language and protocol classes.

She might have been fascinated by all this, and certainly

she would have enjoyed it a lot more, if her head hadn't been quite so full of her husband.

Ever since those three days at the oasis he was all she could think about. What he'd told her about his childhood had shocked her. To be kept alone and apart from everyone, denied friendship and even simple human comfort, must have been horrific.

It made her wonder about the ferocity that burned in his eyes and the sense of volcanic emotions simmering just below the surface, kept tightly leashed and locked down. How would such loneliness have affected such a passionate man?

Well, she didn't need to wonder. He'd told her. He'd been broken and the consequences had been awful. And so terribly unfair. Because it wasn't his fault he'd been pushed to breaking point.

Her throat tightened, her eyes prickling with unexpected tears. That night at the oasis he'd told her about it so flatly, so emotionlessly, and yet she'd seen the rage that burned bright in his eyes. Rage that was still there even all these years later. And not only that, it seemed to her that he was still punishing himself for that youthful mistake, denying himself the emotional outlet that he so clearly needed.

Why do you care so much about this?

Charlotte pushed the book she'd been reading off her lap and stood, pacing over to the windows and back to the couch again, restless.

She cared because she knew what it was like to be pushed into making a mistake that you wished you could take back. And she cared because he was her husband. Because he was a kind man, no matter that he said he wasn't, and he believed in what he was doing. Because he was passionate.

Pacing back to the windows, Charlotte looked out sightlessly at the rose bushes and the fountains, her heart beating far too fast for comfort. She couldn't stop thinking about him. Couldn't stop thinking about those three days she'd spent with him.

It hadn't been the same after that first night, though the sex had been incendiary. It hadn't been the same since they'd returned to the palace either, with them seeing each other only when Tariq needed her physically. Their bed the only place where it felt as if they communicated fully with each other. Where they were joined and words weren't needed…where their pasts were irrelevant.

What would it be like if they had that feeling outside the bedroom too?

Ah, but there was no point thinking about that. It was impossible. He'd told her their marriage would only be a physical one, that he couldn't give her any kind of emotional connection. She'd thought she'd have no problem with that, but maybe she did.

You never wanted a marriage like your parents', but what if that's how yours ends up?

A cold thread wound through her, making her fingers feel icy. That could happen, couldn't it? Tariq might strive for detachment, but she would always be able to sense the hidden currents that shifted beneath his hard, merciless surface. She could feel his anger and his passion, see it in his eyes, sense it burning him alive.

And then it would be like it had been at home, with her parents' bitterness and animosity battering her, surrounding her. With her wanting to take away their anger and pain but not knowing how. Until the day she'd broken away and run from it all, and made everything ten thousand times worse.

You can't run away now, though.

No, she couldn't. She was married to a king and she couldn't leave even if she'd wanted to. But she didn't want to. She wanted to stay, to help him, to turn her marriage into something good for both of them.

Except what could she do when he was determined to stay detached?

Carefully, she went over what he'd told her out at the oasis again—about the dreadful childhood he'd had, with no one and nothing to ease his loneliness.

Lonely, that was what he was. So maybe all he needed was a friend. Someone to talk to, to confide in. Someone who wouldn't make any emotional demands on him.

She could do that, couldn't she?

She could be his friend?

'I have been looking for you.'

There was no mistaking the dark, deep voice that echoed through the room, making her jump.

She turned, looking towards the double doors that were standing open. Tariq's tall, muscled frame was filling the doorway. His hot golden stare found hers and her mouth dried, her cheeks heating.

She knew that look. He had it when he wanted her. And he often did during the day, coming to find her wherever she was and taking her by the hand, leading her to his rooms or to somewhere secluded, where he would strip her bare and take her, with that familiar ferocity molten in his eyes.

He didn't speak afterwards, just left her burned to ashes where she stood while he turned away and went back to doing whatever it was he'd been doing before he'd come to find her, apparently satisfied.

She had the sense that he wanted something from her in those moments, that it wasn't simply sex, but she never knew what it was.

Perhaps she might have an answer to that now.

He was in dark charcoal suit trousers and one of his exquisitely cut business shirts, this one in dark blue, making his bronze skin seem richer and highlighting the gold of his eyes. She was struck, as she always was, by the raw, stark beauty of him. By how amazing it was that a man like this was hers.

He is not yours, though. And he never will be. Just as you will never be his.

The sliver of glass sitting inside her twisted—a sharp, unexpected pain that seemed to radiate out from the centre of her chest.

Which was ridiculous. She'd never thought he would be hers and she'd never wanted him to be. So where this pain was coming from she had no idea, and it was best she simply ignored it.

He turned and locked the doors, then turned back, his stare becoming even hotter. 'Come here,' he ordered darkly.

She could feel her own need start to rise, ignited by the way he looked at her. It didn't take much to set her burning these days—not when he was around. But she couldn't let it get to her, not right now. She needed to say something first.

'Wait.' She took a steadying breath. 'I have something to say.'

His gaze narrowed. 'What?'

Okay, good. He was prepared to listen. 'I've been thinking about what you said at the oasis. About your childhood.'

His inky brows pulled down in a scowl. 'That has nothing to do with you.'

'Yes, it does. You're my husband. You told me once that everything about me is your business, which also must mean that everything about you is mine.'

A certain kind of energy was gathering about him now, dark and electric and absolutely mesmerising. His golden stare held her fast, frozen where she stood, and the warning glitter in it made it obvious that he didn't like what she'd said.

But that was too bad. She hadn't let herself be intimidated by him since she'd arrived here and she wasn't about to start.

'I do not want to hear about this now,' Tariq growled, advancing on her. 'I have other needs first.'

But she knew what those needs were, and she had a suspicion that they weren't only to do with sex. That it was the forbidden connection he came in search of whenever he was in this mood. He would accept it if she offered it without strings. Without any need for him to return it.

'Or we could sit and talk.' She lifted her chin, looking him in the eye. 'Conversation, Tariq. You remember how to do that?'

He didn't stop, his lean-hipped hunter's stride closing the distance between them, his tiger's gaze on hers. 'I do not want to talk.'

She didn't have any time to evade him. One minute he was nowhere near her, the next he was gripping her hips and pulling her close.

She flung up her hands, pressing her palms against his hard chest, holding him away. 'I'm not trying to take anything from you or make you give me something in return,' she said, trying to master her own helpless physical response to him. 'I'm not going to demand anything from you. Just… If you need a friend, I can be one for you.'

He went very still, staring down at her, his eyes glittering. 'A friend?' He said the word as if he had no idea what it meant. 'Why would I need a friend?'

'Everyone does.' His chest was hot beneath her palms, his muscles like iron, stiff with tension. 'Even kings.'

'You are mistaken.' His fingers tightened on her. 'I have no need of a friend. Ever.'

But she could see behind the desire in his eyes and she knew what drove him. Because she felt it in herself. He wanted a connection just as badly as she did.

'How would you know?' she asked softly. 'When you've never had one?'

He made a deep, dismissive sound, pulling her closer, fitting her hips against his so she could feel the hard, demanding length of him through the silk of her robes.

'I have Faisal. And I have other advisors.'

Her heart clenched tight. Was that what he truly thought friends were? His royal advisors? An old family servant? But of course he would. He had no other reference, did he?

'They're not friends, Tariq.' She pressed her fingertips to the warm cotton of his shirt. 'They are employees. And that's not the same thing.'

He ignored her, taking her mouth in a hot, hard kiss that left her breathless and unsteady on her feet.

'You should sit down,' he growled. 'And stop talking.'

The kiss left her lips tingling, with the dark, rich taste of him on her tongue, and it would have been easy to let him keep going. To stop pushing him, to let him do what he wanted and make her mindless with pleasure right here in the library.

But that, in essence, would be running away again. That would be hiding under the table the way she'd used to do, or running into the woods. Curling around her pain like a wounded animal and keeping it inside, not letting it leak into the atmosphere and make everything worse.

Yet running hadn't solved anything. It had only caused her even more pain. She couldn't do that again. She had to make a stand.

Her hand slid from his chest and up, to cup his strong, beautiful face. 'You do know what a friend is, don't you?'

The gold of his eyes was like a sword spearing through

her, full of sharp edges. 'Of course I do not,' he snapped. 'As you said before, I have never had one.' He pulled away from her suddenly and gestured to the low couch nearby. 'Sit down, Charlotte.'

Another order. And calling her 'Charlotte' meant he was displeased with her.

She studied the look on his face. He was angry, that was clear, and he didn't want her pushing him. Didn't want her reminding him of the past that still so obviously hurt him and the mistake he'd made because he was human, because he'd been a boy who'd desperately wanted someone.

She could show him that, couldn't she? She could show him what it was like to have someone. A friend and a lover. A wife. A support. It would mean opening herself up and not demanding anything from him. But that was what you had to do when you wanted to tame a beast, wasn't it?

Slowly and carefully you fed it your heart.

'Charlotte,' he repeated, low and dark. 'I gave you a command.'

His eyes glittered like golden flames burning behind glass and she was reminded of what she'd thought weeks ago: this man was a volcano. Harsh and cold on the outside, while underneath he seethed, molten with rage and passion, burning up inside because all those emotions had nowhere to go.

Well, maybe she would give them an outlet. That was what a friend would do.

'Your father was wrong, by the way,' Charlotte said steadily, moving over to the couch Tariq had indicated. 'He shouldn't have brought you up the way he did.'

She sat down, arranging her robes around her and folding her hands in her lap. Then she looked up at him.

'No one can live in a vacuum, let alone a child. They'd suffocate.'

His face was impassive as he moved to where she sat, standing in front of her, hard and cold as granite. Yet the heat in his eyes was as unyielding and merciless as the desert sun.

'This conversation, wife, is over.' His voice was rough and hot, full of lava and gravel. 'Spread your legs for me.'

Tariq's heart was beating far too fast, and it felt as if the hungry animal in his chest, the one he kept caged and leashed, was sinking its claws into him once again. If he wasn't careful it would claw him to pieces entirely—and who knew what would happen then?

He remembered the disgust in his father's eyes as he'd looked at Tariq from across his desk…

'You are a disgrace,' Ishak had said angrily over the constant ringing of the phone, with the consequences of Tariq's betrayal already reverberating through Ashkaraz. *'After everything I have taught you, you have learned nothing.'* His father's expression had twisted. *'You are unworthy, Tariq. Unworthy of being my heir. Unworthy of being my son.'*

The memory shuddered through him and he shoved it aside, concentrating instead on the woman sitting calmly on the couch in front of him, her blue gaze steady on his.

His chest ached, and a strange and molten anger was seething inside him. He didn't know what she was talking about. A friend? That was nonsense. What did he need a friend for? He'd never had one, it was true, but then, he'd never needed one.

He didn't need anyone.

A lie. You need her.

But only for sex. In fact, since coming back from the oasis it seemed as if sex with his wife was all he thought about. He couldn't concentrate on his duties, on the work he needed to do. Instead he found himself stalking the corridors of the palace in search of her, hard and aching. She would always give him what he wanted. And yet afterwards, when he should have been well sated, all he felt was hollow. Empty. Like Tantalus, for ever drinking and for ever thirsty.

It was inexplicable.

He felt it now as he looked down at her, sitting on that couch in a spread of sky-blue silk. An aching emptiness. A hunger. A thirst.

She was wrong about suffocating in a vacuum. You'd only suffocate if you needed air to breathe, and he didn't. He'd trained himself to live without it. In fact, he'd prove it to her.

'You heard what I said.' His voice was too low and too rough. 'Do as you are told.'

She didn't protest, spreading her knees, her blue eyes full of the same understanding he'd seen in the firelight that night at the oasis.

'Did you know that one night I ran away from home?' she said quietly. 'My parents had been arguing more than usual and I couldn't stand it. I stayed out all night and they ended up calling the police.'

Tariq ignored her, dropping to his knees in front of her. He put his hands on her thighs and pushed them apart, spreading her wider.

'They searched for hours,' Charlotte went on. 'I heard them calling my name but I didn't answer. I didn't want to go back home and listen to all that shouting. They found me, though, and dragged me back.'

Why was she telling him this? He didn't want to hear it. He wanted to hear nothing but her gasps of pleasure and her sighs. The way she called his name just as she was about to come.

He took the hem of her robes in his fists.

'My parents were so angry. And my mother decided that I was too much trouble to fight over, so she let Dad have custody of me.' Her voice wavered slightly. 'Even though he didn't really want me.'

The material was soft in his hands, the scent of her body sweet. His hunger was pulsing in time with his heartbeat and he didn't know why he'd stopped. Didn't understand why that tremble in her voice had made his chest ache.

'I know you may not want me either,' she continued. 'Not for anything more than sex. But if you need someone to talk to or just…be with, I will be that person for you.'

The words hurt—sticking inside him like thorns, piercing him right through. Which was ridiculous.

He didn't want someone to talk to or 'be with'—whatever that meant. He had Faisal. He had his council. And as for her—well, he needed her for one thing and one thing only.

'Be silent,' he growled.

Understanding glowed in her eyes, as if she could see those thorns in his heart. As if she knew how much they hurt and how hard he was fighting them.

She said nothing, only looked at him. And for some reason her silence made him feel even worse, so he jerked her robes up to her waist, uncovering her, not caring if the fabric ripped.

He had to do something to take away the terrible understanding on her lovely face. To strip it from her, turn her pretty eyes dark, make her blind to everything but pleasure. Make her need him.

Prove that you do not need her?

Yes, and that too. Because he didn't. He needed nothing from her but her body.

Under her robes was a pair of loose trousers in the same fine silk, and the material parted without any resistance as he tore them from her, along with the lacy knickers she wore underneath.

She didn't stop him, but he felt her tremble as she was finally bare under his hands, her skin warm and as fine as the silk he'd ripped from her.

His heart was beating so loudly he couldn't hear a thing, and the edge of hunger inside him was made sharper by the scent of her arousal.

He looked down at the soft, damp nest of curls between her thighs, her skin pink and slick. His hands on her pale flesh looked rough and dark—as if they would tear her as he'd torn the fabric of her robes.

You are unworthy. A disgrace.

He growled again, shoving her thighs wide, wanting to look at her and not listen to his father's voice in his head.

She was so pretty. So delicate. And this was all he needed from her—nothing more. Certainly not friendship. Nothing that would threaten the walls he'd built around himself. Nothing that would threaten his detachment. He was perfectly fine, here in his vacuum.

He slid his hands up her thighs, losing himself in the feel of her beneath his fingertips. Then higher still to the heat that lay between. She sighed as he touched her, parting her wet flesh gently, and the soft, needy sound shivered through him.

Yes, this was how it should be. Her needing him. Her desperate for him. Not the other way around. Never that.

Yet his hands were shaking as he held the soft folds apart, and he was breathing so fast it was as if he couldn't get enough air. And he was ravenous, suffocating in his vacuum, and she was the air he needed to breathe.

He should have stopped then—if only to prove to himself that he could hold himself apart from her. But he couldn't. The hunger was too much to bear.

Leaning forward, he bent his head between her thighs, running his tongue directly up the centre of her sex, desperate for a taste.

She jerked, a soft cry escaping her, but he didn't stop, The hunger was sinking its claws deep into him. He slid his hands to her hips and held her still as he began to explore her, the taste of her exploding in his head, a salty-sweet burst of flavour that made him even harder and more desperate.

'Tariq…' she gasped, twisting in his grip. 'Oh…'

The pleading note in her voice was exactly what he'd been hoping for, so he didn't stop then either, teasing the hard little bud with his tongue and then dipping down, circling the entrance to her body, before pushing inside to taste her deeper.

He wanted her as hungry as he was. As desperate. As frantic. He wanted that terrible knowledge in her eyes gone. She looked at him as if she'd seen inside him and seen the lonely little boy he'd once been. The boy who'd broken under his father's lesson.

The boy who was unworthy, a disgrace to his name.

He would never let himself be that boy again.

She cried out, her fingers tangling in his hair, her grip on him bordering on pain. But that only sharpened everything deliciously, making him growl yet again against her wet flesh and loosen his grip on her hip, sliding his hand beneath the soft curve of her buttocks. Then he tilted her so he could taste her even deeper, making her groan and arch in his hold.

A dark satisfaction at the sound of her cries unwound inside him, along with a deep possessiveness that he couldn't hold back. He would make her forget all this friendship nonsense. Make her forget so completely she'd never think of it again. Yes, and he'd make her forget that her father hadn't wanted her, that her mother hadn't fought for her. He'd make her forget about everything but him and what he could give her. She wouldn't need anything else and neither would he.

He pushed deeper with his tongue and she writhed, her body trembling harder as he brought her to the brink. And then he pushed her over with another wicked lick, holding her tightly as she sobbed and twisted between his hands, the climax riding her hard.

Her scent was all around him, her taste on his tongue, her heat so close, and abruptly his own need tightened its grip around his throat, threatening to choke him.

He let her go, pushing himself back from her. She made a glorious picture, leaning against the back of the couch with her face a deep rosy colour, her eyes glittering and dark with the after-effects of pleasure. Her legs were spread wide, there was the sheen of moisture on her inner thighs, and her sex was open and wet and ready for him.

He reached for the rest of her robes, pulling them away from her until she was sitting there naked, surrounded by blue silk, like a jewel in the middle of fine tissue paper.

'Lie down,' he ordered hoarsely, and rose to his feet, not taking his gaze from her as she did as she was told, lying back on the couch, naked and beautiful and ready for him.

He couldn't wait to undress. He simply undid his trousers and freed himself, then joined her on the couch, settling himself between her spread thighs. She reached for him but he pushed her hands away, guiding himself to the entrance of her body and thrusting home.

Charlotte gasped and arched beneath him, her silky thighs closing around his hips, her breasts lifting. Her silvery lashes came down, lying on her cheeks, her mouth was slightly open. For a second he couldn't move. Could only gaze down at her beneath him, the grip of her sex around him and the heat of her body blanking his mind utterly.

And it should have been enough. It shouldn't have made him feel so hollow, as if there was something more. Something so close he could almost touch it.

'Look at me,' he demanded roughly, before he could stop himself. 'Look at me, Charlotte.'

Her lashes lifted at his command, her gaze meeting his, and a hot, intense electrical charge pulsed straight through him. For a moment it felt as if he held something in his hands, something ineffable and beautiful, that would break if he gripped it too hard.

There was tenderness in Charlotte's eyes, a warmth that had nothing to do with sexual heat, and she put out a hand, cupping his cheek as if he was the precious thing, the thing that might break.

His chest ached, a heavy weight pressing on it. The consequences of the vacuum in which he'd been trying to breathe for so long. The vacuum that seemed to be suffocating him, after all.

Yet not when she touched him. The contact of her fingers on his cheek, the clutch of her sex around his, the heat of her body and the warmth in her silver-blue eyes were all lifelines containing oxygen.

It felt as if they were the only things keeping him alive.

He took a shaken breath, then another, and when her fingers trailed along his jaw the pressure on his chest lifted. He took another breath, right down deep into his lungs, and it felt like the first breath he'd ever taken.

And when he moved inside her, deep and slow, it felt as if the pleasure was another lifeline too, another strand connecting him to her.

Her lovely mouth curved, her darkening gaze holding

him as fast as the grip of her sex around his shaft, and he couldn't look away.

She could see him. She could see who he was deep down inside. She could see that lonely little boy and she was reaching out a hand to him. She was pulling away the barriers around his heart as if they were nothing but paper. Putting out her hands and holding him.

Holding him as if he was worth something.

He couldn't stop her. Couldn't stop himself from wanting that touch, craving the way she held him, reaching to grasp all the lifelines she was throwing him.

He moved faster, harder, holding on tight to her as he drove into her, their shared breathing fast and ragged in the room. And her hands were on him, stroking him lightly and easily as he drove her down into the cushions. As he felt the pleasure beginning to take him apart.

'Charlotte…' He hadn't meant to say her name—not like that. Not so deep and dark and desperate. 'Little one…'

Her arms were coming around him, her thighs tightening, embracing him in a way no one had ever held him before. The immensity of his hunger was a tidal wave of need washing up inside him, all the years he'd spent alone crashing down on him.

But he wasn't alone. Not now. Because now he had her. She was his wife and she could never leave. She was safe.

The thought stayed with him as he tore her hands from his body and pushed them up and behind her head, holding them down with his own. And it glowed brightly as he thrust harder into her, the couch shaking with the force of it, burying all the heat and desperation inside her with every flex of his hips.

And she met every thrust, panting and as wild as he was, his name on her lips as she arched and moved beneath him, the pleasure becoming more intense, more raw with every movement.

It was too much to look at her. The wild blue of her eyes ripped him apart. And he only had time to shove his hand between them, stroking her sex hard and sure, feeling the wave of her climax hit as she convulsed beneath him.

Then he was following her, his own hitting him, stealing every breath from his body and every thought from his head.

Minutes or maybe hours later, the feel of her hands drifting down his back returned him to himself and he tried to shift his weight off her. But she made a little protesting sound, her nails digging into his hips, clearly wanting him to stay where he was. So he did, propping himself up on his elbows instead and looking down at her.

She didn't speak, and neither did he, and for long moments he simply let himself be lost in the endless blue of her eyes.

'My father wanted to disown me when he found out what I had told Catherine,' he heard himself say, giving her the final piece of himself—the piece he'd told no one else about. 'He called me a disgrace...said I was unworthy.'

There was tenderness in her eyes, and sympathy too. 'Your father was wrong about a lot of things, Tariq. And most especially that.'

He wanted to disagree with her, but that was a question for another day. Right now there were more important things to do. Like picking her up and carrying her to his bed. And then maybe, after they had sated themselves again, they could even have a conversation.

'I am not letting you leave, *ya amar*,' he said. 'You understand that, do you not? You are mine.'

Something in her face relaxed—a tightness he hadn't noticed before. 'I know. You've said that before, believe it or not.'

'I am not joking.'

One fair brow rose. 'Were you joking before?'

'Let us just say that I did not know that I was in a vac-uum.' He paused, holding her gaze. 'And that I needed air in order to breathe.'

CHAPTER ELEVEN

CHARLOTTE WAS IN the middle of yet more language lessons with Amirah when one of the palace servants knocked on the door of her suite, issuing a summons to Tariq's study.

It had been a week since he'd taken her in the library, when it had felt as if the earth had shifted beneath her and something had changed between them. She hadn't been able to stop thinking about how he'd said he needed air to breathe, and had looked at her intently, as if *she* was the air. He hadn't said it outright, but she'd felt it. As if he'd finally discovered the connection that had been forged between them back in the oasis.

He was such a lonely man—a man desperate for someone—and she'd tasted desperation in his kiss. Felt it in the way he'd taken her. It had made her heart twist in her chest, made her want to give whatever she could, coax his rare and beautiful smile from him. Make him laugh. Take the loneliness from him and give him comfort instead.

So she'd spent time over the past week doing things with him that weren't based either around sex or his duties as ruler. Things that friends did together. A relaxed dinner by the fountains, talking about nothing in particular. Watching a movie in the palace's own cinema. An outing into the city, where he'd shown her a few of his favourite places. A horse ride into the southern hills.

They had been special moments. When he hadn't been

the king and she hadn't been his queen. When they'd simply been Tariq and Charlotte, enjoying each other's company.

She didn't know why she wanted to do this for the man who was keeping her from her family and friends and who'd pretty much forced her to marry him. But she didn't let herself think too deeply about it. Being with him made her feel less lonely, and that was enough. In fact, for the first time in her life she felt wanted—and not only that but needed too. Needed by a king.

That fact alone had given her a courage and strength she'd never known possible.

After the summons arrived she let Amirah go for the rest of the day, then made her way through the palace corridors to Tariq's study.

He was sitting behind his vast desk as she came in and closed the door behind her, glancing up from his computer screen as she approached.

This past week she'd been the lucky recipient of quite a few of his smiles, but not today. His expression remained grim and a sense of foreboding stole through her, making her feel cold. Then he stood and came around the side of the desk, and abruptly she felt even colder.

'What is it?' she asked as he approached.

'I've just had word that your father had a heart attack last night and has been taken to hospital.' His voice was level and matter-of-fact as he stopped in front of her, reaching for her hands and taking them in his own.

Shock echoed through her. 'I don't...' She tried to get her brain working. 'Dad's in hospital?'

Tariq's fingers were warm as they wrapped around hers, and when he drew her to him she didn't resist, needing the strength of his tall, muscular body, because suddenly she was afraid she might fall.

'Yes.' His deep voice calmed her somewhat. 'As I said, he had a heart attack.'

'How bad is it?'

'They're not sure. I spoke to your father's doctor myself, and it appears that it may take some time to see how severe the damage is. But it's entirely possible that he'll make a full recovery.'

Charlotte swallowed. Tariq's warmth surrounded her, and the heat of his skin burning against her numb fingers comforted her.

Her father wasn't perfect, but he was her father all the same, and although he hadn't exactly made her feel wanted, he *had* taken care of her after her mother had left. He'd fed and clothed her, given her a roof over her head and ensured she'd got a decent education. He'd never been actively cruel or abused her. But now he was sick. Now he was alone...

She couldn't bear the thought of that. He might not be the world's greatest dad, but that didn't mean she could leave him in hospital with no support. He had no other family except her. Besides, she wasn't like her mother—she couldn't simply walk away when someone needed her.

Charlotte lifted her head and stared up into the hard gold of her husband's eyes. 'I have to go to him. I have to go back to England.'

There was sympathy in Tariq's expression, but his voice when he spoke was firm. 'The borders are closed, *ya amar.* You may not leave.'

'This is different. Dad's ill.'

Yet he only shook his head. 'It does not matter. I cannot let you go.'

'Why not?' She frowned, not understanding. 'Surely this is allowed? He's sick. And there's no one else to take care of him.'

The planes and angles of Tariq's fiercely beautiful face

hardened, the warmth that had been there before fading. 'That is what a hospital full of doctor and nurses is for, is it not?'

'But…he's my father, Tariq. And it won't be for long, I promise.' She squeezed his hand in reassurance. 'I'll just see that he's okay and then—'

'No.' Tariq's voice was flat, and all sympathy drained abruptly from his expression.

She blinked at his tone, instinctive anger licking up inside her, and opened her mouth to tell him he was being unreasonable.

Then she caught a glint of what looked like fear in his golden eyes.

Her anger disappeared as quickly as it had risen.

'What's wrong?' she asked quietly, because it was clear something was. 'This isn't just about Dad, is it?'

His features had turned forbidding, as if she'd seen something he didn't want her to see.

'You are my sheikha. You cannot simply leave the country whenever the mood takes you.'

'This is not a "mood", Tariq.'

The glint in his eyes blazed unexpectedly, his grip on her hand tightening. 'I do not care. You are my sheikha and your place is by my side.'

Her heart clenched at the intensity in his face and the fierce note in his voice. At how much he needed her. And part of her didn't want to push him or argue, because she liked it that he did.

But this was important to her. And, anyway, she would come back. It wasn't as if she was going for good.

'I know,' she said, trying to sound calm. 'But it won't be for long, I promise. Only until I know what's happening with Dad and then I'll be back.'

The ferocity in Tariq's expression didn't lessen. 'You

have no idea how long it will be. And what if he needs long-term care? What if he is hospitalised for good? What will you do then?'

'I'll work something out. It won't be an issue.' She reached up to touch his cheek, wanting to soothe him. 'Please don't—'

But he didn't wait for her to finish, releasing her all of a sudden and turning away so that she touched nothing but empty air.

Charlotte stared after him as he stalked back to his desk, her heart beating faster. Something was wrong and she didn't know what it was.

'What is it?' she asked into the tense silence. 'You know I'll come back. I will, Tariq. I promise.'

He was standing with his back to her, looking out over the gardens through the window, the line of his powerful shoulders stiff with tension. 'I have been promised things before. Promises mean nothing.'

'But, I can—'

'No.' He turned sharply, pinning her with that fierce, hot stare. 'If I let you go, what will bring you back? Me?'

She stared at him, bewildered. 'Of course. You're my husband.'

'A man you were forced into marrying. A husband who keeps you here against your will.'

'Yes, you've done those things, but it's different now. I said I'd stay and I meant it. I'm your wife, not to mention your friend. I would never walk out on you.'

'No,' he said flatly. 'I cannot risk it.'

'Tariq—'

'My father kept everything that was good from me when I was growing up and I told myself that I did not need it. But you have made me see things differently, Charlotte. This week you have made me see what I have been missing. You have made me see what I need. And now I have that I do not want to give it up.' Fire burned in his eyes, a deep, fierce amber. 'I told you that you were mine and so you are. And I do not give up what is mine. I will not.'

He *was* afraid—she could see it in his eyes. He was afraid she wouldn't return.

'You can trust me,' she said, trying to calm him. 'I give you my word.'

Anger flashed across his intense features. 'Do you think that I am a skittish horse that needs soothing? I have been lied to before, so do not think that your "word" will work.'

Of course. Catherine and her promises to him. But, no, this went deeper than Catherine. This was about his father. This was about himself.

Automatically, she opened her mouth to say something that would ease his anger, and then stopped.

Why? Why are you always placating him? When you know he's being unreasonable?

That was a very good question. And it was a question she didn't have the answer to. But, no, that was wrong. She did have the answer. She just didn't want to acknowledge it. She wanted to pretend it didn't exist.

Except it did exist.

It was staring her in the face and had been for weeks.

She always wanted to soothe him and comfort him because he mattered to her. Because she loved him. She'd been in love with him since the moment he'd taken her in that tent at the oasis.

Charlotte's chest tightened as the knowledge swept through her, overwhelming her, making it hard to breathe, making her feel dizzy.

Her mouth was as dry as the desert and she was afraid. Because she knew all about love. Love was pain. Love was listening to her parents scream at each other over her head. Love was watching her mother give up on her and walk away. Love was the ache that cut deep inside every time her father looked at her as if she was nothing but a nuisance to him.

Love was giving everything and getting nothing in return.

She stared at her handsome husband, her heart roaring in her ears. Stared at the man to whom she was slowly, little by little, giving away the pieces of her soul. And he was taking it. He was keeping it for himself and giving her nothing back.

And you've done that before, haven't you?

Of course she had. With her father. Being quiet and good for him...not causing a fuss as a child. Helping him with his career and being his dogsbody as an adult. Trying and trying to get him to look at her with something more than impatience and frustration. To see her as his daughter and not the millstone around his neck that she suspected he thought she was.

You tried to make him to care. But he never did. And now you're doing the same with Tariq.

'You're very clear about what you want,' she said suddenly, hoarsely. 'But what about what I want? Does that not matter at all?'

His expression was hard. Cold. The mask of the sheikh.

'What has that got to do with anything?'

'Answer the question.'

Something flickered across his face and then it was gone. 'That is not a requirement.'

An empty, hollow feeling opened inside her. He didn't care what she wanted, which meant he didn't care about her.

Did you expect that he would?

Maybe she'd hoped. Maybe that was why she'd never looked too closely at her own feelings. Because she knew she wouldn't be able to bear the disappointment if he didn't feel the same way. But he'd told her in the tent at the oasis that theirs would only be a physical marriage, and she'd been okay with it back then. She hadn't expected or wanted more.

Except things had changed. He'd given her physical pleasure, made her feel beautiful, and then, over the past week together, he'd given her his friendship. He'd made her feel interesting and special. Desirable, sexy and brave. He'd made her feel needed.

And that was the problem.

He'd made her want more.

He'd made her want to be loved.

'It's a requirement for me,' she said, her voice cracking.

And just like that the fierce expression on his face closed, like the door of a furnace shutting, depriving her of all its light and all its heat.

'In that case perhaps you are not as suited to life here as I expected.'

His voice was hard as stone, his gaze as pitiless as it had been that day she'd fainted in front of him.

'Perhaps it would be better if you returned to England, after all.'

Somewhere deep inside her she felt a tearing pain.

So much for all your hopes. If he can give you up so easily, then he really doesn't care.

He stood on the other side of the desk and the distance between them felt vast, cavernous. He was so isolated, and so lonely, and there was a part of her that wanted more than anything to bridge that gap.

But she wasn't the same woman she'd been a couple of weeks ago. She'd found a strength inside her she hadn't thought possible. And she was tired of giving everything of herself to someone who would never give anything back. She didn't want to do it any more.

So if he expected her to soothe and placate him, to beg him to let her stay, he was in for a surprise. Because she wasn't going to. She wasn't going to demand he tell her why he'd changed his mind either. If he wanted to sit here in splendid isolation, in his arid life in a vacuum, then he could.

She wouldn't stop him, not this time.

Charlotte drew herself up, looking him in the eye even as her heart shredded itself in her chest. 'Fine,' she said. 'Then you can arrange for me to fly out tonight.'

A fleeting look of shock crossed his face before it was quickly masked. 'Charlotte—'

'No,' she interrupted, furious and heartbroken, everything hot and raw. 'You will damn well listen to what I have to say. I'm not choosing to leave because I want to. I'm choosing to leave because you haven't given me one single reason to stay.'

She found she was shaking.

'You made it clear what our marriage was. Right from the beginning you told me, and I thought I was okay with it. I thought I didn't want more. But I've changed my mind.'

She met his gaze head-on.

'I've decided I do want more. I want a real marriage, Tariq, emotional as well as physical. I want love. Give me that and I swear no power on earth will make me leave you.'

He was suddenly still, as if she'd turned him to stone. And the silence deepened, lengthened.

'I cannot,' he said at last, roughly, as if it had been dragged from him. 'That is the one thing I cannot give you.'

It wasn't a shock. It wasn't even a surprise. And maybe that was what hurt most of all. She knew he couldn't. And whether it was a case of him not being able to or simply not wanting to, it didn't matter.

The outcome was still the same.

Charlotte ignored the desert that had taken the place of her heart. She didn't plead with him, didn't beg. Didn't ask him why. All she said was, 'Then I have to leave.'

The mask of the sheikh had settled back over his strong features once again, and there was no emotion at all in his eyes. 'I will have Faisal handle your travel arrangements,' he said, without any discernible emotion. 'You will, of course, let me know if you discover you are pregnant.'

That hurt—as he must have known it would.

But she didn't let it show.

She turned on her heel and left him there.

Tariq stood in front of the window for a long time after she'd gone, staring out at his beautiful gardens and the fountains playing, desperate for the peaceful scene to calm the sudden and terrible rage that clawed up inside him. Desperate to find his detachment, the black silence of his vacuum.

But it was nowhere to be found, so he stayed where he was, unmoving. Because if he moved even a muscle he wasn't sure that he wouldn't go running after Charlotte, pick her up and toss her over his shoulder, carry her into his bedroom, lock the door, throw away the key.

He couldn't do that, though. No matter how much he wanted to. No matter how much the pain in her silver-blue eyes had felt like glass sliding under his skin. Or how her request for love had made that glass slice through his soul. Or how her leaving had made him feel suffocated, left to bear the crushing weight of his isolation alone.

No, he couldn't go after her. Couldn't give her the one thing—the only thing—she'd ever asked of him.

He couldn't give her love.

He'd worked too hard, borne too much, to give in to those terrible betraying feelings. Being true to his father's teachings, keeping himself isolated—that was all he could do now. And if he felt as if he was dying inside, then that was his own fault. He'd been the one to think he could have friendship and pleasure, that he could have her smile and her laughter—all the things he'd been missing in his life and all without consequence.

Little by little she'd got past his walls and he should have stopped her days ago. He'd let her get too far and this was the result: his detachment, the thing he needed to be a good king, cracked and broken.

'Does what I want not matter at all?'

Tariq stared sightlessly at the fountain, her voice and the break in it replaying in his head. He'd told her that she was his, that he would never let her go, but the moment she'd said those words and he'd felt something inside him twist and crack he'd understood.

She had to leave. She made him feel too much. She made him *feel*, full stop. And that was a very bad thing. It compromised the very foundation he'd built his life upon, not to mention his reign, and that he wouldn't allow. He couldn't put himself and what he wanted first because he was responsible for an entire nation. And keeping it safe was his primary objective.

Even if that meant keeping it safe from himself.

He'd put his country at risk once before because he'd been too much a slave to his emotions. He couldn't do it again.

'I want love, Tariq. Give me that.'

No, not even for her.

It was a long time before he permitted himself to move. A long time before he turned away from the window, forcing himself to make a few calls, arranging the travel details for her himself.

Then, once that was done, he shut himself in his office, leaving instructions with his guards that he was not to be disturbed under any circumstances.

And he threw himself into work.

A week later and he still hadn't granted anyone an audience or interview. He'd refused meetings. Even requests for casual conversation had been ignored.

Everyone had been turned away from his door.

He didn't want to see anyone. He didn't want to talk to anyone.

He had to shore up the cracks in his armour that Charlotte had created and he could only do that alone.

The week turned into two and then three.

Faisal came at least once every day, demanding admittance, but Tariq ignored him.

Yet he still couldn't find any peace.

One evening he headed to the palace baths, as he had every night since Charlotte had left, unable to sleep and tortured by a warmth that wasn't there. By memories of soft curves and hair like moonlight. Of deep blue eyes that had looked at him as if there was something worthy in him when he knew there wasn't.

He flung himself into the water, driving his hands through it as if he was digging himself out of a hole, or pulling himself up a sharp cliff, swimming on and on. Driving himself into the spurious peace of exhaustion.

That exhaustion never lasted, though, and once it had passed the ache would return, bringing with it the intense longing and the sense of suffocation. As if the air he needed to breathe was being depleted and he was slowly choking and by inches dying.

You need air. You need her.

He forced that thought from his head, driving himself harder through the water.

No, he'd been fine before she came to him and he would be fine again. All he needed to do was hold fast to his detachment and these sensations would pass. They had after Catherine and they would again—he was sure of it.

His hand hit the end of the pool again, but this time, sensing someone standing there, he stopped and stood up, pushing his hair back from his eyes.

Faisal stood at the edge, his expression impassive.

'How did you get past the guards?' Tariq demanded gracelessly. His temper these days was on a hair trigger. 'No one is permitted to enter.'

'I knocked them out.' Faisal's tone was short. 'You need new guards.'

Tariq scowled. He didn't want Faisal here. He didn't want to talk. He wanted to continue swimming until his muscles ached and he was exhausted, the feeling of being suffocated gone.

'What do you want?' he asked. 'Tell me, then get out.'

Faisal stared at him a moment, then said with unexpected savagery, 'You're a fool, Tariq. Sulking in your palace alone. Why did you send her away?'

Tariq felt his hands clench into fists and he had to force the anger away, get himself under control. 'I do not recall asking for your opinion, Faisal. And be careful what you say—'

'Your father was a fool too,' the old man interrupted harshly. 'He closed himself down completely after your mother died—did you know that? He never got over it. He isolated himself and then he did the same to you.'

Tariq went still.

'I told him it was wrong,' Faisal went on. 'That just

because he had lost his wife it did not mean that his son should not find happiness and companionship. But he ignored me. And now look what has happened.' The old advisor virtually spat the words. 'You have closed the borders of your country and your heart. You are him in everything but name.'

Abruptly the weight sitting on Tariq's chest increased, like a vice crushing him, the vacuum pressing in. He should command Faisal's silence, tell him to get out, but he couldn't speak.

'Do you know what happens to a tree with its roots cut?' Faisal asked, suddenly quiet. 'Or to a fire starved of oxygen? It dies.' There was a pause. 'Your insistence on your father's outdated lessons may not end up killing this country, Tariq. But it will certainly end up killing you.'

The water was cool, but suddenly he was burning up. The emotions inside him, the anger and desperation and longing, were too strong and too powerful. They were inescapable and there was nowhere for them to go but inward. And now they were eating him alive.

'Perhaps,' he heard himself say roughly, 'that should have happened years ago. Before I betrayed Ashkaraz in a rush of foolish temper.'

Faisal was silent, but Tariq couldn't look at him. He couldn't bear to see what was on the old man's face.

'No,' Faisal said at last. 'No, that is not true. It was your father who betrayed Ashkaraz. If he had brought you up with love, rather than harshness, you would not have been so lonely. And if you had not been so lonely you would not have been angry with him. You would not have turned to Catherine.'

'You cannot say that—'

'I can and I will,' the old man interrupted. 'You are a good king, Tariq. But you could be a great one. Better than your father ever was. Because you have what he lacked: a strong and passionate heart. You just need to use it.'

His jaw ached, along with every muscle in his body. He felt as if he was standing on the edge of a cliff, the ledge crumbling beneath him. 'Detachment is what makes a great king, Faisal. Not a strong and passionate heart.'

'That is your father talking.' Faisal's voice was uncompromising. 'And he was wrong. Love is what makes a great king.'

A few weeks ago he would have ignored the words. Now they settled into him, through the chink in his armour that Charlotte had left there.

He didn't know how long he stood in the chilly waters of the baths after Faisal had gone, watching the light filter down from the hidden windows in the ceiling, his heart beating fast and getting faster, the emotions inside him burning him alive.

If love was what made a great king, then that was something he couldn't be. Because what did he know of love? It was his father's grief and pain. It was Catherine's empty promises. His own anger and betrayal…

That's not all it is.

He caught his breath, memories coiling through him. Charlotte's gentle hand on his skin. Charlotte's smile as she looked up at him. Charlotte's arms around him, holding him close.

'I want love,' she'd said—as if she knew exactly what it was, as if it was something to be deeply desired and longed for and not something that led to pain and betrayal.

Faisal isn't wrong. If your father had even let you have one friend, one connection, would you have gone to Catherine that night?

Perhaps he wouldn't. Perhaps he wouldn't have been so lonely and so angry. So desperate for any connection that he'd let his father's mistress seduce him. Perhaps if his father had brought him up with love he'd understand what Charlotte wanted.

You can understand now.

The thought made air rush abruptly into his lungs and he found himself gasping, as if he'd forgotten how to breathe.

'You have what he lacked...' Faisal had said. *'A strong and passionate heart. You just need to use it.'*

And to do that he needed to open it. To stop fighting his emotions. To embrace them, make them part of him.

So he did. He stood in the water, his hands in fists, his skin getting cold, and instead of fighting the feelings inside him he set them free, let them rush through him like oxygen down an air line.

And suddenly everything became clear.

He loved Charlotte Devereaux.

He'd loved her for weeks.

She made him better. She made him stronger. She made him compassionate and merciful and protective. She made him humble.

She made him whole.

She made him the king he should be for his people.

And if he wanted to be that king he needed her at his side.

Give her a reason to be there, then.

His heart was beating far too fast and his hands were shaking—because there was only one thing he could offer her and that was himself, and he was honest enough to admit that probably wasn't enough. She'd told him she'd wanted love from him, but maybe after the way she'd left, after the way he'd treated her, she had changed her mind.

But he had to go to her and offer it anyway. He needed to show her that what she wanted mattered to him. He needed to tell her that she was loved. That she was his queen, and to death and beyond would remain so.

Tariq moved to the edge of the pool and hauled himself out. It was late, and he should go to bed, but he wasn't tired. Instead he dried himself off and went straight to his office.

He worked through the night, putting various and very necessary things in motion. And then, just as dawn was breaking, he finally put through the call he'd been waiting all night to make.

'Ready my jet,' he ordered, when one of his assistants answered. 'I will be flying to London as soon as possible.'

CHAPTER TWELVE

CHARLOTTE SMOOTHED THE blanket over her father's knees as he sat in his favourite armchair beside the fire in the living room and ignored his fussing. Luckily the heart attack had been mild, and the doctor was incredibly pleased with his progress—but he was a terrible patient. He wanted to be back in his office at the university, putting together a new lecture or organising a new dig, not sitting 'mouldering' at home. At least, that was what he kept saying to her, as if he was expecting her to do something about it.

'I don't have my laptop,' he said peevishly, readjusting the blanket. 'How am I supposed to prepare anything when I don't have my laptop? I need you to go into my office and get—'

'No, Dad.' Charlotte interrupted, before he could get into a list of all the things he needed. 'I have a job interview tomorrow, so you'll have to wait.'

It was for an office job, doing administrative tasks, and she'd been surprised she'd got an interview, given her lack of work experience. But she'd felt a vague sense of satisfaction that she'd managed to score it. Now her father was better, and would be returning to work in the next week or so, her own life could resume. Not that she knew quite what that life was going to look like.

One thing was clear, though: it wasn't going to be what she'd had before.

When she'd come back to England she'd been caught up in her father's illness and looking after him, too busy to think about what her next move might be. But since he'd been released from hospital, and she'd had to move into her father's mews house in order to look after him, she'd had time to make a few decisions. And one of those was that she wasn't going to be returning to work for him.

She was done with men who did nothing but take.

She was going to do what *she* wanted for a change.

'You don't need a job.' He fussed with his blanket yet again. 'You can be my assistant. The new one isn't working out as well as I'd hoped.'

Once upon a time Charlotte might have leapt at the opportunity. But not now.

Not since Tariq.

The thought of the man she'd left behind made the wound deep inside her soul ache, but she shoved the pain away. She'd made her choice and she didn't regret it. And if sometimes at night, when she couldn't sleep, she wished she'd confronted him when he'd told her he couldn't give her love, then what of it? It didn't change what had happened, and it was far too late to confront him now anyway.

The borders of Ashkaraz were closed to her and so was its sheikh's heart.

'Thanks, Dad, but, no,' Charlotte said firmly. 'It's time I started living my own life, making my own choices.'

Her father scowled. 'The new girl doesn't do things the way I like them.'

'Then I'm afraid that's your problem, not mine.'

'Charlotte…'

'What?' She gave him a very direct look. 'I'm your daughter, not your servant. Not your dogsbody. Not any more. I have things *I* want to do.'

He was silent a moment. Then, 'You've changed. What happened in Ashkaraz?'

It was the first time he'd asked her, and Charlotte debated for a moment whether or not he deserved an explanation. But perhaps it would be good for him to hear a few home truths.

'I had my heart broken,' she said flatly. 'And I realised that for years I've been trying to prove myself to a man who took what I had to give him and never saw me as anything more than a nuisance. And even though I gave up a piece of my soul to come back and help him recover, he hasn't even said thank you. Not once. Is that enough of an explanation for you?'

Her father at least had the grace to look ashamed of himself.

There was a long, uncomfortable silence. Then he said, 'I'm sorry. I know I haven't been the…best of fathers. But, well… You look at lot like her. Your mother, I mean. And sometimes I forget that you're not her.'

Charlotte's throat closed. He'd never talked to her like this.

'It was never about you,' he added gruffly. 'You were a good girl. A good daughter. And I…missed you while you were gone.'

It was as close as her father would ever come to an explanation for his behaviour, and maybe an apology as well. But she didn't need his approval to make her feel good about herself—not these days—so all she said was, 'Good. I'm glad you did.'

He didn't say much after that, and a bit later, discovering that there was no milk for their tea, Charlotte decided that she'd have to brave the rain in order to get some.

She grabbed an umbrella from the stand in the hallway and headed out.

The cobbles in the mews outside her father's house were shiny and slippery, and it was cold. And as the hand clutching the handle of the umbrella went numb Charlotte found herself wishing she was somewhere hot. Where the sun was merciless and the sand was burning. Where neither were as hot as the passion of the man she'd left there.

Her heart squeezed and she had to grit her teeth against a wave of pain. Why was she thinking of Tariq again? Leaving had been the right thing to do. The *only* thing. Thinking of him hurt. Besides, she'd find herself someone else. He wasn't the only fish in the sea.

Except you will never love anyone as you loved him.

The thought was so bleak that she had to stop, because her vision was swimming with tears and it hurt to breathe. Then, as she collected herself and prepared to go on, she noticed someone standing in the mews ahead of her.

And everything in her went quiet and still.

It was a very tall man and he was holding a black umbrella. He was dressed in what looked like a shockingly expensive dark suit, with sunglasses over his eyes despite the rain. But even the suit and the glasses couldn't disguise the sense of authority and arrogance he radiated.

Except Charlotte didn't need that to know who it was.

She would have known him anywhere.

Tariq.

Her poor, shattered heart seized in her chest and she blinked—because surely he wasn't here. This had to be a mirage. Yet despite the blinking he didn't disappear, and, yes, it seemed that he really was here, in London. Standing in the road near her father's house.

Then he was coming towards her, moving with the same fluid grace she remembered, and just like that rage filled her, making her shake.

How dared he come here? After she'd made the horrifically painful decision to leave him. After her heart had torn itself to pieces as she'd walked away. After she'd wept all the way back to London and for days afterwards, missing him so acutely it had felt like being stabbed.

After all that he'd come here. Why? What did he want from her? Was it to hurt her again? Taunt her with what she could never have?

Charlotte didn't wait for him to reach her. She stormed up to him instead, meeting him in the middle of the lane. Then she reached up and tore the glasses from his face so she could see him, holding the familiar intensity of his golden stare with her own.

He didn't move. Didn't speak. Only stared at her.

'What are you doing here?' she demanded, her voice breaking, even though she tried not to let it. 'How dare you? How dare you come here to—?'

It was only then that he moved, throwing away his umbrella as if he didn't care about the rain that was falling around them and stepping under hers. Then he reached for her, taking her face between his hands, and the warmth of his skin was like a bolt of lightning, rooting her to the spot.

He bent and kissed her, his mouth hot and desperate, and the taste of him was so achingly familiar that tears rushed into her eyes, the deep hunger inside her stirring, waking.

Oh, God, how could he do this to her?

She stiffened, ready to push him away, but he'd already lifted his head, the look in his eyes blazing.

'Oh, *ya amar*,' he said fiercely. 'I have been such a fool. I have done such stupid things. Said things I should not have. And all I can say is that I am sorry.' His thumbs moved caressingly over her cheekbones. 'I should have let you go to your father. I should have trusted you to return. And most important of all I should have given you a reason to come back to me.'

She was trembling and unable to stop. Unable to pull away from him either. All she could do was stand there and look up into the blazing gold of his eyes.

'What reason?' she asked, trying to hold herself together.

The lines of his beautiful face took on a familiar intensity. 'You asked me to give you love. So I am here to offer it.'

Her umbrella didn't protect him from the rain and his black hair was getting wet, his suit damp, water was trickling down the side of his face. But he didn't seem to notice. His attention was on her as if he was suffocating and she was the lifeline he needed.

Except it was she who couldn't breathe.

'Be clear, Tariq.' She barely sounded like herself. 'What are you saying?'

'I am saying that I love you, Charlotte Devereaux,' Tariq said in his dark, deep voice. 'I love you, my wife. I have spent the past three weeks telling myself that sending you away would stop these feelings inside me. That once you were gone I could stay detached. Be the kind of king my father wanted me to be. But I could not do it. I could not escape what I feel for you. And I found out that…*you* are what makes me the king I need to be.'

His gaze searched her face, unhidden desperation in it.

'You make me compassionate and merciful. You make me humble. You make me strong. You make me a better man, a better king. And I want to give you back everything that you have given me.'

She felt cold, and then hot, as if she was dying and then coming back to life. 'Tariq…'

His name was the only thing she could say.

Luckily she didn't need to speak, because he went on, 'I want you, *ya amar*. I want to give you all the love you need. And I would leave Ashkaraz if I could, be with you here in London if you wanted me to. But I cannot leave my country. So all I can do is beg you to return with me.'

Her heart felt both heavy and light at the same time, at the ferocity in his eyes, at his desperation and his anguish.

She looked up at him, drinking in every line of his beloved face. 'Then I will,' she said simply. Because this was what she'd been wanting her entire life.

And something blazed in his beautiful eyes—heat like the sun, burning there. 'You would do that? After everything that I did to you? Kept you prisoner…made you marry me? Gave you ultimatum after ultimatum—?'

Charlotte reached out and put a shaking finger on his mouth, silencing him. 'After you gave me pleasure and friendship. Showed me how brave I could be and how strong. After you helped me figure out my own worth.' She pressed harder, feeling the heat of his skin beneath her fingertip. 'Yes, you fool. Of course I would do that.'

'I am not a good man, *ya amar*. And there is much I do not understand. I will make mistakes and I will need you to help me. I am also very possessive of what is mine, and that might be…annoying for you. Are you sure you want to commit yourself to that?'

She blinked back sudden tears, her throat aching with an intense joy. 'I've had some experience of dealing with difficult men, believe me. I think I can handle it.'

His expression turned even fiercer. 'Then you have my word that I will do everything in my power to make you happy for the rest of our lives.'

There was rain on her cheeks, though some of the moisture might have been tears, because the iron band that had been around her heart since she'd left him burst open and her chest filled, her lungs filled. Her heart filled.

And then her umbrella was on the ground too, and she

was in his arms. His mouth was on hers, tasting of rain and heat and the volcanic passion that was part of him.

'Tell me,' he said roughly when she finally pulled away.

'Tell you what? About my dad?' God, how she loved to tease him. 'About the job interview I have tomorrow?'

'No.' That dark intensity was back in his face. 'Do not play with me, *ya amar.*'

Charlotte relented. 'You mean tell you that I love you?'

'Yes,' he said fiercely. 'That.'

'Well, I do. I love you. And I—'

He kissed her yet again, hard, cutting off the words, stealing all her breath and then giving it back to her, so that when he raised his head again, she felt light-headed and dizzy.

'I have a hotel nearby,' he murmured. 'Come with me, wife. I need you.'

'Wait.' She pressed her hands to his hard chest, warm despite the fact that they were both soaking wet. 'You need to tell me what changed your mind.'

And, wonderfully, a fleeting magical smile crossed his face. 'A friend.'

She stared at him in surprise. 'I thought you didn't have any?'

'Turns out I have one at least. Faisal. He told me that the reason that my father brought me up the way he did was because he never got over my mother's death. That he cut himself off and did the same to me.' Tariq pushed her damp hair back from her face. 'Faisal also told me that my father was wrong. That it isn't detachment that makes a great king. It's love.' He searched her face. 'I think I am starting to see what he meant. But perhaps you can show me the rest?'

Her heart was bursting, everything she felt for him flooding out. She reached up on tiptoes and kissed him yet again, because all the kisses in the world wouldn't be enough.

'Yes. Yes, I can.'

And she did.

And even though getting lost in the desert might have been the stupidest thing she'd ever done, it had also been the best.

Because in getting lost she'd found her home.

She'd found her for ever.

She'd found herself.

In the strong and passionate heart of a king.

EPILOGUE

THE KNOCK CAME on the door of Tariq's office, and he'd barely had a moment to acknowledge it before it opened and his wife came in.

She was dressed in a deep pink robe today, and it brought a delightful blush to her pale cheeks as well as highlighting her silvery hair.

He smiled, his heartbeat quickening, her presence already brightening his day. 'What is it, *ya amar*?' He pushed back his chair and raised one brow. 'It had better be good. I have a very important report to read.'

'Oh, it is, don't worry.'

She gave him a secretive smile in return, then moved over to his desk and, ignoring the fact that it was the middle of the day and there were other people around, came around it and sat on his lap as if she belonged there.

Which she did.

'This is highly irregular,' he murmured as she settled back against his shoulder and lifted her mouth for his kiss. 'Perhaps we should lock the door?'

Because he was hard and getting harder and—

His thoughts broke off and he went quite still. She was looking at him with a very particular kind of focus.

'Charlotte? What is it?'

Her smile this time was breathtaking. 'What's "Daddy"

in Arabic again? I feel our child will want to call you something.'

Everything in him became bright, burning. 'Charlotte...' he said again.

She touched his cheek, and everything he'd ever wanted was right there in her blue eyes.

'Are you going to faint, dear heart?' she asked.

But he didn't faint. He laughed instead, and kissed her, filling himself up with her heat, and her brightness, and all the love she'd brought into his life so far.

And all the love she had yet to bring.

* * * * *

MILLS & BOON

Coming next month

THE SCANDAL BEHIND THE ITALIAN'S WEDDING
Millie Adams

"Why did you do it, Minerva?"

"I am sorry. I really didn't do it to cause you trouble. But I'm being threatened, and so is Isabella, and in order to protect us both I needed to come up with an alternative paternity story."

"An alternative paternity story?"

She winced. "Yes. Her father is after her."

He eyed her with great skepticism. "I didn't think you knew who her father was."

She didn't know whether to be shocked, offended or pleased that he thought her capable of having an anonymous interlude.

For heaven's sake, she'd only ever been kissed one time in her life. A regrettable evening out with Katie in Rome where she'd tried to enjoy the pulsing music in the club, but had instead felt overheated and on the verge of a seizure.

She'd danced with a man in a shiny shirt—and she even knew his name because she wouldn't even dance with a man without an introduction—and he'd kissed her on the dance floor. It had been wet and he'd tasted of liquor and she'd feigned a headache after and taken a cab back to the hostel they'd been staying in.

The idea of hooking up with someone, in a circumstance like that, made her want to peel her own skin off.

"Of course I know who he is. Unfortunately... The full implications of who he is did not become clear until later."

"What does that mean?"

She could tell him the truth now, but something stopped her. Maybe it was admitting Isabella wasn't her daughter, which always caught her in the chest and made her feel small. Like she'd stolen her and like what they had was potentially fragile, temporary and shaky.

Or maybe it was trust. Dante was a good man. Going off the fact he had rescued her from a fall, and helped her up when her knee was skinned, and bailed her out after her terrible humiliation in high school.

But to trust him with the truth was something she simply wasn't brave enough to do.

Her life, Isabella's life, was at risk, and she'd lied on live stream in front of the world.

Her bravery was tapped out.

"Her father is part of an organized crime family. Obviously something unknown to me at the time of her…you know. And he's after her. He's after us."

"Are you telling me that you're in actual danger?"

"Yes. And really, the only hope I have is convincing him that he isn't actually the father."

"And you think that will work?"

"It's the only choice I have. I need your protection."

He regarded her with dark, fathomless eyes, and yet again, she felt like he was peering at her as though she were a girl, and not a woman at all. A naughty child, in point of fact. Then something in his expression shifted.

It shamed her a little that this was so like when he'd come to her rescue at the party. That she was manipulating his pity for her. Her own pathetic nature being what called to him, yet again.

But she would lay down any and all pride for Isabella and she'd do it willingly.

"If she were, in fact my child, then we would be family."

"I… I suppose," she said.

"There will need to be photographs of us together, as I would not be a neglectful father."

"No indeed."

"Of course, you know that if Isabella were really my child there would be only one thing for us to do."

"Do I?"

"Yes." He began to pace, like a caged tiger trying to find a weak spot in his cage. And suddenly he stopped, and she had the terrible feeling that the tiger had found what he'd been looking for. "Yes. Of course, there is only one option."

"And that is?"

"You have to marry me."

Continue reading
THE SCANDAL BEHIND THE ITALIAN'S WEDDING
Millie Adams

Available next month
www.millsandboon.co.uk

COMING SOON!

We really hope you enjoyed reading this book. If you're looking for more romance, be sure to head to the shops when new books are available on

Thursday 6th March

To see which titles are coming soon, please visit **millsandboon.co.uk/nextmonth**

LET'S TALK

Romance

For exclusive extracts, competitions
and special offers, find us online:

f facebook.com/millsandboon

🐦 @MillsandBoon

📷 @MillsandBoonUK

Get in touch on 01413 063232

For all the latest titles coming soon, visit
millsandboon.co.uk/nextmonth

JOIN US ON SOCIAL MEDIA!

Stay up to date with our latest releases, author news and gossip, special offers and discounts, and all the behind-the-scenes action from Mills & Boon...

 millsandboon

 millsandboonuk

 millsandboon

It might just be true love...